ALT[illegible] EVOLUTION

THE BOOK OF MARGARET

PAUL A. BROOKS

Altered Evolution

Book Cover by Bruce Rolff

First edition 2023

To those who dare question what we are told is a *fact*.

And to my wife, who has always supported my dreams.

Preface

Let me ask you, should we always accept what we are told as *the truth* if there is evidence it might not be?

There is an accepted 'truth' about our evolution. We're taught it in school. But is it true? There are gaps in our history, leaps in our knowledge, and archaeology that call our time on this planet into question. What happened? Where did this knowledge come from? Where do we come from? Maybe the answers are in the stories, myths, and legends handed down by our ancient ancestors.

Altered Evolution is speculative fiction. A story born from the evidence that suggests there might be more to our origins than conventional science says. A *what-if* story to ask if who we are today results from more than the passing of time and natural selection.

That someone or something changed and molded us into who we are today is both thrilling and terrifying.

Maybe one day we'll know for sure.

Foreword

I woke up that morning with a sense of awe and wonder. It was a feeling of profound connection to the universe, as if I had been touched by something greater than myself.

That feeling had come to me in a dream, a dream of traveling through the stars, nebulae, and galaxies and discovering new worlds. And even though I was just a 6-year-old child at the time, that dream would stay with me for the rest of my life. I can still vividly relive the intense bliss I experienced then floating in space over 40 years later. That dream followed me at different ages and stages of my life, always bringing back that instant and unique connection to the universe.

It was that dream that inspired me to become a physicist, to explore the mysteries of the universe, and to search for answers to the biggest questions of all. And now, after many years of research and exploration, I find myself looking back on that dream with a sense of awe and wonder once again.

What I have experienced is that the universe is far more wondrous and mysterious than we ever could have imagined. And that the origins of life on Earth may be far stranger and more complex than we ever could have guessed.

18 months ago, a discussion with Paul A. Brooks brought back this vivid dream. An inspiring brain shaking conversation, that would be followed by crazy disrupting sessions we had no idea would make us travel through that dream together BUT with a purpose – a musical resolution.

The book you hold in your hands, Altered Evolution, slowly emerged and is a testament to the power of science and the human imagination. It is a journey into a world of wonder and possibility, a world where the boundaries between species and planets are blurred, and where the origins of life itself are shrouded in mystery.

As you read these pages, I invite you to join us on a journey of discovery and exploration, to open your mind to the unfathomable. May this book inspire you to imagine new worlds and possibilities, and see the universe in a new light. And may it remind us all of the limitless potential that lies within us, waiting to be unlocked.

There are moments in life that change the course of our entire being. For me, such a moment came when I was just a child, gazing up at the stars and dreaming of far-off galaxies. Shall Altered Evolution be that life-changing moment we will all share together...

Jean-Philippe Schoeffel, Physicist

Part One

Arrival

One

Numbers, Time, and Idiots

The nine sisters of the ruling council could see how desperate things were. The pained glances at first council sister confirmed they all knew it.

"The numbers don't lie," second sister said. "There are fewer of us now than there have ever been. I fear time is running out."

"Are there any promising results from the last batch of gathered subjects?" first sister said, looking at her, frowning.

"No, and it doesn't matter how aggressive or invasive I get with the experiments. The subjects are just not compatible." She looked away, lowering her head.

First sister stood, casting a dark shadow as she leaned on the table. "What about initiating the cloning program again?"

Second sister leaned back in her chair, folded her arms, and sighed. "We've been down that route before. The problems with cloning persist. Each generation of copies loses something from the previous one, and worse, the further down the generations you go, you end up with a useless, empty shell."

Her disrespect had not gone unnoticed. First sister leaned on her knuckles, glaring at her.

"What about gene splicing, genetic manipulation, re-animation, or synthetic biology? Can you work with any of that?" Fourth sister said, interrupting.

Second sister shot her a sideways glance. "We've never stopped!"

A loud bang filled the chamber as first sister slammed her fists onto the metal tabletop. Everyone jumped. "Well, you're not working hard or fast enough, are you? We need results now. Do you understand, now!" Her eyes drilled into her as she sat.

"Yes, sister, I do. I need more subjects to carry on with my work. I've already destroyed the last batch." Second sister said, fingering the collar of her robe.

A male voice broke the tension in the room. "Ahem. First council sister, we are about to enter the planet's atmosphere."

She spun her chair and stared into the fiery glow surrounding the ship as it descended. "Very well. Return to the bridge and find me a suitable landing site."

"Yes, first council sister," he said, bowing and leaving.

"I'll get you more subjects from here. But you need to get me results, and not just for me, for all of us. You understand that, right? You, more than the rest, understand how urgent the need is?"

"Yes, of course, sister," second sister said.

She turned back to the table and leaned toward her. "Good, there will be no second chance for you, *second sister*!" She clenched her jaw before forcing herself to look away and sat back. "You and fifth sister stay here, the rest of you, leave."

The sound of sliding chairs and rustling robes filled the chamber as the other six sisters left as fast as they could.

First sister closed her eyes, feeling the temperature in the ship rise as it flew through the planet's atmosphere. It calmed her.

"I hope you've found a suitable candidate species, fifth sister?"

"Yes, first sister, there's a species of bipedal hominids I believe will suit very well. They have forward-facing, predator-like eyes, and opposable thumbs, making their hands capable of using tools, and scans show a large adaptable brain. They have no language as they are early in their evolution, but we can give that to them. Physically, they are not unlike us. They don't have our olive skin color, our facial scales, or teeth, and they certainly won't have our reflexes, speed, or strength. We are more similar to the reptilian species in that respect. But several hominid species around the planet may prove fruitful during experimentation, conversion, and training." She gave second sister a tense smile.

"Good. Let's hope you're successful this time, second sister."

"I will certainly do my best."

She fixed her with a stare that made fifth sister's blood run cold. "Your best is required, second sister, but now I need you to do better than that. We don't have time for more failures."

"I understand, sister," she said, looking down.

"Fifth sister, when we land, take a contingent of warriors and gather as many of these hominids as you deem necessary. Don't be shy about it. Take as many as you need. Show no mercy."

"I will..."

The communicator on the table buzzed.

"First council sister, this is the pilot. We should not land. The climate is too cold to sustain us on the surface."

"You mean to tell me you've brought me to a planet I can't even step foot on?" Spit flew from her lips as she spoke.

"Yes, first council sister. I apologize, first council sister." His voice wobbled. "Our sensors are malfunctioning. The last thing they detected was a coronal mass ejection from the sun as we entered the system. Unfortunately, it damaged our sensors and communications array. It's only now that we're inside this planet's atmosphere that we can measure its climate, and I'm afraid the surface is too cold."

"Well, get them fixed, damn it. What about the communication array? How badly is it damaged?"

"We can communicate across short distances, but long-range intergalactic communication is not possible until the array gets repaired."

"What? You mean to tell me I can't talk to my fleet?"

"I apologize, first council sister. Until the array is operational again, it is impossible. I have already notified the chief engineer. He suggested building a communications satellite, first council sister, capable of reaching the fleet, while they attempt repairs."

"Idiot! - I'm surrounded by idiots!"

"If I may, sister," fifth sister said.

"Speak!"

The menacing glare made her choose her next words carefully.

"In the meantime, we could take shuttles, collect a few hominid samples, and run some initial tests in our labs here to see if they're viable. Then use them as labor slaves to build insulated facilities on the surface for us. That way, second sister will have a suitable laboratory to run her experiments on the ground without risking exposure to the cold for the rest of us."

Her face relaxed into a smile. "And we can test the new conversion serum and create more warriors. - At last someone with some sense. Yes, organize it. Let's not waste any more time."

"Yes, of course, sister, we'll start within the hour," she said.

"Do you have everything you need, *second* sister? No half measures this time. Do whatever you need to these hominids and bring me good news."

"I have sister, but I would appreciate and value your input if you have the time?"

The contrition from her subordinate made her smile. "I'd be glad to assist. Let me know when you're ready."

"Yes, of course, thank you, sister."

She stood and walked to the window. "Now leave me," she said with a dismissive wave.

They bowed and left the chamber.

Outside the window, the fiery glow and heat from entering the planet's atmosphere had changed into intermittent, cool blue and white clouds as the ship continued to descend. The view made her shiver.

She sat back at the table, and running her hands over the dents she made, cursed at the desperation of their situation. The communicator on her wrist buzzed.

"We are ready to go, sister." fifth sister said.

"Good. Gather a selection of females for second sister from all the hominid species. Make sure they are old enough to be mothers, and gather some that are mothers already, but leave their offspring. I'm going to need a few of the strongest-looking males as well. Make that your priority."

"Yes, sister."

On the table's communication panel, the light showing a call from the pilot started blinking. She pressed it.

"We have finished our descent, first council sister, and are holding at five thousand feet."

"What's the temperature on the surface?"

"A cold fifteen degrees Celsius, first council sister."

"Hold here then, pilot - but scan the planet's surface for pockets of warmer temperatures. And adjust the ship's internal temperature to compensate. It's freezing in here."

"Of course, first council sister."

She ran her eyes down the columns of numbers again and sighed. Fewer Szateth females were being born. The summary by second sister at the bottom said the hosts from the last planet were not strong enough to carry Szatethess to term. The implanted embryos killed them. She pursed her lips. There weren't many embryos left in storage.

For her, there was something more pressing. The numbers in the warrior caste were dangerously low. *Maybe the hominids here will be good enough*, she thought. *But the numbers don't lie. Without drastic action, I'll lose my network of planets and be the leader of a dead race.*

Neural Blockchain Journal Entry #919

I've lost count of the number of planets we've been to. So far, none of them have had what I need. There are still nine of us, enough to birth the next generation of Szatethess. They are going to have to do their part. If second sister isn't successful with her experiments on this next species, then she's of no use to me. I'll take over, and she'll join her sisters in the harvest.

More important is the need for powerful warriors. My growing network of subjugated planets needs the warriors to stamp out any rebellions by the indigenous species and rule in my absence.

We should be the dominant species in the universe, and we will be.

My mission now is to make sure we have enough warriors. I will find a species that is strong enough. Maybe the males here will be. I'll know soon enough if this planet is the one. Then nothing will stop me.

As for my sisters, it'll soon be time to harvest them and use their eggs to birth new council sisters I can work with. I've been looking forward to it for so long.

First Council Sister - Szateth leader

Advanced planetary research fleet.

Neural Blockchain Journal Entry #009

I don't know what first council sister was expecting. The species from the last planet I had to work with were too weak and there was nothing I could do to alter their physiology to suit our needs.

I need a species that physically is not too dissimilar from us. Fifth sister seems hopeful about the hominid species on this planet. I hope she's right.

If she is, I fear first sister will be more interested in her wars and growing the number of warriors from it rather than the science behind saving our species. To her, it's just a numbers game.

I don't have the same blinkered approach to our survival as her. I think with time we could find an alternative to harvesting and have a more natural way for Szatethess to be born.

I remain optimistic we'll find a species we can blend with.

Second Council Sister
Advanced Planetary research fleet

Two

Workers, Warriors, and Raw Meat

The first wave of shuttles caught her eye as they flew past the window. They spread out, flying off in different directions. She stood, smoothed out her robes, and watched them disappear over the horizon. After her defiance in front of the other council sisters, she wanted to make sure second sister knew her place, as she marched to her lab.

"Is everything ready?" She asked the moment she walked through the door. "Fifth council sister will be back with your new batch of subjects soon."

"Yes, sister. The new straps on the examination tables are better than ever. We'll be able to keep them completely restrained while I carry out the experiments," she said, tugging on one.

"Good. I told her to bring me some males to test the new conversion serum. I need to replenish my warriors, and I need them now."

"In her report, fifth sister suggests the hominid species on this planet reproduce frequently, although their lifespan is relatively short. That increases the potential of the females being fertile younger, producing stronger offspring, and more frequently. If they are a viable source for us to blend with, we can increase their life expectancy by manipulating their DNA blockchain, as you suggested in the meeting chamber earlier, sister. As for the males, some species in the genus look more likely candidates for military service than others. Although perhaps less intelligent. But again, if they prove sufficient for our needs, we can boost that, and teach them in the meta-verse. Fifth sister's preliminary report looks promising, and I'm looking forward to getting them on my table."

"Let's hope you are right. From your numbers, time is running out."

"Of course we do have the option of cryo-stasis, to give us more time if these hominids are not viable, and we need to leave. It may be wise to prepare the chambers."

"Yes, yes, good thinking. I'll instruct the engineers to get the chambers ready. You are proving to be a valuable asset. I hope you continue to impress."

"Thank you, sister."

The communicator on her wrist buzzed. It was the shuttle hangar commander.

"Yes, commander, what is it?"

"Fifth council sister's shuttles have returned, first council sister, and they are full of the hominids, as you instructed."

"Separate the males from the female's commander and Keep them there. Second council sister and I will be there shortly." She pressed the button on her communicator, ending the call. Her eyes lit up. "Come, sister, let's examine the gathering."

∞

Except for the hissing of the shuttle's cooling steam, the hangar bay was silent. The commander had done his job, and the council sisters walked along the line, inspecting the creatures. None of them raised their eyes, and other than the occasional rattle from their shackles, they stood frozen in silence.

Fifth sister appeared out of the last shuttle. "Are there enough of them, sister? I did as you commanded."

"On first inspection, yes, they look sufficient. What's your first impression?" She asked, turning to second sister.

"Favorable, I must congratulate fifth sister on her selection. They look young, strong, and physically similar. Many should survive the serum conversion and experimentation."

"And there are many more groups on the surface to gather from," fifth sister said.

"Good. - I'll expect excellent results. Select the ones you want, but keep a few in reserve," she said to second sister.

She squeezed the biceps of a small male. "Commander, once second council sister has made her selection, you and the warriors can get rid of the rest."

"Yes, first council sister." He bowed.

She looked along the line. "I think there's enough here for you to run your experiments. I'll meet you back in the lab."

"As you wish, sister," second sister said

With a last glance at their test subjects, first sister left the hangar as the commander straightened the line, readying the creatures for the selection.

Second sister walked along the line with fifth sister, pulling on the chains between the shackled wrists of the hominids she wanted, the stinging pain forcing them forward.

"Take these to my lab, sister. Make certain you separate the males from the females and secure them in separate holding cells."

With three warriors, fifth sister marched the creatures out of the hangar. The commander and the remaining warriors force marched the others towards the airlock at the back of the hangar. The ashen-faced males and the crying females made them smile as they tugged on the chains.

"No point in wasting good shackles," a warrior said to the commander, removing them. The rattle of chains echoed when he dropped them in a pile before shoving the hominids through the airlock door. He looked at the creatures through the window as the commander pushed a red button. A warning light flashed and the shrill of an alarm filled the hangar as the airlock's outer doors opened. The vacuum sucked the air and the creatures out into the atmosphere. He could see their mouths open with screams as they disappeared to their deaths. He grinned as he watched the slaughter.

"Enough! Move away from the window and continue with your duties."

"Yes, commander," the warrior said, still grinning as he walked away.

The communicator on the commander's wrist buzzed.

"Commander, prepare and refuel the shuttles so they are ready should there be another gathering today."

"Yes. fifth council sister."

∞

"Ah, good, the subjects are ready for me. Thank you, sister." Second sister said, entering her lab.

Fifth sister smiled. "Yes, everything is ready, as you instructed."

"I can hear and smell their fear," second sister said, flaring her nostrils. "Pump sedation gas into the cells. I need them calm."

"Ah, yes, stressed meat never tastes as good, does it? And there's plenty more where these came from," fifth sister said, laughing, as she flipped the switch, opening the pumps.

"This is delicate work, sister. The subjects need to be taken care of, not tortured. A comment like that demeans my work by suggesting I just hack into their insides and chop bits away before moving on to the next one?"

"No, I didn't mean to suggest that, sister. I know how important your work is. I apologize. Please forgive my ignorance."

The agitated hominids fell silent, shuffling around their cells, their glazed vacant eyes staring into nothing.

"Why haven't you started yet?" First sister said as she entered the lab, carrying her case of conversion serum. "I'd have expected you to have at least one of them open on your table by now?" She put the case on a bench and opened it.

"As I explained to fifth sister, I need them to be calm so I can safely carry out delicate and complex procedures. We've sedated them, so I'm ready for the first female."

"Good. Let's get to it." She opened a drawer, took out a large syringe, and screwed a long lumbar puncture needle to it. From her case, she chose a vial of serum, and pushing the needle through the cap, drew the serum into the syringe. "Let's not waste any more time. There are plenty more subjects where these came from when we need more. - Get me a male, fifth sister, and strap him face down tightly on this table. I need to inject into the epidural space next to his spinal cord, so he must be still."

Fifth sister opened the cell door, grabbing the nearest male. "This sedation gas is effective," she said, leading him to the table. She pulled the ankle, wrist, head, and chest straps tight.

"It is ready for you, first sister."

"It?" Second sister said, snapping back. The sudden objection stopped first sister in her tracks. There was a moment of tense silence. She knew she'd overstepped the mark.

"They are just test subjects, *second sister*. Anyone would think you'd taken a sympathetic liking to these creatures?" first sister said with an unpleasant chuckle.

"I just meant, as subjects, calling them 'it' is rather flippant, ought we not show them some respect, as they may be the progenitors of our future?" As before, she looked down in submission.

Fifth sister shrunk away, out of first sister's line of verbal fire. She knew she'd offended her superior and hoped first sister would come to her defense. She did.

"You want to name your pets? - very well, name them, and let's move on."

"They are hominids, and *homo* in our native language means man. And like us, they are from the dirt, *humus* in our language. So let's call them human from now on?"

"Human, yes, now can we please get to work, or would you like to feed them, walk and groom them before getting on with the more important task of creating my warriors and saving ourselves from extinction?"

The venom in her voice said she didn't need an answer.

"Good." She pushed the needle into the human male's spine. He groaned in tranquilized pain as she injected the serum. "Now, we wait."

"You can go," second sister said, glaring at fifth sister.

She was glad to be relieved and scurried out of the lab.

From the female's holding cell, second sister beckoned the nearest female to the empty table. She shuffled forward, her eyes still vacant, there with no need for physical encouragement. She didn't move as the straps tightened.

"I'll be back to check on his progress shortly. I'll leave you to do your delicate, complex work," first sister said, closing her case as she marched out.

Thank goodness for that, she said to herself, relieved she was finally alone. She slid a cannula into the back of the female's hand, injected anesthetic, and waited for her to close her eyes.

On initial examination, her external reproductive organs didn't look too different from theirs. Her concern was if her internal reproductive system would be strong enough to support the growth of a Szatethess embryo. It had always been the aggressive growth that caused problems with other species she'd experimented on. Their growth and reach had gone beyond what the bodies of the test subjects could withstand, and none survived, killing the embryo.

The scan of this human female's uterus showed the walls were thicker and more elastic than any of the other species she'd implanted. *Hmm, that looks good. Humans might be compatible.* She scrutinized the image on the monitor. *There is only one way to find out.*

She had an embryo prepared for implantation. With the catheter containing the fertilized embryo, she inserted it into the female's uterus. The monitor showed it was in position. She pressed the plunger. A shot of the medium containing the embryo streamed out of the tip. She smiled to herself at a job well done and withdrew the catheter.

The female snored, as she called first sister.

"The scans on the first human female were positive sister, and embryo implantation is complete."

"How long until we know?"

"We will know if the implantation has been successful in two days, sister."

"In the meantime, I suggest you prepare more females in case this one fails. - how is my male subject doing?"

She walked over. "Other than bruising at the injection site, sister, there has been no movement yet."

"I'll give him another hour. If nothing changes, I'll discard this one and begin again with another. - keep me updated."

"Of course, sister."

The female came around and tried to sit up. Unable to move, she screamed and thrashed against the straps, tears filling her eyes.

"Calm now, no one is going to hurt you." She placed a comforting hand on her forehead and wiped her tears away with a cloth in her other. Their eyes met for the first time, and her warm gaze settled her.

She unbuckled the straps, and the female sat up. Her eyes darted around the room, trying to make sense of her surroundings. She offered her a cup of water, and the female gulped it down. She handed the cup back, cupped her hands, and brought them to her mouth.

"Ah, yes I see, drink. Yes, you want more?" She refilled the cup.

Once the female had her fill, she smiled and handed it back.

"It's not so bad after all." Second sister said, holding out her hand. "Come, it's time for you to rejoin your friends."

The female held it, hopped off the table, and returned to the cell with her. Once inside, she smiled at second sister. The others stood frozen, sensing a change.

"I'll get you all some water," second sister said, cupping her hands.

The others looked at the female, not sure what to do. She smiled. The others did the same.

She left the door open as she filled a large jug and took a stack of cups, handing them over to the waiting female, who handed them out and served them.

"What's going on?" first sister said, as she marched into the lab.

The female stopped pouring and looked down.

"Oh, sister. You made me jump." She pressed a hand against her chest. "I was just giving them some much-needed water," she said, coming out of the cell.

"They don't need pampering. They need to get pregnant." She brushed past her and slammed the cell door.

"Yes, of course, sister. But keeping them fed and hydrated ensures their bodies are in a condition to accept the embryos."

"Right, yes, carry on then, but don't get too attached. Their sole purpose is to fulfill our needs, or I'll have them disposed of. You have backup humans, don't you?"

"Yes, but..."

First sister turned away. "And how's my male doing? Is he showing any sign of conversion?"

She followed her over. "No, not as yet. But he is awake. These humans are a lot more..."

"A lot more what?" she said, prodding the injection site. "This male is useless to me." She turned her back on him. "Get me another."

"They are a lot more intelligent than we first thought."

"I'm not interested in how their brains work, just how their bodies can serve me." She put the serum case on the bench and opened it. "Do I make myself clear, *second* council sister?"

From the drawer, she took another needle and syringe, filling it with a new serum. She looked back. "Now, sister. Get rid of this one and get me another."

"Yes, sister, right away.." She undid the buckles holding the whimpering male down.

He sprang off the table, staring directly at her. The look in his eyes told her everything she needed to know, and she retreated. He clenched his fists. The effects of the serum slowed him down and he stumbled toward her. From behind, first sister grabbed his hair, jolted his head back, and rammed the full length of the needle into his ear. He grunted and collapsed, dead.

Gasps and murmuring came from the cells.

"Well, at least there was a warrior's aggression in him," she said, wiping wet fluid off the needle on his loincloth.

"Wha - what, what did you do? He was confused and afraid. You didn't need to kill him. We could have restrained him."

She tutted, stepped over the body, and flipped the switch, releasing sedation gas into the cells. "Quieten down!"

Second sister stood motionless, staring at the dead human, stunned by the callous actions of her superior. "There was just no need for that."

"What did you say?"

The venom in her voice jolted her out of her daydream. She looked up, shaking her head. "Nothing, sister."

"Right, remove this body and strap another on my table."

She pulled the lifeless body to the other side of the lab, out of sight of the cells, and called for two warriors to come and dispose of the corpse.

"I told you not to get attached to these test subjects. They are here to serve us, not for you to bond with. - Now, let's start again."

Second sister opened the door to the male cell and walked another male over to the table.

"Strap him down tight. I want to get this new variant into him before the sedation wears off."

She tightened the last buckle as first sister slid the needle deep into the human's back. He groaned with pain as she pushed the plunger, injecting the new serum. She laid her hand on his shoulder, keeping it there as he closed his eyes and passed out.

"He looks like a good choice," first sister said. "I've dialed back the aggression inducers, added strength builders, and a new compound that should make him totally compliant in this new formula." She ran her hand over his back. "He's nice and muscular, so hopefully, he'll survive the conversion process. Then we'll begin his programming and training. While we wait, impregnate another female. There's no point in wasting time. We have enough subjects for this round of tests."

She caught herself stroking the male's hair and snatched her hand back. "Oh, err, yes, I'll start the procedure now," second sister said.

"Good." She clicked the locks on her serum case. "I'll leave you to it then and be back in an hour. Let me know if anything changes."

Once she'd gone, her ears focused on the murmuring from the cells. The sedation gas had worn off. Inside the female's cell, they were cowering against the back wall. They'd witnessed one of their own being brutally murdered, and all the trust she had earned was gone.

Damn you, sister. She opened the cell door and stepped inside, keeping her distance. The murmuring increased. She lowered her hands to her sides, palms facing forward, and lowering her eyes bowed.

The female she had implanted stepped forward and made the same gesture of water she'd made earlier.

"Of course," she said, smiling and picking up the jug. She left the door open, filled it, and got another stack of cups. When she returned, the implanted female was waiting for her.

The male on the table groaned. She smiled, handed her the cups and jug, and bowed before leaving to check on him. The skin around the injection site had thickened and changed to olive green.

She let out a huge breath and called first sister.

"I hope this interruption means you have something to report?" first sister said, sneering.

"Sister, the male is exhibiting some signs of conversion. Perhaps you could come and look."

"Very well. In the meantime, prepare another male for me, so he's ready when I get there." The line went dead.

A footstep behind made her spin. The implanted female held out the empty jug. "You cannot be out here." Taking her by the arm, she said, "you must go back inside before first council sister gets here." She took the jug and hurried her in. "You," she said, waving at another female. "Come with me." The bewildered female followed her out, and she locked the cell door behind her.

The female didn't move when she walked past. "Come over here." She smiled. "It's going to be okay. I need you to lie on this table," she said, touching it. She still didn't move. "It'll be okay. I promise," she said, escorting the female onto the table.

Her eyes were wide and questioning as she tightened the straps. “Shh,” second sister said, placing her hand lightly on the female's forehead. “It’ll be alright.”

With her female secure, the noise from the male’s cell got louder. Banded together in the back, they were planning. Not taking any chances, she flipped the switch, sedating them again. It went quiet, and she opened the door. They were wandering around, bumping into each other. She grabbed the arm of the nearest male and escorted him out of the cell onto a table. He was bigger and more muscular than the first one. *If the conversion is successful, he’ll make a powerful warrior.*

She was tightening the last straps on the docile male as first sister and two warriors walked in.

“Ah, good. One of each,” she said. She tugged on the straps. “And they’re both ready. Good. I’ve bought these two with me in case there’s a repeat of the earlier incident. They’ll deal with any unruly test sub..., - err, humans.” She put her case on the bench, took out another vial of the same serum, and prepared the injection. “Now, let’s look at you first. Hold this," she said, thrusting the syringe out for second sister while bending over the groaning male. She prodded the olive-colored thickening skin around the injection site. “Hmm, there’s been some progress. - but it’s not enough, hmm.”

“May I continue with the implantation procedure of this female?” second sister asked.

“What - Oh, yes, continue. Give me the syringe.” She held out her hand without looking. “Now, what are we going to do with you?” She squinted. “I know. Let’s try a booster of the same serum. That might work.”

“Or do we need a little more time for the serum to complete its work?” second sister said, hoping to spare him more pain.

"If it were going to work on its own, it would have done so by now. There's been some conversion, as you can see. Maybe more serum would do the trick. And there is no more time. We need to be aggressive with the testing. Or perhaps you don't have the stomach for it?"

"Of course you're right, sister. I apologize," she said, turning away, unable to watch as first sister slid the needle into the male's spine for the second time. He groaned and fell silent.

She pulled the needle out and felt for a pulse. "This one is strong. We might have a winning formula if that doesn't kill him." She chuckled. "What's wrong with her?" she said, flicking her eyes at the female.

She was sobbing and pulling hard against the straps. "Shh now, no, no. It'll be fine. Calm yourself," second sister said, trying to soothe her. She stood shielding her from the males. "Nothing is going to happen to you, shush, now." She injected an anesthetic.

"Thank goodness for that," first sister said as the female went silent. She took another vial from the case. "Let's try this new formula on this one. It is a similar formula to the last one, but I've added some accelerators which should speed up the conversion process. Hopefully, his heart will hold out." She injected a full syringe into the other male's spine. He grimaced. Satisfied with her work, she said, "call me in an hour so I can check on their progress." She locked the case, and walking to the door, said, "I'll leave these two warriors with you, just in case."

"Yes, sister." She lifted the female's feet into the stirrups, spread her knees, and prepared a catheter with the embryo. The warriors stared wide-eyed, then shared a joke and were laughing as she inserted it. "You two, wait outside." She bared her Szatethess teeth, and they fell over each other, trying to get out first.

She realigned her jaw and continued with the implantation. "fingers crossed," she said to the sleeping female as she took her feet out of the stirrups and put her legs back into a more dignified position.

From the corner of her eye, the second of the two human males moved. She checked the time. "An hour… Calm now," she said, walking over. *Well, well.* All the skin on the male's back had converted into a thick olive-colored leathery layer. Although she hated first sister's callous methods, she couldn't deny her progress. "And what about you?" she said to the boosted male. There was no change. Shaking her head, she knew what that meant for him.

Her communicator buzzed. "Right on time." She pressed the answer button.

"Report."

"There has been some progress, sister. Perhaps you'd like to see for yourself."

"Indeed, I'll be right down."

She ended the call and walked back to the female, who was awake. "Well, at least she can't touch you," she said, unbuckling the straps.

The female sat up and looked across at the males. She clung to second sister.

"Don't worry, that will not happen to you," she said, wrapping an arm around her. "But you must understand we need you and your males to ensure our race survives." She helped her off the table and escorted her back to the cell.

"You've done another one, then?" first sister said, booming her voice across the lab as she marched in with her case. "Was the implantation successful?"

"Oh, er, yes, I believe so," second sister said, startled by her sudden appearance. "We'll know for sure in two days. I don't think there's much point in implanting more females until we know if these embryos have gestated. There are very few viable embryos left."

"You worry about making sure the females get pregnant and can carry us to term. I'll get you more eggs to work with."

"There are only nine of us left, sister. Where are you going to get them from?"

First sister placed her case on the bench, opened it, and looked out of the corner of her eyes. "We two are the only ones that matter now. It is we who will save our race. The others are dispensable."

She knew exactly what that meant. And the matter-of-fact way she said it sent an icy shiver down her spine.

To get viable embryos, eggs needed to be harvested. Harvested from newly deceased Szatethess. *Once the other sisters are no longer useful to her, she's going to kill and harvest from them!*

"Don't act so shocked. You knew this might have to happen. I want you to plan for it, and the storage of all the new eggs you'll get."

"Shouldn't we wait until we know if the two implantations in these females have been successful first, before..."

"I have every confidence in your ability. Perhaps you could show me the implantation procedure?"

Why does she want to know? She felt her stomach knot. *Then she won't need me either!*

"But for now, let's look and see what the conversion serum has done to these males," first sister said, turning away.

She caught the murderous smirk on first sister's face, and she knew she was treading on dangerous ground.

"Ah, yes, it's better with the added accelerator. But it's still not there yet," she said, comparing the progress of the two males. "The booster doesn't seem to have done much in this one. Hmm, oh well." She called the two warriors back into the lab. "You two take this one back to the hangar and dispose of him."

They unbuckled the male, grabbed an arm, and lifted him off the table. He didn't move or make a sound.

"Stop!" second sister said. "Might he be of use?"

The two warriors snapped to attention, and to her surprise, the male copied them.

First sister was about to make her pay dearly for countermanding her order and her insubordination, but she saw the male's reaction. She paused. "Interesting how he reacts to authority. Very Interesting."

"We should separate him from the others and see if we can train him. He might not make it as a warrior, but he could as a worker, sister. He and others like him could construct our facilities on the ground." She bowed her head, knowing full well she'd dodged a bullet.

"Good idea. New workers could speed up our progress. We'll need a better way to administer serum two if you want a lot of workers."

"It doesn't need to be as invasive as an injection, sister. What about an aerosol? We could adapt the serum so their mucous membranes absorb it. Then we could release it into a room, creating a lot of new workers all at once."

"I like your thinking. I can create an aerosol. See how well we work together sometimes?" she said with a wry smile. "I still need warriors, so I'll work on that, too. Now let's test and see how well this one takes orders. Take this one over there, then unbuckle and stand this one up."

As commanded, they moved the male they were holding over to the far wall, unbuckled, and stood the other.

"You!" first sister said, pointing and addressing the male. Immediately, his eyes focused on her like a dog, waiting for its master to throw a stick.

"Another good worker," second sister said.

"Agreed. Let's split them into two groups. One to test the conversion serum to make warriors, the other group to be exposed to the aerosol to make workers." She walked over to the bigger male, squeezed the muscles in his arms, and inspected him. "Hmm, yes, he'll make a good worker. Right, you two bring the two worker humans to the hangar, and we'll store them in the room at the back while we make more of them." The warriors marched the two new workers out.

"Get me another male. I want to try this fourth serum formula. It's much more potent and aggressive than the others, so it should work," she said, taking the vial of new serum out of her case and holding it up to the light. "looks like we both have work to do." Attaching a long needle to a new syringe, she drew the new serum into it.

Second sister escorted another male, staggering from the sedation, onto the table. She finished tightening the last strap as first sister prodded for the entry point along his spine.

"It's going to take me a day at least to create an aerosol from serum two to create your workers," she said. The male groaned as she pushed the needle in. As she pulled it out, he convulsed. Every muscle fiber in his body cramped and his face racked with pain. "That's why I ordered the new straps. That's the effect I wanted to see. Good."

He continued to fit for a few more seconds, then stopped, motionless and unconscious, breathing in short, fast breaths.

Carefully closing her case, she said, "call me in an hour with a progress update. Now, we've both got work to do. And if you ever countermand me in front of my warriors again, *second* sister, it will cost you your life. Am I clear?" And walked out of the lab without looking at her.

Emotionally drained by what she'd witnessed, she couldn't answer.

∞

Back in her chambers, first sister collected the ingredients and equipment needed to produce serum two and convert it into an aerosol. It was going to take at least a day to produce a useful quantity. The extra time would be ample to adjust and monitor the progress of the serum she was going to inject into more of the males to make warriors - and prepare for the harvest! She smiled. She was looking forward to that part.

Thinking of her sisters, she called fifth sister. "I need you and the other sisters to take warriors and shuttles down to the planet's surface and get more male test subjects. Go to every continent and land mass on this planet and collect subjects from each one. I've made a breakthrough with the experimental serum and I want to take advantage of it immediately."

"Yes, of course, sister. I'll need to ask what third and fourth sister's availability is before estimating the time to complete your task."

"No need. As of now, I'm making you my third council sister. Take no nonsense from the others. If they object, refer them to me. This takes priority over everything else. I want those new test subjects today, third council sister."

"Yes, sister, immediately. You'll have them in five hours," she said with a new authority.

She laughed to herself as she hung up the call, knowing how temporary the new promotion would be. Then she called second sister to make sure she was on track.

"What progress, sister?"

"It appears your new serum has had the desired effect, sister. Your male has gone through the conversion and survived."

"Finally, some good news. I'll be right there." She checked over the equipment to make sure it was doing its job. New serum two bubbled and hissed as it converted into an aerosol, filling the canisters. She grinned all the way to the main labs.

"There he is," she said, clapping her hands as she entered. All the skin on his back, neck, arms, and legs was an olive green color. It was thicker, more leathery, and tougher than his original human skin. "It looks like the serum has completed the first phase. Have you checked all of him?" She slid her hand up his leg, feeling his new strength.

"No, sister, I thought you would like to do it."

"Ah yes, you thought right," she said, unbuckling the straps.

"Is he safe to release?"

"Yes. I added a little something extra to the formula, so he stays completely still while his body undergoes the conversion. The process radically alters their body chemistry. It's quite violent, really. I didn't want him damaging himself if his body convulsed again. So, I've paralyzed him. He will remain paralyzed until phase two, when he'll shed this skin, completing the conversion. Overall, it should take about a day. - Now, help me turn him over."

"Yes, of course, sister."

He was completely naked. "Everything looks in working order," first sister said, running her eyes over his body.

"It certainly looks that way. His skin looks the same as on his back. His increased musculature looks suitable for a warrior. I would say that humans will give us what we need. Congratulations, sister, you have converted your first new warrior."

"Yes, let's keep him here until he sheds his skin, then I'll start his training, and we'll know for sure. I have worker serum being created in my lab. It will be ready in the next day or so. The newly promoted third council sister, along with the other council sisters, are, as we speak, gathering more human male subjects for us." She rubbed her hands. "Everything is proceeding as I expect them to. Soon, we will have enough workers to build your facility and we can scale the conversion process. All that remains is for you to complete your task. Which I am sure you'll accomplish. How are the implanted females? Are they pregnant?"

"I'll get meaningful scan results tomorrow, sister. The uterus in human females is thicker, stronger, and more elastic than any other species I've implanted. I am hopeful of a positive outcome."

"Good. I'll expect your report tomorrow morning. Take the other side of this table and help me wheel my new warrior into that holding cell. I don't want him disturbed." They pushed the paralyzed human Szateth hybrid warrior into the empty cell.

"It's been a long exhausting day," second sister said, closing the cell door. "There's nothing more I can do today. If there's nothing else, sister, I'll go to my chambers to rest?"

"Yes, rest. Tomorrow's going to be a big day." She smiled at her new toy through the window in the cell door, then spun around. "oh, no, wait!" she said. "Have you started preparing the storage for your new eggs, as I asked you to?"

"I thought I'd wait until we have some test results to work with. I'm not sure there's much point in using up valuable time and resources unnecessarily. Egg storage and embryo preservation are very delicate. It's a procedure that requires focus and precision. I thought it best to work with what we have."

"I know what it takes, *second* council sister." She stepped into her subordinate's space, magnifying her size and authority.

She looked down. "Of course, sister."

"The seven older council sisters are coming to the end of their *useful* lives. But their eggs will be, and I won't miss an opportunity to have them - *help* our work. You understand my meaning?"

She looked up. The glare punching her eyes made her step back. "Yes, perfectly, sister. If I may wait until after tomorrow's scan results, we will know what steps to take next."

Her buzzing communicator ended the intimidation. "Very well, *second* sister. You have another day."

It buzzed again. "Yes, what is it?" she said, turning for the exit.

"The shuttles are returning, first council sister. What are your orders?" the hangar commander asked.

"Have the council sisters sort the males into two groups, commander. Weak-looking, and strong-looking, then put the groups in separate rooms."

"As you wish, first council sister."

"Well, a good day. I'll leave you to rest." First sister gave a weak smile and walked out.

She sat slumped on an empty examination table, shaking her head in disbelief, stunned by first sister's aggression. *She is going to harvest them. I know it. It doesn't matter what I say, I can see it in her eyes.* She hopped off the table and looked through the window in the female's cell door. *There's nothing I can do to protect them, but I'm going to do what I can to protect you. You are our future.*

The two implanted females were standing slightly separate from the others, with a hand on their belly. *Tomorrow we'll know.*

She turned the lights off in the lab and headed back to her chambers. First sister had revealed her plans, and they made her shudder.

∞

The sun was just coming up when she woke from a fitful sleep. The nightmares of failed implantations woke her more than once. There was no way she would get back to sleep now, knowing how first sister would react if the results were negative. She sat up, staring into the gloom, and replayed the implantation procedures in her mind. The scan of their physiology was good, and the implantation procedures went well. There was no reason for them to fail, and the scans this morning would confirm it.

As she flicked the lights on in the lab, she heard uneasy murmurs from the female's cell. She ran to the window. The two implanted females were standing alone. The others, scared by the change in their appearance, made them outcasts. There were no signs of aggression, but she knew better than to keep them in there. She opened the door, and they fell silent. The two implanted females walked out, and she locked the door. "Oh, my," she said. Their skin was turning olive. "No wonder the others are eyeing you suspiciously. Look at you," she said with a smile, reaching into a drawer for a mirror.

They could see what had happened to one another, but not to themselves. She held the mirror so they could see. They held their stomachs and cried.

"No, no, this is a good thing. This will save your lives, and mine, and the others," she said, walking to the scanning table. "Come on over and let me do these scans. So we can see what's happened."

With the monitors set up, she slid the probe over their abdomen. The image on the screen showed the implanted embryo taking root, its tentacles stretching out along the uterus wall in each female. *I can tell first council sister that the females are pregnant.* She pressed print, and the prized pictures appeared from under the monitor. She savored the moment with a slow smile.

"Right now, you two are the most valuable things on this ship." She waved the pictures, then asked, "Are you hungry? You must be hungry, - and thirsty. I'll get you some food."

The two females looked at each other, then back at her, and appeared to nod.

She raised a single eyebrow. "Did you just nod? Do you understand what I'm saying? Do you?" she said, leaning toward them. They froze.

"I didn't mean to frighten you, but do you understand me?" she asked. Her words tripped over themselves to get out.

They looked at each other again, then back at her, but didn't respond.

"I'm sorry, - for a moment I thought... Well, it doesn't matter, I'll get you that food."

From observations of the humans on the surface, they ate mostly fruits, leaves, flowers, bark, and insects, and occasionally cooked some animal meat. The Szateth are carnivores, and the females would need to eat a lot more meat if they were to survive their pregnancies and give birth to healthy Szateth females. She ordered a meat-heavy omnivorous meal to be brought up to her lab.

I'm going to have to keep these two separated from the other females. "Now, let's get you more comfortable with your own room," she said, pointing to the storeroom next to the male's cell. "It's smaller, but once I take the furniture out, it'll be fine for you." The cells had some tables and chairs, but the humans either sat or lay on the floor. She lifted a table, when, to her amazement, the females sat in the chairs. She knew humans were more intelligent than the other species she'd experimented on, which made them suitable candidates in the first place, but this action suggested something else, an instant leap in their level of intelligence. *There's something more going on here.* The thought led her to consider an exciting possibility. *I wonder if the embryos are passing on some hereditary cognitive intelligence. The nod. And now this - could it be possible in a couple of days? And what if it was more? What if our embryos had affected a leap in their evolution? If that were the case, humans would be the answer to the survival of the Szateth.* The hairs on her arms stood at the possibility.

The rattling of the food trolley and the barking voice of first council sister disrupted her thoughts.

"What's going on here? I hope you have an extremely good explanation for all this?" she said, blocking the doorway. Her resentful eyes glared at the females. They stiffened.

Second sister saw their white-knuckled grip on the arms of the chairs. "You must see these, sister." She said, stepping between her and the terrified females.

"This better be good," she said, staring hard at her.

"I assure you it is, sister. Let me show you the images from this morning's scans. They're on the bench if you'll follow me."

"Very well." She shot another glance at the females.

"Here, sister. - And here," she said, pointing to the position of the embryos in the uterus. "-As you can see, the embryos have attached and embedded themselves into the uterus walls in both females. It's unprecedented for things to have progressed this quickly."

"Impressive. How long till they're born?"

"Well, normal human gestation is nine months. We know our embryos are strong and demanding of the host's body. I suspect having made themselves at home, so to speak, the embryos are adapting to human physiology to give them the best chance for survival. I would say the same, about nine months, maybe a little sooner. It is hard to say at this point. They are going to need care if they are to carry our new sisters to term."

"Very well. Good work." Turning to the warriors, she said, "Take the males back to the hangar and put them in with the weaker-looking human males. Show no mercy if they get out of hand."

"Yes, first council sister," they said, drawing their batons.

As ordered, they marched the males out of the cell in single file.

"They, and the others, are going to be your workers and builders.," she said as they marched out of the lab. "There will be enough of them to build the first of your conversion facilities on the surface in the next few days. - In the meantime, I suggest you implant a few more females. Let me know if you need anything to aid in the birth of our new sisters. - Now let me see my new warrior."

Not waiting for second sister, she marched into his cell. The top layer of skin had hardened, become translucent, and was lifting away from the layer below. "It won't be long now," she said to him. "Perfect."

"Should I continue to prepare the room for the two females, sister?" Second sister said, standing in the doorway.

"Yes, do what you think necessary I want nothing getting in the way of our progress now. Tomorrow you will have your first batch of workers, and by the look of things, tomorrow I'll have my first new warrior. - How many experimentation tables do we have?" she said with a cocky smile.

"Four, sister."

"We'll need more. I want to speed things up and inject more males with the conversion serum at the same time. I'll get them made. - We should have a feast. I think there's cause for celebration, don't you?" She smiled and licked her lips.

"Oh yes, sister. And now we know we can impregnate the human females I have enough embryos to add new sisters to our council."

First sister pouted. "Your sentiment and devotion towards your sisters and these humans are admirable," she said. Then fixed her with an icy stare. "It's why you'll never be first council sister." With a sudden sharp breath in, she blinked and looked away. "Arrange the feast. I'll inform the others of the good news. Let's eat something special tonight. Arrange it," she said, marching away.

"Yes, sister." She stared at her back. *And your lack of compassion towards what we have, and for the resource we need, means you won't stay first council sister for much longer.*

She made the two females comfortable for the rest of the day, setting out the furniture and bringing in beds. She clapped and laughed as they tried each new piece without explanation. The new male warrior still hadn't moved, and she'd organized the food. With everything done, she left for the feast.

As she arrived, first sister was giving the others a speech on how she'd created a serum that would convert the humans into workers and another that created powerful warriors. She emphasized how important it was for them to focus on the growth of the Szateth army, and their continued survival no matter the sacrifices. Rapturous applause filled the chamber, and she looked at second sister wearing a knowing smile.

"Ah, second sister, come and tell us of your progress and success," she said, waving at her to come over. "Then we'll eat a special meal to celebrate." The others squealed their excitement.

She took the lounger in the circle next to first sister and told them about the pregnant females. "I'm cautiously optimistic," she said. "The rapid growth of the implanted embryos is unexpected, and I'll be monitoring their development. I don't have enough data to support my assumption yet, but I think these humans could be the key to our survival."

"You're being too modest and pessimistic. Your work, so far, has been exemplary, and your results reflect your efforts," first sister said. The others agreed.

"I need more time to confirm..."

"Time? I know what time it is. It's time for what we've all been waiting for. - It's time to eat." First sister clapped. "Bring in the food!"

They chatted excitedly as the servant workers brought in the meal for examination. He was muscular, magnificent, and meaty! Second sister smiled. He was the larger of the two warriors she had thrown out of her lab for laughing at her female. It was the last mistake he would ever make.

The sisters took turns to inspect and stroke his warm body as they circled him. He looked dazed, unsure of what was happening. All second sister told him was he was there to satisfy them. One by one, they felt his body, then sat back down. When it was first sister's turn, she could see their excited breathing as they waited for her approval. She felt every inch of him. She whispered. Comforting him, he stayed relaxed as she moved behind him. He smiled. The others watched, their eyes wide with anticipation.

A hand slid around his waist and pulled him into her. She was so warm. Another glided through his hair around his forehead. The other sisters, their mouths open, panted as they moved to the edge of their loungers, poised to move.

"Thank you," first sister said, pulling his head back and to the side. He screamed as the searing pain of long, needle-sharp teeth sank into his neck and ripped out the flesh.

She let his body drop to the floor and circled her prey before tearing off the best meat until she'd eaten her fill. The others, jostling for position, waited their turn. Satisfied, she returned to her lounger, letting the sisters take their turn. In a feeding frenzy, they tore gobs of flesh from the rest of the body, tearing it apart. She laughed as they gorged themselves on what she'd left. It was a gruesome, bloody scene, and within minutes, stripped, gnawed bones were all that remained of the warrior. The sisters reveling in their overfed contentment, laid on their loungers, and slept.

Neural Blockchain Journal Entry #920

The warrior serum has not produced the results I need. Second sister has got what she wanted with a serum that creates workers and her females are pregnant. I hope for her sake they deliver new sisters within the nine months, as she says.

This fourth serum formula successfully converts the human male into the warrior I need. I must not lose control of the planetary network I've worked so hard to create. I need those warriors!

Still, the meal went down well. Maybe I shouldn't have taken and fed on a warrior, but he was so tasty that I couldn't stop myself. The sisters appreciated it too.

I'm concerned second sister is developing an attachment to these humans. I need to watch her. Right now, though, I need her to get the females impregnated with our embryos. But there will come a time when she has outlived her usefulness.

She can deal with the females - I need warriors, that has to be the priority.

First Council Sister - Szateth leader
Advanced planetary research fleet.

Neural Blockchain Journal Entry #018

The progress has been impressive. I am convinced the human species can save us. The embryo implantation was a success, and physically they are remarkably resilient, withstanding and adapting to the demands of a Szatethess embryo. I will continue to monitor their progress closely. First sister is oblivious to our embryos' effect on human females. Undoubtedly, they have passed some of their hereditary cognitive intelligence to them. I believe there has been a massive leap in human evolution because of it.

If my belief in their importance is correct, they are to be protected. They could become the dominant hybrid variant of Szateth and Szatethess in the future. I will know soon.

As I thought, first sister has focused on growing her army of warriors. Again, human males are perfect for conversion. I hope she gets the formula for the conversion serum right, although I think she'll be asking for my help soon. She must not decimate their numbers once it is. My concern about her attitude toward humans is growing. Her lack of understanding of their potential and importance is astounding. The meal was a wonderful distraction. First sister seemed pleased with my selection, as were my other sisters.

Second Council Sister

Advanced planetary research fleet.

Three

Success she must keep secret

With the last straps attached to the new examination tables, the engineer workers pulled on them hard to ensure they were secure. Happy with their work, they wheeled them to the lab. Word had gotten around about the feast, and they prayed first council sister liked them. They stood next to them, fingers crossed behind their backs, waiting for her inspection.

Moments later, she marched in, carrying her case. "Ah, at last, I'll be able to convert more warriors," she said, looking at each table and pulling on the straps. "They look perfect," she said to the head engineer worker.

"Thank you, first council sister." He said, uncrossing his fingers.

"You may go."

"Yes, first council sister." He waved at the other workers to leave.

"Good morning, sister. I thought last night's celebration feast *went down well,*" second sister said, laughing and rubbing her belly. She caught the eyes of the last worker, whose face turned white as a sheet.

"Indeed, it did," she said. "And today we'll make more progress with new workers and warriors." She patted the cell door. "I'll refill this cell with some of the strong-looking males I've got in the hangar."

Second sister opened the storeroom door to check on the two females. "How are you two feeling today?" she asked. They smiled, patted their stomachs, and lifted fingers to their mouths.

"Food, yes, of course. I'll arrange some to be brought up for you. Let me look at you first," she said. She took their blood pressure, checked their pulses, and examined them for any signs of the embryos aborting. "Good, everything looks good." She noted the results and called the kitchen for their food.

"How are these two doing?" first sister asked, poking her head in through the door. The females froze.

"Oh, err, fine, just fine. Their blood pressure is normal, and there are no signs of rejection. They're just hungry. So far, everything looks good," she said, offering a reassuring smile to the females.

"Good. Now let's look at the progress of my warrior, shall we?"

Second sister caught up with her as she was leaning over the transitioning male. More of his skin had hardened and lifted away. He was curled up in what looked like a scaly, crispy, transparent skin bag. He still hadn't moved.

"Hmm, another day perhaps," first sister said, prodding it. "Alright." She stood and smoothed her robes. "Let's get some of the other males up from the hangar, so they're ready once I've made more conversion serum four. The new tables should hold them secure." She called the hangar commander. "Bring up nine of the stronger-looking human males to second council sister's lab, Commander."

"Yes, first council sister, immediately."

She ended the call.

"Presumably, you're going to be here playing with your females when they get here?" she said, smirking at second sister.

"Yes, I'll be here, sister."

"Good. Put them in a cell and secure them. It'll take the rest of the day for me to create more serum four. In the meantime, implant at least one more female. It looks like these humans can accept our embryos, so let's get the rest in. I'll be back tomorrow." She walked out without looking back.

Her icy attitude had returned, the joy of last night's celebration a distant memory. "As you wish, sister," she said.

Her nostrils twitched. She could smell the food wafting down the corridor, vegetables, and cooked meat. *How can they eat cooked meat*? When it appeared, she covered her nose and instructed the servant worker to put it down on the table in their room.

As the tray touched the table, they pounced on it, devouring the vegetables, but didn't touch the meat.

"Eat your protein," second sister said, pointing at the meat, pinching her nose.

They looked away in disgust.

I wonder? She called the kitchen and ordered raw meat brought to her lab. "I've ordered something else for you. I think your babies are making your bodies adapt so they get the nutrients they need. After all, you are going to give birth to a human Szatethess hybrid." She pressed a hand against her chest. "This is wonderful."

The meat arrived, dripping with blood, and as soon as the worker left it, they tore into it as she had at last night's feeding frenzy. *Just as I thought*. Once they'd had their fill, they curled up and fell asleep. She smiled, beaming with pride. None of her other subjects had gotten this far.

She hung the clipboard, convinced that Szatethess embryos had successfully blended with humans. It was time to impregnate another female. In their cell, among them, there was a leader she hadn't noticed before. *Perfect, and you'll help the others accept their fate.*

She flipped the switch, releasing the sedation gas. She had built a level of trust and didn't want to upset the females by separating the leader by force. Once the gas made them docile, she escorted the female leader out, got her on the examination table, and gave her an anesthetic, putting her to sleep.

The implantation went well, and she knew she couldn't put her back in the cell. The others would reject her. "When you wake up, I'll put you in with the other two," she said, unbuckling the sleeping female.

"Here are the males, second council sister. Where should we put them?" It was the hangar commander, with six warriors.

"Ah, yes, good. Over in that cell," she said, pointing.

"Come on, move yourselves. Quickly!" He pushed the male at the rear of the column, as the warrior pulled the wrist shackles on the male at the front. The chains on their ankles rattled and dragged across the floor, painfully rubbing their flesh raw as they moved.

She looked away, knowing far worse was to come.

Once inside, the warriors removed the shackles and locked them in. "Would you like me to inform first council sister that the males are here, second council sister?" the commander said.

A cough from behind made her turn. It was the female, awake and sitting up. "No, no, I'll do it. You can go, commander." She waved him away.

"Yes, thank you, second council sister. Come on, let's go," he said to the warriors.

The female had a hand on her belly. She knew something had happened, but didn't know what. She sat frowning and confused.

"Don't you worry?" second sister said, putting a hand on her knee. "Like the other two, you are the most important thing on this ship. Nothing is going to happen to you. I'll see to that. Come and join the other two over in this room?" She held a hand out for the female to follow her.

They were snoring when they went in. They'd been asleep awhile. She checked their pulse. *It's faster than normal, but nothing to worry about. Probably their digestive systems working overtime to metabolize the raw meat.* The new mother-to-be stood, staring at them.

"Come in. They're fine." She beckoned her in. "Just resting. Nothing to worry about." The two females opened their eyes at the sound of her voice. "Look, there's someone else here to join you."

They raised their heads, glaring at her. She was the one who had them stand separated from the others in their group. Now she was standing there, holding her stomach, her watering eyes pleading for their help.

"I expect the two of you to look after her. You can see how afraid she is."

They nodded, put a hand on their belly, and gestured for more food.

"Alright, I'll order more food for the three of you."

They got up and welcomed the new mother in.

She called the kitchen, "I need you to bring the same food up to the lab for my females. Bring the same fruits and vegetables as before, with a mix of cooked and raw meat. Enough for three this time. And bring more every four hours."

"Yes, straight away, second council sister," the head kitchen worker replied.

She watched, fascinated, as the two led her over to a chair. She didn't know what to do. One of them sat showing her, got up, then pointed to her to sit.

Second sister clapped when she did. "Right," she said, smiling at them. "I'll leave you three to rest. Your food will be here shortly." They smiled back, and a tingling surge of warmth spread throughout her body as she closed the door.

She sat at her bench and buried her face in her arms. *We can save our species.* As tears wet her sleeves, she shuddered. *What if first sister finds out? She'll harvest the others straight away.* She raised her head and wiped her face. *I'm going to need help to make sure she doesn't. Ah, I know.*

Neural Blockchain Journal Entry #921

Conversion serum four seems to work. The male is showing signs of conversion and the second, skin shedding stage, looks like it has started too. It's been a good day.

Second council sister seems in line and obedient, but I'm still not sure about her. It's annoying that she is a better scientist than me, so I need her for now.

I'll soon be able to convert more human males into warriors at once, thanks to the new examination tables and restraints. They work very well.

The engineers should be able to repair the ship's damaged communications array, but I want the fleet to know what I've found on this planet, and I want them here. I have designs for a communications array to which I've added an observation array, so I can find the tribes of humans. I will have the engineers build them into a satellite and launch it into a low orbit. Soon I'll be able to speak to the fleet, and with my new warriors, conquer new worlds.

Everything is moving, as it should.

First Council Sister - Szateth leader
Advanced planetary research fleet.

Neural Blockchain Journal Entry #027

My new mother-to-be will learn from the first two.

There is no doubt humans are compatible hosts. The implanted embryos are adapting and getting the human physiology to adapt. They've passed on some hereditary cognitive intelligence, causing a leap in their evolution that would otherwise have taken thousands of years. I wonder if they've altered their DNA.

In short, our Szatethess embryos will make the human females more intelligent as they gestate. When they're born, the hybrids will be like us. At last, we can save our species.

But it is a double-edged sword. I fear that if first council sister finds out how like us the hybrids are going to be, she will harvest my sisters for certain, and nothing will stop her from cementing her position as first council sister with so much support from new sisters. If that happens, she'll strip this planet bare of its most essential resource, the humans.

She is a megalomaniac, a ruthless war-monger, and will try to take what she wants to continue her fight for the conquest of 'her' universe. She needs warriors and workers for that. If she decimates this planet of all the males, we would be back on the brink of extinction again in the next few hundred years.

For our long-term survival, I have to keep it to myself for as long as I can.

The hybrids will be born in about nine months. Between now and then, I'm sure the females will display ever-growing levels of intelligence. I'll have to keep her away from them so she doesn't see it. She'll need to be distracted and kept busy with the warrior conversions. I'll have to convince her I'm as dismissive and unfeeling about the humans as she is.

It is going to be hard. But for the sake of our survival, it has to be done. I am amazed and delighted with the females. The Szatethess human hybrids will save our species.

I will appear to go along with her plans. I'll even help her develop a more efficient conversion serum, as well as manage the building of the conversion facility on the surface, and attempt to convince her of the importance of humans. It may be too late to save my sisters already, and self-preservation may become a priority.

I don't like the way things are going. She must not continue down the path she has chosen. It would be the end for us all.

Second Council Sister
Advanced planetary research fleet.

Four

The stench of death and incompetence.

"The males have arrived at the lab, sister," second sister said into her communicator.

"The serum isn't ready yet. Keep them secure for me," first sister said.

"Yes, of course, sister. Is there anything I can do to help with the serum?"

"No. But can you look and see how my new warrior is doing? Report if there has been a change. I'm with our engineer workers, looking at the designs for my new observation and communications satellite right now."

"Yes, of course, sister. It will be my pleasure. Anything else I can do for you?"

"No, just report any change."

"As you wish," she said. The line went dead.

From the cell door window, she could tell he hadn't moved. "That can't be right," she said, fumbling for the right key. The smell hit her the moment she opened the door. She gagged and covered her nose with her sleeve.

Oh no.

She pressed the sleeve tighter and took a step closer. Like the other species they'd experimented on, human males defecate when they die. Other bodily fluids dripped from his ears, nose, and mouth. The puddle added to the noxious stench. There was no mistake!

Damn. She closed the cell door to contain the stench. Then called first sister.

"This better be good."

"I'm afraid it's not good news, sister. Your new warrior is dead."

"What? - why? He was fine yesterday. Are you sure?"

"I'm afraid so, sister."

"Shit! - This whole day is turning out to be shit! - What are you looking at? Get back to work."

She heard the pitter-patter of nervous shoes hurrying away. "I'll perform an autopsy on the body, sister, and find out why he died."

"Very well. Do it now. I'll be along in a couple of hours."

The line went dead.

She looked through the cell door window, wrinkling her nose, as she called for cleaner workers.

"You're going to need to put coveralls, masks, and gloves on before you go in there," she said when they arrived. "Take all your cleaning equipment in and keep the door shut until you've finished."

"Yes, second council sister," they said, unfolding their coveralls.

"Once the cell is clean, bring the body out," she said, sliding a leg into her own coveralls.

"We're ready, second council sister," a muffled voice said.

"You have everything you need?"

"Yes, second council sister."

"Very well." She pulled her mask down and opened the door enough for them to get in, closing it immediately. She waited as they mopped the sticky puddle of fluid off the floor and sprayed the cell with an air freshener.

One of them gave her a thumbs-up through the window.

She nodded and cracked the door.

They took an end of the table and pushed. The wheels jammed. As they shook the table to free them, the skin bag split, spilling feces and fluids everywhere. They gagged as it splattered to the floor, covering their boots.

She slammed it shut. "Clean it up and do not come out until that cell smells fresh. Do you hear me?"

Through her mask and the glass they couldn't, but the fury in her eyes made it clear. They bowed and picked up their mops.

Two hours later, she heard a knock on the cell door. The cell was clean.

She tightened her mask and opened the door. "Push the table into my lab, over by the bench."

"Yes, second council sister."

She looked around the cell. "Good work, you two."

"Thank you, second council sister," they said in unison, unaccustomed to praise

"Do you think you could deep clean and redecorate that cell for me? I'd hate first council sister to be upset by a lingering smell. You know what can happen when things upset her."

"Of course, right away, second council sister."

They were gone before she reached the body on the table.

Her mask kept the stench of his bloated body at bay. "Now, let's see what killed you," she said.

She tore open the skin bag and examined his leathery skin.

"What news?" first sister said, marching into the lab. "And what's that smell?" She covered her nose and mouth.

"Human males defecate like the other species when they die. That, mixed with the other fluids, it's secreting, and the putrefying flesh gives off this rotting stench of death. I have instructed two cleaner workers to redecorate the cell to eradicate it, sister. There is protective clothing, gloves, and masks in the closet for you over there."

"Good. I can't stand that for much longer." She pulled on the coveralls, gloves, and face mask. "That's better. Alright, what have we got?" She barged in, pushing second sister sideways.

She's testing my loyalty to her authority. She ignored the insult and moved around to the other side of the table. "There's nothing obvious as to the cause of death at this point. What we can see of the Epidermis looks normal, so far. But we should take samples, and samples from the dermis and hypodermis layers to test for toxins."

"What! You're thinking poison? Don't be stupid."

"Well, there's no evidence to suggest that, sister. But we must consider it and test for it. Wouldn't you agree?"

"Right, well, yes, if you want to waste time. Let's get a look at his organs." She grabbed a scalpel, slicing open the skin covering his sternum. "Be ready with the bone saw and rib shears."

She's loving this. The saw buzzed into life when she pressed the button. "Ready, sister," she said.

"Okay, use the saw to score this bone here," she said, running her fingers along the exposed sternum. "Then use the shears to crack the chest cavity so we don't damage the organs inside. I'll get the rib spreader."

For the next hour, first sister cut and sliced into the male's body, removing, weighing, and taking samples from all his internal organs. Second sister assisted without comment on her butchery.

She put the organs in a neat line next to the body. "I see nothing from these that would have caused him to die," first sister said. She huffed.

"Hmm, yes, I agree. Let me run the microscopic, chemical, and microbiological tests, sister. They're laborious and time-consuming. There's no point in you wasting any more valuable time on this. Let me complete the Autopsy for you. I'll report once I have the results."

"So you think you can do it better without me?"

"That's not what I..."

"Very well," she said, stepping back from the table and pulling off the rubber gloves. "You're right. I have better things to do."

The lab door opened and the two cleaner workers pulled in a trolley, with cleaning and decorating equipment on it. They stopped dead at the sight of the dissected body lying open on the table with its organs on display.

"What are you looking at? - Get on with your work, now!" The viciousness in first sister's voice was enough to jolt them away from the gory sight.

They scuttled off into the cell, closing the door.

"Thank you," she said, laughing. "I'll leave you to it and get back to the idiot engineers who can't seem to wire a plug properly, let alone build me an orbital communication and observation satellite. Report once you're done."

"Yes, of course, sister. It might take a while."

"Take your time, but let's get it right." She removed the rest of her protective clothing and threw it in the garbage. "Carry on," she said, and marched out.

"It's going to be a long day, "she said, squeezing a drop of his blood onto a slide. For the next few hours, she made slides from urine, hair, nails, stomach content, and spinal fluid samples, and began testing.

"Second council sister," a male voice said, interrupting her concentration.

"Yes, what is it?" she said without looking up from the microscope.

"We've completed the clean and redecorating."

"Already?"

"It's been a few hours, second council sister."

"Really?" she said. She lifted her head and blinked to refocus her eyes. It was dark outside. "Oh, I lost track of time."

The workers took sideways glances at the dissected body. "We have finished, second council sister. Is there anything else we can do for you?" one of them said, praying they wouldn't be told to dispose of it.

She knew what they were thinking and chuckled. "No, you may go."

"Thank you, second council sister. Have a good evening." They were moving towards the door before he'd finished the sentence.

She went back to her microscope. None of the slides showed anything. She ran her chemical toxicology tests - and there it was.

It was late. *I don't think she would appreciate a call from me now. This news can wait until the morning.*

Neural Blockchain Journal Entry #922

My new warrior didn't make it.

Maybe these humans aren't strong enough to survive the conversion process. Second sister's idea that it was poison is plain stupid.

She knows her place, and I'll keep her in it. It annoys me she's the better scientist, so I'll use her to get the information and the results I need. She'll have a young healthy egg, which will make an excellent addition to the harvest.

Once I have new sisters and an army to command, she'll no longer have a purpose. It's something else I can look forward to. Plus, I want to know how she does the implantation.

I'll be polite and get her to do what I need her to do. She is very humble right now, which isn't like her. Maybe she is coming around to my way of thinking. Although that's more wishful than probable.

You have sealed your fate already, second council sister.

First Council Sister - Szateth leader
Advanced planetary research fleet.

Neural Blockchain Journal Entry #036

First sister is a poor scientist.

Her lack of research and testing has unnecessarily cost a human male his life. Her ambition is greater than her ability, and it will surely cost more lives.

I mentioned it may have been poison, but of course, she disagreed. There is no doubt the serum formula is to blame, and the test results will confirm it.

She has been polite. She thanked me for the first time in a long time. Does that mean she's truly thankful for my help or has my willingness raised some suspicion in her? I don't know.

I'll assume the former and work on the assumption she believes I'm with her.

But I need to be careful.

Second Council Sister
Advanced planetary research fleet.

Five

Callous actions

Lying on her lounger, first sister's heart pounded as the two warriors seduced her with their dance. Well-trained muscular bodies rippled with every sway and step. She was going to have them both. One for pleasure, the other for food!

Ah, but which one for what? Drooling, she licked her lips.

She stood and sandwiched herself between them. Her hands roamed over their bodies. Their warmth, their muscle, their movement, and their size excited her. She chose.

"You stay with me first," she said to one. "You wait outside until I call you."

The chosen one sat waiting for instructions. The other, closing her chamber door, stood outside. Her moans of pleasure made him smile while he waited for his turn.

"You can come in now," she said, so he'd hear. He opened the door. The unmistakable smell of sex lingered in the air. "Now for you." Her voice was soft and dusky. The spent warrior picked up his uniform, and holding his loincloth to cover himself, left.

She patted the cushion next to her on the lounger, eyeing him as he sat.

He closed his eyes, wetting his lips. She moved behind him, her legs wrapping around his waist. Her hand slid around his stomach, pulling him closer. The other she slid through his hair onto his forehead. “Thank you,” she whispered, pulling his head back and to the side, exposing his neck, and sank her teeth in. She drank his warm, velvety blood as he bled out and died.

She pushed his body to the floor, kneeled, and tore into it, ripping off mouthfuls of the best flesh. A feeding frenzy always took its toll, and once she’d had her fill, staggered back from the carcass, collapsing exhausted onto her lounger.

She called for her servant workers. Two appeared. “Clear this away,” she said, her eyes rolling.

They bowed. They knew of her voracious appetite for sex and food and collected what she’d left in a bucket, in silence, in case she chose one of them next.

The satisfied smile on her sleeping face meant they were safe - this time.

∞

The buzzing of her communicator woke her. “Yes, what is it?” she said, rubbing her eyes.

“Good morning, sister. I’m sorry to have disturbed you, but I have the autopsy results. Would you like to come to the lab for them?” second sister said.

“No, tell me now.”

“Very well. According to the toxicology results, the male died from heart failure, brought on by the paralytic agent in the serum.”

"What, shit, did I use too much?"

"That's unclear, sister. It could be you added too much, or the agent itself."

"Damn it! That means the new batch of serum four I've just made is unusable, - all of it. Shit, - I've got to start over. - I don't have time for this today."

"Can I help, sister? It's going to be a few more days until the females make any progress worthy of reporting to you. - I'm happy to produce the new batch for you?"

"Yes, okay. Thank you, sister. Let's review and revise the formula. I need it to work. A new formula must be in production today. Be in my chambers in ten minutes."

"Yes, sister."

Her chambers were on the other side of the ship. First sister, being more of a warrior than a scientist, had little tolerance for poor time-keeping. Everything had to be done with military precision. Her level of intensity to make sure things ran smoothly on the ship matched her temper when they didn't. She needed to show the same level of urgency for things to get done if she was to convince her she was an ally. The slap of her sandals echoed in the corridors as she ran. She made it - just.

She was about to knock when the door opened. "Ah, right on time. Good. Come in. - Shall we make a start?"

The time was another test. She'd waited, clock-watching, on the other side of the door to see if she got there as instructed. She let out a breath. "Yes, sister. Do you have everything we need?"

"Of course, close the door, will you? We're going to be working in this room over here." She walked past her lounger.

Unlike the other sisters who shared chambers and facilities, first sister had everything to herself. A large central living and dining area smelled freshly cleaned, with rooms off it. It was beautifully warm and bathed in a dim, red light. It felt like home, and her eyes drifted around the room, taking in the atmosphere.

"This is my private lab. No one but me, and now you have been in here."

"I'm honored, sister."

"Honor me by producing a serum that works. Let's get started."

The lab was bright and fully equipped. The workbench stretched the entire length of the room. At the far end, she had equipment set up to produce the worker serum and canisters of the aerosol standing to attention in rows on the floor. Where she and first sister were standing was the apparatus producing the now useless conversion serum four. "Well, this is all waste now," first sister said, flipping the switch and shutting off the production.

"Perfect," second sister said, looking in the cabinets above the bench. All the agents, compounds, acids, oils, and extracts to make the serum clearly labeled.

First sister opened one. "This is what I used." She said. "It is a complete paralytic." She handed her the bottle. "And here's how much I put in the serum." She pointed to the amount on the ingredients list. "So, we have a starting point to work backward from."

"Well, it could be just a matter of recreating the serum with a lower dose. I'll make a few small vials with varying amounts of the agent and test it on the males we have in my lab. And we have more of them in the hangar to use if needs be."

"Yes, I like it. I'll let you do your work. Call me if you need me. I'll be with the idiot engineers." She raised her eyes as she left.

"Yes, thank you, sister. I'll have the test samples by the end of the day." She read the list of ingredients, shaking her head.

So you guessed how much of the paralyzing agent to use. A paralytic this powerful stops every muscle from functioning, including the heart. You need to at least know the subject's weight before injecting this. Such an amateur.

Knowing their weight was only half the picture. She needed to know how long, per unit, the paralyzing agent worked for. The first male died without ever waking up, so she had no reference to work back from. She stared at the bottle. There was only one way to know. She punched the bench.

She took a few more bottles from the cabinet and headed back to her lab. *I can't sedate them first either. I need them fully conscious, to get the dose right. Damn, this is going to be hard on them.* She called for two warriors to meet her in the lab.

On the list, she could see the amount she'd used in the serum. She calculated three-fourths, a half, and one-fourth of that measurement and wrote them on the list as she walked. They were an educated guess. She didn't like it, and they would like it even less, but it had to be done. She stood outside the lab, pressing her lips tight. *It has to be done.* With a deep breath, she pushed the door and went in. The two warriors were waiting.

"Can you take three examination tables in there for me?" She said, pointing towards the newly decorated cell.

"Yes, second council sister."

The needles squeaked as she pushed them through the rubber cap of the paralytic bottles. She dragged the plungers back, making sure she got the exact dose into the syringes. "I need you to get me a male, stand him on the scale so I can record his weight, and inject him."

"Should we shackle him?"

"No. And I don't want you to scare him, either. Ask him to come out on his own first. I'm hoping that your presence is enough to make him comply."

"Yes, second council sister."

They opened the cell door, stepped in, and pointed at the nearest male. He shrank back, but when they didn't approach and waved at him to come out, he relaxed a little. The others looked at the floor and didn't move. The two warriors moved aside as the male walked out.

One warrior stood on the scales, stepped off, and pointed to him to stand on it. She wrote the number one on his hand and recorded his weight next to his number on her spreadsheet. He didn't move when she jabbed the needle into his shoulder, injecting him with the three-fourths dose.

"Fingers crossed," she said to the male, recording the time she administered it.

"Take him into the other cell and get him to lie on a table. Do it quickly. The agent won't take long to take effect," she said to the warriors.

His legs buckled, and the two warriors grabbed him just in time. They carried him to the cell and laid him on a table, as instructed.

That was fast! She noted the time it started working next to the other information.

She and the warriors repeated the same process twice more. Giving the half and one-fourth dose to males numbered two and three. The effects didn't start on number two as fast as number one, and even slower with number three. She noted everything.

She felt the pulses of the three paralyzed males, closed her eyes, and prayed for their survival.

"You can go," she said to the warriors. They came to attention briefly, then left.

She let out a large breath. Now she had to report to first sister. She knew she wouldn't be pleased and waited until the lab door had closed before calling her.

"Sister, there's not much more I can do today."

"You've created a new serum already? - I'm impressed. Good work."

"Actually no, sister. But I have three tests running."

"I told you I needed a new serum today. Was I not clear?"

"Yes, of course, and I understand the urgency, sister. We need more warriors for the wars to come. But we need to calculate the amount of the paralyzing agent to add to the serum for it to work as needed. If we get this right, the conversion serum will be fast and efficient. The survival rate of the subjects will be much higher, and you'll get your warriors more quickly. If we don't, you won't. I thought it would be more logical to do it this way."

"I'm not interested in what you thought, or survival rates. There are more than enough human males to be used. They breed like cockroaches. Now, let me be absolutely clear, just get it done!"

She could hear the anger rising in her voice. She expected it, and her next sentence.

"You have one day. Don't make me regret putting the growth of my army in your hands. It would not turn out well for you!"

There it is, - another threat. But she knows she can't do it without me.

"Yes, sister. One day is all I need. Thank you. I won't let you down."

"Pray that you don't."

The call went dead, and she smiled to herself, knowing she liked it when her subordinates bent to her authority. A classic narcissist, who fed off the fear everyone had of her and believed in her omnipotence.

She also knew she was more than capable of carrying out her threats. The threat to the lives of her sisters was real. She knew she'd kill them the moment she found out how intelligent the hybrid Szatethess babies were when they were born. It was already too late for them, and once she'd outlived her usefulness, she'd be of no more use to her either. She had to protect herself, and she had given her the method to do it.

The paralytic, she said to herself, unscrewing the cap. *With some self-preservation chemistry, you will be my life insurance, and I have just what I need right here.* She sucked a biological inhibitor into a pipette and squeezed a few drops into the bottle. *That will do it, and she'll never know she's got the paralytic in her.* With a syringe, she filled two vials of the modified paralytic and dripped in a depolarizing agent. *Until I give her this.*

She screwed the cap on the bottle, gave it a shake, and put it in the cabinet behind the other bottles, then sealed the vials and put them in her pocket to hide in her chamber. *You can't touch me now, sister.*

She went back into the cell to check on the males. They looked dead. But that was to be expected. The paralytic agent relaxed every muscle. She pressed her fingers to their necks and listened to their breathing. Two and three seemed okay. Their breathing rates were low, as were their heart rates. *This is not sustainable over a long period,* she noted her observation. Number one's breathing was shallow. His face looked gray, and his heartbeat was faint. She sighed.

"Just know that your death is going to save many lives, including mine," she said, stroking his hair. "I'm sorry, but there's nothing more I can do for you." She left the cell and went to check on the females. They were finishing their meal when she opened the door.

"Do you want anything?" she said.

The three of them looked at each other, then the female she'd impregnated first looked back and shook her head.

She smiled, and stepping forward, took her hands in hers. "Yes, you understand me, don't you?" She looked at the other two. "You will soon as well. And I'm going to need your help." The first female nodded, followed by the other two. "Thank you," she said, smiling.

Now she had allies.

"Let me check your blood pressure, then I'll leave you for the night." She wrote the measurements in their records before saying goodnight.

∞

She sat up, took a deep breath, and stretched her body awake. Her first thought was of the males. *Have they survived?* She jumped out of bed and threw on her robes.

First sister was already in the lab when she arrived. "Ah, good of you to join me. I've thought about your reasoning for not doing what I told you I needed you to do, and I can appreciate your logic. Talk me through it while we look at the results of your three tests."

"Yes, of course, sister. - The test subjects are in here." She pointed at the cell, her heart pounding as they walked over.

None of them had moved. She checked the time. There were a couple of hours to go until a full day was up. Number one's breathing was raspy. "What's up with this one?" first sister asked.

She felt his pulse. It was weak. She closed her eyes in silent prayer. "I gave him three-fourths of the dose you had in the serum. I think it's too much. He will not make it."

"Pity. He looks strong. Oh well. What about these two?"

She checked their pulse and breathing. "They seem to be fine. The paralyzing agent you're using in the serum is potent. The problem is that we need to create a serum with the right amount, otherwise, they'll all die."

"I know the problem. I don't need chapter and verse, just tell me what you've done, and how you're going to solve it."

"Yes, of course, I apologize. As all the males are of different sizes and weights, we'll need to find an average dose that will allow most of them to survive the conversion process. Your meticulous record-keeping has given me everything I need to have a starting point for the experiments. Given that the amount you had in the serum was too high, I have used three different amounts of the agent on these three male subjects. This one, I gave three-fourths, this one half, and this one, one-fourth. We need to find out how much to add to keep them paralyzed for the day it takes for the conversion to complete. That's the first step. Ordinarily, we would give a dosage determined by their weight, again to avoid overdosing. But we won't have that luxury. We'll need to find the average weight across a good sample number. How many do we have in the hangar?"

"About a hundred, give or take a few."

"And they are of mixed species?"

"Yes. - Your point?"

"Different species might react differently to the agent, adding a further complication. And honestly, more time."

"You don't have it. I need to replenish my warrior numbers now."

"In that case, I'll find an average across all species. Be aware, sister, that the mortality rate will be higher."

"That's acceptable. What do you need to get it done?"

"A larger sample size with an equal number from all the different human species. I'll know in a few hours which of these males has woken on time and remained healthy."

"Very well, I'll get third sister to organize another gathering. And while I think about it, the aerosol version of the worker serum will be ready in a few hours. We'll test it on the group of males selected for the worker serum in the hangar. There shouldn't be any problems with this one."

"That's good news, thank you, sister. I'll be able to start the construction of the conversion facility on the surface, which will speed things up considerably."

"Yes, that's the idea. Now, how are your pregnant females?"

"Oh, they're fine," she said, then changed the subject. "Can I observe when you expose the weaker males to the aerosol in the hangar? I'd like to watch the result of your work, sister?"

"Why not? They'll be yours to use as you see fit, anyway."

"I'm looking forward to building the conversion facility. Once it's ready, we'll be able to feed it with males day and night."

"That's the plan, provided you get the serum perfected. You will get it perfected. Won't you?"

"Once I have the new test subjects, I'll be able to find the correct dose fairly quickly."

"Right. Good. These two look okay," she said, waving her hand at them. "This one doesn't look so good. Just get rid of him."

"I agree. This one had the highest dose. I don't think he'll survive. But these two should. Now I need to see how long the doses I gave them keep them paralyzed. I'm aiming for one day, which you said is enough for the conversion and the shedding?"

"Yes, exactly."

"I'll keep you informed, sister."

"Now what about the female..." Her communicator interrupted her. "Yes, what is it?"

"We have made good progress with the satellite, first council sister. Perhaps you'd like to see it?" the lead engineer worker said.

"It's about time. I'll be there soon." She cut him off.

"Sounds like they've done what you told them to do. That's good news. I won't keep you."

"Yes, at last. Someone who does what they say they're going to do," she said, fixing her with a stare and raising her eyebrows. "I need to check their work. Keep me updated. You know where I'll be." She marched out.

"Of course, sister," she said, smirking. *None of this would be necessary if you'd done it right.*

She heard her call third sister as the lab door closed. "Won't be long now, and you two will move again. I'm sorry you've had to endure this," she said. Tears welled in her eyes as she stood next to number one. *You don't look right at all, and there's nothing I can do for you.*

"I promise you, your sacrifice will not be in vain!" She placed a hand gently on his forehead as the tears ran down her face.

They didn't move. What was waiting for them was a painful and violent conversion to a worker or a warrior. Many more would die, and there was nothing she could do about it. If the females couldn't carry the implanted embryos to term, or give birth to healthy Szatethess hybrids, they'd get executed. If they did, first sister was going to harvest the eggs of the other seven council sisters. Whichever way her thoughts went, death stared back. Her emotions threatened to overwhelm her. She couldn't let anyone see her in this state.

Aware of a presence in the doorway, she turned away, wiped her eyes, and pulled herself together before looking back. Her shoulders slumped as she let out a breath. It was one of her females. "I'm sorry you have to see this," she said.

"Sss-orry." The female repeated.

She stepped back, stumbling into a table. "Did you just.... Oh, my goodness. Say that again."

"Sorry."

"I knew it. - do you understand everything I'm saying?"

She nodded.

"Yes?" she said, nodding back. "Say, yes. If you do."

"Yes."

She reached out, pulled her into the cell, and put a hand over her mouth. "No one must know you can speak. No one, only me. Do you understand?"

"Yes."

"Can the other two speak as well?"

She shook her head.

"No?" she repeated, shaking her head.

"No."

"They soon will. And you must tell them not to unless it's to me. Do you understand?"

"Yes."

"I will come and talk to you all shortly. You'll pick up more words, and we can practice. You can speak to each other, but no one else, only me."

"Yes."

"Now, go back to your room."

The female, frowning, looked at the paralyzed males before going back.

The males! No one had looked in on them for nearly two days. First sister either forgot about them, or she didn't care enough to consider their well-being while a new serum was being made.

She ran to their cell and opened the door. The sores on their wrists and ankles caused by the shackles were untreated and festering. They'd had no food or water in all that time, either. Their eyes fell on her and they bolted, knocking her over.

She sprang to her feet and ran out after them. They had stopped and were looking at the three females who'd heard the noise and came to help. She joined them.

"Please," she said, holding her hands up. "Go back to the cell. There's nowhere for you to go. If you get caught, they will put you to death. Please go back in." She pointed. None of them moved.

The first female started filling a jug with water. The sound of it hitting the bottom of the jug had them looking over at the sink. Once she'd filled it, she walked into the cell and waved them back in. The second female gave each of them a cup and pointed to the cell. Like a pack of animals around a watering hole, they surrounded her. She poured, and they gulped. The third female went in with another jug and gave them more.

Second council sister soaked cloths in a bowl and gave it to the second female, who was standing next to her, guarding her. She took it, went in, and began bathing their wounds.

Maybe it was instinct, or perhaps it was intelligence passed to her by the embryos. She didn't know, but the females took control.

The first female made a gesture for food.

"Yes. Yes, of course," she said and ordered food to be brought up immediately.

The females cleaned their wounds while they waited, and she took in more water and cups.

As she poured the water, something strange was happening. On the planet's surface, humans lived in a patriarchal society, with each tribe dominated by an alpha male. But here the three pregnant females had taken charge, and they accepted it. *Do they recognize the female's superiority?* They were clearly more intelligent than the males. *Am I witnessing human society switch from a patriarchy to a matriarchy, like their own?*

There was no doubt in her mind now humans were the saviors they'd been searching so long for. *First sister must see how vital humans are to our survival. How am I going to get her to do that?* She took a deep breath and ordered her thoughts.

To begin with, she would keep the pretense of being as insensitive towards the humans as she was. Then gradually introduce the idea that they are more useful than they first thought. It was going to be difficult to hide her true feelings.

On the plus side, she'd be able to explain her actions to the three pregnant females and get their help. There wasn't much she could do for the males, save make them as comfortable as she could, while the new conversion serum did its work. She shuddered at the thought.

The females were doing a great job, and there was still an hour before the paralyzing agent wore off the males. She went to check on them, taking their pulse and checking their breathing. Male one's pulse was weak and his breathing shallow. He was going to die. Numbers two and three were okay, but it was of little comfort.

"Second council sister, are you in here?" a voice said.

In the lab, three kitchen workers with big trays of food and even bigger smiles on their faces were standing there.

"Yes. Put them on the bench, will you?" she said.

"Yes, second council sister."

They did as instructed, bowed, and left.

She closed the cell door on the paralyzed males to leave them in peace and poked her head into the other male's cell.

"Their food has arrived," she said to the first female, who nodded and followed her to get it. She gripped the handles as they walked in with the trays, expecting a hungry mob to attack. They didn't. They waited wide-eyed while they put them down. The first female looked and nodded at each male. None of them moved. Their eyes didn't leave her as they left the cell. She nodded at them through the cell door window and they pounced on it.

Her skin tingled at what she'd witnessed. *They've accepted her authority.* Her females and their children would be the leaders of a new human society. "Back in your room now, please," she said. "Remember, don't speak to anyone but me. No one else must know. I'll be back in a while."

She needed to get some distance between herself and what was happening in the lab, to give herself time to think, and headed for the hangar.

She walked, lost in thought. The only way she could get first sister to think of the humans as more than cannon fodder for her army was to show her they had evolved into a species that would save them. She had to show her that the embryos had passed on some of their hereditary cognitive intelligence and that they now controlled the males. But doing so would put her sisters more at risk.

Still not sure of the best course of action, she entered the hangar bay. "Where are the males being kept?" she asked the commander.

"In the two big rooms at the end of the hangar, second council sister."

"And separated, weaker and stronger in different rooms?"

"Yes, second council sister. The strong in the left, the weak in the right."

"Good, I'll inspect them now."

"Very good, second council sister. If you'll follow me."

"Have they been any trouble?"

"Two of the stronger ones tried to escape their room." He chuckled. "First council sister had us secure them, then throw them out the airlock. We shackled the others, and it's been peaceful ever since."

"I'm not surprised. They're probably terrified."

"Here they are, second council sister."

As strong as they were, they were in a bad way. "Have you fed them and given them water?"

"No, second council sister. Our instructions are not to, as further punishment for their disobedience."

"What?" she said, glaring at him. "Well, I'm instructing you to now. Feed them and give them water commander. The weaker males as well." She looked back at them and cringed. "Remove those shackles, and have a medic worker treat their sores. If you don't, most of them will die."

"But first council sister told me..."

"I'll speak to her about this and tell her you had become concerned that her males would die without proper care. And knowing how important they are to her, you asked me if you could provide for their basic needs."

"You would do that for me?"

"Yes, of course, commander. You do a hard job here, and you deserve rewards and recognition for it. Which I'm sure first council sister will lavish on you when I tell her."

"Thank you, second council sister. I'll get them food, water, unshackled and treated immediately."

"Very good, Commander. I'll leave you to it." She knew he would obey her instructions, and she walked back to the lab.

Back in her lab, she heard movement coming from the cell with the paralyzed males. She unlocked the door. Male number three was awake, huddled in a fetal position in the far corner. He looked pale and his whole body was shaking.

She grabbed a blanket and wrapped him in it. "I'm glad to see you awake," she said. He stared at her, pulling it tighter. She felt for a pulse in male number one's neck. She sighed. "I'm sorry your friend had to die. He would not have felt any pain. I won't forget him." Moving over to number two, she was relieved to feel the beat on her fingers. She looked at the clock. "He should be awake, too. He might have had too much. I hope he'll be okay. We'll see when the effects wear off."

She called for two warriors to come and take the body away. "So, now I know a quarter of the amount first council sister used is a survivable dose. At least in your species of human," she said to male three. He shrank into the blanket as she approached. "Be calm," she said, lowering her voice. "No one's going to hurt you. I just want to feel your pulse and take your blood pressure. If you'll let me?"

He'd stopped shaking, and color was returning to his cheeks.

"Please, come and sit here," she said, patting the chair. He didn't move. She pointed to him, and sat, showing him what she wanted him to do. He tried to stand. The paralytic hadn't completely worn off, and she helped him to the chair.

She took his pulse and blood pressure. "Good," she said, writing them down.

She felt male two's pulse again. It was weak, but he was alive. On his notes, she wrote she thought half the original dose would likely be too much. She added that should he would wake, the effects of being paralyzed for so long might have damaged him. She suspected oxygen starvation, which would have impaired his brain function, making him mentally and physically disabled. As for male one, the note simply said, - deceased.

Two warriors arrived to take his body. "Take this body and cremate it," she said. "And send two more warriors up to my lab."

"Yes, second council sister," they said, lifting the body and putting it on a stretcher.

Once they'd gone, she turned to male three. "What shall I do with you? Hmm. Come with me. You can spend some time with the pregnant females." She waved for him to follow. *I wonder what they'll do with him?* She smiled.

They were eating when she opened the door, and his eyes lit up on seeing the food. The first female rose out of her chair. Something in her movement and demeanor made him stop and stand still.

"They'll look after you," she said as she shut the door.

She prepared three more injections of the paralyzing agent with a one-fourth dose. *Let's see if you're a good average for the serum.* She flicked the syringes, removing air bubbles. The warriors arrived as she finished.

"Ah, well," she said. "Wait here while I open the cell door, then follow me in." The males stared at her, then shuffled to the back when the warriors stepped into the doorway.

"Don't worry," she said. "Everything is going to be fine." She smiled, reaching for a different species from the first three, gently placing a hand on his arm. "Please come with me," she said. He didn't resist.

She would test three different species, numbering them four, five, and six. She weighed them, injected them, and crossed her fingers as the warriors carried them into the cell. Tomorrow she'd know.

Male number two from the first tests still hadn't moved. She had a biological inhibitor that would counteract the paralytic agent. She prepared two injections, one with the inhibitor, and one with a massive dose of the paralytic, which she hoped she wouldn't need. The inhibitor would work quickly. A few moments later, he moved.

He turned his head toward her. She could see the pain in his eyes and squeezed his hand. Her chin trembled. "I'm sorry," she said.

His eyes rolled and he could no longer focus. Holding back the tears, she injected the paralytic. All she could do was give him a quick, painless death. She held his hand as he passed away. She recorded the effect of using half the original dose in her notes.

The events of the day had taken a physical and emotional toll. She splashed her face with cold water and stared blankly at the wall. She still needed to come up with a good plan to keep all the humans and her sisters alive. First sister was interested in new warriors and new sisters to reign over, and she didn't care how she got them. She'd found a dose that would keep the males alive while they suffered through the conversion, and she'd have to come to terms with that. After drying her face, then checking on the males and the females one last time, she switched off the lights and headed to her chambers. *Perhaps sleep would bring some peace and some answers.*

Neural Blockchain Journal Entry #923

It seems like I'm surrounded by idiots.

Why is it that when I give an order, it doesn't get obeyed? Am I too soft? My predecessor certainly wouldn't have put up with any insubordination. No one understands how vital it is to build my army. I need them otherwise the planets in the network will rebel against us. An iron fist is what I need to keep them in check, and the warriors to do it. I will have them. On a more positive note, second sister seems to be more compliant. My previous concerns about her may have been a mistake - but I'll keep working and watching her.

She needs to work faster. Her excuse for not getting a new serum in production as I asked her to, and her request for more testing time, is not getting the work done. She needs to understand that test subjects are disposable, there are so many of them. I don't care how she does it. She must get me a working serum soon. Or I'll harvest her. It's as simple as that.

I admit she's a better scientist than me, and her willingness to help has been worthwhile. She knows she needs to get results and I expect she will. But she has a good egg - hmm, decisions, decisions.

First Council Sister - Szateth leader
Advanced planetary research fleet.

Neural Blockchain Journal Entry #045

I've said it before - first sister is a poor scientist.

She's a rank amateur. I can't believe she's our leader. She leads by fear, nothing more.

She does not know how important humans are to us. I don't think she cares.

All she sees are warriors for her army. I understand we need them, but it is she who has allowed the ranks to become decimated with her ridiculous strategy of fighting on multiple fronts.

They are the actions of a despot. We do not need a leader like that. Her willingness to waste life is unpardonable. I must protect them, my sisters, and myself.

She seems to have softened her attitude toward me, so perhaps my plan to get her to trust me is working. I will get results, but not for her, for the humans.

It is becoming more difficult to keep my emotions and my attachment to humans under control - But I must if I am to succeed.

If I succeed, we'll have everything we need, and over time, we'll secure the survival of our race.

I'll need to be careful and steel myself against her callous actions and attitude.

I don't doubt she'd harvest me - given the chance.

Second Council Sister

Advanced planetary research fleet.

Six

His time will come.

The buzzing of the communicator on her wrist woke her. It had taken her a long time to fall asleep, and she didn't want to open her eyes.

"Who is disturbing me?" she said out loud, pulling her arm out from under the warm blankets. The caller id read first council sister.

What could she possibly want so early?

"Yes. Good morning, sister," she said in the most polite tone she could.

"Ah, I thought you might like to join me in the hangar. I'm about to expose the weaker males to the worker serum. Unless you have something better to do?"

"No, no. I'd love to see it in action. Give me ten minutes to dress. I'll be right down."

"Very well, we'll wait. But we are ready now, and I've got a busy day. Don't be long."

First council sister was checking the time as she walked in, a minute late.

"Good of you to join us," she said. "I was about to start without you."

"Apologize, sister. I couldn't find my notes."

"Right, well, I have a busy day ahead, so let's get on with it. Open the valves, commander."

The hiss of the aerosol canisters sprayed a light green mist filling the room. The males shrank away, huddling together in the farthest corner. In seconds, the mist was so dense they could no longer see them.

"How long should we leave it in there?" first sister asked.

Second sister pressed against the window. "I'm not sure. I can't see what's happening. It won't take effect as fast as a direct injection of the serum would. So let's leave it until the mist settles."

"These look healthy," first sister said, looking at the powerful males in the room next door. "Second council sister told me of your concern that they should be in top condition for me. Good work, Commander. I commend you. I'll send you a female to enjoy as a reward."

"Thank you, first council sister."

"What do you think of the look of these?" she said calling second sister over.

"I'm sure they'll be fine," she said without turning from the window.

"I want you to look, *second sister*, and see how magnificent they'll be as my new warriors."

She huffed. The mist still hadn't cleared enough for her to see, so she tore herself away.

"Well, what do you think? - don't you agree, once you get the serum right, they'll make powerful warriors?"

"Oh yes. They look perfect for your purpose."

"How long until it's ready?"

"I have a test of the paralyzing serum running on three new males as we speak, sister. We will have a result by the end of the day. If successful, I should be able to start the production of a new conversion serum first thing tomorrow."

"Good. Time is not on your side. I want no more failures."

"Yes, I'll get it done for you. Third sister is going to gather more human males, I believe?"

"Yes. I need them."

"Well, can I ask if she waits until I know which is the best species for you to use for warriors? The others we can use as workers."

"Why not just scoop up a load at once, then sort them when they get here?"

"It'll be more efficient, and you'll get your warriors more quickly if she selects the species that will survive the conversion. There's no point in wasting the other species. I could have them for workers. And as long as this worker conversion goes well, I'll have enough workers to build the first facilities on the ground."

"Hmm, I would get my warriors into training more quickly."

"Yes, and they will make a powerful army for you."

"Very well. I'll instruct her to hold off until we know which species to gather."

She glimpsed across to the other window. The mist was settling. "Finally," she said, leaving first sister to admire her males alone. From the window, all she could see were bodies lying on the floor.

"Commander, vent the room," she said.

"Wait," first sister said. "Let me see, then I'll decide if we should vent the room."

"Yes, of course. My enthusiasm sometimes gets the better of me. Forgive me, sister."

"It looks like the aerosol has done something. But it is hard to tell from out here. Yes. Commander vent the room."

He closed the spray valves and switched on the extractor fans. The whirring sucked what remained of the green mist out into the atmosphere.

"It's clear, first council sister." The commander said.

Second sister shot past her and the commander to be first in the room. First sister, scowling, followed her in.

The males were lying in a heap on the floor, making it difficult to examine them. "Get me two warriors in here, commander. I want them rolled over and lined up whilst they are unconscious," first sister said.

Second sister didn't wait. "Look, sister," she said, kneeling next to one of them. "Can you see this green residue around their eyes, nose, and mouths?"

She crouched next to her, pulled his mouth open, and lifted an eyelid. "Hmm, yes. It seems they have inhaled the aerosol, and some will have gotten in through their eyes. A good result, wouldn't you agree?" she said, wiping her fingers on the male's clothing.

Two warriors appeared. "Drag them into a line so we can see them," she said.

"Yes, first council sister."

"It looks like you'll have your workers. Put them to work immediately. Get them to build a compound on the surface where we can keep them, and let's get my conversion facility built," she said, as the warriors dragged the unconscious human males.

“They are ready for your inspection, first council sister,” one of them said.

“You can look,” she said to second sister, getting to her feet and smoothing her robes. "I've got things to do."

She didn’t hesitate. Visions of male number one dying flooded her mind. “Is this the serum with the accelerator?” She checked for a pulse, and they were breathing. She smiled and her shoulders relaxed. They were fine.

“Yes, it should speed up the conversion process. - Well, is it working?”

“They are alive. Heart and breathing rates have elevated presumably to compensate for the effects of the serum." She lifted the male’s covering, exposing his torso. “And look at this, his skin has a faint olive green color to it.” *Like the pregnant females.* She thought to herself.

First sister leaned in to see, “Ah, yes, good. Like the other two workers. I’d say it worked, wouldn’t you?”

“We’ll know for sure once they come round. If the aerosol’s conversion time is comparable to the injected serum three, then I’d say they’d come around in another hour, maybe. But yes, it looks like it.”

“I don’t have the time to hang around for that. You can wait. Report to me once we know,” she said and marched out of the room.

“Yes, of course, sister.” She waited until she’d left. “Do you think you could get some coveralls for these males, commander?”

“Yes, second council sister. But I think we only have orange.”

“That’s fine, commander. I want them all to look the same. And if they’re all wearing orange, they won’t be able to hide.” She laughed. “Call me when it’s done, and they’re awake. I’ll be in my lab.”

“Yes, second council sister. And thank you for your kindness. First council sister is sending me a female as a reward.”

“She’s what? - one of my human females?”

"Yes, I believe so. It's been a long time since I had a female. Thank you, second council sister." He licked his lips.

She could feel the rage building inside, and fought to control herself. He'd question her attachment to them otherwise and report it to first sister.

"May I choose her for you, commander? I have the perfect one for you." She clenched her jaw.

"Honored if you would, second council sister. I hope she is, err shapely, I like my females, bigger."

"I'll see what I can do. - Call me once the males are ready," she said, walking away to hide the anger on her face.

"Yes, second council sister. Of course."

She stopped, and without looking back said, "I may ask a favor, commander, in the future. I assume you'll grant it?"

"It would be my pleasure. Whatever you need, please ask second council sister."

"Good," she said and walked on. The thought that the commander was going to get one of her females to use and pleasure him made her feel sick. Hard as it was, she'd have to bear it to maintain her ruse. As she entered her lab, first sister was there, looking at the females through the cell door.

"Can I help you, sister?"

"No, no. I just need one of these females for the commander. You have no objection, do you?" she said, looking at her and narrowing her eyes.

"No, not at all. The commander told me of your gift, and I asked if I might choose for him."

First sister looked back into the cell. "I don't know how you're going to choose. They all look the same to me," she said, chuckling to herself. "But go ahead."

It was an impossible choice. The only criteria she had was the female needed to be of a heavier build. There was only one like that, so there was no choice. She knew what was in store for her, and couldn't look at her. She just pointed.

"That one," she said, closing her eyes. She'd sentenced her to a fate worse than death, and the painful knot in her stomach was her punishment.

The commander had a sadistic reputation. After he beat her, he'd rape her, over and over. She would wish for death before her ordeal was over. He would grant it.

"Get that one," first sister said, pointing her out to the two warriors. "Don't shackle her. I don't want too many blemishes on her skin before he gets her."

Second sister turned away, unable to watch as the warriors grabbed the screaming female and dragged her out.

"Take her to the hangar commander and give her to him with mine and second council sister's compliments."

"Yes, first council sister." They dragged her away.

First sister grinned, knowing full well what was going to happen to her.

"Alright, now that's done. Let me see your pregnant females, then the three males you're experimenting on."

She couldn't answer, trying to block out the fate that awaited the female they'd just carted away.

"Second sister, wake up!"

She squeezed her eyes. "They are in this room, sister," she said, pointing.

The communicator buzzed on first sister's wrist as she reached for the door handle. "Damn it. What now?" She answered the call. "What is it?"

"I apologize, first council sister. There is a problem with the cloaking shields on the satellite. Could you give us your guidance?"

"I'll be there directly." She cut off the call. "Remind me to cull those idiots in engineering when they're done building my satellite. I'd better get there before they really screw things up. I'll look in on the pregnant females another time. Keep me updated with news of the males. I want an answer, so I can tell third sister which species to gather."

"Certainly, sister."

They smiled as she opened the door. *That was fortunate,* she thought, wanting to keep their transformation secret a little longer. The male sitting in the chair was naked. He looked tired. She smiled at the females, knowing full well what had gone on in her absence. They giggled.

"I see you've had your fun?" she said, raising her eyebrows. They giggled again. "Alright, that's enough fun for now."

She took his arm, pulled him out of the chair, and gave him his clothing. "Let's put you back in the cell with the others," she said as he covered himself. "Looks like you could do with the rest."

She looked back and smiled as he staggered out. He still had the number three on his hand. She knew first sister would want him to be injected with the new serum first because of it. He looked back at her as she closed the cell door and gave him a weak smile.

It was getting harder to keep her emotions in check. Her mind wandered back to the fate of the female she'd selected to entertain the commander. *How could she ever consider giving another female, as a gift, to a known abuser, rapist, and killer? Did she have any regard for the humans, or any other life form, at all?* She knew the answer, and inside, she screamed.

The hardest part was knowing there was nothing she could do. She would have to look away and ignore every cruelty she saw inflicted on the humans, her humans. With the conflict inside growing, her only solace was knowing she had found their saviors. Now she had to make sure nothing, and no one prevented her females from giving birth to the next evolution of Szatethess.

She was right about one thing. She thought. *There are a lot of humans on the surface, mostly males. It will be easier to keep her focused on building her army. With fewer females than males, it makes them even more precious. I'll do what I can for the males by getting the formula right, which will please her, but I'll focus on the females.* These few moments to gather her thoughts gave her time to pull herself together.

The males in the cell next door still hadn't moved. She checked the time. There were a few hours left before the paralytic would wear off. She checked to make sure they were still breathing. They were.

Her communicator buzzed. It was the hangar. She took a breath, and gritting her teeth, answered, "Yes, commander."

"It's the first officer here, second council sister. The commander is unavailable at the moment."

She relaxed her jaw. "Yes, first officer, what is it?"

"Your worker males are awake and dressed in the orange coveralls as you requested, second council sister."

"Thank you, first officer. I will be there to inspect them in a few minutes."

She took one more look at the motionless males and closed the cell door. On her way, part of her hoped the commander wasn't there when she got there. In her mind, she'd already played through tearing his head off and feasting on him for taking one of her females. She wasn't sure if she could stop herself if she saw him. As she got closer, she still didn't know what she was going to do. Her body was telling her to rip him open and eat his insides in front of him, as he died screaming. Her mind was telling her it would ruin everything if she did. She was still battling as she rounded the corner and entered the hangar.

"Ah, I'm excited for you to see your workers, second council sister," the first officer said as she walked in.

His being there and enthusiasm took her by surprise. She paused and looked around before she spoke. "No commander I see."

"No, and I don't think we'll see him for the rest of the day."

fortunately for him, she thought.

"Show me then, first officer," she said, unclenching her jaw.

"This way, please," he said, pointing and taking the lead.

She could see them through the window as they approached. Their skin was a light olive green made more obvious by the orange coveralls they were wearing. There was no confusion or fear on their faces, they were just standing there - waiting. She smiled and entered the room.

"Look at me," she said.

They instantly focused on her.

"You are my workers and you are going to be my builders."

They didn't understand what she was saying, but recognized her authority.

"First officer, come in here, please."

"Yes, second council sister."

"I need to prepare injections of P9R to stimulate their brains so they can learn, understand and speak our language."

"Oh, I see," he said. "Is that what you gave me?"

"Yes, exactly. We give it to all males. I need these to speak and understand instructions, too."

"Oh, err, I see."

"Good. Well then, keep them in here. Feed them, give them water, and keep them calm whilst I'm away. I'll be back with the shots in a little while."

"As you wish, second council sister."

"Good work, first officer," she said. "I'll be back."

Her steps felt lighter as she walked back to her lab. The worker serum had been successful. She had her first batch of new workers. Once they'd had the P9R injection and training, they'd build the facility on the surface. *First sister is going to be pleased,* she said to herself.

Back in her lab, she looked in on her females. Food had arrived before she got there, and they were too busy eating to notice her looking through the window. They looked contented, so she left them to it and prepared the P9R injection.

When she'd administered P9R before, she'd had to prepare individual syringes. To speed the process, she'd given the engineering department a design to make an automatic self-refilling injector syringe. She took it out of its case. "It fits perfectly," she said out loud, squeezing the trigger. Its elegant design and efficient operation were ideal. *Perhaps they're not as useless as you think. You just don't know how to treat them so they do their best work.* She said to herself, remembering what first sister had said about the engineers. This was going to be the first chance she'd had to use it.

She poured the P9R neurogenic compound into the injector supply bottle. There was enough to give to the workers in the hangar, but she'd have to make more for any new workers and warriors.

"Another thing to add to my to-do list." She said, swirling around what remained of the compound in its container.

"Hello," she heard a small voice say.

She looked in its direction, and there stood the first of the pregnant females, with blood all around her mouth, smiling. She wiped her mouth on her sleeve. "Hello," she said again.

"You shouldn't be out here, my dear." She had her finger on the syringe's trigger, and the female winced.

"Oh, no, this isn't for you," she said, putting it back in its case.

The female smiled and made a drinking gesture.

"Ah, water," she said, mimicking the gesture back to her.

"Yes, water," the female said.

"Of course. Let me get it for you and I'll bring it in."

The female watched as she filled a jug and got some cups.

"You can get water yourself when you want it," she said, showing her where she kept them.

"Yes," said the female.

"Good. Let's go back in."

She filled the cups, and all three of them gulped down the water like it was the last drink they were ever going to have.

"Are you feeling alright?" she asked, feeling the first pregnant female's forehead.

"Hmm, no temperature. Alright ladies, let me check your blood pressure." All three were fine. "Just thirsty then?"

"Yes," the first pregnant female said.

"Well, you know where to get water when you need it. - Now, I've got more work to do. I'll check in with you later."

She looked in on the paralyzed males, checking their breathing and heart rates. The clock said she should have enough time to administer the P9R to her workers and get back before the paralytic wore off.

The neurogenic P9R compound would take a few weeks to alter the male's brains, making them capable of speech - if injected intramuscularly. That would not be acceptable to first sister. She would inject directly into their brains. P9R was a fascinating compound. It created neurons that migrated to the networked language regions of the recipient's brain from the hippocampus, enabling the ability to understand, comprehend and produce language - they learned to talk. It was an invention she was proud of, and it impressed first sister when she could give *dumb animals,* as she called them, orders they obeyed.

She'd have to scan a human brain to find the hippocampus and sedate them to make sure they remained perfectly still as she injected them.

"First officer, can you send two warriors to my lab? I need them to carry some equipment for me," she said into her communicator.

"Yes, second council sister, right away."

She found her portable scanner and a canister of sedation gas. They arrived as she'd got them.

"I need you to carry these for me back to the hangar. - Be careful with this one. It's a sensitive medical scanner and I don't want it damaged."

"Yes, second council sister," they said, picking up the equipment.

Back in the hangar, her new workers watched her set up the scanner in their room.

"Connect the sedation gas to the pump, first officer. You know how to do it?"

"Yes, second council sister. It'll take a minute for me to hook it up."

With their eyes glued to her, the males waited to be told what to do.

"The canister is ready, second council sister."

"Thank you, first officer."

She checked to make sure the scanner was ready. "Lay down," she said to the males. They didn't move.

"First officer, can you come in here, please?"

"Yes, second council sister."

"I need the males to lie down. I'm going to give the order again, to you, so they can see what to do."

"Of course, second council sister."

She said it again. He lay down. And they understood.

"Perfect, thank you, first officer. Shall we go?"

They left the room and secured the door. "Release the gas," she said.

He opened the valves, and the gas hissed as it fed its way into the room. She watched through the window, waiting for the sedation gas to do its job. In moments, their previous alertness evaporated into a stupor.

"Vent the room," she said.

He turned on the extraction fans.

"Let's give it a minute for the gas to clear."

Once inside, she ran the scanner over the nearest worker's head.

"Fascinating," she said as the image appeared on the monitor. "Ah, there you are."

"First officer," she said, calling him in. "Hold this here, will you?" She gave him the scanner's wand. "Hold it still while I inject him."

She aimed the automatic syringe to just below his ear and squeezed the trigger. A small dose of the P9R shot into the male's brain, right into his hippocampus.

"Excellent," she said. "Now, let's do the others before the sedation wears off."

They repeated the scan and injection procedure on all of them.

"Thank you, first officer," she said, putting the syringe back in its box.

"Can you get those same warriors to take this equipment back to my lab?"

"Yes, of course, second council sister." He called the two warriors back in. "Take this equipment back to second council sister's lab and take care not to damage it."

"Yes, first officer."

"Make sure they have food and water when they come round," she said to the first officer as she lifted the eyelid on a worker, checking his pupil's reaction with a penlight. "They may have headaches, so have an analgesic put in their water to dull it. Keep a close eye on them over the next week. Make sure they're cared for. Send one of your hangar workers every day to talk to them. They need to hear someone speak. I'll be back then to test their language skills. Then we'll start their construction training."

"Yes, perfect, second council sister."

They locked the door behind them. With a last look through the window. "Good work today, first officer," she said. "I'll report that you were a great help in the commander's absence to first council sister."

"Thank you, second council sister. I'm pleased to have been of service."

The P9R injections had gone well. Her workers had made good progress. She beamed to herself as she walked back to her lab. She was thinking about the next step for the formulation of the new conversion serum when she nearly bumped into the commander coming out of his quarters.

"I apologize, second council sister," he said, swerving to avoid contact.

She flinched, then seeing who it was, felt an instant seething in the pit of her stomach, and sneered at his satisfied grin. She looked away, ignoring his apology. *I'm going to wipe that grin off your face,* she thought to herself, as he carried on.

The two warriors were packing her equipment away when she walked in. "Thank you," she said. "You may go."

Her heart hammered in her chest. Her reptilian nature almost got the better of her. Had she slaughtered the commander right there in the corridor, she knew it would have ruined everything. *His time will come,* she said to herself.

The groan from the cell with the three paralyzed males snatched her out of her daydream. She grabbed her notes, excited to see what was going on.

In the cell, males four and five, the two bigger species of the three, were awake. They were sitting with their heads in their hands, not completely free of the effects of the agent yet.

They looked well, but she checked their pulse and blood pressure to make sure. Number six, the smallest of the three species, still hadn't moved. His pulse was weak and thready, and she sighed. Not wanting him to suffer, she got another dose of the paralytic and injected him before he came around. She held his hand as he took his last breath.

"First officer, can you send two warriors up to my lab, please?" she said into her communicator.

"It's the commander, second council sister. Yes, of course, I'll send them straight away."

"Good," she said and ended the call.

"Now, let's check the two of you," she said to four and five. She flashed her penlight in their eyes. "Pupil's response is good. You're fine." She noted no adverse effects on their charts.

"Come with me," she said, waving for them to follow. She led them back to the cell with the other males, none the worse for wear. As she locked the cell door, the two warriors appeared.

"In that cell." She pointed. "Take the body for a cremation? Do it respectfully. His death gave us the answer first council sister needed. She will hear of it if you don't."

"Yes, second council sister," one of them said. They came out with the body of number six. "We will wish him well on his journey to the next life, second council sister."

"Good. Thank you," she said as they left.

She called first sister. "Are you free so I can update you on my progress, sister?"

"Yes, and I would welcome some good news. I need a break from these idiots. - Go ahead."

"I have a result of the paralyzing agent tests. It looks like two male species would survive the conversion and make fine warriors for your army."

"At last. Well, that is good news. When can I expect a working serum?"

"I will need access to your lab again, sister, so I can produce conversion serum formula five with the adjusted paralytic dose."

"Right, well, you can't use it today. I'm going to be tied up here correcting all the mistakes these so-called engineers have made. Sunrise tomorrow morning."

"Yes, sister. I will be there."

"Be sure you are not late. - Oh, and good work," she said offhand.

"One more thing, sister, before you go."

"What is it?"

"I have administered the newly converted workers with the P9R neurogenic compound."

"So, what, we've got to wait weeks before they are any use to you? I told you more delays are unacceptable."

"Well, the good news is that human physiology is not unlike ours, and I injected the P9R directly into their brain's hippocampus. It'll be a week at worst before we can begin their training. - It could be quicker with your warriors, as they are the strongest two human species."

"Well, that is good. I commend you."

"Thank you, sister."

"Tomorrow then, at sunrise."

The call went dead.

The death of the male left a bitter taste. She dug out a tissue, sniffed, and wiped her nose. She vowed not to forget his face.

The secret of her females gave her hope, and she shed some happy tears. She needed to see them. Out of politeness, she knocked on the door before entering. They greeted her with a smile, and she shared their meal. Over the next few hours, she taught them to speak.

Neural Blockchain Journal Entry #924

Second council sister might be the ally I need after all.

She's more accommodating than before and has made some good progress. Although I wonder how much she would have made if I hadn't pushed her.

I have to admit that my plans to build an unstoppable army would be more difficult without her, - at this point.

I wish I could say the same about the engineers. If second sister's workers turn out the way I hope, I will feast on the idiots, take some of the new workers, and train them as engineers. But I need that satellite to work and I need it now.

Second sister will have a new conversion serum for me within the next day, and I'll ramp up the conversions. Yes, lots to look forward to. Nothing will stop me now.

First Council Sister - Szateth leader
Advanced planetary research fleet.

Neural Blockchain Journal Entry #045

First council sister should not be our leader.

Her callous, no, murderous treatment of one of my females cannot go unanswered. I'm not sure what I'll do yet, but I must do something.

Her focus, right now, is away from the females and firmly set on the males. She's desperate to build her army, and I hold the key.

I will mix the conversion serum formula for her and she can test it on the males in the hangar. I know it will work.

She will, I'm sure, try to take *all* the males from the compatible species, but I'm going to have to limit her over-enthusiasm, or at least temper it. She needs to see that taking more than she needs will mean there are fewer for her to take in the future. It's basic, animal husbandry.

And I want the commander - dead!

Second Council Sister
Advanced planetary research fleet.

Seven

He tasted so good.

As promised, she knocked on first sister's chamber door as the sun brightened the corridors.

"Right on time," she said, opening her door, still in her sleeping robes. "Good. Come in."

"Thank you, sister."

"Give me a few minutes to dress. Take a seat while you're waiting."

"Thank you, sister." She sat on the big lounger and gazed around. She couldn't help but admire the trappings that came from being the first council sister.

"Right. Shall we make a start? I assume you have the test results with you?" first sister said.

"Yes, of course, sister." She smiled, tapping the clipboard.

"Follow me then, and let's make a conversion serum that works this time, shall we?"

She didn't answer. First sister seemed to have softened her attitude towards her. Now was not the time to ruin it. She followed behind into the lab.

"I'm going to leave you to it again. You don't need me to help you, do you?"

"I should be able to create serum five from the results I have, and from the ingredients you used in serum four."

"Good. I'll get back to those idiot engineers and put them on the right track. The end of the day is enough time to get serum five into production, yes?"

"I believe so. You have everything so clearly set out and labeled. It shouldn't be a problem."

"I'll leave you then. You know where I'll be if you need me."

"Yes, sister."

She wasn't lying. First sister had everything labeled and lined up with military precision, making the lab feel lifeless and sterile. It was the workspace of someone who could only follow instructions, someone who lacked imagination and creativity. There was no mistaking whose lab it was. She shivered.

Right, let's mess this place up a bit, and get this done, she said to herself. Over the next couple of hours, she set up the apparatus and double-checked the quantities of the ingredients, especially the paralytic. With everything set up, she hit the start switch. The smells and the heat coming off the apparatus as the ingredients cooked and blended into serum five gave the lab a warm, comfortable feel. She smiled as the new serum dripped into the vials.

She called first sister. "Conversion serum five is in production, sister. It will be complete and ready for the morning."

"Good work. I knew I could rely on you to get it done. I've made good progress here too. - Take the rest of the day and entertain yourself. Would you like me to arrange for a warrior - or two for you? I'm going to indulge myself this evening."

She knew what that meant for the unlucky one. "I thank you, sister, but no, I have more work to be getting on with."

"As you wish. Can I finally instruct third sister to gather from the two human male species you've identified for warrior conversion?"

"Yes, but can I suggest she doesn't take too many from any one tribe?"

"I want them all, *second sister,* and I will have them."

"Yes, of course, sister, but might I suggest you leave enough so they can breed with the females to produce more for you? It seems foolish to take them all, and those you leave will keep you supplied for years to come."

"Hmm, - just so, just so. I'll instruct third council sister to take ninety percent."

"Might I suggest forty? It would leave a healthy breeding population."

"This is not a negotiation," she said. "I want my warriors."

"Yes, I, of course, understand sister."

"However, will sixty percent satisfy your proclivity for preserving their numbers?"

"Yes, sister. I apologize if I've overstepped, I was thinking more long-term. You are wise to preserve their number to allow them to reproduce for you."

"Agreed," she said. "I'll set third sister to the task."

She ended the call, pleased she'd saved almost half of them.

Mating and breeding, first sister thought to herself. *Hmm, I wonder how humans do it.*

"We are ready to test the propulsion system, first council sister," the chief engineer said, interrupting her thought.

"Very well. Let's hope for your sake it goes well."

She stood behind the protective screen, watching the monitors while he began the test. He held his breath, set the propulsion system to full power, and pressed the ignition button. The monitors showed enough of an increase in energy output to launch the satellite.

"Power it down," she said. "We have it. Now work on the observation and communication arrays."

"Yes, first council sister," said a relieved chief engineer.

She grunted.

"Third sister," she said into her communicator. "Meet me in the hangar in ten minutes. I have instructions for you for the next gathering."

"Yes, sister."

"I've done the hard part for you. Keep me updated with your progress on the internal systems," she said to the chief engineer as she marched away.

She marched everywhere, full of the swagger and attitude of someone who knew they were in charge. She loved it when the crew stood aside at attention in the corridors as she strode past. Today was no exception.

She was pleased to see third sister waiting as she entered the hangar. "Ah, good. Come with me. I have instructions for the next gathering."

"I enjoyed my last trip to the surface so much," third sister said. "The humans stampeded when they saw our shuttles. We corralled them and scooped them up. It was glorious."

"Well, this time, thanks to the conversion serum tests, I need you to be more selective with the males you gather."

With third sister almost running to keep up, she walked over to the room where her males were being kept.

"You see these two species of male," she said, pointing to the larger males in the group.

"Yes. They are magnificent, sister."

"Only gather these. Leave the others. And don't take them all. I need you to leave about forty percent of them so they can breed with the females and produce more for me. I need to preserve my stock so I can sustain my warrior numbers long into the future."

"Ah, yes, that's clever, sister. I'll give the other crews those instructions."

"Very good. Now assemble them. You leave for the gathering in a few hours."

"Yes, sister."

She called the shuttle pilots, their crews, and the warriors she used last time to meet her in the hangar's briefing room.

"Where is the commander?" first sister said, looking around. She spotted him inspecting a shuttle. "Ah, Commander, there you are. I trust you enjoyed your reward?" she said with a sly grin.

"Yes, first council sister, very much. Thank you."

"And did you make a mess like the last time?"

"I have had it cleaned up, first council sister. Nothing remains."

"Excellent, Commander. Carry on."

It is turning out to be a good day. She thought as she marched back to her chambers. Next was to check on the progress of serum five. She expected everything had gone to plan. Second sister wouldn't dare disappoint. And her day would get better. She had been dreaming and looking forward to this while they searched for a compatible species to blend with. It had taken many years, but now it was time. She clapped and took in a deep breath. *At last, the harvesting of her sisters.*

Other than the journals with events and comments she recorded, every first council sister held private files on her council sisters, passed down from the previous first council sister. It was her duty to keep them updated and added to when new sisters replaced the old. It was especially important to log every detail of any harvest. Goose bumps ran down her spine as she added a sheet of paper to each file, and wrote the title - Harvest Details.

The files contained information about the sister's blending, the name of the planet, and the implanted species. Thoughts, concerns, threats, suspicions, and anything else that could be useful and used against her if needed. Of particular interest was their age.

Council sisters three, four, five, six, and seven were nearing their prime, and although older, council sisters eight and nine, she hoped, had a viable egg. Either way, she would still harvest them. When she took their eggs depended on the females delivering healthy Szatethess hybrids. Assuming they do, the harvest will be shortly after, in about eight months. Her heart raced as she wrote her notes.

She'd had the lower levels of the ship, remodeled to look and feel like the hunting grounds of their home planet. She loved it down there and would often spend time there alone, basking in the heat and bathing in the dim red light of the artificial sky. Here she would hunt her sisters, one at a time, and harvest their eggs. She smiled as she marched, and it reminded her to see if second sister had prepared a storage facility for them. When she entered her chambers, she hit the call button and could hear a communicator buzzing.

"Yes, sister," second sister said, appearing from the lab.

"Oh, you're still here," she said, ending the call. "Good. I assume everything is going well, and the production of serum five is making good progress?"

"Oh, yes, sister. You should have a batch ready to use in the next few hours. I just wanted to be here in case any issues needed some creative tweaking to keep the production on track."

"And, were there?"

"No, no. So far it's going well."

"Excellent. Now, I asked you to prepare a storage facility for new eggs. Have you done that?"

"No, sister, not yet. It is on my list to do."

"Well, don't leave it too long. I want one made ready."

"Very well, sister. I'll bump it up my list."

"Good. You may go."

"Thank you, sister. Can I observe as you administer serum five?"

"I'll be in your lab first thing in the morning. There are males ready, I presume?"

"Of course, and they'll be the ideal test subjects for you."

"Good. And third sister is shortly going to gather more from the surface, then there'll be a plentiful supply."

"I look forward to it, sister. Till tomorrow then."

"Yes, yes," she said, waving at her to leave.

Once she'd gone, she pulled out and read the files on her sisters. *Yes, they are ready.* She said to herself, grinning.

She saw a movement from the shadow. "You."

A worker was doing his best to hide and jumped when she shouted. "Yes, first council sister, how can I serve you?" he said, shuffling into the light.

"Arrange for a warrior to entertain me this evening."

"Yes, first council sister, immediately," he said, turning to leave.

"Wait. - make that two."

He saw her eyes light up. "Yes, of course, first council sister." He swore he could see her drooling.

The evening entertainment and meal ordered, she called third sister. "Are you ready to depart for the gathering?"

"Yes, sister. We are standing by, waiting for clearance to leave from the commander."

"What's the delay?"

"I do not know. But we are ready to go."

"Where is he?"

"I'm afraid I do not know, sister. He was here, now I can't see him."

"Find him. I'll be there shortly."

"Yes, sister."

The cleaner worker reappeared. "I have organized your entertainment for this evening, first council sister."

"That was quick. Maybe I should make you the hangar commander." She laughed.

He didn't reply. "Get on with your work," she said, locking the files in her desk drawer. He hurried past her, his cleaning products rattling in the bucket, and disappeared into her bed-chamber.

She took a cleansing breath to calm herself, got up, and marched out. Third sister was holding the commander's arm as she strode in. The look of terror on his face when he saw her pleased her. He looked down.

"Well, commander. Why have you held up my gathering?"

He didn't answer.

"First council sister asked you a question, commander. Answer her, now," third sister said.

"There isn't enough hydrogen for the fuel cells, first council sister."

"What? Why not? - Didn't I tell you to make sure they were ready for relaunch when they got back from the last gathering?"

"Yes, first council sister. But I've been so busy, and then you gave me the female, I - I - forgot to generate more hydrogen to recharge the fuel cells."

She glowered. Third sister had seen that look before and backed away. The mistake was going to cost him.

"How long?" she said. "How long will it take you to correct your mistake and recharge the fuel cells, commander? So I get my males from the surface?" She took a step towards him.

"Just one day, first council sister," he said, trying to make the time sound shorter.

"Just one day?" she said, grabbing his wrist. "Just one day?"

He didn't resist as she lifted his arm. His eyes, wide with fear, met hers. "I apologize for my mistake, first council sister," he said, his voice shaking.

"One finger," she said, holding his eyes in a grip as strong as the one she had on his arm. "That's what your *mistake* will cost you. - One finger."

"Whaaat?"

She struck forward with lightning speed, opening her mouth and clamping on his first finger. Her teeth scythed through the skin and ligaments, then crunched through the bone, biting it off.

He screamed as blood spurted from the open stump, spattering her face. She released him. He grabbed it and screamed again as he squeezed to stem the flow.

She spat his severed finger onto the floor. It landed at his feet. "Any longer, commander, it'll cost you a lot more. Am I clear?"

"Yes, first council sister," he said, gritting his teeth through the agony.

"Get it done, or it will be the last thing you do," she said. "Stand your crews down, sister. We'll resume the gathering tomorrow, once the commander has refueled your shuttles." She licked the blood from her lips and wiped her face. "Now, I have an appointment with two warriors in my chambers. - Get that wound seen to, and heed my words, commander."

"Yes, - first council sister," he said before the color drained from his face, and he slumped to the floor.

The first officer and the other warriors in the hangar watched the extreme punishment in stunned silence. "Well, help him up," third sister said. The first officer volunteered two warriors, who grabbed an arm each and hoisted the moaning, bleeding commander to his feet.

"Take him to medical," she said.

"Yes, third council sister, straight away." They held him up as he staggered out, squealing from the pain.

"Have this blood cleaned up, and dispose of that, first officer," she said, pointing to the cruelly amputated digit and the puddle of blood on the shiny floor. He instructed workers to get a bucket of water, and sponges to wash it away. The worker picked up the finger, and it splashed as he dropped it into the bucket.

"Right." She wrinkled her nose. "Carry on," she said to the first officer as she left.

None of them looked at her. They were reeling from the ruthless treatment they'd just witnessed.

∞

The two warriors sat the commander on the edge of the examination table in the medical bay. "She shouldn't have done that, - she shouldn't have done that," he said, repeating over and over, still gripping the stump.

"Let me look at that," the doctor said.

"She shouldn't have done that, - she shouldn't have done that."

"Maybe. But let me save what I can of what's left and take away the pain for you."

"She shouldn't have done that, - she shouldn't have done that."

"Can you lay him down for me?" The doctor said to the warriors.

"He's right, you know," one of them said, "she shouldn't have done that." They laid him down.

"Hmm, so which one of you is going to complain to her, then?" the Doctor said, injecting an anesthetic into his arm.

They didn't reply. "I thought not," he said. "You can go now. He'll be fine in a few days."

The warriors left the sedated commander, grumbling under their breath.

Neural Blockchain Journal Entry #925

I am surrounded by incompetent fools.

I taught the hangar commander a lesson today he'll never forget. And it served as a reminder to the others that I expect things to be done to a high standard, and on time, or there will be consequences. Plus, he tasted so good.

Second sister has started the production of conversion serum five. I'm confident it will work and give me the warriors I need.

We will administer the first batch tomorrow.

I must give her credit and say that her work, and work ethic, have impressed me. Maybe I've been wrong about her?

The hangar commander had better get my shuttles launched tomorrow, or I will treat myself to more of him.

First Council Sister - Szateth leader
Advanced planetary research fleet.

Neural Blockchain Journal Entry #054

I have convinced her, finally.

I've done what I set out to do. I have created the formula for conversion serum five and began the production of it for her. She would not take the blame for the failure of serum four. On top of her narcissism, and belief in her omnipotence, she's got a responsibility deficit disorder.

I overheard two warriors complaining about how she'd treated the hangar commander. Not that I have any sympathy for him, but to bite off one of his fingers in front of everyone was too much.

It's a shame the commander's mistake couldn't delay the gathering for longer. Maybe there's an opportunity to nurture his hatred of her?

The pregnant females can now communicate with me. I have told them to keep it between us for now. They agreed and told me of their feelings toward first sister. The feeling is mutual.

The good news is she's still well and truly focused on the males. I'll continue to encourage that.

Second Council Sister

Advanced planetary research fleet.

Eight

Serum Five and P9R

"Good morning," first sister said, entering the lab. "I see you've anticipated my needs."

"Good morning, sister. Yes, the examination tables and syringes are ready for you." Two large warriors walked in. "And made sure we have some protection with these warriors."

"Well. Let's get on with it then," first sister said, looking over the two warriors. She opened the case full of the new serum five vials. "The three males that survived your tests, they are in there?"

"Yes, sister."

"You two, go get me the males with the numbers, err." She looked at second sister.

"Three, four, and five," second sister said.

"Three, four, and five written on their hands. I want them first. Bring them out one at a time, and secure them face down on these tables."

"Yes, first council sister."

"Wait. - Don't force them. Invite them out of the cell," second sister said to the warriors. "They'll be easier to manage if they're not scared to death."

"Well, let's sedate them first," first sister said, frowning.

"We shouldn't, sister. There's a possibility that sedation, on top of the paralyzing agent in the serum, could cause an overdose and kill them."

"Ah, yes, good thinking." The two warriors stood there, looking blankly at first sister. "Well, you heard her, do as she says. Get me number three, and do it gently."

"Yes, first council sister."

"I'll be sending third sister down to the surface to get more males today," she said, picking up a syringe and jabbing the needle through the cap of a vial.

"Yes, and I heard about the delay caused by the idiot hangar commander. Not to carry out your orders when he knew how important this mission was. Well, I've never trusted him," second sister said.

"He won't be making that mistake again, for sure," first sister said, laughing.

"No, I guess not."

"Do you think me harsh?" She pulled the plunger, drawing serum into the syringe.

"No, sister, not at all. I'd say he was lucky you were so lenient. I'm not sure I would have been that restrained."

"He won't be that lucky next time, I assure you. Besides, he tasted extremely good." They laughed.

Male three approached the sisters, flanked by the warriors. He was pale and sweating and didn't resist when they strapped him to the table.

With the syringe ready, she felt for the entry point on his spine. "Here we go. This better work," first sister said, pushing the needle into his spine.

His cry cut right through her.

"I'm sure it will," second sister said, stroking his hair like a mother soothing a baby in pain. Moments later, he was still.

"Push the table into that cell and loosen the straps," first sister said to the warriors. "How long until we know for sure it worked?"

"Assuming we have the formula correct. A day to complete both phases of the conversion."

"Hmm, let's hope you're right," first sister said, raising her eyebrows.

Another veiled threat. She was tired of them now.

"Bring number four and let me stick this in him, too," first sister said to the warriors.

"I'd like to check number three's pulse and blood pressure. If you'll allow me," second sister asked.

"Yes, yes. If you think it is necessary."

"Just to be sure."

"Very well."

She looked back as she walked to the cell. She could see the syringe, and the maniacal grin on her face, while the warriors strapped him to the table. *I can't watch. She's enjoying herself too much. There is no need to torture them like this.*

From inside the cell, she heard his pain. It made her feel sick, knowing these males were going to suffer.

"Well, is he alive?"

She stood aside as the warriors wheeled in number four and parked him next to number three. "Yes, he's stable," she said back into the lab.

"Alright then. Let's speed this process up. Grab a syringe, you can do one at the same time. - Bring number five, and another one for second council sister," she said. The warriors grinned, brought them out, and strapped them down.

She saw her hesitation. "Well, go on, slide the needle in. It's not that difficult. Watch," she said. "Use your fingers to find the space. Line up the needle at this angle and - push." The male groaned.

Her stomach knotted, but she had no choice. She screwed her face as she slide the needle in. He groaned, and moments later, was still and quiet.

"There, not so difficult after all," first sister said. "Right, let's get the rest of them done."

They injected the others and the warriors wheeled them into the cell and loosened the straps. She checked their heart rates and blood pressure.

"Satisfied?" first sister asked.

"Yes, sister, everything looks good. I would like to check on them regularly until the conversion is complete."

"Good idea. And if anything goes wrong, you might have time to fix it. - I'll leave you to it then . I'm going to call third sister to start the next gathering."

"Yes, sister." She watched her march out and make the call.

∞

"Meet me in the hangar, third sister. I want you and the others to launch for the gathering."

When she got there, third sister and the commander were waiting for her.

"I trust you have fueled my shuttles, commander?"

"Yes, first council sister. It won't happen again."

"See that it doesn't." She dismissed him with a wave. "Are you ready to go?"

"Yes, sister," third sister said, smiling at the power they had over the crew.

"And you're clear with what's required of you and the other crews?"

"Yes, sister. Only gather sixty percent, and leave the rest for mating with the females."

"Correct. Although if you see a few extra, you think would make powerful warriors, take them."

"I will, sister."

"Happy hunting, then. I look forward to seeing what you bring back for me." She stepped back.

"Alright, everybody, to your shuttles, we've got work to do for first council sister. Now, let's go." The pilots and crews scrambled to their shuttles.

"Clear the hangar," the commander said over the tannoy, then sounded the launch alarm.

First sister entered the observation room, as the commander pulled the lever opening the hangar doors. She watched as the shuttles took off and flew out, dispersing in all directions. She rubbed her hands in anticipation of a good yield.

"That's how you carry out my orders, commander," she said, glaring at him.

"Yes, first council sister." He looked down as she rebuked him, hiding the contempt he had in his eyes.

As she marched away, his eyes followed her out. His stump throbbed, reminding him of what she did.

∞

In the lab, second sister checked the progress of the males. Their skin was turning olive green and thickening. They were panting rather than breathing smoothly, and their heart rates and blood pressure were higher than normal. *I hope you survive.* She wrote her observations in their notes. Now all she could do was wait.

To take her mind off the males, she went to speak to her females. She knocked.

"Come in," they said.

They were eating and invited her to join them.

"Thank you, ladies, nothing for me, but please carry on."

"We heard our males in pain earlier. What is it you want from us?"

"If first council sister had her way, she'd want and take everything. And once she'd had it all, she'd move on to another planet. What you heard was first council sister giving your males the warrior conversion serum."

She explained their mission, their search for a compatible species to blend with, first council sister's need to dominate the universe, and her never-ending demand for new warriors.

"But I believe you humans could be our saviors," she said.

"She is on a path to self-destruction if she takes all our males," one of them said.

Astounded by the logic, second sister knew the fetus inside her was the one talking. "You're right, and I have told her so myself. Look, I am not in a position to stop her from doing exactly what she wants. But I am trying to manipulate the situation so we all survive."

"Is there anything we can do to help?"

"Not right now, but there may come a time. Just remember what I've said. Don't let anyone know you can speak. Make them think you are still as you once were. I will protect you from her, but to do that, I have to help her with the conversion process. Do you understand?"

"Yes, but the pain she's inflicting on our males, - it's barbaric."

"I'm embarrassed to say it is, yes. The current conversion method is barbaric. I've never had enough time to work on an alternative, before another gathering, and first council sister's insistence on getting them converted immediately. I've done what I can to make the process less painful. The sacrifice your males are making means we'll all survive." She got up to leave. "I hope they survive. She will harvest me if they don't."

"What did you say?"

"Err, no, nothing. Now, I must check on the females next door. And I have a neurogenic compound to make. Is there anything you need before I go?"

"No, we are fine. Please take care, second council sister."

"Thank you, ladies," she said, closing the door.

The females had food and water, warmth and shelter, everything a tribe of hunter-gatherers needed. *You've never had it so easy*, she thought to herself. *And you've got no idea how important you all are.* They looked contented, and she wanted to keep them that way.

There was work to do if she was going to keep first sister's attention on warriors and workers. First, a new batch of P9R needed to be produced for the newly converted warriors.

The conversion process dulled their wits and tore out any ideas of self-identity, which is how first sister liked them. She wanted powerful, unquestioning automatons, whose only purpose was to follow her orders or die trying.

At their present level of evolution, humans hadn't developed the use of language, and the conversion serum would hamper any further development unless it had some help. P9R would give them an evolutionary boost, the ability to understand and use language, and to carry out her orders.

The chemical structure and molecular formula for P9R were simple. She knew it by heart, having made it often enough. She had everything she needed to prepare it in her lab. *I could solve two problems at once,* she thought, as she put the apparatus together. *If I use a larger storage unit, at minus twenty, it could store new embryos as well. That will please her.*

It didn't take long before P9R was dripping into the vials. This wasn't a job she enjoyed, so she made a lot of it when she did. With the storage unit open, her hands shook, and she shivered in the cold as she carefully placed each vial into the storage unit. With the last of them placed in the unit and enough space left for embryos, she closed and secured the lid. *Thank goodness that's over,* she said to herself, pulling off the protective gloves and breathing warm air into her hands.

Her communicator buzzed. She shook life back into them so she could answer the call. "The shuttles are on their way back. Join me in the hangar's observation room. Then we'll inspect the males once they're all in," first sister said.

"Yes, sister. I'll be right there."

Before she left, she checked the males. They were motionless, and the room felt cold, like a morgue with corpses on slabs. She got closer to hear their panting breath, and there was a significant change in the texture of their skin. The conversion was well underway. She closed the cell door behind her as if trying not to wake a sleeping baby.

When she got to the observation room, an excited first sister was waiting for her. "Today I get my warriors. That is as long as third sister has carried out her orders correctly."

"I'm sure she has, sister. And as you requested, I've prepared a storage unit for any new embryos."

"Aha, yes. Good work. I have a feeling today is going to be another good day."

The shuttles flew in. "Close the hangar doors, commander," she said, once the docking clamps had secured the last of them.

"Yes, first council sister." He pulled the lever and the heavy outer doors closed with a thud, and hissed as they sealed.

"All clear, first council sister," he said. He still couldn't look at her.

Third sister was busy barking orders to the warriors to get the males out and lined up ready for the inspection when they got down onto the hangar floor.

"Do they need to be shackled?" second sister asked, seeing the red raw skin on their ankles.

"They are wild animals and need to know who's master here. So they will remain shackled until they do. Are we clear?" first sister said. Then walked on ahead.

She heard a sound from behind her.

"Ahem."

It was the commander. She hadn't realized he'd followed. He walked past her, giving her a sideways look like he knew something. She ignored him and caught up with first sister.

"We gathered the males you required, sister. These species are a lot more boisterous than the others," third sister said.

"Looks like you have outdone yourself," first sister said, walking the line. "Don't you think so?" she said, looking at second sister.

"It certainly looks that way. Congratulations, third sister," second sister said.

"Thank you. It is my honor to serve."

"Put them in the room over there with the other males ready for conversion."

"The room on the left, sister. The other room has my workers in it," second sister said.

"Yes, of course." She turned to the warriors. "March them into the room on the left, over there."

The warrior at the end of the line closest to the room tugged hard on the first male's shackles. "This way," he said. The male squealed as the shackles bit into his wrists. He moved to get away from the pain and the others followed like a long serpent undulating around the obstacles in the hangar. Third sister went with them.

"We have enough conversion serum five for these males?" first sister asked.

"Yes, plenty, sister," second sister said. "And there will be more than enough P9R for them as well. Your new warriors should be ready for training in the next seven or eight days."

"Perfect. There, see. I was right, a good day."

"Indeed, sister," second sister said, as third sister jogged over to them

"The males are secure and ready, sister," she said.

"Good. Walk with me," first sister said.

The two of them walked off. Alone, she looked at the floor and sighed.

"May I speak with you, second council sister?"

"What?" she said, surprised by the voice.

"May I speak with you?" It was the commander.

"What do *you* want?" she said, trying to hide her hatred of him.

"Forgive me, second council sister, but I noticed you have a, err, how should I put it, a fondness for the humans?"

"I don't know what you mean, commander."

"I have observed there's a marked difference in the way you treat them as opposed to first council sister."

"What of it?"

"Knowing, as I'm sure you do, first council sister's uncaring attitude towards them..."

"Be very careful with what you say next, commander."

"Forgive me, second council sister. I'd like to help, if or when you might need that favor you asked me for. If say you want to get anybody off the ship, for example?"

"I'll bear that in mind, commander." She stared at him and walked away. *Hmm, you may regret that,* she said to herself, heading back to her lab.

Further down the corridor, she could see first and third sister walking toward their chambers, deep in conversation. Third sister's rise through the ranks had sent ripples of uneasiness through the other council sisters, particularly the demoted fourth sister, who already felt humiliated.

The loungers in the main relaxation area were empty when they entered the chambers. "I am impressed by your work. I wish your other sisters were as efficient as you," first sister said.

"Thank you, sister. I understand how important this mission is."

"Yes, I can see you do. You deserve a reward for it."

"It is unnecessary, sister. It is my duty to further your goals where I can."

"Whilst that is true, you deserve something for your commitment. Tonight, two handsome warriors shall entertain us. You shall join me in my chambers, and we'll enjoy one each."

"Thank you, thank you, sister."

"What's all this noise in here..." fourth sister said, striding into the chambers. "Oh, I apologize, sisters. I didn't know.... How can I help you?"

"I was just talking in private to third sister, here," first sister said.

"Of course, forgive my intrusion."

"I presume you've moved your belongings to the fourth sister's chambers and allowed third sister to take up residence in your old chamber?"

"No, sister, not as yet. I've been so busy."

"What is it with everyone being too busy to do what needs to be done? The commander knows what a mistake that is. Make the time."

"Yes, sister. I'll do it now."

"Good. Shall we go to my chambers, third sister so that we can continue uninterrupted?" she said raising her eyebrows, staring at fourth sister.

"Yes, sister, I'd like to hear what else you have to say."

Once they'd left, fourth sister, feeling degraded, simmered with anger. *And in front of another sister. How is that allowed?* she said to herself.

∞

Back in her lab, she checked on the males. The top layer of their skin had hardened and lifted. They were in the second stage of the conversion process. Tomorrow they would shed this skin, and emerge new warriors. Their breathing was normal and feeling their pulse, their heart rates were strong. It was working.

"Second council sister, are you in here?" She heard a voice say from the lab.

"Yes," she said, walking back out. "Ah, first officer, what do you want?"

"I apologize for the intrusion, second council sister, but first council sister instructed me to bring these to you."

He pointed to the chain of shackled males shuffling in, flanked by a squad of warriors.

"Put them in that cell over there," she said.

"Bring them in," the first officer said. "Put them in there and remove their shackles."

"Move!" said the warrior at the front of the chain as he shoved the first male. The others had no choice but to follow.

They filed past the first officer, their shackles dragging on the floor. "If this is what we have to work with, it's going to be a long war," he said, watching them shuffle past.

"Don't let first council sister hear you say that."

"Oh, err, no. I meant no disrespect..."

"Calm yourself, first officer. I know what you meant. I think we can keep that between the two of us."

"Thank you, second council sister."

"Prisoners are secure, Sir," the lead warrior said.

"Very good. Back to the hangar. Carry on," he said, and the squad marched out.

"If that's all, second council sister?"

"Yes, that will be all. Thank you, first officer."

She waited for him to leave before looking at the males, oblivious to their fate.

"Bring me enough food to feed thirty male omnivores," she said into her communicator to the head kitchen worker.

One of the pregnant females opened their door and said. "Can we help, second council sister? We saw our males coming in. They are going to be frightened, and a large group like that can be unpredictable. We thought we could calm them down for you."

"That would be very helpful. I have called for food for them. If you bring in the water, I'll take in the cups."

"Let us go in first. They won't attack if they see their kind first."

"Yes, very good."

She turned the lock, and all eyes were on the door. The pack of males stepped forward, ready to charge as the door opened, but stopped when they saw three of their females walk in.

Again she saw it, the authority these three females now had over their males. She smiled and walked in behind them. Their eyes narrowed, but they took the cups she offered, and drank the water their females poured.

"Thank you, ladies," she said as they left the cell.

They made it back to their room moments before the kitchen workers arrived with the food.

"Leave it on the workbench. I'll take it into them."

"Very good, second council sister," the head kitchen worker said.

They were still drinking as she took the food in. She put it on the floor in the middle of the cell. They didn't move. As soon as she'd left and locked the door, they pounced on it.

There was nothing left for her to do in the lab: the females were in good spirits, the new gathering of males was secure, and the nine new warriors were in the second phase of the conversion.

"First officer," she said, calling him. "Give me an update on my workers. Are you making sure they are healthy and stimulated, with someone speaking to them daily?"

"Yes, second council sister, as you ordered. They are making good progress, with reports that they are trying to mimic sounds and speech already."

"Thank you, first officer. Good work. Notify me of any changes."

"Yes, second council sister."

Her communicator buzzed with another incoming call. "How are my new warriors?" first sister asked.

"They are doing well, sister. I think you'll have the first of your warriors ready for P9R on schedule tomorrow."

"Wonderful. Third sister and I are having some entertainment tonight. Care to join us?"

"Thank you, sister, but I have a stack of paperwork waiting for me in my chambers."

"Very well. You're going to miss out on a spectacular meal. Oh, and has the next batch of males arrived to you yet?"

"Yes, sister. Secured and ready for you for tomorrow."

"Excellent. I'll meet you in your lab."

The call went dead. Although she felt she'd earned more trust with first sister, she didn't like the Commander knowing she cared for the humans. *I'll deal with you, commander,* she thought to herself.

∞

She was in her lab before first sister arrived and looked in on the nine males. They were doing as expected. She ran her fingers over the top layer of their skin. it was hard, scaly, and ready for them to break free. The paralytic still had them in its grip. *It won't be long now.*

First sister walked in with her case, and an entourage of warriors, as she was coming out of the cell. "How are they?" she said.

"They are fine, sister. Would you care to look?"

"No. Let's get the new batch injected."

"But we don't have any examination tables."

"That's what these warriors are here for. I don't have the time to do just nine. I want all these males converted today. They're going to hold them down while I inject them. "

"But, sister..."

"But what?"

She couldn't answer without giving her feelings away. "Let me clear some space on the floor first."

"Yes, yes, good idea." She pointed to two warriors. "You, and you, help her move these benches."

The screeching assaulted their ears as they dragged the heavy benches over to the walls. With space now in the middle of the floor, she ordered the first male to be brought out. There was no consideration of how scared they were this time. Held secure, and forced face down on the floor, first sister, unconcerned, felt for the first injection site. He howled as she slid the needle into his spine, and they held him tighter. A few moments later, he was silent and still.

"Take him back in and bring me the next one." She said, preparing another injection. "This shouldn't take too long."

There is that maniacal smile again. I can't be a part of this. I have to get out of here. "If you don't need me, sister. I'd like to check on my workers. The P9R may have taken effect already."

"You're of no use to me. Yes, go check on your pets."

"Thank you, sister." She left without looking back. *She is being even more vicious than usual.* "First officer, meet me in the hangar. I want to discuss the new workers," she said, calling him.

"Yes, second council sister."

As she walked past the sister's chambers, fourth sister came out. "Good morning, sister," she said.

"Is it?"

"My goodness, what's wrong?"

She told her how first sister had humiliated her in front of third sister. "I'd be careful if I were you. She'll be after your position next. The way first sister is treating everyone these days has our sisters rattled," she said.

"I don't want to sound like I'm making excuses for poor behavior, but she is under pressure to complete our mission. You've seen the numbers, and know how critical it is for us to succeed," second sister said.

"I apologize, sister. But I wonder if she's lost sight of it, and just wants to build her army to fight her wars? Perhaps something has to be done."

"What do you intend?"

"What can I do? As fourth sister, I work in maintenance now. I have tighter restrictions, more work, less free time, and even less access to her. - But you never know."

"Know what? What do you mean?"

She snorted. "There's only so much we'll take," fourth sister said and walked off.

For a moment, she stood there, trying to process what she'd said. *Discontent among the sisters, the commander hates her, the first officer will help, and I have the females.* "Things are about to get interesting," she whispered.

In the hangar, the first officer was there to meet her.

"Ah, first officer. Shall we look at the worker's progress?"

"Hello, second council sister. Yes, and the last worker to go in this morning was a cleaner worker, second council sister. He talked to them about the tools he was using. He reported they listened, and nodded, in what he said looked like some understanding of what he was saying."

"Did they speak at all?"

"He didn't say so."

"Okay, well, let's test them ourselves, shall we?"

Her new workers immediately got in a line and stood to attention when they entered. She grinned. Their eyes glinted with growing intelligence.

"Bring in the head construction worker, would you, first officer? I think we should start their training?"

"Right away, second council sister."

"Alright," she said, addressing the line. "I am pleased with your progress. You will be my construction workers. You are to build a compound, where you will live, and the first of what may be many conversion facilities. In return for your efforts, we will make sure you receive food and water and get fair treatment."

"Here is the head construction worker for you, second council sister," the first officer said, standing in the doorway with him.

"Ah, good. Come in and meet your new construction workers," she said.

"Yes, thank you, second council sister."

"Here is your new leader," she said, pointing to him. "You will follow his commands. He will teach you everything you need to build the compound and facility buildings. Do everything he says, without question, and I will reward you for your obedience. Fail, and you will suffer the consequences."

They nodded but made no sound.

"I know you understand, and I need you to speak and say, 'yes.' First officer, come here, please." She took his hand and touched his fingers to her throat. "Yes," she said. Then touched his fingers to his throat, and had him say yes, to feel the vibration of the sound.

"Do the same to the workers, first officer, so they can feel it."

He went along the line, repeating the same process. They felt and heard the sound. When he'd finished, they were all trying to mimic it.

"Thank you, first officer."

"Silence," she said, clapping her hands to get their attention. They stopped. With her fingers touching her throat, she said, "Yes." And one by one, they repeated it.

"Well done, all of you. Now we just have to keep working on it," she said.

"Amazing, second council sister," the first officer said.

"The P9R is working. It's how we learn to speak, by listening, understanding, copying, and praising."

"Teach them every tool and every technique they need to build my facility," she said to the head construction worker. "Don't expect them to get everything right the first time. Be patient. They will learn quickly. In the meantime, I will instruct the engineer workers to install and power a meta-gate in here for you. You can send them into the metaverse and teach construction techniques there. I'll have them draw a new set of plans for the compound and the conversion building. You'll have them to you in a few days. Are you clear?"

"Yes, second council sister."

"Right, I will leave you now. If you need anything, liaise with the first officer, and he will see you get what you need."

"Yes, second council sister." He bowed.

"I need you first officer if you'd come with me."

In the main hangar bay, they stood by the largest shuttle. "I require more of you, first officer. I need you to re-fit and insulate this shuttle enough to withstand the cold on the surface."

"Yes, second council sister, I can do that."

"You have until my construction workers are ready to build my facility on the surface. A week maybe."

"I will have it ready for you, second council sister."

"Yes, first officer. I believe you will." Her communicator buzzed. It was first sister. "Excuse me, I have to take this."

"I want you back in the lab. I have nine new magnificent warriors, and they need P9R immediately?" she said through the communicator's speaker.

"Yes, sister. That's good news. I'm on my way," she said and closed the call. "Things are going to plan, first officer. Carry on with the re-fit. I'll be in my lab if you need me."

She passed two of her sisters, talking in the corridor on the way back. They stopped when they saw her.

"Sisters." She nodded, walking by.

"Sister." They said in unison, their eyes following as she passed.

The hairs on the back of her neck stood up, sensing the change in their attitude.

"Come and see them," first sister said as she walked in.

The cell door was open and when she went in, the nine warriors were sitting on the examination tables. They turned and looked as she entered.

"Aren't they just perfect?" first sister said, clapping.

"I'd like to examine them."

"Go ahead. Go on, do what you need to do. But they are perfect."

Stepping over layers of dead skin, she examined the first one. "It certainly looks like the conversion has been successful," she said, taking his pulse, blood pressure, and temperature. "Pulse is strong, blood pressure is normal and his core temperature elevated to that of a

Szateth warrior's." She ran her hand over his skin. "It feels thick and tough, and there's a considerable increase in muscle mass."

"They are perfect. The P9R, give it to them."

She examined the last two warriors before answering. "Congratulations, sister. You have your first new warriors."

"The P9R. How long does it take to work?"

"Well, I've just been to see my workers. I administered P9R a few days ago, and they have made remarkable progress. Sister, I believe humans are the species we've been searching the universe for. The males are compatible with the serum for workers and warrior conversion, and the females are adaptable to bear us new sisters. They are going to save our race, sister."

"Yes, yes, but how long will the P9R take to give me warriors capable of being in my army?"

"Judging by the workers, sister, just a few days. Then you can begin their training, and I'll be able to build on the surface, giving us a more permanent solution."

"Aha, I knew you could do it. Soon I'll have an army big enough to rule with. The P9R, give it to them."

"Yes, sister."

She's still not interested in the females, that's good. She prepared her automatic injector syringe.

"Is this storage unit big enough for new embryos?" first sister asked, running her hand over the lid.

"Yes, sister, the others I have are in that smaller storage unit over there on the bench."

"How many do you have?"

"Another six."

"Hmm, okay, not so many, then. We may have to change that now we have a bigger storage unit."

She pretended not to hear. "The P9R is ready, sister," she said, screwing the cap tight on the injector supply bottle.

"Good. Get it done then."

Nine pairs of eager eyes fixed on her when she went back into the cell. They didn't react as she raised the syringe. She knew where to inject the P9R and they didn't move or flinch as the needle entered the space just below their ears. Within a couple of minutes, she was done.

"A few days, you said?"

"Yes, sister. But I'd like to monitor them over the next few hours in case there is a reaction. I'm not expecting any adverse effects, I'd just like to be certain. They are going to need some stimulation if the P9R is going to do its work, sister. I would recommend that you have your training officer or a ranking officer come and speak to them so they can learn."

"Very well. And tomorrow you'll give P9R to the others in the cell. Good, I'll have third sister prepare for the next gathering."

"Where are we going to put them all, sister? Space on board for new warriors is very limited."

"We'll build sleeping racks for them in the room in the hangar. They won't be in there for anything other than resting. They'll be training other than that."

"Might I suggest an alternative?"

"I'm listening."

"My workers are almost ready to build the compound and the conversion facility on the surface. I'm having the first officer refit and insulate a shuttle so I can manage the construction on site. Why not have my workers build a big compound? Then you can have these training, housed, and guarding the workers and newly gathered males at the same time."

"Hmm, interesting idea."

"You could train them in combat and security, preparing them for the wars to come. Once the conversion facility is complete, it would be a very efficient production line for you."

"If everything happened in the same place, it would save space and time. Hmm."

"And I'll have suitable chambers constructed for us, so you could visit and supervise their training. If we shift the entire operation to the surface, sister, we'll be able to gather and convert as many males as you wish, and whenever you wish."

"Yes, yes, your reasoning is sensible... Yes, alright, let's do it that way."

"I have new construction plans being drawn up, and the shuttle should be ready in a couple of days. In time, I would say, for my workers and your warriors to transfer to the surface and begin constructing our future."

"Very good work. I commend you."

"May I ask, sister, if fourth sister could assist me?"

"Very well, although you might find her help worthless. Although at least I wouldn't have to endure her miserable moods. Yes, take her."

"Thank you, sister. I'll inform her of her new role."

"Very good. You have everything under control. I'll be in the lower levels if you need me. Carry on."

"Congratulations again, sister."

She waited until she'd left before calling fourth sister. "Can you come to my lab, sister?"

"Yes, sister. I have a few minutes before I have to resume my maintenance duties."

She wondered for a moment what she was going to say. She didn't want fourth sister to know the full extent of her feelings towards the humans, and first sister. But she wanted her to suspect she might feel the same towards first sister as she did.

I could nurture her dislike and grow it into something I could use. This is too good an opportunity to miss.

"You wanted to see me, sister?" fourth sister said, as she walked into the lab.

"Yes, come in sister. Take a seat. I have something to ask you."

"Thank you, sister. I hope you don't think my outburst when we spoke earlier means anything. I was just in a bad mood, I would never..."

"Don't worry, sister," she said, cutting her off. "I have some sympathy with your thoughts. That's why I've asked you here."

"Oh?"

"Yes. Look," she said, scanning the lab for listening ears, then lowering her voice, "I believe the humans are the species we've been looking for. The males make for perfect warriors, and the females can carry and give birth to our new sisters. First sister knows that but is so focused on gathering the males to grow her army that she may, as you said, have lost sight of our primary mission. Third sister is intent on helping achieve her goal, so I think it will be down to us, sister, you and I, to prioritize the survival of the Szateth, above all else."

"You are right, sister."

"Are you with me, sister? Can I count on your help and support?"

"Of course. What do you need me to do?"

"I would like you with me on the surface. To help supervise the construction of the compound and conversion facility."

"It would be my pleasure, sister. But I don't think first sister will allow it. She seems to have it in for me by taking my rank, and then so viciously degrading me in front of third sister."

"I've already cleared it with her. Between you and me, sister, she said she'd be glad to see the back of you. Now, although I can't give you your rank back, I can give you a position and your dignity by asking you to help me directly. Will you, sister, help me save our race?"

"Yes, sister, I am so grateful. Thank you. Whatever you ask of me, I will do."

"It would mean leaving the ship and your sisters for long periods."

"If it means I'm away from first sister, I'm happy with that."

"We will leave in a few days. I will let you know when once I have a clear idea myself. There are a few things still to do."

"Anything I can help you with?"

"Not with the preparations they are in hand. But you could let the other sisters know, although you might not want to tell third sister, about your new position. And stay on first sister's good side."

"If she has one."

"I would keep remarks like that to myself if I were you. You must be on your guard. You never know who's listening."

"Yes, sorry, sister."

"You may speak freely with me, of course, but only me."

"I understand."

"Right, well, thank you, sister. I'll call you when it's time to leave. You should get back to your work."

"Thank you again, sister. I'll wait to hear from you."

She watched as she virtually skipped out of the lab and smiled to herself, having planted the seed.

"Second sister," a voice said from behind. It was the first of the pregnant females waving for her to come into their room.

"We saw what happened today to our males, second sister. How could she be so cruel? Is there nothing you can do?"

"I wish there was, I honestly do. But if there is any suggestion I'm not with her to help her, I will not see another dawn. I have to grit my teeth and bear the terrible way you are all being treated. I am so sorry. You know we are not all like her?"

"Yes, but now we know what's happening. It's difficult."

"I know. But you must if we are all to survive. You won't have to witness it for much longer. I am moving down to the surface and taking the new warriors and workers and the other females with me."

"What about us?" They said in unison. "Can't we come with you?"

"I will ask, of course. But you may well be safer here. Besides, I'll be here most days and first council sister will be more interested in what's going on there, anyway."

They didn't answer and slumped in their chairs. "Honestly, you'll be safer, and as your pregnancies progress, more comfortable here."

"If you say so," the first pregnant female said.

"If I thought otherwise, you would be coming. Ladies, the three of you can save our race. I know it, first council sister knows it, we all know it. Nothing is going to happen to you. You three are our most precious humans. But you have to keep yourselves to yourselves. Don't draw attention, at least not yet."

"Alright, we'll play the dumb humans for you."

"I'm sorry, but it's for the best. Now I have more arrangements to make. I'll look in later." She'd done everything she could for them. It was for the best that they stayed, but her insides were in knots, thinking about leaving them.

As she walked to the hangar, it was hard to be positive about what was happening. Even the atmosphere felt heavy. On the bright side, she told herself she had allies in fourth sister, the females, possibly the first officer, and definitely in the commander.

Her mood lightened when she saw the first officer. He was talking to the commander.

"Ah, commander," she said, interrupting. "I'd like to borrow the first officer."

"Of course, second council sister," he said, stepping away.

"Shall we see what progress the workers are making?"

"Yes, second council sister. And I think you're going to be pleasantly surprised."

She could hear them talking before she got to the room. "That's wonderful, first officer," she said, peeking in through the window. Inside, she could see construction equipment being taught and used.

The lead construction worker came out when he saw her. "I am amazed, second council sister. Your workers are almost ready. They know enough to start construction. They are learning so fast, it's hard for me to keep up."

"How much more time do they need before I can send them down?"

"At this rate, five days, no more," he said.

"That's how long you've got to get my shuttle ready, first officer, and I need you to create another resting chamber for fourth council sister now as well."

"It's almost ready now, second council sister. The new chamber will take a reconfiguration of the layout inside, but it will be ready for you on time."

"I commend you for your work, both of you." She saw the commander approaching. "I only wished all the crew were as efficient as you," she said, walking away.

In the corridor outside the hangar, she heard the distinctive slap of first sister's sandals, along with smaller steps, marching toward her. She spun to escape back into the hangar, but it was too late.

"Sister," she heard third sister say.

Damn it. "Yes," she said, turning back. "Good afternoon, sister."

"I was just telling third sister here about my new warriors and your females," first sister said. "How are they all doing? Shall we see them together?"

"They are fine, sister. If you'd like to come this way." She led them toward her lab.

"Between the two of you, third sister, my army will regain its strength in no time."

"As it needs to, sister, there are wars to win and rebellions to quash. You need warriors to do that."

"Quite so," first sister agreed.

"The nine warriors that have had P9R are in there, third sister and the males going through the conversion process are in there," second sister said, as the lab door swooshed closed.

"Has the training officer been in to speak to them?" first sister asked.

"Not that I'm aware of, sister."

"Right, leave that with me. I'll get him here now, and he can stay here until they understand and speak."

Third sister stood blocking the cell's doorway. "Is it normal for them to be this still?"

"Yes, I added a paralytic agent to the conversion serum to stop the convulsions so they don't damage themselves," second sister said.

"And can they feel every bit of the conversion?"

"Yes, they do."

"Ah, the wonders of modern drugs." Third sister chuckled.

"Why haven't you been here, training officer?" first sister said into her communicator. The anger in her sister's voice.

"I apologize, first council sister. I've been stuck under a mountain of paperwork." They knew that excuse would make things worse.

"I don't care about paperwork. You've heard what happens when my orders don't get carried out? - Get down here and talk to your recruits, get someone else to do your admin."

"Yes, first council sister. I'll be there in a..."

She cut him off. "He'll be here in short order," she said. "Now show me your females."

"These in here first sister are the ones waiting for implantation," second sister said, directing them to the cell.

"Why haven't they been done?" first sister asked.

"With only six embryos left, sister, I thought it prudent to wait until after the first trimester of the three that are pregnant. To make certain the human female is compatible."

"Hmm, show us those, then."

"They are in here." She opened the door.

"Well, let us in then," first sister said.

She closed her eyes as she opened the door. Neither of them saw her as they barged in.

"There's not a lot of change in them, other than the bump in their abdomen, and their skin color, then?" first sister said.

She stepped inside the door and saw the three females sitting on the floor, like the females next door.

Her eyes widened. "N-no, sister. It doesn't look that way," second sister said.

"Are you alright, sister?" third sister asked.

"Oh, err, yes, sorry." She blinked rapidly to refocus her eyes. "Their blood pressure and heart rates are normal, and they eat well."

"Yes, so I see," first sister said, reading their charts. She put the clipboard on the table. "Not as exciting as my warriors, are they sister?"

"No, not at all," third sister said with a smirk.

"Let's leave second sister to run her experiments on them."

She stepped aside as they walked out, and they didn't see her give the females a knowing smile.

"Well, I think we can call it a day," first sister said. "Tomorrow you'll give the P9R to the warriors in there, and in a few days, we can send them with the other nine down to the surface with your workers and start the building. Shame about the females. I was hoping to see a similar improvement in intelligence to the males. Perhaps they have smaller brains?"

Ha, you carry on thinking that. "Yes, first sister, I think you are right," she said, to stroke her ego.

Once they had left, she opened their door again. "Well done, ladies. Good night."

They smiled, and she closed the door.

The training officer appeared, carrying his bedroll. "I'm reporting as ordered," he said.

"You are lucky she needs you, training officer."

The look on his face said it all.

"They are in there," she said, pointing to the cell. "Make sure they can speak by the time she gets back, training officer, or I guarantee you'll lose more than a finger as the commander did."

"Yes, second council sister. I'll do my best."

"Let's hope it's good enough. I can stall her until late morning tomorrow to give you a bit more time, but that's all."

"Thank you, second council sister."

"And you'll owe me one."

"Yes, second council sister, thank you."

"Well, goodnight then," she said. He disappeared into the cell.

∞

The supply bottle of her syringe needed topping up with P9R for tomorrow. She pulled on the thick leather gloves to take another vial out of the storage unit. The air instantly cooled when she opened the lid. She grabbed the nearest vial, closed the lid quickly, and put it on the bench to warm. It worked better when it was at room temperature.

It would need a few minutes, so she took the time to look in on the males to check on their progress. Like the nine in the cell next door, their skin was changing color, lifting, and hardening, getting ready to be shed. They were panting. She pressed her fingers to their necks, feeling their pulse. It was fast like the others, but now she knew this was normal, she wasn't concerned.

She couldn't lie. She was looking forward to the next few days: seeing her workers improving their speech and building skills, the move to the surface, her pregnant females would be safer, and she'd be away from first sister. *Yes, there is much to look forward to,* she thought, pouring the P9R into the supply bottle. With one last look around the lab, and everything ready for the morning, she switched off the lights.

The tension of the day fell away once she got into her soft, warm bed, and she fell asleep straight away. It felt like only a few minutes when she woke up sweating in a panic. "The females!" she said out loud. It took her a moment before she realized where she was, and that she'd had a nightmare.

She sat up wide awake. *That felt so real,* she said to herself. *More than a nightmare, it felt like a memory.* The empty feeling in the pit of her stomach was still there as she remembered the look on first sister's face as she ordered their deaths. There was no way she was going back to sleep now.

Although it hadn't happened, her heart was pounding. It took more than a few deep breaths to calm down before swinging her legs over the edge of her bed and getting up. The clock said she'd slept longer than she thought, and the sun was just coming up when she pressed the button to lighten the blackened force-field-protected window. *An early start then,* she thought as she stretched. The memory of the nightmare faded as she dressed.

Other than the occasional hiss of the air pumps and the gentle rhythmic tap of her sandals, the ship was eerily quiet on her walk to the lab. When she got there, apart from the light on in the cell with the nine warriors and the training officer, it was in darkness. She switched the lights on.

The training officer was in front of her before she knew it. "Good morning, second council sister," he said.

"Good morning, first officer. I trust you had a successful night?"

"Beyond successful, second council sister. The warriors are... well, come and see for yourself."

She followed him over, not sure what to expect.

"Attention, council sister on deck," the training officer said.

The warriors snapped to attention.

"Eyes right!"

They stood motionless, like columns of granite. Their eyes filled with discipline and pride, fixed on her.

"Well, I don't know what you've done to them, but they are magnificent. First council sister is going to be more than pleased with their progress. I commend you, training officer."

"They are like sponges, second council sister. I tell them once and they do it. No question, no hesitation. Do we have more of these human hybrid recruits?"

"This is wonderful, training officer. Yes indeed, we do. You'll have thirty more in the next day or so. I will administer their P9R later this morning when first sister arrives. Keep up the good work, training officer. I will check on your new warriors, then I'll be in the lab if you need me."

"Thank you, second council sister."

Impressed by the warriors, she gave them a majestic nod as she left the cell.

"At ease," she heard him say.

The warriors had taken little care of how they laid the males after their serum injections. They littered the floor. As she stepped between them, she could see the conversion process was nearly complete. It would be a few more hours before the paralytic wore off and they could shed their outer skin, but it was further confirmation that serum five worked. *It is going to be difficult to stop her now.* She thought.

A kitchen worker arrived with the first meal of the day for the females.

"Good morning, second council sister. Shall I take the meals in?"

"Take the food in for the females in the cell, and I'll take the food in for the three pregnant females for you."

"Very good, second council sister." He flipped the switch and a dose of the sedation gas flooded the cell.

"What did you do that for? Can't you see they are calm and compliant?"

He shrank back as she stepped towards him.

"I apologize, second council sister. I thought that was the procedure I had to follow when entering a prisoner's cell."

"Look at me," she said. "Do not use the sedation gas unless a council sister tells you to. Am I clear?"

He could feel how close she was and saw the anger in her eyes. "Yes, second council sister."

"The lives of these humans are more important than your miserable life. Take the food in now, then get out of my sight before I enjoy a meal of my own."

He scurried into the cell and back out again, bowing respectfully, before disappearing back to the kitchens without another word.

One of the pregnant females was watching through the window and opened the door to let her in with their tray of vegetables, fruit, and raw meat.

"Good morning, ladies," she said, placing the tray on the table. "I hope you slept well?"

"Good morning, second council sister. Yes, we did, thank you."

"I think we can be a little less formal. Call me second sister."

The four of them sat around the table and tucked into the meat.

"Second sister, would you have eaten that worker?"

"My goodness me, no, but the males need to know their place, and the threat of being eaten alive puts them in it. Besides, unlike first sister, I'm much pickier about the meat I eat." The four of them laughed.

"Look at the time," she said. "Now, first sister will be here soon. Remember, no talking and act like the females next door."

"Yes, second sister."

As she left the room, first sister walked into the lab.

"Everything under control?"

"Yes indeed, sister. Everything is ready, and there is news about your nine warriors."

"What news? They had better be alright."

"Training officer, bring the warriors out," she said, calling out to him.

The cell door opened and the training officer marched out, followed by nine disciplined, powerful warriors. They lined up, ready for her inspection.

"Attention, the first council sister is on deck," he said.

They instantly came to attention, standing straight, with their shoulders back and chests out.

"Impressive, training officer, very impressive," first sister said, walking the line. "Do they speak?"

"Not as yet, first council sister, but they understand, and will obey without question."

"Really?"

"Yes, first council sister," he said, unable to hide the pride in his voice. "Just give an order."

"You, step forward," she said, pointing to one of them.

The warrior in the center took a step forward.

"Do not move," she said, drawing her knife.

She raised it so he could see it. He didn't move. She placed the tip of the blade against his throat, just breaking the skin. He didn't move. Her eyes fixed on his as she dragged the tip of the blade down his throat onto his sternum. She stopped just below his ribs. He did not move. A thin trickle of blood flowed past her blade.

"Impressive," she said, holding his stare.

Second sister saw the grin, the same one she'd seen on her face when she was enjoying the torture. She knew what was coming, and closed her eyes just before first sister plunged the knife deep into his stomach. He did not move and made no sound.

Frustrated, she twisted the blade and tore it across, ripping open his abdomen. Now he groaned, and she hummed with delight as his guts spilled out onto the floor.

She stepped back as he fell forward - dead.

Second sister opened her eyes. Neither she nor the training officer moved. Both were speechless after witnessing such a violent and despicable act.

“Impressive,” first sister said. “You are to be commended, training officer. They, as you said, obey without question.”

Second sister turned away, as tears welled in her eyes. “I’ll prepare the P9R,” she said, struggling to keep first sister from hearing the wobble in her voice.

“Yes, good. - and have two of these warriors clear this away, training officer.” She waved the blood-covered knife at the eight still standing at attention and the body on the floor.

“Yes, first council sister.”

He gasped as she casually licked the blood off the blade, savoring the taste. Once she’d cleaned it, she slid it back into its sheath and stepped over the body.

“They still haven’t shed their skin,” she said, looking at her new warriors lying on the floor in the cell. “I’ll come back in a couple of hours to watch you give the P9R. I need to eat. All this excitement has made me quite hungry. - Carry on training officer. I expect the rest will speak by the end of the day?”

“Yes, first council sister,” he said, staring at the guts steaming on the floor.

“Conversion and the ability to take orders, and all within two days. That too is impressive. Serum five is a masterpiece. I’d imagine you could start sending your workers and these warriors down to the surface tomorrow. See you in two hours.” She marched out of the lab.

"You'd better get his body cleared away, training officer," she said, still unable to turn around.

"Yes, second council sister."

She slammed her fists on the bench. *Why, why, why would she do that?* she said to herself, gritting her teeth. She sat in silence, trying to understand the mind of a psychopath.

"Ah, sister, any news on when we'll be going down to the surface?" fourth sister said, striding into the lab, breaking the silence.

"Not now, sister."

She caught the movement of the warriors picking up the guts next to the dead warrior in the corner of her eye. "First sister?" she said, wincing at the sight of it.

Second council sister nodded.

"I'll come back later," she said.

The time passed by in a blur, and before she knew it, first sister marched back in. "Are my warriors ready?"

"Oh, um, I haven't looked, sister. Shall we check together?"

"Why not?"

As they got closer to the cell, they could hear movement from inside. First sister looked through the window, and she moved aside, smiling, to let second sister see. All thirty were on their feet, shed skin crunching as they stepped on it.

"I'd call that another success, wouldn't you?"

"Indeed. I'll get my syringe."

First sister opened the door, calling for the training officer to join her. Her new warriors trained their eyes on her, and on the training officer when he walked in.

"See how they're looking at me?" she said. "A warrior's stare. Get them into lines so second council sister can inject the P9R."

"Yes, first council sister."

He maneuvered the warriors into three ranks, making sure there was enough space between them.

"They are ready for you, second council sister," he said.

One by one, she injected the neurogenic compound just below their ears, and like the others, they did not move.

"Wonderful," first sister said, rubbing her hands. "Stay tonight, training officer, and do whatever you did last night. Use the other eight to help you with their training."

"Yes, first council sister," he said, standing to attention.

"Tomorrow evening, sister, you can begin transporting them to the surface and start building my conversion facility."

"I'd like to take the pregnant females. To monitor their progress. And once the housing compound is complete, transfer the other females as well."

"There's no need for that. You can visit your pets when you visit the ship. I want the females here with me."

"I understand, sister. Will you have time to check and record their progress, take their measurements, adjust their food, and bring regular food and water for the other females as well, or should I appoint someone to do it for you?"

"Are you questioning my ability to look after a few females?"

"Of course not, sister. I only meant with your schedule it would be easier for you if I or someone else did it for you."

"No need. It will be done. You concentrate on building my conversion facility, so I can send third sister out on another gathering. That is your role now. Are we clear?"

"Of course, sister. I will make all the arrangements. It will be a day to remember."

"Very good. Carry on the both of you." She marched out.

"Change of plans, first officer," second sister said, calling him. "I will need the shuttle ready to go tomorrow evening."

"It will be ready for you, second council sister."

She called fourth sister to inform her to be ready to depart for the surface tomorrow evening. She could hardly contain her delight.

"Have them clean this cell, training officer. Then take them and the other eight back to the hangar, and the room in there. You'll have more space to instruct them there instead of in this cramped cell."

"Yes, second council sister. Thank you."

She wanted him and the warriors out of her lab and away from the females. He showed the warriors what he wanted to be done. They carried out his instructions without hesitation.

"The cell is clean, second council sister. Shall I march them to the hangar, now?"

"Yes, training officer. And good work today. I look forward to seeing their training on the surface."

"Thank you, second sister. I'm sure they'll be an asset to first council sister's army."

"I'm sure they will."

He bowed to her. "Form ranks!" he said to his new warriors.

There was a chaotic sound of running feet, then the rhythmic sound of marching as the column left the lab.

She had to break the bad news to the pregnant females and sat staring at the door to their room wondering how she was going to tell them first sister was going to be looking after them.

There's no point in putting this off. She knocked on their door and went in.

"Ladies, there is no easy way for me to say this, but I have asked first sister if you could accompany me to the surface. But she denied my request."

"We know, we heard." The first pregnant female said.

"You will be better off here. It's safe, warm, dry and you'll have as much food as you want."

"Yes, second sister," they said and looked away.

"I will be back every other day to see you, and I'll send my assistant, fourth sister, to check on you."

"Yes, second sister."

"Please ladies, it won't be forever. You'll be with your new babies and me sooner than you think. First sister knows how important you all are. You will have the best care, I assure you."

"We know, second sister."

"Good. I will come and see you tomorrow before I leave and introduce fourth sister to you. She knows nothing about you, so remember, don't speak."

"Yes, second sister."

They still hadn't looked at her. "Right, well, I'll see you all tomorrow then."

Tears welled in her eyes as she closed the door. She had failed them and needed a distraction to take her mind off saying goodbye. It came from the commander when he called her.

"What do you want, Commander?"

"I have the first officer with me and he informs me your shuttle is ready. Would you like to inspect it?"

In her mind, she saw another opportunity before she answered.

"Yes," she said, "stay there with the first officer, commander. I'll be there with fourth council sister in a few minutes."

"As you wish, second council sister."

She called fourth sister and asked her to meet her in the hangar.

"Ah, good. You're all here," she said when she got there, "Commander, I'd like to introduce fourth council sister."

"It is an honor to meet another council sister," he said, bowing his head.

"The commander has been very helpful, sister, and I'm sure he can be called upon to be so again. Should we need him?"

"Of course, second council sister. Whatever you need me to do."

"That is good to know, commander," fourth sister said. "Second council sister has made me aware of your punishment carried out by first council sister. How is your hand?"

"The first officer and I are going aboard to check we have everything, sister," second sister said.

"Very good, sister," fourth sister said with a smile. She turned her attention back to the commander.

He lifted his bandaged hand. "It is on the mend, fourth council sister. Thank you for your concern." It throbbed, and he gripped it with his other hand.

"It still causes pain?"

"Yes, fourth council sister."

"I will bring you something to relieve it."

"Thank you, fourth council sister. And if there is *anything* I can do for you, please ask."

"Sister, come on board and see our new accommodation," second sister said from the top of the shuttle's ramp.

She nodded to the commander, who bowed as she walked onto the shuttle.

"As I was explaining to second council sister," the first officer said. "We have insulated against the cold on the surface. You will be more than comfortable. Second council sister's chambers are there, and yours fourth council sister, if you'll follow me, is over here."

"I have my own chambers?" she said, following him down a narrow corridor.

"Yes, fourth council sister, on second council sister's insistence. Please go in and inspect it. I'll be happy to make any changes."

Inside it had everything she needed: a luxurious lounger, an enormous bed, and the warmth and light of their home planet.

"This is perfect, first officer. Is yours the same sister?"

"Yes, apart from the lab I had built as well."

"Do you have any pain relief in your lab I can give to the commander?"

"Yes, let me get you some."

"First officer, you have done well. I commend you," fourth sister said.

"Here you are, sister. Give him these," second sister said, handing her some pills.

"Thank you."

"Well, first officer, if there is nothing else to show us, fourth council sister and I will move our belongings on board."

"Certainly, second council sister. I will be in my office should you or fourth council sister need anything more."

"Thank you first officer, you can leave us now."

He bowed and walked off the shuttle.

"What do you think of our new home?"

"It's wonderful. When do we leave?" fourth sister said, beaming.

"Pack what you need. We leave tomorrow evening."

They walked off together.

"I'm going to check on my workers and the progress of the new warriors, sister. Then I'll be heading back to pack myself. I suggest you do the same."

"I'm going to do it now. I'll see you back here tomorrow," fourth sister said, her eyes sparkling.

"No, meet me in my lab first. I want to introduce you to the pregnant females before we leave."

"Yes, of course, sister."

She stopped to give the commander his painkillers on her way out. "Here, commander, take these."

"I am most grateful, fourth council sister. And if there is ever anything I can do for you in return, please ask."

"Yes, commander, I will."

He bowed low as she walked away.

As she walked over to the room at the back, her workers were busy packing tools and equipment. Not wanting to disturb them, she looked in on the training officer and his recruits. The warriors were in eight small groups, making sounds that were developing into speech.

"How are they doing?" she said, walking in.

"Attention, there's a council sister on deck."

All thirty-eight of them fell silent immediately, made ranks, and stood to attention.

"As you can see, second council sister. They are doing well. They are already trying to speak. Some are better than others, but the original eight are helping with that, as they now understand and speak perfectly."

She eyed the ranks. "They look the part, training officer."

"They'll be ready for combat, gathering, and security training tomorrow, as first council sister instructed."

"Very good, training officer. Carry on," she said, leaving the room. The rumble of voices started again as she closed the door.

The atmosphere in the corridors felt lighter as she strolled back to her lab until...

"Ah, good evening, sister. Are you ready for your move to the surface, with fourth sister?" third sister said, blocking her path.

"Yes, sister, thank you for asking. We are looking forward to the work we can do there."

"I'm sure," she said as she got closer. "Oh, and don't worry about your females. First sister and I will take good care of them," she said, stepping aside to let her pass.

Her eyes burned deep into hers. "That is your job now until I say otherwise. So I expect you will."

"Of course, sister," she said, bowing her head.

What a bitch. She walked into her lab.

She had a working lab on the shuttle so she could afford to pack light. She took mobile computer equipment and her new favorite toy, her self-filling syringe.

She had what she needed and took it with her to the kitchens. It was busy in there. It was almost mealtime for the crew. The kitchen workers were frantically trying to get everything done on time.

"How can I help you, second council sister?" the head kitchen worker said in his meek little voice.

"As you may have heard, fourth sister and I are leaving the ship for the surface tomorrow."

"Yes, second council sister, and may I say we will miss you being on board."

"Thank you. I want you to make sure the females, all of them, eat regularly. It's especially important for pregnant females. Can I rely on you?"

"Yes, of course, second council sister."

"And I'd like you to report to me directly if you notice they are not eating, or if they seem unhappy or unwell. This is a vital job. Will you do it?"

"Yes, second council sister, it would be my honor."

"I take comfort knowing their well-being is in your hands."

There was a loud crash of plates smashing on the floor. He looked around and sighed. "Please forgive me, second council sister."

"Of course," she said, and he was gone.

Back in her chambers, all, except third sister, were in the living area talking as she walked in.

"We are sad that you and fourth sister are leaving us," fifth sister said.

She looked at them all. "Thank you, sisters. We will be back on board most days."

"We wish we were coming with you," sixth sister said.

"I would like that too. But first sister needs you to keep the ship functioning."

"Things are changing, sister. It's not like it used to be," fifth sister said, looking at the others. They were nodding.

"Change is inevitable, sisters. I believe the humans are going to save our race, and that we can blend with a new species, strengthening our DNA again."

"Are there enough Szatethess embryos to ensure our survival, sister?" ninth sister asked. The others murmured.

She hesitated before answering. "Of course, sisters, there are plenty. Soon we'll have more sisters. We'll need to build ships for them, and a bigger table in the council chambers." The lie made her feel cold inside.

"We wish you well, sister, and you fourth sister," fifth sister said.

The sisters hugged and said their goodbyes.

Lying in bed, she couldn't help thinking about the lie. She knew first sister would harvest them the moment the females gave birth. *What did fifth sister mean when she said, 'things are changing?'* She had her head kitchen worker spy in place, so she'd know if things were going wrong. She must keep the females safe. A lot depended on them delivering healthy Szatethess hybrids. The commander needed to be dealt with, and fourth sister's growing dislike for first sister required nurturing. It was the middle of the night before she finally drifted off to sleep.

She slept late. It was halfway through the morning before she got up and dressed. There was some last minute packing to do, including the all important vials of paralytic, which she wrapped carefully hiding them amoung the rest of her things in her bag. With a last look around, she put her bag over her shoulder, and with a box of lab equipment, she headed to the hangar. The ship felt deserted as she walked along silent, empty corridors. That changed as she got closer to the hangar.

The first officer and the commander were there, making the final departure arrangements.

"Everything is ready for you, second council sister," the first officer said. "Can I take those for you?" He reached for the box she was holding.

"Good. No, I can manage. Have you seen fourth council sister?"

"Yes, second council sister. She was here early this morning with her belongings. She is excited to be working with you."

"Yes, she is, isn't she? Carry on first officer."

He bowed and barked orders at some hangar workers to tidy their mess away.

The hum of the hydrogen filling the fuel cells, and the hiss of release valves filled the shuttle as she went aboard, and then silence once she closed her chamber's door. She took a deep, cleansing breath, kicked off her sandals, and sat on her lounger. The calmness of the surroundings relaxed her. She fell asleep, staying much longer than she thought.

Her communicator buzzed, waking her. "Sister, shall I meet you in your lab?" fourth sister asked.

"Yes, I'll be there presently." When she looked at the clock, it was late afternoon. She slid her feet into her sandals and walked back to the lab.

"I apologize, sister. I lost track of the time. Let me introduce you to the females."

They were sitting on the floor when she opened the door. They looked at the two of them but didn't get up.

"Well, I can see they're pregnant, but I was hoping there would be more, err, I don't know what, just more."

"Yes, they will take a bit of getting used to. And they will need to get to know you, too. They might surprise you yet."

They looked away.

"What do you want me to do with them?"

"Nothing other than say hello every time you come back onboard. Make sure they seem happy, have eaten, and just speak to them. You never know, they might answer you back."

"I doubt it, looking at them."

"Time will tell. But will you do that for me?"

"Yes, of course, sister."

The first female looked back at her with a wry smile. Fourth sister missed it.

"Well, shall we go, then?" second sister asked.

She nodded eagerly. "Let's get off this ship."

In the hangar, the first officer and the training officer were marching the warriors on board. The workers, with all their equipment stowed away, had taken their seats.

"I hope you weren't planning on leaving without saying goodbye," first sister said, striding into the hangar.

"Of course not, sister," second sister said.

"Well then, I know you'll get the facility built for me quickly, won't you?"

"Yes, sister, we'll get it done."

"Very well. Report your progress. I expect great things." She ignored fourth sister.

They both bowed before going aboard.

"Clear the hangar," the commander said over the tannoy before sounding the launch alarm.

"I really hate her," fourth sister said.

"Yes, I know," second sister said as the ramp closed. "Change is inevitable."

Neural Blockchain Journal Entry #926

At last, things are coming together. Conversion serum five works. I have thirty-eight new powerful warriors. This planet is full of human males capable of surviving the conversion process. They take orders very well and are so easy to train. I'm going to get the numbers back up to full strength in no time.

Second sister is proving to be a valuable asset. Between her and third sister, I will accomplish what no other first council sister has accomplished before. I will rule the universe.

With the construction of the housing compound and the conversion facility, I'll soon have a non-stop warrior conversion conveyer belt running all day, every day.

As much as I dislike her, fourth sister will be useful to second sister. They make a good team and seem close. Maybe I've miss judged her too?

I'll soon be able to turn my attention to the harvest. Everything is going as I planned.

First Council Sister - Szateth leader
Advanced planetary research fleet.

Neural Blockchain Journal Entry #063

Of course conversion serum five worked. I'm not as incompetent as she is.

She is a monster. There was no need to kill that warrior. She did it because she could. She is becoming more unpredictable, and it has unsettled the sisters.

Fortunately, she and third sister know how important the three pregnant females are, so they shouldn't abuse them. I don't think I'll be able to contain myself if they do.

I have a couple of new allies, fourth sister and the first officer, who I know I can count on to help come the time. The commander remains a resource I will use up at some point.

Once the new facility is complete, there will be another, larger gathering, and I'll need to limit the numbers she gathers to maintain the human species for our future.

I don't like how the sisters are feeling, and I hated to have to lie to them. But how could I tell them?

With the way we are all feeling, change is inevitable.

Second Council Sister

Advanced planetary research fleet.

Part Two

Project Residentz

Nine

A conversion conveyer belt

The sisters stood on the open deck of the shuttle and looked across the construction site. In the month since they landed, the workers had made good progress.

"What's happening to the weather? It's got a hell of a lot colder lately," fourth sister said, shivering and pulling her top robe tighter around her body.

"Brr, yes, it's cold, nothing like home, is it? The season has changed for the worse. They don't seem to mind it, though," second sister said.

Despite the weather, the workers had built their living compound, a separate secure area for gathered humans, and had made excellent progress building the conversion facility. The warriors guarded the entire site as the workers set about their tasks.

"Good thing, really. If we had to build it, it would never get done," fourth sister said, blowing warm air onto her hands.

The wind was getting up, and there was a hint of snow. "Well, that's true. - Damn!" second sister said, wiping a cold flake off her face. "Let's go back inside to the warm."

They hung their top robes near the warm air vents in the main chamber in case they needed to go outside again. They spread out the plans for the whole construction site on the conference table.

"I'm a little concerned we don't have a big enough secure area to house the humans being held for conversion," fourth sister said, smoothing the paper over the area she was talking about. "You know first sister is going to increase the number of gatherings and ramp up the number of conversions once the facility is ready?"

"Hmm, I know. We could take down the far wall, extend these two right up to the side of the mountain, and use that as the back wall. It shouldn't take too long and will double its size," second sister said, running her finger to the mountain on the plans.

"Or we could just try slowing her down and preserve the human males."

"That would be the ideal, sister. I must be rubbing off on you."

"That's no bad thing. I know our sisters would follow you," fourth sister said, hoping she had judged her right.

"What do you mean?"

"Oh, nothing. Just thinking out loud."

"I'm flattered if you're saying what I think you're saying. But it's unlikely unless first sister steps aside."

"She certainly won't - *step* aside. She loves the power too much."

"Well, that's that then. For now, let's think about how we satisfy her and try to make things a little easier for the humans." Her communicator buzzed. "Talk of the devil," second sister said. She answered the call. "Yes, sister, how can I help?"

"You can help by telling me how much longer it will take you to get the facility up and running."

"A few weeks, sister, maybe another month."

"Really? I understand the compound is secure and you're fitting the interior of the conversion facility."

They looked wide-eyed at each other. "How does she know that?" fourth sister mouthed. Second sister shrugged.

"To get the quality of finish, you'd expect, sister, it will take a few weeks."

"I don't care about the finish. It doesn't need carpets and flowers. You're not building a hotel, you're building me a conversion facility. One week, sister. Then I'm sending third sister on the first gathering to start the facility working. One week, are we clear?"

"Yes, sister. I'll have it ready."

"Good."

The call went dead.

"How?" fourth sister said.

"I don't know. But someone is keeping her well informed. So let's shelve the idea of extending the secure area and redirect some workers to complete the internal fixings."

"I'll see to it, sister."

"Tomorrow I'll be going back to check on the females. How were they when you last saw them?"

"Huge! The babies are growing fast," fourth sister said, chuckling. "They looked tired, but so would you if you had to lug that extra weight around all day?"

Second sister laughed. "They are in their second trimester now." Her tone darkened. "They shouldn't look overly tired though if they're getting the proper care. I hope they are. I'll find out tomorrow." She rubbed her eyes. "I'm going to retire to my chambers and make a list of what we need from the ship."

"Well, I'll see you tomorrow when you return. Good night, sister," fourth sister said.

In her chamber, she poured herself a drink, typed the list on her computer tablet, and sent it to her personal computer on the ship, reminding her to get first sister to produce more serum five.

She's right. It is getting colder, she thought, as she cocooned herself in her blankets. As the warmth spread through her body, an idea grew before falling asleep.

The knock on her door woke her. "The first officer's shuttle had just landed to take you back up to the ship, sister."

"Very well. When he comes aboard, tell him I'll be there presently."

"Yes, of course."

She could hear the muffled voice of fourth sister telling the first officer to wait in the main chambers as she washed and dressed. Fastening her thickest robe, she was ready to go.

"Good morning, first officer. Shall we go?"

"Good morning, second council sister. Yes, of course."

"I'll leave our project in your safe hands, sister," she said, walking by.

"Project? What project?"

"I'll talk to you about it when I get back." She needed to say it out loud to make her idea real.

Outside, the wind and the temperature had dropped. "Let's get a move on, first officer. I don't want to be out here any longer than necessary."

"It's not far, second council sister. And I have raised the temperature on my shuttle for you."

True to his word, they were on board, and in the warm, heading back to the ship before she suffered too much.

The shuttle docked in the hangar, and she pressed the button to lower the ramp. The commander was there to meet her.

"Welcome back on board, second council sister."

"Thank you, commander. I trust you are well?" she said, trying to sound as caring as she could.

"Yes, thank you, second council sister. My finger is healing nicely," he said, holding up the deformed stump.

"I understand you and fourth council sister have been in communication with each other."

"Yes, second council sister, we have a lot in common."

"I thought you might."

"Do you object, second council sister? I will cease all communication with her if you do?"

"No, not at all, commander. If the two of you have the same interest, then carry on."

"Thank you, second council sister."

"Now, I must get to my lab."

The moment she left the hangar, she felt it, a heavy oppressive atmosphere, worse than before. *Something has changed,* she thought.

As she got close to her lab, she could hear whispering. She couldn't hear what was being said, and it stopped as she turned the corner. Once one of the five sisters recognized her, they surrounded her and the whispering started again. All of them talking at once.

"Sisters, sisters. Please, one at a time. What's going on here?"

"Thank goodness you're back," fifth sister said.

"Well, let's not skulk in the corridor. Come on into my lab."

They shuffled in behind her, arguing about who was going to tell her.

"Tell me what?" she said, cutting off the childish chatter. None of them spoke.

"You are the highest ranked council member, fifth sister, so you tell me."

"Very well," she said. "It's third sister. She has become so much like first sister it's hard to tell one from the other."

"She's trying to improve herself. That's a good thing, isn't it?"

"Not when it's at our expense." There was a murmured agreement.

"What do you mean?"

"She's re-assigned our duties, giving us more work and less time to rest. She's even moved into your chamber and had hers converted into a lab, where she and first sister spend a lot of their time together."

"I see. Well, it's not surprising as fourth sister, and I have moved to the planet's surface. After all, she is the next highest-ranked council sister, and our absence has unfortunately created additional work for the rest of you."

"And we were all delighted when fourth sister got the chance to work with you. We accept the additional work, sister. We are keeping the ship functioning as it should. What we can't accept is that she didn't take on any of the extra work herself, or the self-righteous I'm-better-than-you attitude that came with the reassignments." Fifth sister's mouth curled into a sneer.

"Have you spoken to first sister about this?"

"No, we haven't been able to. Our workloads and additional restrictions mean we rarely see her. Other than when she's with third sister in her lab, but even then she ignores us when she leaves. It feels like something is going on that we don't know about. I have to say it's reaching the point where we may have to do something about her. Is there something going on, sister? Something we don't know about. Is that why you've abandoned us? Because that's what it feels like?"

"There is nothing I know of, sisters." She lied, - again. "As for third sister, do nothing you will regret. You may not like her as a person, but as she is a council sister, you must respect her rank. However, I will speak to her before I leave. I haven't abandoned you, sisters. Please, don't think that. You are welcome to come down to the surface and visit anytime you wish."

They looked at each other, pursing their lips, and reluctantly nodded. "Very well, sister. All we ask is you do what you can for us. It's almost unbearable, and I don't know how much longer we can go on like this," fifth sister said, speaking for the others.

"I will always do what I can for you, sisters, you know that. I will talk to you in chambers this evening after I've spoken to them both, and before I leave."

"Thank you, sister," fifth sister said. The others nodded and smiled as they left.

I hate this. She said to herself, closing the lab door behind them. *Why has third sister got a lab? She's no scientist. Why is first sister ignoring them? What's going on here?*

She was still frowning when she opened the door to see the three pregnant females. They jumped when they heard the door open.

"Hello, ladies," she said.

They stood up, the fear in their eyes turned to joy when they saw who it was.

"Oh, second sister, we are glad to see you." The three of them hugged her.

"Hay, hay, what's all this about? I'm sorry I haven't been to see you for a couple of weeks. We had to speed up the time to complete the facilities on the surface."

"It's getting harder not to talk, second sister," one of them said.

"We need more food, too," said another.

"And we need to leave this room. As we get bigger, it gets smaller."

"Okay, look, I'll see if you can move to a more suitable chamber. I can't promise anything, but I'll try. I'll make sure you get more food, and next time I'll come with fourth sister, and you can let her get to know the real you more."

"Yes, thank you, second sister."

"How are you feeling? The three of you look good."

"We are fine, second sister. We have been looking after ourselves. Other than you, fourth sister, and the kitchen worker who brings the food, we rarely see anyone else."

"You haven't seen first sister or third sister?"

"No, not for a while. But that's alright with us."

"It's not alright with me though. You need to be monitored, and your records updated."

"It's nice to see you and have someone to talk to."

"I'll make sure they take care of you, and yes, I've missed you as well. Now, let me take some measurements and bring everything up to date," she said, setting up the blood pressure monitor. "Take a seat, ladies."

She recorded the blood pressure for all three. "Hmm, it's a little high. Could be you're not getting enough to eat or enough exercise. But you feel okay yourselves?"

"I've had a couple of twinges of pain over the last few days," the first pregnant female said.

"Have you mentioned this to anyone?"

"Well, no. You told us not to speak, and no one's been in to see us."

"But you've felt the babies moving?"

"Oh yes. Sometimes it feels like they are trying to claw their way out."

"Right, well, I've made a note. I think we need to make sure you get enough food and you need some exercise. If we get those sorted out, I'm sure things will settle down again."

"Thank you, second sister."

"I'll see what I can do about getting you moved to more suitable chambers and increasing your food. I'll be back again before I leave," she said, packing the blood pressure monitor and record sheets away.

I knew she wouldn't do it; she said to herself, walking to the kitchens.

"Where is the head kitchen worker?" she said to a worker who was washing the pots.

Startled, he splashed water on the floor. A council sister had never spoken to him before. He recognized her immediately. "He is over there, second council sister. Shall I get him for you?"

"No, carry on with your work."

"Yes, second council sister, thank you."

He saw her approaching. "How can I help you, second council sister?"

"I need you to increase the daily amount of food you give to the pregnant females."

"Of course, second council sister."

"Have you seen anything out of the ordinary that you think I should know about?"

"No. Second council sister."

"Very well then. Just make sure you give them enough to eat, please."

"Of course, second council sister."

"And please report anything you think I might want to know about. Anything out of the ordinary, no matter how small it is."

"Yes, second council sister."

The kitchen worker was still cleaning up the water as she walked past him. She called first sister. "Can I update you, sister?"

"Yes, come to my chambers."

"Thank you, sister. I'll be with you in ten minutes."

As before, first sister opened her chamber door exactly ten minutes later. She was there.

"Punctual as ever," she said, standing aside to let her in.

"I know how busy you are and I don't want to waste any of your time, sister."

"How considerate of you. Give me your report," she said, leading the way to her lab. The production of more conversion serum five was well underway. "I trust my facility will be ready?"

"Yes, sister. It will be rough around the edges, but it will be functional."

"Good. Now, what else?"

"I understand third sister has taken my chamber and is using hers as a lab under your supervision."

"What of it?"

"If I may speak plainly, sister. There is a better use for that room and third sister will never make a scientist as good as you, and her time would be of more value fitting out the shuttles for larger gatherings, to speed things up for you."

"Hmm, you make a good point. What do you want the chamber for?"

"I thought about moving the pregnant females into it, sister. They are getting bigger, and closer to their time to birth our new sisters. I thought it would be better if they were closer to the others, who can monitor them more frequently."

"No. Don't be ridiculous. The chambers are ours. A human will never have one. They are to serve as incubators, nothing more, and you would do well to remember that. They will stay where they are."

"I understand, of course, sister. I have checked on their progress. Their blood pressure is higher than I'd like, which is concerning. I'd like to have them monitored daily. I have ordered more food, as the babies are growing, but they will need exercise to keep them healthy."

"I'll see to it."

"I have no objection to third sister using my chambers whilst I'm away, but perhaps she should leave the science to us. We are at a critical stage, and I was going to ask you to send serum five down to us. The facility is ready to store it. Third sister can certainly manage the transportation. Or perhaps you could bring it yourself and inspect the facility, suggesting any improvements we should make? I think productivity and harmony on board would improve if she removed the lab, and you gave her chambers to fifth sister to use until such times as we are back?"

"Yes, good idea. We'll both come down. Third sister will need to see the secure area, to get an idea of the numbers it can hold. I'm not overly interested in the concerns of our sisters, you know why. However, it would be easier, come the time, if things are calm onboard. I'll have third sister remove the equipment and inform fifth sister she can move in. Or you could do it for me?"

"I'd be happy to do it for you, sister. While I think about it, fourth sister and I have already planned for an extension to the secure area, using the side of the mountain as a natural barrier. It would double its capacity, and won't take long to build."

"Forward-thinking, I like that."

"When can we expect you on the surface?"

"Two days. It's going to take till then for the production of this new batch of serum five to finish. Good work." They both watched as serum dripped into the vials.

"One more suggestion, sister, in the interest of efficiency. Should we move the production of serum five down to the facility so we can produce it in-house? We could use the equipment from third sister's lab? Is that where she is now?"

"Yes, very well. Again forward thinking. Yes, she's there. Tell her to put it on board the shuttle, ready for your return to the surface."

"Thank you. With your permission, sister, I'll give her your instructions."

"Very good. See you in two days."

At least I can put third sister in her place and show I have their interests at heart, she thought. Her victory lightened the atmosphere as she strode towards the chambers.

They were in the living area chatting in a tight group when she entered. "Where is third sister?" she asked.

"In her lab," fifth sister said, pointing to it.

She didn't knock. She went straight in. "Ah, sister, there you are," she said, leaving the door open. "I have new instructions for you."

"Oh. err, yes hello sister. I wasn't expecting you."

"Never mind. I asked you to keep a close eye on the pregnant females, but you haven't. Why is that?"

The chatter outside stopped.

"I haven't had the time. *First* sister is instructing me on the basic manufacturing principles of the conversion serum, and I have to follow her instruction."

"Quite so, sister. I have new instructions for you. First, you are to dismantle this equipment and take it along with this storage unit to my shuttle. I will use it to manufacture and store serum five in the facility below. Second, you are to give fifth sister these chambers for her use."

"I don't take instructions from you. I take them from first sister, and only her. She won't like it if I tell her you've interfered with my experimentation."

"Careful, sister. That sounds like insubordination. I am second council sister, and you will do as I order."

"I'm going to call first sister for clarification."

"As you wish."

Third sister huffed and walked into her bed-chamber. The chatter outside started up again, and turning towards them, she grinned. It stopped when third sister came back into the lab. "I apologize, sister. I will do as requested by first sister immediately."

"That's very good to hear. Now will you tell fifth sister or shall I?"

"If you would, please."

"Fifth sister, would you come in here?"

"Yes, sister, what can I do for you?"

"There, see, third sister. That's how you address a high-ranking council sister."

Third sister looked at the floor.

"Once third sister has cleared and put all this equipment on my shuttle, this will be your chamber. I am allowing third sister to occupy mine until we live aboard again."

"Thank you, sister, and to you, third sister."

Third sister grunted, she didn't look up.

"Good," second sister said and left the lab. Outside, the others were smiling. "Well, sisters, I have to get back. Lots to do at the facility. Remember, you are welcome anytime."

"Safe journey, sister," they said in unison.

There was one more stop for her to make before flying to the surface. She had to give the females the bad news. She knocked before going in. They were eating, and it looked like the head kitchen worker had done as he was told. There was a mountain of food, mostly raw meat, and they were tucking in like it was their last supper.

"I have to say goodbye, ladies. I will be back in a few days, once the facility on the surface is operational. You've got the food, good."

"Would you like to join us, second sister?"

"No, but thank you. First council sister has once again denied a request to give you better chambers. She has promised, however, that someone will look in on you, and that you will have daily exercise."

"Well, that's something," the third pregnant female said.

"I am sorry ladies, I'm trying, but you must endure it for now."

None of them said anything. They looked at her and nodded.

"Thank you, ladies. I will be back as soon as I can. In the meantime, if there is any repeat of the pain in your abdomen, show it when someone comes in."

They nodded again.

As she left their room, something in the back of her mind was telling her there was more to the pain the first female was feeling.

In the hangar, the shuttle was ready for her. The lab equipment and all the compounds to make the serum were onboard, and the first officer was at the helm, running through the pre-flight checks.

"It was good to see you, second council sister," the commander said.

"Thank you, commander. Do you have a message or anything you'd like me to give to fourth council sister?"

"Perhaps you could tell her I'll call in a couple of days?"

"I shall."

"Thank you, second council sister. Safe journey."

She knew she'd be back to see the females after the gathering in a couple of days, but her concern stayed with her.

∞

"At last. It's been bugging me all day," fourth sister said, ambushing her the moment she walked into their conference chamber. "Now, please tell me - what project?"

"At least let me get my top robe off, then I'll tell you. It's lovely and warm in here." It was enough to take her mind off the females.

"Yes, sorry sister. It's been going around my head all day, wondering if I've missed something important."

She hung her top robe by the warm air vents, then explained. "No, nothing like that, sister. I have been thinking about what you said when you mentioned we should preserve the number of males. We should have an ongoing project to monitor and preserve a minimum breeding number. I brought this idea to first sister before the last gathering. She was receptive to the idea, but we'll have to remind her of it and rein her in."

"She won't like that."

"No, she won't, and we may end up having to take steps ourselves. So, for now, let's keep this project between us."

"What should we call it?"

"Well, the humans live here. It's their home, their residency, and we want to protect them. So, let's call it Project Residents, but with a z, to give our project the symbolic and spiritual meaning of completion and new beginnings driven by females of valor."

"Yes, wonderful sister, Project Residentz, it is."

"How has the work inside the facility gone today?"

"These workers amaze me. Nothing stops them, they just keep going. So much so that the facility will be ready for the next inspection by tomorrow."

"That is good news. First and third sisters will be here for it, and with a new batch of serum five, the day after tomorrow. It's been a long trying day, and I'm going to have a warming nightcap before going to bed. Care to join me?"

"Yes, good idea. We should toast our new project as well."

"Let's have a shot of the good stuff to celebrate."

Fourth sister poured a finger measure of their favorite drink into two small glasses. "To Project Residentz," she said, raising hers.

"Project Residentz."

They clinked their glasses and emptied them in a single swig, closing their eyes as the liquid warmed as it went down.

"That was lovely, thank you," fourth sister said.

"Yes, it was. Now, I'm ready for my bed. Tomorrow, we should inspect the compound and facility to make sure everything is ready for first sister to see it."

"Yes. Goodnight sister."

In her chamber she looked at the two vials of modified paralytic, giving them a shake before putting them in the pocket of her top robe. The feeling of security they gave her made her smile.

∞

Two warriors and the training officer standing to attention waited for the sisters at the bottom of the shuttle's ramp, ready to escort them around the construction site. The weather was getting worse, and the cold-blooded sisters shivered as they walked down to meet them.

"Good morning, training officer. We do not need guards. I'm sure the workers are going to behave."

"Yes, of course, second council sister. Security details are part of their training. I hope you won't mind them coming along. I assure you they won't be a bother."

"Very well. I have no objection. Do you fourth council sister?"

"No, none at all."

"Thank you, council sisters. My warriors are ready for your inspection, and the lead construction worker is waiting for you at the entrance to the compound."

"Let's get this inspection done," fourth sister said, pulling her collar higher.

The warriors and their training officer followed behind as the sisters trudged across the muddy ground.

"Good morning, council sisters," the lead construction worker said. "I have the honor of showing you around today. I apologize, but the ground is soft underfoot, so please take care as we walk. What would you like to see first?"

"Let's start with the living compound," second sister said. "Then the secure area, and then inside to get out of this cold." She put her hand in her pocket cradling the vials.

"Yes, second council sister. This way, please." He led them in.

The compound was an ample open space, split into two areas, surrounded by a fence with guard towers in each corner. "This area is for the warriors, and the other over there is for your workers."

"These huts, are they all the same?"

"Yes, fourth council sister. They are identical."

"I'd like to look inside this one."

"Of course, fourth council sister. Please." He stepped aside and followed her in.

"The wire fence isn't particularly secure," second sister said to the training officer, pulling it back and forth.

"It doesn't need to be, second council sister," he said. "Once the conversion process is complete, none of the warriors or workers consider escape. It's more to represent the border of the compound than to keep anyone in."

"Ah, yes. Very good. And the guard towers. What are they for, then?"

"More for training, second council sister. Although, as you'll see, we have some fully trained warriors posted in the towers in the secure area."

"The accommodation huts are more than suitable, sister." Fourth sister said, coming out.

"Well, the living compound is ready for full occupancy, would you agree, sister?" second sister said, looking around again.

"Yes. It's ready."

"Thank you, honorable council sisters," the lead construction worker said. "We will build a meta-gate room in this compound in the next few days, once you've approved everything, second council sister."

"Right, yes good. The secure area then, if you please."

"This way, honorable council sisters." He led the way through the conversion facility and out through the only door in what was the serum room.

"My goodness, these walls are high," fourth sister said, shielding her eyes from the sun as she looked at the top of them. "It feels like a completely different place."

"Yes, as per your plans, fourth council sister, the males need to feel isolated from their world. There is no way in, other than from the air.

As you can see, there is a landing pad at the far end. And only one exit through this door."

"If I may add, council sisters," the training officer said. "With the six guard towers, there is no escape once they're in here."

The sisters could feel the eyes of the guards watching them.

"So I see," fourth sister said.

There was nothing else to see besides some simple shelters in the middle. It was secure.

"The far wall, sister, that's the one I propose to take down. Then we extend these two side walls right to the side of the mountain," second sister said.

"It would make the secure area huge, sister. Is it a good idea based on what we talked about..."

"It's a good idea to have expansion plans in mind, don't you think?"

"Oh. err, yes, of course." Fourth sister knew from the look she got she'd slipped up.

"Good. Now, can we see in the serum room. It needs to be ready?" second sister said, turning to the lead construction worker.

"Yes, second council sister. I think you'll like how everything is," he said.

Stamping the mud off their boots, and blowing warm air into their hands, they went back in. There were rows of examination tables, benches, drawers, and cabinets full of chemicals and compounds to make serum and compounds

The lead construction worker said, "it's a conversion conveyer belt, council sisters, as you requested: the males get injected with serum in here, then moved into the side room over there to go through the conversion process. Once they've gone through it, they're moved to another room for your P9R to be administered second council sister, which frees the examination tables for another group. Then they're housed in the living compound for training."

"Very efficient," second sister said.

"From the number of examination tables, second council sister, the living compound will have to expand."

"Yes, it will," she said. "I commend you, lead construction worker, you have exceeded expectations. First sister wants everything operational for her inspection tomorrow."

"It will be ready."

"Yes, it looks like it to me. Thank you for the security detail, training officer. I think we'll make our own way back. And thank you for the tour of the facility lead construction worker. You are both dismissed." They bowed and left.

"Well, this place is going to make it hard to stop her now," fourth sister said going into one of the side rooms.

"I'm afraid you're right." She reached into her pocket, and opening a cabinet, hid the two vials at the back before fourth sister appeared again. "Let's get back to the shuttle, shall we?"

Their boots squelched through the mud, and they cursed the weather as they walked back to the shuttle. Second sister said, back in the warm, stripping off their outer layers and boots. "You need to be mindful of what you say, sister. I don't think they caught it but remember first sister is getting information from someone. You must be careful."

"I know, sister, I will be," fourth sister said.

"Good. Especially tomorrow."

Her cheeks flushed, and she looked at the floor.

"Well, everything is ready, unfortunately. After her inspection, first sister is going to want to start the conversions as soon as she can. Now we have to figure out a way to protect a healthy number of males."

Neural Blockchain Journal Entry #927

At last, my army will soon be ready.

I hate to admit it, but second sister has done a good job getting the facility ready in good time. I'm sure the fourth sister did the leg-work for here, but that's what she's there for.

I'm looking forward to seeing it. She wouldn't dare invite me down without it being ready.

Those damn females are getting more demanding, or maybe it's second sister wanting them treated more like us than like humans. That will never happen. I think I made that clear.

Tomorrow will be a landmark day. I'll take the serum to the facility, third sister can go on a gathering, and the facility will be fully operational by the time she unloads the males in the secure area.

Nothing is going to stop me now.

First Council Sister - Szateth leader
Advanced planetary research fleet.

Neural Blockchain Journal Entry #072

The atmosphere on board the ship is toxic.

The sisters were so rattled, if I hadn't put third sister in her place, I think they would have taken matters into their own hands and dealt with her. They are calmer now, but I had to lie to them again, and I hated to have to do it.

I am worried about the females, and I knew first sister wouldn't care for them properly. Hopefully, I've resolved that too.

As for their new chambers, perhaps it was a leap too far to think she'd agree to let them have chambers with the sisters. But as long as they get exercise and good food, they should be fine. They only have about three months left.

Fourth sister and the commander are getting cozy. That could be useful.

Now the facility is ready, I don't doubt, first sister is going to take full advantage.

I have to keep her from taking all the males. They are our saviors, and Project Residentz is going to be theirs.

Second Council Sister

Advanced planetary research fleet.

Ten

A spy, and heads on spikes

A blip appeared on the monitor in the shuttle's cockpit. The beep told them they were coming.

"They're on their way, then?" Fourth sister asked, walking in to join her.

"Yes. Is everything ready?"

"Yes, sister. The honor guard is in place. They'll escort her here."

"All the construction workers are out of the building, and the warriors are in place?"

"Yes, sister. We are ready to receive her."

"Here we go then. Let's meet her at the bottom of the ramp."

The shuttle's landing legs sank into the mud as it touched down. Steam hissed from the engines as they slowed to a stop, and the ramp opened.

"Attention," the training officer said.

The eight warrior honor guards dressed in crisp parade uniforms, four on each side of the ramp, snapped their heels together. First sister marched down between them, followed closely by third sister.

"Honor guard left turn. By the left, quick march."

At the bottom of the ramp, she lifted the hem of her top robe clear of the mud, as she and the honor guard marched over to meet the sisters, followed by third sister, who didn't and struggled to keep up.

"Honor guard, halt," They stopped on command, and first and third sisters took the last few steps without them.

"Welcome sister," second sister said, ignoring third sister.

"No time for pleasantries. Show me my facility."

"Of course, sister. If you'd like to come this way, we'll get out of this cold. I'll show you the plans of the facility and where we think we might need to extend it."

"You and fourth sister take the serum down to the facility, then wait there for us there, and I want you to tell me how many males we can get in the secure area," she said to a shivering third sister. "Training officer, you can dismiss the guard."

"Yes, first council sister."

"Now, let's look at these plans." She walked up the ramp of second sister's shuttle ahead of her.

"Something to drink to warm you, sister?" second sister asked as they entered the conference room.

"Oh, err, no. Just talk me through these," she said, leaning over the drawings on the table. "Show me where your extension would be on these plans?"

"Right here, sister," she said, pointing to the secure area. "As you can see, if we extended the secure area over to the side of the mountain, it would easily double the size of the area, doubling the holding capacity."

"Hmm, well, yes, but I have some plans of my own. I want you to drill into the mountain and cut out a cavern instead."

"Instead of extending the walls. Yes, yes, that's brilliant, sister. We cut a big holding area right out of the rock."

"Exactly, and we cut a tunnel straight into the secure area. We have mining equipment, don't we?"

"Onboard the ship, yes."

"That's what I want you to do. Then we churn out new workers and new warriors without running out of space. And have a Meta-gate built in there as well."

"Yes, sister. That's wonderful."

"Right, let's get over to the facility and make sure the other two have done what I've told them to do."

Outside, the temperature had dropped. "Would you like a warmer robe, sister?"

"No, this one's fine. Now come on, let's get over there," she said, striding across the wet mud, ignoring the cold.

Fourth sister was filling the last of the syringes when they walked in. First sister stopped. "Well, just look at this place," she said, unable to contain a grin. "I commend you."

"I couldn't have done it without the help of fourth sister." She smiled at her, and fourth sister gave her a grateful nod.

"Hmm, I'm sure."

The emotionless response crushed her, and red-faced fourth sister looked away.

"We are fully operational, I take it?"

"Yes, sister."

"Right then, take the shuttle and gather me some males, third sister. Let's use this facility for what I've had it built for."

"Yes, sister." She smirked at the other two, bowed, and left.

"Not much more we can do here until we get some males. How about that warming drink? Fourth sister, you wait here and inform us when the shuttle lands in the secure area."

"Yes, sister," she said, shivering, hoping to follow them back. She could feel the cold seeping into her bones.

"Here, take my top robe," second sister said, unfastening it.

"Thank you, sister. The temperature has really dropped."

First sister huffed and walked out.

"Try to keep warm. It'll soon be over," second sister said, touching her arm.

"Come on." She heard from outside.

"Better go. I'll be back later, with a hip flask of the good stuff for you."

"Thank you, sister. I'll be fine. I'll call as soon as she lands the shuttle."

To keep warm, she kept moving. She re-arranged the examination tables, running them along the wall with the first right by the door.

Her communicator buzzed. "First sister told me you're waiting. Are you ready for the first batch of males? I am moments away."

"No, I am not ready. You should have warned me you were on your way back. I'll need help here to secure all the males. You will need to fly in a holding pattern. I will call you when I'm ready."

"There is no fuel for that. I'm coming now."

She knew she'd done this on purpose to make her look incompetent in front of first sister, again!

"Can't you keep them onboard until we're ready, then?"

"No, if we keep them sedated for too long, it might damage them."

"I see. Once you land, have your warriors corral the males by the door. If they're in a tight space, we'll be able to control them."

"Very well, sister. Sedated, they are docile, but once out in the fresh air, it's going to wear off and they'll try making a break for freedom. Be ready. I have informed first sister her males are here," she said and cut off the call.

"Damn you, third sister."

She needed warriors in the serum room ready to secure the males. The shuttle was on final approach and she needed them now. She called the training officer. "I need a dozen warriors in the serum room now."

"My warriors are on a gathering training exercise, fourth council sister. It will take some time to get them to you. I'll order them from the guard towers."

"Get them in here. I need them now. Third council sister is about to land with the first males."

"As soon as I can, fourth council sister."

She opened the door to the secure area as the shuttle landed. Its engines whined as they powered down. The ramp opened, and a dozen large human males staggered out, followed by warriors, cracking whips and shouting.

"Bring them over here, and guard them closely. We are not ready for them yet," fourth sister said, waving them over.

The warriors pushing and whipping the males herded them towards the door. In the fresh air, the sedation gas wore off, and panicking, they ran in every direction, to the walls, the shuttle, and the door. A few attacked the warriors. She looked on in horror.

"What is happening here?" first sister said, marching into the serum room.

"I err..."

She didn't let her finish. She barged fourth sister out of the way, knocking her to the floor, and ran out into the secure area.

"Are you okay, sister?" second sister asked, helping her to her feet.

"This is third sister's fault. She knew I wasn't ready but landed, anyway."

The sound of a dozen pairs of running boots got louder as the warriors charged through the serum room, and out into the secure area to join the fight.

"We need to control this situation. We'll deal with third sister, later. Come on, sister," second sister said, following the warriors.

She couldn't move and looked on as first sister and the warriors violently beat and whipped the males into submission.

First sister lined them up against the wall. "Choose two, sister," she said to second sister.

"What?"

"Get out of the way... I'll do it." She grabbed one, then another, pulling them out of the line.

"This is *your* doing. *Your* inability to do as instructed, fourth sister," she said, stamping on the back of their knees so they collapsed. She grabbed a fistful of the first male's hair, jerked his head back, drew her knife, and sawed the blade across his throat. Fountains of blood spurted forwards, staining the sand red. The male gurgled, and letting go of his hair, he fell, dead. With a look of sheer terror, the second male knew what was coming. He squeezed his eyes tight, anticipating pain, and showing no mercy she cut his throat the same way.

"Cut off their heads and mount them on spikes, so they know what will happen if any of them try to escape," she said, casually tasting the blade, before wiping the rest of the blood on the dead male's loin cloth. "Bring the others into the serum room, one at a time."

"Yes, first council sister," said the warrior nearest to her.

She glared at fourth sister and swept past her without saying a word.

Third sister appeared out of the shuttle and sauntered across the sand, ignoring the dead humans, grinning.

Second sister grabbed her arm and leaned in. "I know what you did," she said in a whisper.

"I don't know what you mean, sister," she said, breaking the grip and walking into the serum room.

"Don't dwell on it, sister. She'll be leaving soon," second sister said, as fourth sister watched her saunter away. "now, steel yourself. I'm sure first sister will have more to say."

"I'm sure she will," she said, clenching her jaw.

As they closed the door behind them, first sister was waiting. Third sister, standing behind her, was almost drooling at the chance to see her sister get punished.

"You have disappointed me, fourth sister. I assumed you would have had everything ready for my visit today. Instead, I find a facility in disarray and inadequately guarded, humans running riot and attacking my warriors, and putting me in danger. You are fortunate I remain uninjured."

Third sister smirked, and second sister saw it. "If I may interject, sister."

"No, you may not, second sister, be quiet," she said, glaring at her.

Third sister smirked again hearing second sister being put in her place.

She looked back at fourth sister, her eyes hard with rage. "If you were one of my ship's crew or a human, I would have you executed on the spot for your reckless stupidity, but as you are a council sister, you are fortunate I cannot. You still have council duties, so I will allow you onboard the ship to perform them, but you will leave the instant they are complete. There will be no social interaction with your sisters and you are no longer entitled to chambers. Until I say otherwise, fourth council sister, you are now banished from the ship." She paused just to see her reaction. "You will remain here on the surface and serve in the facility. You are to make sure it runs smoothly and produces the warriors I demand. If you fail, it will be the last mistake you make. Am I clear, fourth sister?"

"As you command, first council sister," she said and looked down, pretending to be submissive.

"Until I call for second sister to return to the ship, you may stay in your chambers onboard her shuttle. After which you will have to make do somewhere in here."

"Yes, first council sister. As you command."

"Now, bring the first male in. I want this facility operational."

There was nothing she could say, nothing even second sister could say to change her mind. Humiliated again, in front of her sisters, she vowed it would be the last time.

She opened the door and ordered the first male to be bought in. The warriors grabbed hold of the one nearest, dragged him in, and strapped him face down on the first table.

He groaned as first sister slid the needle into his back and injected the serum. "Take him in there," she said to third sister, who wheeled the paralyzed human into the next room.

"Bring in the next one," she said to the warriors. "Let's keep it going."

The conversion conveyer belt had started.

"Well, that works," she said, withdrawing the needle from the last male's spine. "A good day's work... We will leave you now, second sister, and return to the warmth of the ship. How long until the shuttles are ready to hold more than a dozen human males, third sister?" first sister asked.

"By the end of tomorrow, sister."

"Good. Expect the next gathering to start the day after tomorrow, second sister. Make sure everything is ready. I don't want a repeat of today's disaster. I will come down too to make sure there isn't."

"Very good, sister. We will manufacture more P9R. I have everything I need for that. These males will have gone through the conversion and be ready for it by then. Perhaps you would bring the compounds for further production of serum five when you return?"

"I will indeed. Just make sure you're ready."

"We will be."

She grunted. "Come on, third sister, let's get out of this cold and get something good to eat on the ship," first sister said.

"Yes, I'm ravenous, sister," she said, smiling in contempt at the two sisters.

"I will see you again soon, second sister," first sister said, not even looking at fourth sister, as the two of them walked out into the secure area.

They stood in the doorway and watched as the shuttle took off. "I'm sorry, sister," second sister said.

"It wasn't your fault," fourth sister said.

She looked across and shook her head. A warrior held a spike, while another jammed the severed head onto the point. The second head lay at his feet, blood dripping onto the sand from his neck.

"She still doesn't see how important the humans are to us." She closed her eyes and turned away. "After today, it's going to be hard to slow her down. I'm going to have to be direct with her. I'll go to the ship tomorrow and confront her."

"Good luck with that, sister," fourth sister said.

"Hmm. Can you get fresh sand to cover over all that blood? The spikes will have to stay until after her next visit, but we don't need to see the blood on the sand."

"Straight away, sister."

"Once it's done, come back to the shuttle and we'll discuss her plans for the mountain. And don't worry, I'm sure something will happen that will change her mind about you."

"Yes, I'm sure it will," fourth sister said, unable to hide the sarcasm in her voice.

They shared a knowing look. Second sister nodded, then headed back to the shuttle, leaving her in the cold quiet of the serum room.

She thought she was alone until she heard a voice whispering. It was a male voice. Whoever it was, he didn't want anyone overhearing the conversation. She moved closer.

"Yes, first council sister... thank you, yes I am enjoying the females... of course... I will continue to report on both of them."

It was the training officer. She couldn't believe it. *He's her spy*, she said to herself, struggling to accept it. *Second sister needs to know.* She crept away.

He came into the serum room moments later, "Oh, fourth council sister? I didn't realize anyone else was here."

"I was outside in the secure area, making sure they properly cleaned it up. I'm about to go back to the shuttle. Did you want something?"

"I have the warriors needed, fourth council sister."

"A little late now."

"I informed second council sister and apologized for the time it would take to get them here."

"Well, they are here now."

"I will have those posted to serum room duty to be on standby in the living compound. They will be here in seconds when needed. Will you tell second council sister they are at her disposal?"

"Of course, training officer. Good work. Now, if you'll excuse me, I must get back to the shuttle."

"Of course, fourth council sister."

Another name to add to my list. She said to herself, wading through the mud.

She struggled to pull her wet muddy boots off, then sat for a moment, thinking about what had just happened while trying to warm her toes with her hands.

Second sister saw her sitting on the floor by the ramp. "Come into the warm, sister. I want to go over what first sister has proposed."

"And I have some news for you, too."

"Sounds ominous."

Fourth sister picked herself up, and unfastening her top robe said, "I know who first sister's spy is."

"Tell me," she said, checking the hallway to see if anyone was listening, before closing the conference room door, "who is it?"

Fourth sister, hanging up her robe, said, "you will not believe it. It's the training officer."

"The training officer? How do you know?"

"I overheard him saying he'd continue to spy on us for her."

"But why? I can't believe it. Why would he do that to us? It makes no sense?"

"She's bribing him, - with females."

"My females?"

"I guess so, and I don't think there's anything we can do to stop it."

Her face flushed. *She using my females again. That cannot go unanswered.*

Her instinct for revenge screamed in her mind. She closed her eyes, fighting for calm.

"Are you alright, sister?"

Fourth sister voice was enough of a distraction, and as she opened her eyes an advantage presented itself. "We should use him to feed her with information we want her to have."

"Yes, I like that. Let's do it."

"You're going to have to be even more mindful about what you say around him now. Seriously, sister, be very careful from now on."

"Yes, of course."

"I know you can. Now, let's have a look at what first sister is proposing. I think it might be a good idea. She liked our extension plan, but wants to change it by cutting a cavern to hold more males inside the mountain."

"Won't that make it harder for us to get males out?"

"Yes, and no. Yes, in that more males are going to get swept up in larger gatherings, but if you think about it, we could hide some of the better males and get them out under the cover of darkness, without the guards seeing anything."

"Okay, but how?"

"She wants a tunnel from the cavern straight into here." She said, running her finger from the mountain to the secure area. "What if we build a tunnel of our own?"

"An escape tunnel?"

"Exactly, and your banishment has given us the perfect opportunity."

"How?"

"You will be here to manage the escapes. You can manage the changing of the guards and use the time between rotations to get some of them out."

"It won't be very many. If too many go at once, it'll get noticed."

"Good point. You'll have to work something out."

"And who's going to dig the tunnel?"

"You and I. We can't trust anyone else to do it."

"I don't know how to use mining equipment."

"Me, neither. We'll have to learn in the metaverse."

"I see."

"Tomorrow, while I'm on the ship, survey the mountain. Find the best position for the cavern and the tunnels."

"I will. Have you thought about what you're going to say to her yet?"

"No. I think I'll be direct and go from there. You could let slip to the training officer you think the cavern is a good idea."

"Yes, sister. I'll see you tomorrow when you get back."

"Let's use her spy against her. He can be our screen so she can't see what we're doing. Good night."

∞

The temperature dropped overnight. The mud was hard and slippery as she stood at the bottom of the ramp, waiting for the first officer to land the shuttle that would take her to the ship. She still didn't know what she was going to say as she crunched across the cold ground toward it.

"Good morning, second council sister. It's a fine clear sky today."

"It's just cold first officer, shall we go?"

"Of course. Please come aboard, second council sister. I'll have one of the crew bring you a warming drink." He barked the order.

A minute later, a worker handed her a cup. Its warmth seeped into her hands as she stood next to him in the cockpit as they took off.

She snorted when the training officer appeared from a hut in the living compound. *There he is.*

Shielding his eyes from the winter sun, he watched as the shuttle rose from the ground.

First sister was there in the hangar as the shuttle docked. "Good morning, sister. I wasn't expecting you today. You know I'm coming down for tomorrow's gathering. There are no problems, I hope?"

"No, sister, none to concern you. We are looking forward to it. I came to see how the females are, and I was hoping to see you, too."

"Oh, what's so important that it couldn't wait?"

"I want to talk to you about third sister."

"I see. Meet me in my chambers in an hour." She walked away.

"Thank you, first officer. Please make sure the shuttle is ready to go. I shouldn't be too long."

"Yes, second council sister."

The atmosphere was oppressive as she walked to her lab. It was in darkness when she got there. *What's going on?* She felt along the wall for the switch and flicked it on. The light greeted her with silence.

She opened the human females cell first. They were sitting in a circle, some rocking back and forth. The rest stared at the floor. None of them looked at her. There was nothing for them to do, nothing to stimulate them, and the smell of rotting food made her gag. No one had been in to clean up.

A shiver ran down her spine. *The pregnant females!* she thought. She rushed to open their door. They were gone. The dents in the pillows and rumpled sheets meant they'd slept their beds in, and there was food left on the table. *Where are they?* Her mind was racing when she heard the clink of chains.

A bored-looking warrior holding a chain like a leash led the shackled pregnant females into the lab.

"What's going on here?" she said. "And get those shackles off them now."

Shocked at the voice, he reached for his weapon, then seeing her, realized who it was. “Oh, yes, second council sister. Straight away.”

He scrambled to get the keys off his belt and dropped to his knees to unlock the chains. The females stood passively, almost regally, as if waiting for a lower life form to do what he'd been told.

“What were you doing with these females?”

“Taking them for a walk, second council sister. First council sister told me I must do it every morning.”

“Right, yes, very good. Although I don't think there's a need for shackles, do you? They are pregnant, and where are they going to go?”

“I don't know, second council sister. But that's what we have to do to prisoners.”

“They are not prisoners. Do not shackle them again. They will follow you without restraints. Do I make myself clear?”

“Yes, second council sister.”

“Leave us.” She waved him away.

“Yes, second council sister,” he said, coming to attention before marching out.

They smiled, “we are glad you are here, second sister.”

“I am too. How have you been?” She read their record charts.

“We have more to eat now, and a warrior comes to take us for some exercise.”

“Hmm. And from now on, without chains. No one's been in to take your blood pressure, I see,” she said, seeing the blank spaces on the chart. “I'll do it now.”

She tightened the monitor's cuff around their upper arms and pressed the button to inflate it, noting the readings as the air hissed its escape.

“Have you had any more stomach pain?”

“Only minor. We are all getting them,” the first female said.

"All of you?" She frowned.

They nodded.

"Your blood pressure is still higher than I'd like, and if you're all getting pain, I want you monitored more closely."

"We are fine, second sister."

The clatter of trays being wheeled into the lab made them silent.

"Here we are then," the head kitchen worker said as he pushed the trolley into their room. "Oh, good morning, second council sister. It's good to see you."

"Yes, good morning."

"I thought I heard voices?"

"No, just talking to myself, and even then, I'm not sure I get a decent conversation." She laughed.

"Oh, I see," he said, putting the trays of food on the table.

The females dived in.

"Same as last time. These animals have no manners."

"Enough of that."

He bowed his head, squeezing his eyes tight, preparing to accept her punishment.

"Is it you bringing their food every mealtime?"

"Yes, second council sister. I want to make sure they're getting enough food, as you've instructed."

She could hear the stress in his voice. "I commend you," she said, touching his shoulder.

He looked up with a tentative smile.

"Now, I'd like you to do something else for me."

"Yes, second council sister," he said. No council sister had ever treated him so well. Let alone compliment his work. "What would you like me to do?"

"See this chart?"

"Yes, second council sister. But I must tell you, I cannot read."

"That's okay, all I want you to do is to call me if any of these spaces here in this column remain blank," she said, sliding her finger down it so he could see.

"So, you want me to tell you if there is no writing in them?"

"Yes. Can you do that for me?"

"Of course, second council sister."

"Thank you. There will be a reward for you."

His eyes fell on the females. "Oh, thank you, second council sister."

She fought back the urge to bite something off him, for the thoughts he was having. She swallowed hard. "You may go," she said. For now, she needed him to be her eyes.

The females shrank away when he looked at them like playthings. Intellectually, they were far superior, but physically, they couldn't stop him if he wanted more than to talk.

"Do not worry, ladies. No one will touch you," second sister said.

"We've seen some of our females from next door being taken and brought back a few hours later. We know what's been happening."

"I will put a stop to it, but I have to leave you now, and it will be a few days before I can return."

"Thank you, second sister. See you soon."

Anger bubbled below the surface as she left their room. *I have to put a stop to the females being used as rewards.* She had to convince first sister of their importance.

She took a deep calming breath before knocking on first sister's chamber door.

"Come."

First sister was lying on her lounger sipping a drink when she went in.

"You wanted to talk to me about third sister," she said, putting her glass on the floor.

"Yes, as well as some other things."

"Okay." She pointed to a chair. "What about third sister?"

She sat and crossed her legs. "You know she set fourth sister up. She could have waited before landing to give us time to get the warriors in place."

"Yes, maybe she did. But you told me everything was ready."

"And they were. We weren't expecting you to send third sister on a gathering. You told me it was an inspection visit. If you'd told me there would be a gathering, I would have made sure we had sufficient security in place, but you didn't."

"Watch your tone. Remember who you are talking to here. Let me be clear. It is my facility that you are building. This is my ship, and it is my fleet when they get here, and they are my sisters to praise and punish. They are my humans to do with as I see fit. Nothing here is yours. It is all mine, and I allow you to use what's going to be of benefit to me. Tell me you understand that!"

"Yes, I understand sister."

"Good. We've made such progress, you and I. It would be a shame to spoil it. Perhaps I've been overly lenient with third sister. She is a brown nose and lords it over the sisters, and maybe I was hard on fourth sister. But they know who's in charge. Now, what are these other things you want to talk to me about as well?"

"The humans, sister."

"What about them?"

"The numbers of males you intend to gather won't keep a sustainable number for population growth."

"I will have my army first, and deal with the human population after."

"Of course, sister. It's vital that you do, but do you need all of them now?"

"I don't understand the feelings you have for this species. They are fodder, nothing more."

"No, sister. They are much more. If you'd taken an interest in their physiology as I have, you would realize that the human species is what we've been searching for. None of the others we've experimented on even come close. The humans will reverse our dwindling numbers if you don't take them all."

"The males are perfect for conversion. We will find another for blending."

"But we don't have to if we manage the population correctly. We can blend with the human females and Szatethess will be born. We can cultivate more males and convert them to your armies. This planet and the human species, sister, could be the next evolution for our Szateth race. We could make this planet our new home."

"This ship is my home. Don't make me repeat myself."

"I see, sister." Her heart sank. "What more can I do for you?"

"Be ready for tomorrow's gathering. I want my facility running at full capacity."

"It will be, sister."

"Is there anything else?"

"The pregnant females, sister. Their blood pressure is still high, and they are experiencing some abdominal pain. Will you ensure they get monitored daily, whilst I am on the surface?"

"How long until our new sisters are born?"

"Maybe three months."

"Hmm. Very well. They get a walk every day as you requested, and I will make sure someone sees and checks on them. Is that good enough for you?" She picked up her glass and drank its contents.

"Yes, sister. Thank you."

She beckoned the servant worker, holding the drinks bottle over. "Leave me now. I have some entertainment and food on the way."

"Yes, sister, and I will prepare for tomorrow." Her bow went unnoticed as she left. *More dancing and death. She didn't listen to a word I said. There's only one way to change the mind of a monster*, she thought, looking at the commander as she boarded the shuttle. *And you're going to help me.*

Neural Blockchain Journal Entry #928

I have my first conversion facility.

It feels like getting it's been a long haul, to get it but it's going online. I will soon have all the warriors I want.

Third sister has been a help. She's an ass-kisser, but she's my ass-kisser and will do whatever I want her to do. Although her setting up fourth sister was a little over-the-top. But I enjoyed banishing her, so maybe it wasn't so bad.

It's a pity I had to dress down second sister. Well, they all need it sometimes. But she's fully onboard.

The facility is excellent, and I'll get it extended into the mountain. Then look for a site for a second holding facility.

Everything is going as I want it, and the food tastes sweeter when things are going well.

First Council Sister - Szateth leader

Advanced planetary research fleet.

Neural Blockchain Journal Entry #081

She's never going to understand.

It doesn't seem to matter how blunt I am with her. She will not see how important humans are.

Her insistence on getting her army first is going to ruin the human species. It is all she cares about.

Putting a spy on the surface to report on us is underhanded. She may well regret that.

Her attitude and banishment of fourth sister were terrible. Let alone what she did to the human males. What a stupid thing to do.

I'll make sure Project Residentz is successful with fourth sister's help.

I will say first sister's dislike of fourth sister (I don't know why she's taken a dislike to her?) is pushing her closer to some sort of revenge.

It's an encouraging development.

Second Council Sister

Advanced planetary research fleet.

Eleven

Too late to save them. She has to go.

"Is everything ready, sister? They will be here within the hour," second sister asked.

"Yes, I've ordered warriors to the serum room. They're ready to restrain the males. There will not be a repeat of the last incident."

"Alright, good. Have you put the survey report in the conference chamber as well?"

"It is on the table with the facility's construction plans."

"Everything is ready. Let's get down there."

The biting cold wind cut through their robes as they walked across the hard ground.

"I can't believe she's banished me to this," fourth sister said, pulling the collar up.

"It hasn't happened yet, sister. Come on, let's get inside before we freeze to death," second sister said, striding ahead to reach the door.

She got inside first with fourth sister on her heels. They stamped on the spot, trying to get some feeling back into their toes.

"The wind is cold today, council sisters," the training officer said.

"You have mastered the obvious training officer."

"My apologies, second council sister. My warriors don't feel the cold. It must be what remains of the human physiology that makes them used to it."

"And now you're a master of biology, too?"

He had the good sense to change the subject to something relevant to today's events. "Perhaps you would like to inspect your warriors, second council sister? They will prevent another incident like the other days."

She heard the submission to her authority. "Forgive my aggressive retort, training officer. The cold affects my mood. I envy their resilience," she said, thinking it was better to keep him sweet.

"Of course, second council sister. They are waiting in here if you would like to follow me?"

"Lead the way," she said, smiling. "Fourth sister, will you escort the newly converted warriors into the other room and prepare a syringe for the P9R injection, please?"

"Yes, sister."

The warriors stood to attention as she entered the serum room. "Impressive, training officer. How many here?"

"Twenty, second council sister. These, plus the warriors onboard the shuttle, should provide enough security."

"I believe you're right. I commend you."

"I understand this will be one of the biggest gatherings yet."

"Where did you hear that?"

"I, err, overheard first council sister saying something about a refit for the shuttles during her last visit, so they could hold more, and I guessed that's what it meant."

"You'd do better than trying to guess what first council sister wants, training officer, and concentrate on your job. You'll earn hers and our respect for a job well done."

"Of course, second council sister. I just want to make sure I cover all hers and your needs, so everything runs smoothly."

"Well, I'm impressed, and I'm sure first council sister will be, too. Have most of them stationed outside and ready to corral the males into here," she said, reassuring him he'd gotten away with his slip-up.

"Yes, second council sister," he said.

He barked orders and opened the door to the secure area. She turned away as a blast of icy wind hit her face.

"The new warriors are ready for P9R, sister," fourth sister shouted from across the large room.

"Thank you, sister. I'll be right there," she said, raising her voice above the noise of running warriors and the wind. The last one closed the door behind him. She shuddered, welcoming the quiet and the shelter from the cold as she walked across the room.

"Let me show you how this is done, sister," she said, picking up the syringe. "You may as well learn how to do it."

She showed her the place behind the ear for the needle to enter and pushed it in. "You need to take your time and not go too deep. Get one of those portable scanners and you'll see the position and depth for the needle."

Fourth sister held the wand close to the entry point, and the image appeared on the screen. "Ah, yes. I see," she said.

"Good. Now, there's an easier way to reach the required area of their brain." She injected the compound and carefully removed the needle. The warrior didn't move.

"I had this made," she said, showing fourth sister her auto-refilling syringe. "You set the needle depth here and the dose here. Once calibrated, you can safely administer the compound to a lot of them in one session."

"I can use it?"

"You might as well. Let me show you how it works." She injected another warrior. "Now you," she said.

Fourth sister copied her. "That's much simpler. Thank you, sister."

"They will need someone to stimulate their brains and help them learn."

The training officer poked his head into the room. "I see the shuttles, second council sister."

"Ah, good. Thank you, training officer. Can you get a couple of your warriors to clean up the shed skin in the other room and wheel the tables back out, please?" She saw his frown of disapproval. "It's just for today. I will get some cleaner workers down here tomorrow."

"Of course, second council sister, right away."

"Well, we'd better go out and meet them, sister."

"Must we?" fourth sister said, fastening her robe to the top.

"Well, I'd better. Why don't you go back to our shuttle and lay out your survey report, and we'll meet you there?"

"Thank you, sister. I think the less time I spend with her, the better."

Two warriors with brooms came in with the training officer. She nodded her thanks. "I agree," she said, opening the door. "Damn this wind. I'll see you onboard shortly."

Fourth sister walked quickly towards their shuttle while the fleet of shuttles landed. The ground crunched under their weight. None of them powered down their engines. The ramp of the lead shuttle opened and first sister marched out.

"I trust everything is ready?"

"Yes, sister, and we've administered the P9R to your newest warriors. They are magnificent."

"It's going to be a good day," first sister said, raising her hands. One by one, the shuttles took off in different directions to gather males.

She shivered, not because of the cold, but at the prospect of first sister decimating this precious planet of all its males. "The report from the survey of the mountain carried out by fourth sister is ready for you to see in the conference room."

"Anything interesting, or drillable?"

"I believe so, sister."

"Aha, told you it was going to be a good day. Let's go then." She marched away across the hard ground.

"Can I get you a warming drink, sister?" fourth sister said as they hung up their robes.

First sister scowled. Then, remembering the conversation with second sister in her chambers, she offered a faint smile. "Yes, alright."

"Can I pour one for you as well, sister?"

"Yes, thank you, and get one for yourself," second sister said.

She nodded, took the lid off the decanter, and poured the drinks, while first sister read the report.

"So we can drill out a cavern, by the looks of it, and dig a tunnel into the secure area."

"Yes, we believe so, sister," second sister said.

"Well, this calls for that drink."

Fourth sister put the tray on the table and handed them both a shot glass.

"To my new army." First sister raised her glass, swigged back the warming liquid in one mouthful, and slammed her glass on the table.

They looked at each. "To the new army," they said, emptying their glasses, and slamming theirs next to hers.

"Let's wait in the serum room to see what the shuttles have brought us., I don't need you this time, fourth sister. You may remain here."

"As you wish, sister," she said, putting the empty glasses on the tray, and leaving the room.

"I see she's still angry with me."

"You banished her to suffer this cold weather, sister."

"Hmm, well, she doesn't have to like it. She just has to do what I say. She'll get over it, or not. It doesn't matter, does it?"

"Absolutely not."

"Right. Are you ready?" first sister said, putting her robe back on.

"When you are, sister."

The two made their way outside. First sister marched away, and she matched her stride to keep pace. The extra speed got them into the warmth sooner.

"That wind is bracing," first sister joked.

"No, it's just damn cold." They laughed.

"There don't seem to be many warriors in here," first sister said, walking into the serum room. "Has she screwed up again?"

"Ah, no sister. Most of them are outside in the secure area waiting for the shuttles to arrive, to corral and secure the gathered males the moment they get off."

"Right. Good."

"Your new warriors are through here, sister." She pointed and led the way. "We gave them P9R this morning. If it takes effect as quickly as last time, they should be ready for combat training in a few days."

"Ah, yes, look at them. They are magnificent."

"Good afternoon, first council sister," the training officer said, appearing from the room being cleaned.

"Good morning, training officer. I hope you're pleased with your recruits?"

"They will make excellent warriors, first council sister. With more to come in a few days?"

"From today, you will have a steady influx of recruits to train for me."

"I look forward to it, first council sister. In a few short weeks, you will have your first battalion trained and ready for deployment."

"That's what I like to hear. I presume everything else is satisfactory?"

His eyes darted across to second sister, then back again. "Yes, first council sister, everything is as you'd expect it to be."

"Good." The activity in the room next door caught her attention. "Err, why are warriors being used for cleaning?"

"Second sister said it was just for today. I would have -"

"That's right," she said, cutting him off. "It is just for today. I have already put in a call to the first officer asking him to send a contingent of cleaner workers. They'll be here tomorrow."

"Do they have much more to do, training officer?"

"No, the room will be clean in the next few minutes, first council sister."

You weasel, she thought, staring at him. *You're going to regret that.*

"Good, carry on training officer," first sister said.

"Once they've finished, you can join them outside to help coral the males," she said to get rid of him.

"As you wish, second council sister." He bowed and left.

"How many males can we expect per gathering, sister?" she asked

With an exaggerated sigh, first sister said, "I would have had more if I had all nine shuttles, but you have one and I've left one for general use." She paused, then talked her through the math. "Seven shuttles, one for each continent on this planet. Each one holds thirty males, so a maximum of two hundred and ten. But some continents are huge, so with the extra weight, longer flight times, and limited fuel capacity, it's more likely to be half that unless we get lucky."

"It's a good start, sister."

"It's a slow start." She looked into each of the rooms. "As long as this facility is efficient, I'll have meta-gates with holding facilities built around the planet to transport the males into the cavern without having to use shuttles."

"That would be quite something, sister. This facility is ready."

Her communicator buzzed. "It better be," she said, tapping the answer button

"The shuttles are on their way back, sister," third sister's voice said.

"We're about to find out how ready it is." She opened the door to the secure area.

"Make sure you have control of the humans when they come down the ramp," she said to the training officer.

The first shuttle landed, and the hiss from the ramp opening told them to be ready. Sedated, disorientated males staggered down met by the warriors, cracking whips, shouting, beating, and pushing them into a tight bunch towards the serum room door. Overwhelmed by the brutality they did not resist.

"That's how it should go," first sister said, picking up a syringe while a warrior restrained the first male on a table.

Over the next few hours, the shuttles returned, with all the males subjected to the same cruel treatment. Second sister stood helpless, as the warriors dragged in a terrified male and strapped him down. The scream of pain as first sister savagely injected the serum was excruciating. She couldn't stop it and wiped her tears on her sleeve as she checked their breathing and blood pressure, and tried to make them more comfortable.

In a few hours, the facility had gone from silent to deafening screams of pain to silent again as the side room filled with the paralyzed males.

First sister looked on with a satisfied smile. "There, I told you it was going to be a good day."

Emotionally drained, she couldn't answer.

"Right, I'll leave you to monitor them, and give them the P9R."

"Yes, sister," she said. It was an unconscious answer as she looked at the rows of human males silently enduring the pain of conversion. She looked at the floor.

The training officer re-appeared. "Looks like a successful day, first council sister."

Second sister looked up and glared at him.

"Yes, it was, training officer," first sister said, grinning. "Now, stand your warriors down and get ready for the next wave of recruits."

"I have already started, first council officer."

"Wonderful. Carry on, training officer."

He gave the orders to the warriors in the serum room and outside and marched them away.

"There's a good and loyal warrior," she said. "Right, my shuttle is waiting. I will expect your report in a couple of days. Then we'll decide when to drill into the mountain and expand this entire operation."

"Very good, sister," she said. She couldn't look at her.

"Good work today." She was waiting for the customary, thank you. When it didn't come, she huffed and walked out into the secure area, across the sand, and boarded the shuttle on the landing pad.

Second sister stared unseeing as the ramp closed and the shuttle took off. The horror of the day's events had numbed her senses. She didn't feel the cold as she walked back to her shuttle. At the top of the ramp, she pressed the button to close it, went to her chambers, slumped onto her bed, and fell asleep.

Locked in a nightmare, and powerless to resist, she saw the fleet arrive and heard the screams of human females being used and violated. She saw males corralled and converted, then doing the same to other human males. All the time, in the background, first sister was laughing and saying '*we have more*' until there were none left. She woke soaked in sweat, knowing the nightmare would become a grim reality if she didn't stop it.

Her communicator buzzed. Her eyes flew open with an overwhelming feeling of dread. It was the head kitchen worker. "What's wrong?"

"The pregnant females are ill, second council sister. I have informed first council sister who said she would deal with them. But you asked me to let you know if anything out of the ordinary happened."

"What is wrong with them?"

"I do not know, second council sister, but they will not eat and they're holding their stomachs as if in pain."

"When did this start?"

"I don't know for sure, but when I went in with their food this morning, they hadn't eaten yesterday's meal."

"I need to speak to first council sister. Thank you for calling me," she said and ended the call.

Her finger hesitated over the call button. *She'll know I have a spy onboard if I ask her about the females. Damn it. It would be better if I got up there myself. I need a shuttle.*

She called the first officer. "I need a shuttle, first officer."

"Yes, second council sister. When would you like one?"

"Now, if you please."

"We are currently refueling after yesterday's gathering. It will take about two hours before I can send one for you."

"What about the reserve shuttle? Send that."

"I am sorry, second council sister, but it is undergoing essential maintenance, and is not available."

"Can you get me one any faster?"

"Is something wrong, second council sister? Can I help you with anything?"

"No. I just need to get up there."

"I will prioritize the fueling of one of them and dispatch it as soon as I can for you, second council sister."

"Thank you, first officer. I know I can count on you."

"Of course, second council sister. I look forward to seeing you." He ended the call.

Two hours, damn it, she said to herself. *Stomach pains in all of them, and now not eating? What's wrong with them? Could be the food, but the first female told me about the pain before, and she ate the same food as the other two. Don't think it's the food. I need to examine them to be sure.* It was then that she realized she was wearing yesterday's dirty clothes. *Damn it. Right, I need to get cleaned up.*

She turned the shower on and took her clothes off, waiting for the water to heat. *It isn't obvious what was wrong with them. It could be as simple as the food, as they hadn't eaten the previous meal, I don't know, and first sister is going to treat them. She knows nothing about them. Damn it, I need to get up there.*

Steam filled her shower stall, and she stood under the hot spray, wishing the time away.

Three hours later, there was still no sign of a shuttle. Frustrated and pacing the corridor, she called. "Where is the shuttle you promised me, first officer?" she said as soon as he answered.

"It is on its way to you now, second council sister. I apologize for the delay. The fuel cells had depleted more than expected, so it took longer to charge them. It should be with you in minutes."

"Very well, first officer."

She opened the ramp, and saw the shuttle on approach.

"I see it. Thank you."

As soon as it touched down and the ramp opened, she ran over, ignoring the cold.

"Welcome aboard, second council sister," the pilot said.

"Yes, thank you. Can we go, please?"

"Of course," he said, pulling the levers to power up the engines.

In moments, they were airborne, and her shuttle got smaller as they rose closer to the ship. She stood at the ramp as the shuttle docked and hit the open button as soon as it came to rest.

The first officer was there to greet her. "Welcome onboard, second council sister. I'm sorry for the -"

"No problem, first officer. I have to run."

Her boots thumped as she ran through the corridors. She slid along the floor to slow down at the entrance to her lab and almost bumped into first sister coming out.

“Well, well, sister. What’s the hurry? I didn’t think I’d see you today. With my new warriors going through the conversion, I need you to be monitoring them for me. Why are you here?”

“Oh, I, err, checked on them before coming up, and, err, I needed to get some, err, more needles for my automatic self-refilling injector syringe.”

“And you couldn’t ask for them to be brought down with the cleaner workers?”

“Well, I thought as they’re doing fine, and it’s been a few days since I came up, I thought I would see our sisters, and while I was here, I thought I might as well look in on the females, too.”

“I see. Interesting. It’s as if you had a crystal ball or something?”

“Is everything okay?”

“It is funny that you should ask. It’s almost as if you knew.”

“Knew what, sister.”

“That the females are unwell.”

“Oh, what’s wrong with them?”

“I think it’s just their food. I’m having their diet altered to all meat.”

“Ah, well, if that’s what you think.”

“It isn’t anything serious.”

“Perhaps I could examine them, as long as I’m here?”

“Very well. As long as you’re here, let’s look together then, shall we?”

First sister turned, shoved the door open, and marched back in, leaving her to catch up. She stopped outside the female's room and looked in through the window. “There, as you can see. Nothing to worry about.”

Second sister joined her. “They haven’t eaten their -”

“That’s not surprising, as they have upset stomachs. It’s just their bodies adapting to suit our new sisters. Nothing to worry about.”

"What's their blood pressure like, any vomiting, any blood, or discharge?"

"They are fine. Do not worry about these females. We will take care of them for you. They have months before you need to be involved with them again. It's more important that you make sure my warriors are healthy. Now, get what you need, see your sisters, then get back to my warriors. Unless you think I'm being unreasonable?"

"No, of course not, sister," she said, looking through the window. "It's just that -"

"It's just that what? What is it? You don't think I can do as good a job as you looking after some human females, do you?"

"No, sister, I'm sure you can, but I'd like to -"

"To what? Are my instructions not clear?" She stepped into her personal space.

She felt the intended intimidation. "Perfectly clear, sister. I'll get back."

"That would be wise," first sister said, waiting for her to move away from the window before blocking her view as she looked back. "Contact me once my warriors are in the living compound. So I can send the shuttles out on the next gathering."

"As you wish, sister. I'll see our sisters, then return to the facility," she said, opening the door to leave.

"Haven't you forgotten something?"

She stopped and turned, her mind racing to remember.

"Needles for your injector, wasn't it?" first sister said, answering the blank expression she saw on her face. "That's what you said you came all this way for, isn't it?"

"Ah, yes, thank you, sister. I almost forgot. Clean needles reduce the risk of transmitting infection, and I wouldn't want your warriors out of commission because of a dirty needle."

"Definitely not." She watched her grab a handful of needles from the drawer and leave. *She must think I'm stupid. Needles, really? She knew about the females. That means she's got someone watching and reporting to her. Oh well, it's only fair, I suppose.*

Damn her for not letting me see the females. She clenched her fists as she strode into the hangar. "Take me back to the facility," she said to the pilot, who was leaning against one of the shuttle's ramp hydraulic struts. He jumped at the growled order.

"Yes, second council sister. At once," he said and ran up the ramp.

"Ah, second council sister, can I speak with you?" the commander said from across the hangar.

She waited for him to finish his jog over to her before answering. "What is it, commander?"

"Could you give fourth council sister a message for me, please? Could you tell her I've done an inventory of the mining and tunneling equipment? There's more than enough for your plans."

"What plans?"

"Fourth council sister mentioned something about mining a cavern and digging some tunnels."

"*Some* tunnels?"

"Yes, second council sister. That's what she said, and we've got everything you need. May I offer my help?"

"Perhaps, commander," she said, looking to see if anyone could hear them. No one could. "Please keep this information to yourself."

"Of course, second council sister."

"Good. Thank you, commander. Now, I need to leave. Carry on."

He smiled and walked over to his office to alert the hanger crew the shuttle was leaving. *You're digging your own hole,* she said to herself and boarded.

Over the tannoy, the commander alerted the hangar crew, then opened the hangar doors. "Let's go, pilot," she said.

"Yes, second council sister."

The shuttle flew out into the blue sky.

She stood, looking out of the cockpit window. *You'll regret it, sister, if anything happens to those ladies.* She ground her teeth.

As the shuttle touched down, she hit the ramp's open button and walked down before it fully opened. She jumped off; the ground crunched as she landed and the icy air reminded her where she was and would stay until first sister got what she wanted. She stomped across to her shuttle.

"There you are, sister. You've been gone for hours. You left without a word. Is everything okay?" fourth sister said, seeing her walk up the ramp.

"I have a message for you from the commander. He's got everything for the cavern and the tunnels. You said tunnels, plural. What have I said about being careful with what you say?"

"It's only the commander, sister. He's on our side."

"I hope so, sister. What have you told him?"

"Nothing other than we'll be digging a couple of tunnels."

"I told you to keep the details of Project Residentz to yourself."

"I didn't tell him about Project Residentz. I only mentioned digging tunnels. What harm could that do?"

"The details are a secret, sister. I told you to keep it between us. What if he mentions *tunnels* to first sister? She suggested *a* tunnel and will want to know why she'll need more. Who else have you mentioned anything to?"

"No one, sister. Only the three of us know."

"A secret, sister, is private knowledge kept between two people. As soon as someone else knows, it's not private, it's news, and now we need to control the flow of it because he thinks he's part of something. We'd better hope he's true to his word."

"He will be. He hates first sister."

"I hope so. I know you've been talking to him, but please, watch what you tell him, and don't give him details." Fourth sister looked upset. She rubbed her eyes. "Look, it's been a rough day, sister, and I'm not myself. I need to spend some time on my own. If you don't mind, I'll see you tomorrow, and we can get the P9R injected."

"Of course, sister. I'll be more careful."

She tried unfastening her top robe as she walked into her chambers. Her fingers were still cold, and she was having trouble getting them undone. "Damn these things and damn first sister," she said to the room. With a hand on each side, she ripped the robe open, pulled it off, threw it into the corner, and sat heavily on her bed.

"Why doesn't she understand how important human females are?" She said to the universe. There was no reply.

"You're a great help. What else are you going to throw at me?" She took a deep breath to calm herself. "Well, at least I have a scapegoat if things go wrong. I guess I should be thankful for that," she said, flopping back on the bed and closing her eyes. She slipped from the physical into the dream world, where the universe answered - with the same nightmare.

The communicator buzzed on her wrist. She felt it before she heard it and woke up with a start. The memory of the nightmare filled her mind. It was so vivid.

"Good morning, second council sister," the head kitchen worker said. "I thought you should know the females haven't eaten again and they do not look well. First council sister gave them an injection last night and I think it's made them worse. She is with them now."

An incoming call beeps on her communicator. It was first sister. "Thank you for telling me. She's calling me now." She switched calls.

"Good morning, sister."

"As you may already know, the females are unwell and worse than yesterday."

"I see. How are they worse?"

"You'd better come up to see them. I have sent a shuttle for you."

"Yes, of course. I'll be ready."

She threw her robes on and went into the cockpit so she could see the shuttle arrive. It was landing as she got there. *That was fast. Too fast. It's bad, I know it.*

She hit the ramp's open button and sprinted to the waiting shuttle. Its ramp was still closing as it took off.

"Get me up there, pilot, best speed," she said.

He throttled up, and the hard acceleration pushed her back in the chair. A feeling of dread blocked out every other thought.

There was no time for the customary pleasantries and greetings a council sister receives when docking. Sprinting down the ramp and out of the hangar, she ignored them all.

The lab door hardly slowed her as she crashed through it to get to their room. "What's happened to them?"

"Ah, you're here. You made good time."

"I got here as fast as I could." Her eyes darted to each of them. They looked pale and weak. "What's wrong with them?"

The first female coughed, spitting blood from her mouth and nose.

"What's wrong?" she asked the female. Lifting her head from the pillow, cradling her in her arms. Her eyes bulged, and gasping for breath, coughed again, splattering her face with blood.

"What did you give them?"

"They weren't eating and bled on their bed sheets. Their blood pressure and heart rates were high, and I felt they were in danger of losing our new sisters."

It was then she saw the syringes. "What was in those? What did you give them?"

The other two lying in a fetal position holding their stomachs moaned. "What have you injected them with?"

"Careful how you speak to me!"

"You can see how distressed they are, sister. Whatever you gave them, it hasn't helped. It's made things worse. Now please, what was it, and perhaps I can fix this?"

"Worker serum."

"What!"

"A small dose, to strengthen them."

"What? No. We created the conversion serum for males. Their bodies will reject it. They have Szatethess DNA and need a blood transfusion from a sister. Now."

"I see."

"Do you? Do you sister? Why didn't you call me before taking matters into your own hands?"

"I didn't need you for this experiment."

"Experiment?"

"To see if we could make the females stronger. They could bear more sisters if they're strong like us."

"But that's not how things are -"

The first female coughed more blood, gasped, and went limp.

"She's not breathing. Help me with her."

She laid her flat, tilted her head back, blew air into her lungs, and began chest compressions.

"Sister, please, help me."

The other two began coughing. Blood spilled from their mouths and nose, and they gasped for air.

"Sister, please, we must save them. Call for more help."

"It's pointless. This experiment is a clear failure. Let's not waste time on them," she said, as they gasped their last breaths.

"No!"

"Calm yourself. They're just humans."

She looked up from the dead female covered in her blood, fighting back the tears, unable to speak.

First sister chuckled. "We have more."

A moment from the nightmare flashed. It was real. "You're a bi..." The room began to spin.

First sister stood over her. "Stop being so so pathetic. Pull yourself together. You're no good to me like this." She turned to the door. "Guards, get in here."

The room went black.

When she woke, her eyes darted around, before focussing on a familiar voice. It was fourth sister and she was back in her chamber.

"I'm so sorry, sister. Here, drink this, it'll make you feel better," she said, sitting on the edge of her bed holding a cup. "The warriors who bought you back told me what happened."

"They're dead, sister. I couldn't save them, and I wasn't there to stop her. She didn't care about them, she used them like experimental animals. But they were more, so much more. They were like us, and they would have given birth to sisters who were just as intelligent and powerful as us. Perhaps even more so, and happy to live on this planet. How could she be so callous? I tried to tell her, but she's so determined to conquer the universe that she's forgotten what we need. Forgotten that if we don't find a new host species, the Szateth will join all the other species that are extinct because of her. We have to stop her."

"I know, sister. I know how much they meant to you. There was nothing you could have done. We are not the only ones who see she's lost sight of our primary mission. Our other sisters know it too, and we think it's time for a change of leadership. We are all behind you, sister. So what now?"

"You're suggesting a leadership coup? It is an ugly game you want to play, sister. Have you got the spine for it?"

"We all have."

"Well, I'm flattered, but how do you know I'm right for the job?"

"Because you care. You care about us, and our survival. That's why we're here, now, having this conversation."

"You think more of me than you should."

"I don't think so, and it's time for a change, so what now, sister?"

Sitting up and taking the cup, she said, "Payback."

Neural Blockchain Journal Entry #930

Real success.

The conversion facility works. Apart from there not being enough warriors to control the human males at the first small gathering, because of fourth sister's incompetence. She has and will pay for that, despite third sister setting her up. But all that doesn't matter. In the end, it went well, and the incident was not repeated during the second gathering.

Using refitted shuttles to gather males takes too long. It's not efficient. I'll go ahead with my plans to cut a cavern into the mountain and build the meta-gates and the holding facilities on the continents around the planet. With a squad of twenty warriors at each facility to corral the males through the gates, I'll be able to convert more.

It's a pity about the females dying. Second sister took it hard, but we've got more. I'll use them after the harvest.

Now, it's time to call for the fleet.

First Council Sister - Szateth leader

Advanced planetary research fleet.

Neural Blockchain Journal Entry #090

She has to go.

There's no convincing her of how important human females are. She's blinkered and wants nothing more than to build her army. She has endangered our future.

Fourth sister and the commander are getting cozy. They will serve as my scapegoats if things go wrong. I feel sorry for my sisters. They are going to be harvested. They have to be now. Human females are the hosts we need, they are our future. They will give birth to the next and greatest evolution of our race.

Maybe I should have told another sister how advanced the pregnant females had become. To my shame, it's too late now.

The nightmare I've been having is more like a premonition. I'm sure it's the universe telling me things have to change. There is only one course of action left to me. To ensure the survival of our race,

She has to go.

Second Council Sister

Advanced planetary research fleet.

Twelve

Warehouse, tunnels, and senseless murder

"Where is my chief engineer?" first sister said, marching into the engineering department.

"He is working on your satellite, first council sister. In the clean room," an engineer said, bowing.

"Good," she said, going over to the observation window. She pressed the intercom button, "how much more is there to do chief engineer?"

He dropped his wrench and held his breath as it narrowly missed a power cell and clattered to the floor.

"You're lucky that didn't damage it."

"First council sister. I apologize. I wasn't expecting you."

"Well, when can we launch?"

"There is still an issue with the shields, first council sister. We can shield it from view, but radiation is another matter entirely. The sun is very active and if we launch now, it won't survive the effects of a coronal mass ejection, or from a stellar coronal mass ejection. The internal systems are too sensitive. We'll have to adapt it before installation."

"That is not the news I want to hear, chief engineer. If you're not up to the task, perhaps I should replace you and have you entertain us one evening. What do you think?"

"I will get it done for you, first council sister. We will not rest until it's finished."

"I expect nothing less. Have you repaired the ship's communications array and sensors yet?"

"No, not as yet, first council sister. We will need shielding material for that as well, but I have prioritized the work on your satellite. I know how important it is."

"That's what I like to hear. Fortunately for you, the success of my conversion facility has bought you some time. I want to build meta-gates and holding facilities on all continents. I'll need engineers to build them for me. Put a team together and make sure they are ready when I call for them."

"Yes, first council sister, immediately. Building the meta-gates will add additional strain on the supply of shielding material we have."

Her eyes narrowed, and he backtracked. "But I'm sure there's enough for us to achieve everything you need, first council sister."

"Good," she said, turning to leave. "One more thing, chief engineer, just in case. Can you dance?"

"No, first council sister, not at all."

"Pity, but it doesn't really matter. I'll be back for that team chief engineer," she said, walking away.

"Yes, first council sister," he said. Once she'd gone, he took a deep breath, letting it out slowly.

∞

Second sister was looking over the plans when fourth sister came into the conference chamber. "Here sister. I think we should dig the entrance to our tunnel here," she said, stabbing her finger into the drawing of the excavated cavern. "In this corner. We could manipulate the positioning of the lighting so this area stays in shadow."

"That looks good. I have news, sister. She's called for a full council meeting to give us the *good news* about her progress. She's sending a shuttle for us."

"Her progress? I see. Well, we'd better be ready."

"I'll take this opportunity to meet with the commander and arrange for some of the equipment to be secreted away and put onboard the spare shuttle. He can bring it without having to record the flight."

"Okay, well, don't give me any of the details. We know what needs to be done. Keep the how to yourself until we need to share things."

"Yes, sister. I'll get things moving."

Dressed in their formal council robes, they waited for the shuttle to land.

"The only reason I can bear this cold and filth is because of what's coming next," fourth sister said, lifting her robe as they squelched across the ground.

"Keep your voice down."

"What, there's no one -"

Second sister looked over to where she heard marching boots. "Good morning, training officer," she said, looking back at fourth sister and raising her eyebrows.

"Good morning, council sisters," the training officer said. "First council sister has asked that I bring some warriors up to today's council meeting for inspection."

"I see. I didn't know she spoke to you directly."

"She does occasionally, second council sister."

"Well, it's quicker than going through the proper chain of command. Get them on board, then."

He saw her displeasure and marched the warriors onto the shuttle without another word. None of them spoke during the short flight.

The first officer and the commander were there to greet them as they walked off the shuttle.

"Take them straight to the council chambers, training officer," she said as the warriors marched past her.

"Yes, second council sister."

"Welcome aboard, sisters," the commander and first officer said.

"Thank you, commander," fourth sister said. "Will you be available at lunchtime? I'd like to talk to you."

"Yes, of course, fourth council sister. I'll be in my office."

"Good, I will see you then."

He smiled at second sister as they walked out of the hangar.

"What's that all about?" asked the first officer.

"Oh, err, nothing," the commander said. His face flushed.

"If you need me for anything, commander. I'm happy to help, especially if it helps second council sister."

"I'll bear that in mind, first officer. Come and see me after lunch."

∞

"It's good to feel the warmth of the ship again," fourth sister said, as they approached the council chambers. They could hear chattering and laughing. "I think they're waiting for us."

"Hmm, yes. Let's get this over and done with, shall we?" second sister said, painting a fake smile on her face as they entered.

"Sisters, welcome. Come in and take your seats. Now we are all here we can start," first sister said, pointing at the empty chairs at the far end of the table. Third sister had sat next to first sister which, by rights, should have been the second council sister's seat. The slight had not gone unnoticed.

The chamber fell silent, waiting for first sister to start the meeting.

From the head of the table, she rose. "Sisters, thank you for attending. I want to update you on the monumental progress we've made in replenishing the numbers of my warriors. After an uninspiring start, I can announce second sister has perfected the conversion serum." She paused and waited for a round of applause. Third sister started, and the others followed.

"I have my first conversion facility on the surface, which second sister, along with fourth sister, has completed and made operational. We have carried out two gatherings so far, successfully converting and training new warriors. - Bring them in, training officer." She directed their view to an anteroom door.

The door opened and six warriors marched in and stood to attention behind first sister.

She beamed with pride. "Aren't they magnificent?" she said, again waiting for applause. Third sister obliged.

"Within weeks, I will have enough warriors to begin the next phase. I am going to build meta-gates and holding facilities guarded by these warriors all over the planet. The males will get transported to the conversion facility via the meta-gates, speeding the process. Soon I will have the warriors to suppress any uprisings and encourage more planets into our network. Sisters, we *will* rule the universe."

Third sister stood clapping, a second later the others joined in. As it died down and they returned to their seats, first sister said, "this is the planet we've been looking for, sisters. I intend to call the rest of the fleet. I have a communications satellite being built as we speak -"

"What about our primary mission? To find a species to stop us from dying out as a race." the ninth and oldest sister said. They all stared at her, amazed by her boldness. "I thought second sister had successfully implanted our stored Szatethess embryos into three human females. What of their progress, sister?"

"Another failure. Human females are not strong enough to carry a new sister to full term. Although I believe a blood transfusion at around the end of their second trimester with blood from us will mean that they will be. We will begin again tomorrow with more implantations, and I will expect each of you to donate blood."

She looked at second sister to see if there was going to be an objection. When there wasn't, and second sister looked down at the table, she smiled at her victory.

"Thank you for attending," she said, rising from her chair. "I'm sure you are as delighted as I am at the progress."

Third sister stood clapping. The others knew they should do the same. First sister left the council chambers to the sound of thunderous applause.

"Why didn't you say anything?" fourth sister said to second sister under her breath. "We would have backed you up."

"It wasn't the right time. She had third sister, the training officer, and the warriors with her."

"Yes, that makes sense."

"What does?" third sister said from behind them.

"Oh, hello sister. I was just telling second sister that it makes sense to use meta-gates for transport as opposed to shuttles."

"Oh, right?"

"We need to get back, so if you would excuse us," second sister said, getting right in her face.

"Oh, err, of course, sister." Third sister backed away.

"Nice to see you though," she said, as they left the chambers.

"Sorry sister, I didn't see her behind us," fourth sister said, wringing her hands.

"We must be even more on our guard now. Have your meeting with the commander, but make it quick, and I'll meet you back on the shuttle."

They separated as they got to the hangar. It was a few minutes before fourth sister joined her on the shuttle.

"Everything alright?"

"Yes, everything is ready to go, sister. We can start tomorrow."

"Good. I'll leave it in your capable hands, then. I'll be here to implant the last of our embryos."

Neither of them spoke on the flight back. They didn't know if the pilot was to spy on them, like the training officer.

Once the shuttle had taken off, fourth sister said, "She's unbelievable. She points the finger when something goes wrong and takes the credit for everything that goes right. That meeting was a total waste of time."

"Not entirely, sister. It allowed you to organize equipment to start our project."

"Well, I suppose so. The commander is with us. I've never known a converted worker promoted to the position he's in with such hatred for a sister before."

"You'd feel the same if she had bitten off your finger too. More so, as it was in public. I still don't think you should trust him, though."

"I think he'll be okay."

As they approached their shuttle, the ramp came down automatically and they stomped the mud off their boots as they walked up.

"All I'm saying is, be careful. Let's have a look at the plans for the cavern, the tunnel into the secure area, and make sure they will not see ours."

"I think we need to go in the opposite direction and out this side of the mountain." Fourth sister slid her finger in the direction she wanted to go.

"That is a long tunnel to dig. And what's on the far side of the mountain?"

"I think it's dense forest, so there's plenty of cover and places to hide."

"We could help them start a new colony, instead of them trying to get back to their tribes, where they'll get caught in another gathering. We could teach them to survive unnoticed. Can you survey the far side?"

"If I can use the shuttle when it gets here, I could, yes."

"Escape and education. I like that idea. Find somewhere secluded, but large enough to create a colony."

"A new colony. I like it, but we're going to need help, sister."

"One step at a time. We must appear to be carrying on as normal." She looked at the time on her communicator. "I'm going to retire for the evening. I want to get up to the ship early in the morning. We've got lots ahead of us, sister, but we have a beginning."

"I'll get the survey done, then we can take another step. Goodnight, sister," fourth sister said, smiling.

She had trouble getting to sleep. Every time she closed her eyes, she would see the terrified faces of the females as they died. When sleep came, she was grateful.

It was sunlight streaming in through the window that woke her. She tutted. She'd forgotten to darken the windows, and the brightness made her squint. The thought of getting up wasn't something she looked forward to. Today was the day she was going to implant the last six Szatethess embryos. *Just a few more minutes,* she grumbled, pulling the blanket over her head.

Stop all this self-pity. There are things to do, she chided herself and threw the blanket back. She called the hangar. "Yes, second council sister, how can I help?" the first officer said.

"Good morning first officer, can you send down a shuttle for me, please?"

"It'll be with you within the hour, second council sister."

"Thank you," she said.

She dressed and was ready when fourth sister came out of her chambers and joined her in the cockpit.

"Good morning sister," she said. "Can you get that survey done today? I want to take that next step."

"It's already done, sister."

"Really? When?"

"During the night, sister. The commander was doing the graveyard shift, and it's a good time for him to hide and do things without drawing attention."

"That's fantastic. Mining equipment as well?"

"Some. It was more of a test run to see if anyone took any notice. We've got a few plasma and laser drills. The rest will come once we're excavating the cavern. He'll be able to hide more and have good reason to have it if he gets asked about it."

"Fantastic. Let's discuss it when I get back this evening."

"I look forward to it, sister."

She saw the shuttle land. "Yes, me too. See you later."

The cold hit her the moment she lowered the ramp. They'd noticed it getting colder over the last few weeks, and the days were getting shorter, which, they agreed, was a good and bad thing. She looked at the mountain as she crunched across the frozen ground and thought about their plans during the flight.

The first officer was there to greet her when the shuttle docked. "Good to have you on board, second council sister," he said.

"Thank you, first officer. Everything okay?"

"Yes, thank you for asking. May I speak with you before you leave this evening?"

"Of course, first officer. I have a full day in my lab, and won't be leaving until this evening. You'll be here?"

"Yes, or please call me."

"Very well. We'll speak this evening," she said, leaving the hangar. *I wonder if he noticed the commander's little jaunt out last night?* She frowned. *Guess I'll find out later.*

First sister was waiting for her in her lab when she got there. "Ah, good. You're here," she said. "These are the last of our embryos?" She had the lid of the storage unit open and the cold was escaping.

"Yes, sister. The last six. Could you keep the lid closed? The P9R is in there as well, and it must remain cold."

She let it go and it slammed shut.

"You'll be implanting them today?"

"Yes, sister, that's why I've come aboard, and I think I have a care plan to stop the rejection at the end of their second trimester. It was you who suggested it at the council meeting."

"Ah, yes. Remind me?"

"The transfusion, sister."

"Ah, yes, that's right. It makes sense they'd need some of our blood to bolster the deficiencies of their own."

"I was thinking the same, sister. Particularly our blood plasma to carry the nutrients their bodies will need to cope with the demands of the babies and deliver a healthy sister."

"Exactly. With only these six, and another seven, you can't afford to mess this up."

"It's precision work, and they'll need constant care. With that in mind, I'd like to propose we move pregnant females into ninth sister's chambers from the start of their second trimester, so they are more comfortable and have our sisters there to care for them daily."

"I've already told you that will not happen. They are going to stay here. I will, however, allow you to make their room more comfortable. Once they are born, we will take our new sisters into chambers, but the humans will remain here. I have further plans for them once they've given birth." She flashed a sly smile.

"May I ask what plans, sister?"

"Nearer the time. Now, let's get the implantations done."

"It's exciting to know we are soon to have more sisters with us."

"Yes, yes, it is. I look forward to instructing them," she said, as third sister walked in.

"You wanted me, sister?"

"Ah, yes. I want you to plan another gathering for tomorrow," she said. Then, looking back at second sister said, "I assume the facility is ready for the next males?"

"Yes, sister. I apologize. I forgot to mention your new warriors are about to be moved into the living compound."

"Not a problem." Her expression said otherwise, before looking at third sister.

"Get the shuttles ready. I want more warriors ready in the next few weeks."

"Yes, sister," she said, smirking at second sister. "And while I remember. There will be a team of engineers coming down to you tomorrow to build the meta-gate."

"I was going to ask you when they were going to build it," second sister said.

"And I want you to instruct a crew of construction workers to build a warehouse," first sister said to her. "It makes sense to store the materials and equipment for the cavern excavation, and the building of the other holding facilities, on the surface. We might as well keep the materials for meta-gates there as well."

"Yes, sister, good idea. You're pushing ahead with your expansion plans sooner than expected," second sister said, touching her throat.

"I see no point in waiting now the facility is fully operational."

"Yes, it is, and in a matter of weeks, we could have a constant supply of males feeding it day and night."

"That's the goal. Now, unless you need my help, I'll leave you to get on with the implantations."

"Thank you, sister. I can manage."

"Well then. I'll see you in a few days. To see how the excavation of my cavern and tunnel is progressing." She left without a goodbye.

I can't wait for that, she said to herself, watching her leave. She took a deep breath, trying to cleanse her mind of first sister's self-absorption.

As she prepared the catheters and scanners, part of her was looking forward to watching the females evolve as the embryos grew and made them more like her. To care for them, enjoy their company, and help them give birth. The other part dreaded what first sister might have planned for their future. *I'll deal with that come the time, but for now, there is work to do*, she told herself.

The females in the cell were not in the best condition. She chose the healthiest looking, and the six lucky females received an embryo over the next few hours. Rather than putting them back in that bare cell with the others, after every implantation procedure, she took the female to the room next door.

It was hard for her to go in. The memory of the first three females and the horror of their deaths was still raw, but she knew they were better off separated from the others in the cell.

She watched the new females as they got used to their surroundings, and like its previous occupants, they knew what the furniture was for. She smiled, called down to the kitchen, and asked the head kitchen worker to bring them food as they settled in. It was too early to say with certainty whether the embryos had accepted their new hosts, but their actions suggested it.

"Welcome to your new home, ladies. We'll get to know each other over the next weeks and months."

They looked at her and smiled in recognition.

"It's a pleasure to see you again, second council sister," the head kitchen worker said, as he walked in holding a tray full of fruits, vegetables, and raw meat. The females shrank away from the unfamiliar face.

"It's okay, ladies. This worker is a friend. He'll bring you your food."

They relaxed, hearing the calming tone in her voice.

"Put the tray on the table so they can see you do it. And I'd like to thank you for watching the other females for me. Would you do the same for these?"

"Of course, second council sister."

"I'd like you to watch what they eat, to start with. When you see they are leaving more of the fruits and vegetables than they eat, reduce the amount of those and increase the amount of meat."

He nodded his understanding.

"Come with me a moment," she said and led the way to look through the window of the cell next door

"What do you know of the females in here?"

"Not much, second council sister. I'm told to slide a tray of leftovers through the door."

"Right, well, let's change that. From now on, bring them the same fruits and vegetables, but with cooked meat. Can you do that for me? I want them better treated."

"Yes, second council sister. I don't like to see other animals suffering."

"Oh, they are more than animals. Much more, as everyone will soon see."

"What do you mean, second council sister? What are they?" he said, looking through the window again.

"Nothing you need concern yourself with. Just bring them good food. Can you do that?"

"Yes, second council sister, of course," he said, looking down.

"Thank you," she said. "I value and commend you for your loyalty."

He looked up, standing straight as if to attention. "If there is ever anything I can do for you, second council sister. Please ask."

"I will, thank you," she said. "Carry on," addressing him as though he were an officer.

He smiled, bowed, and virtually marched out.

It had been a long day, a successful one, and there was one more thing she had to do before going back to the surface. She looked in on the mothers-to-be and the females next door. They were peaceful and resting. With one last look around the lab, she flicked the lights off.

What am I going to tell the first officer if he asks about the commander? She thought as she walked to the hangar. *Maybe it was a test flight, or fourth sister had asked him to bring her something. Or maybe I just tell him he's helping us to overthrow first sister. Well, maybe not that.* Lost in her thoughts, she nearly walked into him as she entered.

"Ah, first officer. You wanted to see me?"

"Yes, second council sister," he said, looking around. "I know the commander is helping you, and fourth council sister. I want to say, if you need me for anything, I'm happy to help too."

"Well, that's between fourth council sister and the commander, first officer. Nothing to do with me. I am not privy to their private conversations. What is it you think you know?"

"My apologies, second council sister. I may have miss read an observation. I hope I haven't offended you?"

She paused before answering. "Not at all, first officer. You know you can always ask. And thank you for your offer. I will keep it in mind."

"Thank you, second council sister. Your shuttle is waiting," he said, directing her to it.

"Have a good evening, first officer," she said, walking onto the shuttle.

You escaped that one. She closed her eyes as the shuttle left the hangar.

Fourth sister was waiting for her when she entered the conference room. "Can we expect new sisters in a few months?" she asked.

"I hope so. The implantations went well, and the females were acting in the same way as the others did. As long as first sister keeps her hands off them, they should give birth in about nine months."

"That's good. I've been going over the survey and I think I've found the perfect place for the colony."

"Fantastic. Show me."

"Here, sister," she said, pointing to an area on the map that showed no detail. "It looks blank, as you can see, but it's covered in lush vegetation. There's a water source and material for buildings. If we build it correctly, you won't see it from the air, and if we can get some shielding material from the engineers, the ship's sensors won't pick it up. That's the hard part."

"I have some news on that. Engineers are coming tomorrow to build the meta-gate in the living compound. Among the materials is going to be shielding. We'll take some, a little at a time, until we have what we need."

"Aha, yes. Another step, sister. She's helping us without realizing it."

"Maybe you can get your commander to re-direct some, our way too?"

"I'm sure he could. I'll arrange it."

"Well, that's it for me today. I need to get some sleep. Goodnight sister."

She fell asleep quickly with things to look forward to, with no nightmares or memories to disturb her.

The following morning, they were waiting for the engineers. As the shuttle touched down, they went to meet them and walked them down to the living compound where they were to build the meta-gate. Like the warriors and workers, the cold didn't seem to bother them either, so after introducing them to the training officer in the living compound and calling for the head construction worker to meet them, they left the engineers and retreated to the relative warmth of the serum room.

"First council sister wants a warehouse built to store equipment and materials. Where will you build it?" second sister asked the head construction worker as he walked into the serum room.

"Good morning, council sisters," He bowed. "It would be easy if we built it on the side of this facility -"

"No, don't do that," fourth sister said, cutting him off. "Build it close to our shuttle and the shuttle landing area. That way, the materials won't have to move too far to be stored, or to be transported for use." Her eyes flicked across to second sister.

"Yes, that's a better idea," she said. "Build it where fourth council sister suggested."

"Very good, second council sister. I'll order the construction materials sent down from the ship and we'll start building today," he said, bowing and leaving the shivering sisters.

She tucked her hands under her armpits. "That was a good idea. We can take what we need and move the materials straight to the colony from the landing pad. And if we orientate the building correctly, anyone watching from here won't see a thing. Once they've constructed the main warehouse, I'll build a secret room for us to store our materials."

"Yes, even better, sister," fourth sister said.

"I suggest we crack the whip, so to speak, and get this warehouse built. The next gathering is tomorrow."

"So soon?"

"She wants her warriors, and we need to protect as many males as we can. Are we ready for the next group of males to arrive?"

"I'll instruct the training officer to have warriors here first thing in the morning, ready for when the shuttles land."

"Right, shall we get into the warm and go over the plans for the excavation of the cavern and tunnel? She's going to want a progress update when she comes down in a couple of days, and I want the excavation underway."

"She's coming again? Well, I'll be over at the mountain excavation site, so I don't have to see her."

"Hmm, probably wise. Come on, let's get back," she said, opening the door. Heavy rain and icy wind assaulted their exposed faces, making their walk through squelching mud more miserable than usual.

With their hands wrapped around a warm cup, they got to work. "I don't think we can delay her anymore, sister," she said, leaning over the plans. "Your survey has found the best position under the mountain for the cavern, and she knows it. And to dig two tunnels under her nose, without it going unnoticed, will be nearly impossible."

"Hmm, maybe not," fourth sister said, leaning over the plans next to her. "See here?" She pointed to the back of the mountain. "That's what I was going to tell you yesterday, sister. During my survey for a location for the colony, I noticed a cave opening in the mountain. So I scanned it. Sister, a whole cave system leads almost to where we're going to excavate the cavern."

"Really? how far up to it?"

"Maybe twenty meters. We could dig that and break into the caves in a single night. We'll be able to get some males away sooner than we thought."

"Well then, sister, that's it. All we need are the materials, and maybe, just maybe, we can save our species."

"I think that calls for a drink," fourth sister said, touching her forearm.

"Not yet, sister," she said, looking out the window. "Let's celebrate once Project Residentz is in operation."

Outside, the first of the shuttles with the warehouse building materials landed, and the sisters watched as a crew of construction workers from the compound unloaded it and began the construction of the warehouse.

As soon as one shuttle had unloaded and taken off, another landed, and so it went on for a few hours, landing, unloading, and constructing the pieces of the warehouse jigsaw.

She walked over. "Very impressive," second sister said to the head construction worker, her voice echoing around inside the empty warehouse. "I commend you for your speed and efficiency. First council sister will be very pleased."

"Thank you, second council sister. We are waiting for the delivery of the mining and digging equipment, and construction materials for the other compounds and meta-gates."

"When is all that being delivered?"

"It's on its way now, second council sister."

"Well, this is very impressive," fourth sister said, stamping mud off her boots as she joined them from the cold. "You've built the warehouse exactly where I want it. I commend you."

"Thank you, fourth council sister. Equipment and construction materials are on their way, and we'll begin the cavern excavation tomorrow."

"Wonderful. So shall we," she said, her stomach fluttering.

Second sister's scowl made her blush, and she looked away.

"I have a copy of the excavation plans on our shuttle for you," second sister said, directing his attention back to her. "Come and collect it once the equipment has arrived, and it's stored away."

"Yes, thank you, second council sister."

"Good. Let's leave them to it, shall we, sister?" It wasn't a question.

"Yes, sister," she said, too embarrassed to look up.

The groan from the landing gear of the next shuttle landing echoed in the warehouse, giving them the chance to retreat. They didn't speak until they got back.

"Damn it, sister. How many times have I got to remind you to watch your tongue?"

"I know, I'm sorry. The excitement of starting Project Residentz got the better of me," she said, looking at workers unloading equipment.

"We don't know if she's got anyone else spying on us. Be more careful."

"The commander."

"What? The commander is a spy as well?"

"No, he's the pilot of that shuttle. Look."

They saw him standing at the bottom of the ramp, looking toward them. "I'll call him to come on board," fourth sister said, pressing the call button on her communicator.

He answered and walked over. "Good evening, council sisters," he said with a bow.

"Good evening commander," second sister said. "I'll leave you with fourth council sister." She left the two of them watching the workers from the cockpit.

With military precision and efficiency, they were passing the equipment along the line from the shuttle to the warehouse. She went back into the cockpit as the commander, walking back to his shuttle, came into view.

"He's had two of everything loaded, so we can take what we need," fourth sister said.

"Good. I think we should -"

"I have come for the excavation plans as instructed, second council sister," the head construction worker said, catching them off guard.

"Oh, err, of course. Wait there, I'll get them for you."

"You sneaked up on us. We didn't hear you come in. Maybe you should be a warrior instead."

"I apologize, fourth council sister."

"Here," second sister said, handing him the rolled-up plans. "Fourth sister will accompany you and your crew tomorrow to help you get started."

"Very good, second council sister. I shall look forward to working with you fourth council sister."

"I will meet you on-site tomorrow morning," fourth sister said.

"Thank you, and goodnight, council sisters." He bowed and left, clutching the plans.

She pushed the button that closed the ramp. As it rose, she saw the engineers walking toward the commander's shuttle. "The engineers have finished installing the meta-gate. I think we have everything we need for Project Residentz. Learn what you can about operating the equipment from the construction workers tomorrow and use the metaverse to learn the rest. You are going to have to dig our tunnel into the caves."

"I'm looking forward to it. I'll have it done in no time," fourth sister said, unable to hide her delight.

"I'll make sure first sister doesn't get to know about it. Tomorrow is going to be a big day. Let's call it a night and get some rest.."

"Yes, goodnight, sister."

∞

She slept well again and woke refreshed. It was later than her usual time to rise. The shuttle was quiet. There was none of the clumsy banging, crashing, and awful singing that was normal when fourth sister was onboard.

She must have left already. Good. In time too, she said to herself, as first sister's shuttle came into view.

She put on her thickest top robe, wrapping it tight against the cold, and went out to meet her. "Good morning, sister."

"Good morning. Look at that, now that's what I call a warehouse. Shall we go in and get out of this wind?" She didn't wait for an answer, taking the lead. "Well, this is quite something," she said, looking at racked equipment and materials. "And they built this in a day?"

"Yes, sister, quite remarkable," second sister said, blowing warm air on her hands. "The worker serum works, and the head construction worker has taught them well."

"Is everything here?"

"I believe so, sister."

"Remarkable."

"And we have a construction crew with fourth sister over at the mountain site already excavating the cavern. We'll have it ready in a few days, sister. Then we can scale up."

"Wonderful. And the Meta-gate?"

"Installed and online. Perhaps you'd like to inspect it before we go to the excavation site?"

"I would, yes. Lead the way. And remind me to reward the head construction worker, will you?"

"Yes, of course, he deserves it. This way," she said.

"So efficient," first sister said, taking a last look around before following her out.

First sister caught up and marched alongside her. "They built the Meta-Gate in the living compound?"

"Yes, sister. It gives the workers and the warriors easy access to the metaverse for training," she said, opening the door to the Meta-gate room.

"They are something to behold, aren't they?" she said, feeling the smooth stone that framed the gate. "Instant communication and travel between gates, and access to the metaverse, a place to learn, relax and live if you want to. A technology handed down to us from, well, we don't know who. I am in awe every time I see one."

"They are amazing, sister, and the one we build in the cavern will allow us to convert more males," second sister said, telling her what she'd want to hear.

"I've sent third sister on another gathering. This time she'll be bringing the biggest group of males yet for conversion. And we'll begin building the holding facilities and Meta-gates around this planet soon."

"That is good news, sister. Shall we head over to the excavation site, to check on progress?"

"Yes, let's do that. I'm looking forward to seeing it."

"If we go through the facility, I can make sure all the warriors for the gathering are in place and ready for when third sister gets here."

"Good idea."

Fourth sister had done her job. All the warriors were there, positioned and waiting to abuse and subdue the unsuspecting human males as they forced them off the shuttle and into the serum room.

"Everything is ready, sister."

"Let's not waste time. Let's get over to the mountain. I want to be back for the first shuttle landing."

It was quite a long walk, and she struggled to keep up battling the wind and rain as first sister marched on. She couldn't feel her fingers or nose when they got there.

The head construction worker met them at the entrance. "Good morning, council sisters. It is an honor to see you, first council sister." He bowed low.

"I have to commend you. Your work so far has been exemplary. I am impressed."

"Thank you, first council sister. The new workers are fast learners, and highly productive. Can I show you our progress?"

"Yes, do."

"As you can see, we've excavated this large atrium area with the stairs in the center going down to the cavern level. You and the other council sisters can enter the cavern from here."

They walked over to the stairs and started down.

"Forgive the noise and smell, council sisters. We are removing rock to create the cavern."

Saws, drills, plasma, and laser cutters sliced and vaporized the rock. While other workers cleared debris. It was going to be huge and growing in front of their eyes.

"Where is fourth council sister?"

"I do not know, first council sister. She was here," he said, looking around.

"I'll find her, sister," second sister said.

"I'm here, sisters," she said, putting a plasma cutter down and taking off a protective mask.

"Why are you working?" first sister asked.

"I want to get some experience using the equipment, sister. I saw no harm in it."

"You are a council sister. You do not work, you control workers to do it for you. I despair, fourth council sister. How ridiculous you are," she said, staring hard at her.

Fourth sister stared back and would not look away. Second sister stepped in before her defiance caused a fatal escalation. There was only one punishment for challenging a first council sister.

"We should get back, sister," she said, distracting her before she thought of it. "I'm sure third sister will arrive soon."

"Hmmm. Let's leave fourth sister doing what she loves best, digging in the dirt." She sneered and marched away.

Second sister exhaled her relief, glared at fourth sister then ran to catch up with her. They got back to see the first shuttle landing in the secure area.

"I'm sure she thought she was helping by knowing how the equipment worked, sister."

"Well, her actions better further my goals or she'll pay a heavy price. She's lucky you were there and I've got other priorities. Besides, her time will come."

∞

The warriors whipped and beat the males, corralling them towards the door to the serum room. One of them stumbled and fell under the heavy beating. He tried to get up, but it was too late. Two warriors viciously attacked him for falling behind. When they finished, the gaping wound on the back of his head meant that he would never get up again. First sister laughed and third sister smiled from the top of the ramp. Second sister's heart sank.

"Right, I'll leave you to it. I assume you'll be coming to scan the females tomorrow?"

"Yes, sister," she said, unable to take her eyes off the dead human.

"Good, see you then."

Tears welled in her eyes as the sadistic first sister stepped over the body.

With all the males processed and undergoing conversion, she walked back to her shuttle, alone in the dark. Fourth sister was already back.

"Tell me you'll have our tunnel ready in a few days, sister," she said, opening the door to her chambers.

"It will be ready. What's wrong, sister? What's happened?"

"Good. This cannot go on for much longer," she said, before going in and closing the door behind her. She stripped off her robes and stood under the hot shower, hoping the water would wash away the memory of the cold-blooded murder she'd witnessed, and wept.

Neural Blockchain Journal Entry #931

There's been actual progress. The conversion facility runs like clockwork. It's so efficient I can scale up. The excavation and tunnel construction is underway, and in a few days, it will be ready to receive and hold males.

Materials to build the Meta-gates around the planet are tight, but the chief engineer assures me we have enough. I hope so for his sake. Once I have my holding facilities, meta-gates, and a consistent flow of new warriors, she'll have seven more from the harvest - I am so looking forward to that. Then I will expand our fleet with new ships and sisters to captain them for me.

Next on the list is to get the satellite launched. The chief engineer is feeling the pressure now. Which is a shame because stress spoils the flavor of the meat. Everything is moving as I predicted, and once the satellite is online, I'll send for the fleet.

Second sister didn't appreciate the deaths of the three pregnant females, but now she's got six new pets to play with, she'll have to get over it.

First Council Sister - Szateth leader
Advanced planetary research fleet.

Neural Blockchain Journal Entry #099

Senseless murder. I've got to hold it together now, but she's making it harder every day. She enjoyed watching that human male being brutally murdered, and there was nothing I could do about it.

With the cavern being excavated and fourth sister having found a place for our new colony, it's down to her to get it completed as soon as possible. But it's going to take time, and more males are going to suffer before it's ready.

I'm going to give her another focus - the females. I'm going to let her see how they evolve. Then she'll see how important they are. I want to know what her plans are for them after they give birth - I'm worried about that.

If I can get her to focus on something other than warrior conversion, even for a short time, I can stall the process, giving fourth sister time to build what we need for Project Residentz to succeed. Pregnant females are the best option for that. We are going to need allies if the project is to remain undetected. Fortunately, her threats and demands alienate people, which will make recruitment simpler. Not too much longer now, before I can save our race.

Second council Sister

Advanced planetary research fleet.

Thirteen

Assassination, escape, and an unexpected ally.

"Warmer weather at last," fourth sister said, putting her thick outer robes in her closet. *First sister was right, I do like digging in the dirt, but not for the reason she thinks.* Over the last few months, she has been doing everything possible to make Project Residentz a reality. Looking at the callouses on her hands, she chuckled to herself. *If only she knew,* she thought.

She heard a knock. "I'm going up to the ship for the council meeting and to check on the females," second sister said through the door. "Do you need me to pass on any messages or anything?"

"Well, as I'm no longer welcome to attend her meetings of self-worship, could you ask the commander for more construction and shielding materials, sister? We're taking a lot more material from the forest than I'd like to build shelters, and we mustn't thin it too much, or we risk exposure, but the colony needs expanding."

"I will. I have a feeling she's going to give the go-ahead for the rest of the holding facilities and the Meta-gates to be built, which means a lot more material stored in the warehouse."

"She knows the cavern is big enough to hold a lot more males."

"I know, and I don't like it. It means a lot more suffering too. So far, with her enthusiasm for the females and their progress, I've kept her distracted enough to keep the number of gatherings down."

"You've done an amazing job to keep her looking the other way, sister, while I've gotten some males to the colony. Thanks to the P9R, they are easy to teach and train. They build everything, and are becoming effective warriors."

"Thank you. But it's not enough, I need to save more, and she's got something else in mind for the females once they've given birth. They are nearing their time, but she won't tell me what it is. I'm worried about it, to be honest."

"Maybe we can get them to the colony, too?"

"I will certainly try, though getting them off the ship would be difficult."

"Something else to ask the commander about then."

"You could be right. I'll pass on your message, sister, and see you tonight."

She stood at the bottom of the ramp, waiting for the shuttle from the ship to land. She shook her head, her mind unable to come up with anything that first sister might have planned for them. As it came to rest and the ramp lowered, she walked over. The pilot welcomed her onboard, and she flicked him an acknowledging smile. *What could it be?* Her mind poured over past comments and conversations on the flight. As the shuttle docked, she had nothing.

"Welcome aboard, second council sister," the commander said, meeting her as she stepped off the ramp. "It's a pleasure to see you again."

"Ah, commander, can you arrange more construction and shielding materials for fourth council sister?"

"Yes, of course. Although..." he said, looking around to see if anyone was within earshot. "Although shielding is becoming harder to get."

"We need it, you know why. As soon as you can, then. And I may ask you for my favor soon, commander."

"Yes, second council sister. Whatever I can do to help."

She gave him a weak smile and left the hangar for the meeting. *Fourth sister is right,* she thought as first sister congratulated herself on the success of the warrior conversion program. Her megalomania was hard to listen to, but she applauded with her other sisters in all the right places to keep her happy. The last item on the agenda was her order for the additional holding facilities and Meta-gates to be built. She stood and applauded with the rest.

As the clapping died and the sisters began filing out, first sister called to her. "Stay, second sister."

The other sisters glanced at her. She smiled as they passed her.

"How are the females?" first sister said, once the chamber had cleared.

"I was just going to see them, sister. Would you like to accompany me?" she asked.

"No, I've better things to do. I need to get my satellite launched."

"I see. Well, I'll give you a report once I've spoken to them."

"They must be ready for their transfusion, yes?"

"I'll establish that today, sister. We have enough donated blood?"

"Yes, but check anyway. It's in the large storage unit."

"Very good, sister."

"Tell me, were the other three like these? Could they speak? Were they intelligent?"

"Yes, and I was going to surprise you with them. Then they fell ill, and you suggested the solution. Which I think is a genius call, sister."

"The blood should give them the strength to carry and birth our new sisters. Then we'll..." She looked around. "Then we'll prepare to get you the rest. Now, I must get on."

"Can I ask what you plan to do with them once they've given birth?"

"It's something, well, more of an experiment, really," she said with an excited smile. "You don't need to worry about it. Leave me now."

"Yes, sister." She faked a smile back, bowed, and left. *What, what is it?* She asked herself, walking to her lab.

"Good morning ladies," she said, opening the door to their room. "How are you all today?" When they didn't answer right away, she knew. "Are any of you having abdominal pains?"

"Yes, but they are not too painful."

"May I check your heart rates and blood pressure?"

None of them objected. It was something they were used to having checked. She noted the results on their chart and she could see from the results it was time to talk to them about the transfusions. "Ladies, your blood pressure is high. That, coupled with abdominal pains, is something we've seen before."

"You mean there were others of us pregnant before?"

"Yes, three of you. Do you remember them?"

"Vaguely, then they disappeared. We assumed you'd moved them elsewhere."

"I wish that was the case. They experienced the symptoms you're exhibiting now, and sadly, passed away."

"Are we going to die too?" one of them said. There was a nervous murmur.

"No ladies, don't worry. We know what happened and know how to treat you. At this stage of your pregnancy, your babies exert too much strain on your human systems and it needs help to provide them with what they need. If we don't, your bodies will sacrifice themselves for them. We need to give you the strength to provide what your babies are demanding. They are half Szatethess, and that half is stronger and more dominant than your human half, so you need blood from a Szatethess, from us, the council sisters, which will give you the strength you and your babies need to survive and thrive."

"Your blood will stop the pain?"

"Yes, and it will help prepare your bodies for giving birth in the next few months."

"And when do we need it, second sister?"

"I'd like to give it to you now before the pains get worse and your blood pressure gets any higher."

They flicked nervous glances at each other.

"It's perfectly safe, ladies," she said. "You'll sit, or lie down if you prefer. I'll put a small needle into a vein in your arm or hand connected to a tube and a bag of our blood. The blood runs through the tube and into your vein. It's safe, painless, and will give you what you and your babies need."

They looked at one another again and sat down.

"Good, thank you, ladies. I'll get what you need and do the transfusions now."

The head kitchen worker came into the lab as she was taking the bags of blood out of the storage unit. "Good morning, second council sister. It's nice to see you."

"Yes, and you. Thank you once again for taking good care of the females."

"It's my pleasure, second council sister, and have you seen the others in the cell are doing better now, too?"

"I haven't, no, not yet," she said, putting the bags of blood in the warmer. "But that is good news. Thank you."

"I'll put the food in with the pregnant females first, then in with the others."

"Wait, I'll take it into the pregnant females. You take it into the others if you would."

"Of course, second council sister," he said, taking the bottom trays of food off his trolley. They turned their noses up at the smell of cooked meat.

The timer on the blood warmer pinged. "Thank you. Your work is more vital than you know, and I commend you for it," she said, taking the bags of blood out and placing them on a tray next to tubes and needles. "Please keep it up, and inform me of any changes, as before."

"Yes, second council sister," he said, bowing. The food almost slid off the tray.

"I'll see you again," she said, walking into their room.

He heard her snigger as he slid the tray in through the cell door hatch.

She hung a bag of blood for each female, attached a tube and needle, and slid it into a vein of their choosing. She stayed while the bags emptied into their arms. "How are you all feeling?" she said, putting the empty bags and used needles in a bin.

They looked wide eyes at one another again. "Good. I think, strong, and starving. We need food," one of them said.

The others licked their lips.

"Hungry? I have what you want."

They moved to the edge of their seats, mouths open, poised, and ready. She smiled. It reminded her of how a feeding frenzy takes over.

"I will see you in a few days," she said, putting the tray of raw meat on the table. She closed the door behind her, then looked back to see what they would do. They pounced, biting, tearing, and gorging themselves.

They'll be fine, she thought to herself as she left the lab.

She called first sister. "I have given the females the blood transfusion, sister. It was time. The effect of our blood was immediate. They are more and more like us every day."

"That's good news. And the idiot engineers have finally completed my satellite. It will launch later today if you'd like to stay around and watch?"

"I would, sister. It will give me a chance to catch up with our sisters and monitor the females over the day."

"Make sure they are healthy and happy. I need them in top condition."

"Yes, sister. Call me when it's time for the launch, and I will join you on the top observation deck."

"I will expect you then. An all-around successful day," she said, chirping.

A happy first sister meant the atmosphere on the ship was lighter than it had been. She felt it walking through the corridors to the sisters chambers. The crew was openly chatting to each other, not whispering or falling silent when a council sister approached. It was a refreshing change.

Apart from third sister, who was organizing the transport of the materials for the holding facilities and Meta-gates, the others were there. "Good afternoon, sisters," she said.

"Good afternoon sister," they replied together.

"How are you all? It's been a while since we've spent any time together."

"Things have improved, sister," fifth sister said.

"As long as things are going her way, anyway," ninth sister said.

"She's got third sister doing all the running around for her, which keeps her out of our hair at any rate," sixth sister said.

There was a collective laugh.

"Her plans for galactic domination are moving forward?" ninth sister asked.

"You mean her new warriors? Oh, yes, a steady stream of recruits is coming out of the facility now."

"Yes, we're seeing more of them up here, hovering around her. And I hear her communications satellite is ready?"

"Yes, that's right. It's launching today."

"Well, the sooner our fleet gets here, and we can go to other ships, the better."

The others agreed.

"Will you stay and eat with us, sister?" sixth sister said.

"I would be delighted to thank you."

Seventh sister clapped, and a troop of kitchen workers appeared with trays of meat. They looked nervous, placing the trays on the table surrounded by loungers, each one occupied with a powerful, hungry council sister. They placed the food and scurried away.

For the next few hours, they talked, gorged, and drank before falling asleep. The kitchen workers waited for them to rest before clearing away the gnawed bones.

Second sister woke with a satisfied smile. There was no doubt when things went wrong for first sister and her attitude changed, it would spark a mutiny. It would take them all to overthrow her, and as she looked at them sleeping, knowing what first sister had planned, she doubted they had enough time left. She sighed.

Her communicator distracted her from the unease. It was first sister.

"Yes, sister," she said, answering the call.

"We are ready to launch. I will start the countdown from the observation deck. If you come now, you won't miss it."

"Yes, sister. I'm coming now."

She looked at her sisters, as if for the last time, before tip-toeing out.

"You're just in time. There, look," first sister said, pointing to the back of the ship. A few seconds later, a dark knife-shaped object rose above a column of white smoke. "There it goes. Finally, I'll be able to see where all the human tribes are right across this wretched planet, and summon the fleet."

"Congratulations, sister."

"This is a great day. I'll be able to build my army faster and reunite with our other sisters here. I've decided we will make this planet our new home."

"You mean to stay?"

"Why not? I'll convert all the human males into warriors. There's more than enough to replenish and even grow my army. With all the ships here, I'll deploy them across the network of planets, controlling and expanding from here."

"And what of the females? What do you have planned for them?"

"It's going to surprise even you." She laughed.

"How, sister?"

"You'll see. And as this is going to be our new home, we need to warm the climate. I've decided I want to live on the surface. I'll get the chief engineer to build the energy generators and climate converters."

"I wish you'd tell me, sister."

"All in good time. Now, leave me. I have to make sure third sister has organized the materials and warriors for the holding facilities and Meta-gates."

"Yes, sister. Congratulations again."

She left feeling sick. *I knew it. She's going to take them all, and now she wants to terraform the planet as well.*

She walked faster. The sense of urgency burning. It was quiet in the lab when she got there, but she had to know the females were alright after their transfusions. She knocked before going into their room.

"I'm sorry to disturb you, ladies. Can I take your blood pressure again before I leave you to rest, please?"

They smiled, seeing the concern on her face, and lined up without a fuss. Their blood pressure was excellent, and none of them were experiencing any abdominal pain. Their heart rates and moods were strong, and wishing them goodnight, she headed for the hangar.

The pilot welcomed her on board. "Take me back, pilot," she said, sitting in a passenger seat. There was a knot in her stomach as the shuttle descended. She stood at the top of the ramp as the shuttle landed, desperate to get off and tell fourth sister of first sister's plans, and that the satellite could scan the surface. They were going to have to take extra precautions and Project Residentz was going to have to save more.

As it lowered, she hitched up her robes and strode across the ground faster than first sister marched straight into the conference room. "We're about to have a big problem, sister," she said, looking over the area of the map that hid the colony. "The satellite she's just launched can scan the planet's surface. It might find the colony."

"I see. Hmm, we'll have to boost the shielding. I'll get onto the commander to get more." Fourth sister sensed her distress.

"Can't we go underground? We've got the equipment."

Fourth sister stared in thought. "I'll have to survey the area and check the soil. We may have an issue with supporting and shoring any excavation, and if there are any water courses underground or inflow from surface water, we'll have a problem. If we sever or damage tree root systems, they could fall, exposing the surface. It makes sense to go underground, but it might be too dangerous, and it would need more time and construction materials."

"You've learned so much in the metaverse, sister. I trust your judgment. Let me know, but we need to move fast. The satellite comes online in a couple of days."

"I'll contact the commander and see when he can get what we need. We'll fly over and scan the area to see if it's possible."

"There's something else. She's planning on making this planet our new home. She's going to send for the fleet, take *all* the males, and terraform, so we can live on the surface."

"But if she takes all the males, we'll be back in the same situation we're in now in a few years."

"Exactly. It's bad, sister, and she still won't tell me what she's going to do with the females once our new sisters are born. Whatever it is, that won't be good either. I don't know how to stop her."

"I do."

"How?"

"Don't worry about it, sister."

"I need to sleep. I'm going to retire. It's been an exhausting day. I'll let you make your call."

"Leave it to me, sister. I'll sort things out."

"Thank you," she said. She smiled, leaving her to call the commander.

She fell asleep the moment her head touched the pillow, but the nightmare came back with a vengeance. The fleet, the beaten males, the screaming females, with first sister in the background laughing and shouting for more. She woke in a cold sweat, knowing she had to stop her.

It was the early hours of the morning, there was no way she was going to get back to sleep. She was too restless to even try. *Maybe a drink will help me sleep.* She poured herself a large glass and swallowed a mouthful. The liquid warmed her insides as it went down. From the window, she saw a shuttle land and fourth sister walk off. She threw on a robe and stood at the top of the ramp. She couldn't wait to hear the results of the survey.

"Oh, sister. I wasn't expecting to see you awake. Everything alright?" fourth sister said, surprised to see her standing there.

"Yes, just a bad dream, and I want to hear the results of the survey. I've poured myself a drink. Would you like one?"

"Yes, I need one. It's not good news, sister. The soil and structures are not suitable for excavation."

"Damn. What do we do now?"

"I don't know, sister. The commander said the shielding material is in very short supply, and it's getting harder for him to get any. We're going to have to put Project Residentz on hold before they discover the colony."

"But she will not stop the gatherings. There will be many more, especially now she's ordered the other holding facilities and Meta-gates to be built. There must be something we can do."

"Maybe it's time to consider an alternative solution, sister."

"What do you mean?"

"I mean a direct replacement. You for her, and there's only one way that can happen."

"You mean a coup? Or are you suggesting an - assassination?"

"I do. It can be done."

"I don't want to know. But whatever you do, it needs to be done soon. Third sister is getting materials, equipment, and warriors ready to build the other facilities around the planet. They'll start in a day or so and be finished in a week."

"We already have a plan."

"By we, you mean the commander?"

"Do you want to know?"

"No."

"Leave it to us then."

"As we can't go underground, we could look for another site for a new colony. When we find one, you'll need to survey it to make sure it's suitable. Hopefully, there'll be enough time. Then we'll have options."

"That's a good idea."

They clinked their glasses, studied the map, and chose another site. Silently, they both knew which option was best.

∞

"Ah, there you are," first sister said, meeting third sister in the corridor on her way to the engineering department. "Have you got the construction materials ready to take down to the warehouse?"

"Good morning, sister. Yes, I am on my way to the hangar now to supervise the storage."

"Good. I'm about to send for the fleet. It's going to be a good day. Report your progress when you're back."

"Yes, sister. It will be good for all of us to be together again."

"I'll expect your report later," first sister said. The sound of her sandals clapping on the floor was lighter, more joyous, than their usual heavy marching slap.

"Are we ready, chief engineer?" she said, swinging open the door to engineering.

He dropped his pen. "Oh," he said, picking it up and looking up at her. "Y-yes, first council sister. Sorry, yes, please come this way."

Her presence made everyone nervous, just the way she liked it.

"Is it online now?"

"I thought you might like to bring it online and send the first message, first council sister."

"Wonderful. Yes, I would."

"If I might suggest you send our position as a text message first, the other council sisters will have a hard copy of it before making a voice call."

"Very well. Let's get started."

On the monitor she could see the satellite holding a near-polar orbit, waiting for instructions.

"You bring it online here, first council sister," he said, pointing to the switch. "Type your message and hit the send key."

"Yes, I've got it."

She flipped the switch and seconds later - *online* - flashed on the monitor. The message she typed was simple, instructing all ships in the fleet to converge on her position in the Orion arm of this spiral galaxy. The key made a satisfying *click* as she pressed it - *sending message* - flashed on the monitor.

"Now I want to speak to them. I assume I can call them all at once?"

"Of course, first council sister. Just select 'all' on the keyboard, then transmit, and speak into the microphone."

As instructed, she tapped the keys to call them all. She waited, but nothing happened.

A bright flash stabbed out the side of the satellite, then - *offline* - flashed in red on the monitor.

"What is this, chief engineer?"

"I don't understand," he said. "May I run a diagnostic, first council sister?"

She stood aside, glaring. The engineers, watching, backed away.

"I don't understand. It worked in all the simulations," he said. His fingers frantically typed instructions on the keyboard, and she took a step closer to him.

"Well," she said. "Can I call my sisters or not?"

He could feel her breath on his neck behind him. It was hot and heavy.

"Well, chief engineer."

"I apologize first council sister. A call is not possible. The explosion destroyed the communications array and damaged the observation array. But your text message got transmitted. I don't understand, it was perfect during..."

"That's disappointing, chief engineer. How long before they receive the text message?"

"I'm not sure, first council sister.," he said, his voice wobbling. "A transmission into deep space degrades and slows the-"

"HOW LONG!"

He punched some keys. His whole body shook. "Fifteen thousand years, first council sister," he said, bowing low.

"W what? You mean to tell me I can't communicate with my council sisters because you couldn't do one simple thing? I needed that satellite. I needed my sisters here so we can send warriors and expand our race. You've prevented that, Chief Engineer. Now I've found the resource I need for my army, you're telling me they won't hear about it for thousands of years? You may well have just killed us all."

She growled and ground her teeth. He lifted his head, and the color drained from his face as she grinned. "I am so sorry, first council sister."

"So, I've got a chunk of useless metal floating around that might take a picture or two of the planet's surface if it feels like it. Tell me, chief engineer, what am I supposed to do with it?"

Paralyzed with fear, he couldn't answer.

"Send me two warriors to the engineering department," she said into her communicator.

"I'll start again, redouble my efforts. I won't rest until you can call your sisters." The words spewed from his mouth as two large warriors appeared. The other engineers buried their heads in paperwork or stared at monitors.

"First council sister, please..."

"Take him," she said. "Guess we're going to find out if you can dance after all." She laughed.

The others ignored his screams as they dragged him away.

"You," she said, pointing to a startled engineer coming out of the clean room. He froze on the spot from the force of her voice. "You will be my new chief engineer. Now, get the long-range communications working on this ship."

He hadn't seen the chief being hauled away. "Oh, err, yes, first council sister."

There was a deathly silence as she flung open the door. Her heavy march matched her mood, and everyone held their breath until she'd gone.

"Prepare him for my entertainment tonight," she said to the warriors, before turning down the corridor that took her to the hangar.

"Yes, first council sister," they said, knowing exactly what that meant. So did the ex-chief engineer. He soiled himself.

She didn't run anywhere, but her angry marching pace increased, determined to get to the hangar before third sister left for the surface. The shuttle's ramp was closing as she got there.

"Hold that shuttle, commander," she said with a growl.

He contacted the pilot, instructing him to stand by, and the engines powered down.

The ramp lowered, and third sister walked down. "What's the hold-up, commander?"

"That would be me."

"I apologize, sister. I didn't see you there."

"Open your eyes then. You should be mindful of who's around you at all times."

"Yes, sister," third sister said, knowing better than to say anything else.

"Good. Shall we go? I'm coming to make sure this day doesn't turn out to be a total disaster. Come on," she said, marching up the ramp.

Third sister followed without question. They sat in silence on the flight down. Third sister could hear her grinding her teeth and shivered at her rage. She hit the open button, and the ramp lowered as the shuttle touched down. "Get these materials stored," she said, without looking at her

"Yes, sister."

She marched across the sludge, towards second sister's shuttle, ignoring the mud sticking to the bottom of her robe. Fourth sister saw her coming.

"First sister is here," she said through the door of second sister's chambers. Then stood at the top of the ramp to greet her.

"This is an unexpected pleasure, sister," she said, as first sister walked up the ramp.

"I have no time for you. Where is she?"

Her dismissive attitude stung, and she replied in kind. "What do you want her for?"

"None of your business. Tell me where..."

"I'm here, sister," second sister said, appearing from her chambers.

"I need to speak with you. Alone."

Fourth sister snorted and walked away.

She waited for her to leave, then said, "I cannot call the fleet."

"What? Why?"

"My satellite, the idiot chief engineer built, exploded when I tried to call. They don't know where we are, or about the resource we've found."

"You mean the males?"

"What else?"

"So we've no way of communicating with our other sisters?"

"That's what I said, didn't I? It was his last mistake. Why am I surrounded by idiots? Can you tell me that?"

"What about the ship's long-range communications array?"

"Damaged by radiation. I have told the new chief engineer to get it fixed, or else he'll end up the same way as the last one."

"I understand." She grinned.

"Understand this." She exhaled, and for a moment, looked defeated. "We're cut off, sister, incommunicado, out of reach, lost."

"If you look at it a different way, sister, it's an opportunity for the male species to proliferate. What are a few thousand now, could turn into millions, if not billions, in the future? You'll have a virtually endless supply to tap into."

"What are you talking about? Don't be a fool. You're talking about waiting thousands of years and hoping, hoping their species explode in number, to make them useful to me. Are you crazy? No, better to take them all now, leave this place, and go look for our sisters."

"But sister, the females can carry and give birth to Szatethess, here, now. They can save our species. Surely it's better to stay to develop the humans and warm the planet so we can live here until we have enough to leave?"

"No, I want all the males. I can't afford to let my network of planets go uncontrolled for thousands of years. They'll easily overwhelm my diminished army and gain independence if left all that time. I want my warriors now. I'll put down any insurrection first, then we'll search for another planet like this one. There are thousands of planets with life forms out there. That's what we're going to do. Build the holding facilities and Meta-gates Then I'll harvest the others and have the females give me new sisters, not ones inherited from the last first council sister, ones I control. Then we leave."

"But we'll be back in this same dire situation if we do that, sister. Surely you see that?"

"What I see is another attempt at someone trying to undermine my authority, and a sister not doing what she's ordered to do. Is that what you're doing? Are you disobeying a direct order?"

"Of course not, sister. But it's my job to question your thoughts, as the second council sister. I would not, however, disobey an order."

"Good. You have your orders."

She looked to see if there was any recognition or understanding of the situation they were in. There was nothing, no emotion. She had dead eyes.

"Apologies. I thought you'd be gone by now," fourth sister said, walking into the main chamber.

First sister bared her teeth. "And get this idiot to help you?"

"You have insulted me for the last time. You should have more respect for me. I am still a council sister. - I reject you. You are a pathetic excuse for a first council sister. I call for a vote of confidence with the council."

Second sister stood between them. "Sisters, please, this is not seemly..."

"As is your right," first sister said, more calmly than expected. "It is also my right to suggest the method of your punishment."

"It is."

"Tomorrow then. I will convene the council sisters at noon."

"There is no need for this, sister. I'm sure this planet is affecting fourth sister's thinking."

She slammed her fist on the table. "It is too late. The vote has been called for, and I will see you both in council chambers at noon tomorrow."

She spun and barged passed fourth sister, almost knocking her off her feet. "I will pray for you," she said, as fourth sister regained her balance.

"And I for you," she said, leaning on the conference table.

First sister huffed her derision and walked off the shuttle back toward third sister who was overseeing the unloading and storing of the construction materials.

"Now we have a third option for getting rid of her," fourth sister said, rubbing her shoulder. "I have your vote, don't I? I know I have the others."

"Of course, sister."

She watched her march across the mud from the main chamber window and frowned. *How is she so confident? She's almost swaggering.*

"How much longer? I want to get off this rock. I've got things to prepare," first sister said.

"The last of the materials are being stored in the warehouse now, sister. About five more minutes."

"Good. Let's get going." She stood at the bottom of the ramp.

Second sister watched her speak into her communicator. *None of what just happened has bothered her in the least.* Third sister secured the warehouse doors and walked back. They looked over, then boarded. It didn't take off. *This isn't right, she's planning something.*

A troop of warriors appeared, led by the training officer. They boarded. The ramp closed, and the shuttle took off. A feeling of dread washed over her as the shuttle rose out of sight.

"Right after the vote, I'll recommend they elect you first council sister," fourth sister said.

"If you think it's best, sister. Thank you." She shuddered.

They didn't speak about it for the rest of the day. Fourth sister acted like the result was a foregone conclusion, but she knew first sister better. She saw the odd way they looked over at her shuttle and the squad of warriors. She had something planned.

She didn't sleep well, the nightmare, not knowing what was going to happen with the females, and now a leadership vote she was sure first sister would rig. Daylight couldn't come soon enough. When it did, the morning dragged and as the shuttle arrived, "are you sure about this?" she asked.

"By the end of today, sister, everything will have changed."

I hope you're right; she thought to herself, fastening her council robes.

With certainty, fourth sister walked across to the waiting shuttle, with a not-quite-so-certain second sister.

When the shuttle landed, a worried-looking commander greeted them. The 'confidence vote' had spread through the crew. "Welcome aboard, council sisters."

"Thank you, commander," the fourth sister said.

"I wish you the very best, today fourth council sister."

She smiled, acknowledging the sentiment. Second sister gave him an expressionless glance.

They strode into the council chambers. The sisters were in their usual seats around the table, waiting. They didn't look up or greet them when they sat down. Warriors had positioned themselves behind each sister, and once the door closed, blocked the exit. The room was silent. *Something's wrong,* second sister said to herself, looking around the room. The others, wide-eyed and pale, didn't speak or smile, and the smug look on first sister's face confirmed her fears. *She'd got to them!*

Third sister rose. "Thank you for your attendance council sisters," she said with authority. "I bring this council to order." She hammered the gavel onto the block.

The loud knock had the warriors snap to attention, each one focussing on a council sister.

"Fourth council sister has called for a vote of no confidence in first council sister's leadership. It is a simple yes or no vote. On the ballot paper, the question asked is - are you confident in first council sister leadership ability? You check the relevant answer box. Are there questions?"

"Why are these warriors here?" fourth sister said.

"They are here to ensure a fair vote, sister," third sister said.

"This is highly irregular. It should be a private ballot." She looked at her sisters for support, but none of them said anything.

"None of us will see which way a council sister votes - Continue, third sister," first sister said.

"These two warriors will now hand each of you a ballot paper and wait while you fill in your answers."

They went to fifth sister first. The warrior behind her took a step closer. Surrounded, there was only one safe option - she checked, 'yes.'

In her naivete, fourth sister couldn't see what was happening, she assumed they'd follow Szateth council law. It was unthinkable to do otherwise. But to second sister, it was obvious. This was a setup.

Once the warriors had been to each sister, they stood back, while third sister counted the votes. It didn't take long.

"There is a definite result," she said, handing first sister the ballot papers. "By an overwhelming majority, the council sisters here present have unanimously voted their *complete confidence* in first council sister's leadership ability."

Fourth sister slumped, shocked. Then it became clear. She jumped out of her chair. "Are you all serious? How can you even think she's a responsible, and now even an honest, leader?"

"Warriors, secure her," first council sister said, squeezing and shaking the ballot papers at her. "Lock her in the Brig until I decide how to punish her."

Four warriors surrounded her. "Don't you dare touch me? I am a council sister," she said. "I'll walk there myself." They stepped back. She stood, smoothed her robes, and looked at each of her sisters. "You know I'm right. You will all regret this." She knocked her chair aside.

You don't know how right you are, second sister thought, not able to look at her.

"Take her away," first sister said, standing to assert her authority.

Fourth sister spat on the table, before being escorted out of the chamber. "Now that's taken care of," first sister said. "Does anyone have anything to say?"

Second sister glanced around the table. None spoke.

"This council meeting is closed," third sister said, hammering the block again.

The warriors stood to attention as the sisters rose and filed out in silence. Second sister headed straight for the hangar. A creeping, toxic atmosphere chased her through the ship's corridors as she hurried away.

Somehow word of fourth sister's arrest had already reached the hangar, and the commander looked panicked when she got there. He kept up with her as she walked to the shuttle. "You know then?" she said, whispering.

He nodded.

"Help her. Can you?"

"It's perilous, but I will."

"Good. Get her to the surface. Call me when you're on your way. I'll prepare the hidden room in the warehouse and meet you there. Make sure no one sees you. No one, commander, and do it quickly," she said, walking up the ramp.

"Yes, second council sister. I will."

She ordered the pilot to leave immediately. First council sister had set it up so she could harvest fourth sister first. She had to admire her devious mind. *She's good, she's really good.* Thoughts of self-preservation became a priority. She already had a plan, which would have to be put in place with the help of someone who owed her a favor.

The shuttle left the hangar. She was going to need to speed things up if she was to save herself, the Szateth, and the humans. *The colony is perhaps not the safest place now. If the commander doesn't get her away, especially if first sister sweetened her harvesting with some torture first, she might reveal its existence and location.* Her mind raced for an alternative.

In her shuttle's main chamber, she poured herself a drink to think about what happened. Alone, it felt different from when her sister was there, her noise and terrible singing breaking the peace. The silence felt heavy. She could feel the pressure of it in her ears, as she strained for the comfort of sound. The buzzing of her communicator did nothing to make her feel better. It was first sister.

"Yes, sister."

"You left without a word. I was hoping to speak with you."

"I apologize, sister, but without fourth sister, there is a lot to organize for the construction of your other facilities and Meta-gates."

"I appreciate your sense of urgency. I wanted to ask you if there was anything I needed to know about fourth sister's activities?"

"Like what?"

"There have been reports of her and the commander talking alone."

"About what?"

"Perhaps you can tell me."

"All I can think of is that they would talk about the transportation of construction materials and mining equipment."

"Hmm. Nothing else?"

"Nothing that I'm aware of, sister."

"Very well. I'll expect you'll be building the other facilities and Meta-gates soon, then?"

"Yes, sister. First thing tomorrow morning."

The call ended. *Meta-gates. Of course, I'll build two of my own.*

It had been a big day. It saw the loss of fourth sister, the beginning of first sister's plans for human males, and the beginning of her plans to save them. She'd had fourth sister take all the risks to get Project Residentz started. She had done well, but her carelessness meant she overplayed her hand, allowing first sister to harvest her, without the other sisters suspecting a thing. Now she knew the lengths first sister would go to and how calculating she was, she knew how to play her. She took herself to bed, knowing she was about to throw herself in harm's way. Tomorrow was going to be another big day.

∞

She rose early, calling the head construction worker to her shuttle, and up to the ship to send one down.

"Gather a crew of workers, materials, and warriors ready to build the first holding facility," she said, meeting him at the ramp. "The shuttle is on its way."

"Immediately, second council sister."

"Oh, and I need a list of materials for constructing a facility and a Meta-gate. Do you have one?"

He took a page off his clipboard. "Please, second council sister, have mine," he said, handing it to her.

"Perfect, thank you."

He bowed and left, jogging across to the compound.

They were waiting at the landing pad as the shuttle arrived. She marveled at their efficiency as they loaded the shuttle. They were onsite before midday.

With a Meta-gate, they could go anywhere in the linked network instantly. The process was simple. You took what you needed to build a Meta-gate to the location where you want one, then connect it to the Metaverse, add it to the Meta-gate network, and do the same with another. She planned two of her own. One at the forest colony, and the other at the location she and fourth sister had chosen together.

Once the workers had unloaded, and the warriors set up guard posts, she had the pilot fly her back. "How long until we get to the warehouse?" she asked.

"About two hours, second council sister," he said.

She put her hand in her pocket and felt the list. "Once we get back, return to the ship."

"Yes, second council sister."

Not knowing how long she would have, as soon as she left the shuttle and it took off, she unfolded the list and entered the warehouse. With the parts she needed for her Meta-gates in the hidden room, she covered the door. She was checking to make sure no one could see it when she heard a voice behind her.

"Can I help you with anything, second council sister?"

She spun. Relieved it was a worker, she said, "no, just doing an inventory. Why are you here?"

"We are ready for more construction material at the site, second council sister. We're here to get it."

"Already?"

"Yes, the facilities are basic, second council sister. It doesn't take long to construct them."

"Right, well, carry on then."

He clapped and half a dozen workers filed in, got what they needed, and followed her out. She returned to her shuttle and watched the workers enter the Meta-gate room in the living compound. *If there was a Meta-gate in the warehouse, the workers would get the materials to the site faster, she'll like that. And I could move what I need unseen. I'll suggest it,* she thought. With the planet survey third sister had done on the conference table, with the locations for the other facilities marked, she could see they were in the planet's warmest regions. The location she and fourth sister had chosen for their colony was remote and among cold, snow-capped mountains on the largest continent, far from the others. *She'll never go there.*

She was going to need help to build her Meta-gates and the new colony's buildings. *There was the commander,* of course, but she knew his true nature. He would betray her to save himself without thinking twice, besides she hated him for raping and killing one of her females. He would prove himself useful if he got fourth sister out, but nothing after that, after that his time was at an end. *Who else was there?*

She called first sister.

"What is it?" she asked when she answered.

"We will complete the first facility by the end of the day, sister."

"Well, that's good news. Station warriors there, and tell the training officer to make sure they're ready to carry out the gatherings. Start the next one as soon as this one is complete."

"Can I suggest we move the Meta-gate from the living compound to the warehouse, sister? If we do that, it'll speed up the supply chain, as the workers won't have to collect and carry materials to the compound. They can pick what they need and go straight back from inside the warehouse."

"Hmm, yes, I agree. Get it moved. Anything else?"

"Not for now, sister."

"Keep me up to date. Carry on." She ended the call.

The first part of her plan was in place. To get the Meta-gate moved, she would order the head construction worker to do it.

She found him in the Meta-gate room. It was the end of the day, and the workers were returning. Even though she'd seen the shimmering surface of an open Meta-gate many times, it still mesmerized her. She told him what she wanted him to do as she stared, transfixed.

"We are losing the light, second council sister. Can I move it first thing in the morning?"

"Of course. Inform me once it's done," she said, tearing herself away.

It was almost dark by the time she got back to her shuttle. She shivered, glad to get back into the warmth.

Her communicator buzzed...

"We are on our way, second council sister," the commander said.

She rushed to the warehouse and waited. Moments later, the shuttle's landing gear groaned under a heavy landing. The ramp opened, and fourth sister staggered down. As soon as she was clear, it took off.

She caught a bloodied and bruised fourth sister as she slumped to the floor.

"Oh, sister. What has she done to you?"

She spluttered, blood trickling from her mouth. "She just looked on, laughing while the warriors took it in turns."

"Can you walk, sister? We must get you hidden with the parts in the warehouse."

"Yes, sister."

"Come on then," she said, supporting her weight and helping her to the hidden room.

"You'll be safe here, as long as you remain quiet." She propped her against a wall while she took her robe off and laid it on the floor. "Let me help you, sister," she said, laying her down. "I'll get you food and drink, and I'll bring you a cot to lie in. I'll bring some painkillers, and something for those cuts and bruises."

"Thank you, sister." She coughed and groaned.

"Rest now. We'll get you away to the colony when you can move more easily."

"Hmm." She closed her eyes, wrapped her arms around her bruised ribs, and fell asleep.

First sister had her worked over pretty badly. *Did she tell her about the colony?* She wasn't sure if, or for how long, the colony in the forest would be safe. *She can't stay here.*

She secured the door and slid the racking back to conceal it. There was maybe a day before first sister would be down here tearing the place apart, looking for her. She'd be so mad, she'd organize and join the search herself.

The dark made it easier for her to move about, but she still made sure it was clear before going back to her shuttle. She washed fourth sister's blood off her hands then poured a self a large drink.

Her communicator buzzed...

"Is she safe?" the commander said.

"Yes. For now. We'll need to move her soon."

"The alarm has already sounded. First council sister is furious. She's killed the guards."

"She'll scour the ship first, before coming here. You should keep out of her way, commander."

"I intend to. One more thing. On fourth sister's instructions, I've rigged the fuel cells on the shuttle to explode, so when she comes, she'll be dead before it lands."

"Well, then. I'll encourage her when she calls."

"I'd better go." He closed the call.

There was nothing more she could do. Fourth sister was safe for now, first sister would be beside herself tearing the ship apart, and if the commander has done his job on the fuel cells, which had a sense of poetic justice since it was a fueling mistake that cost him his finger, she would never have to see first sister again. She was right, she thought, *it has been a big day.*

∞

It was early when her communicator woke her. She knew who it was before answering.

"Have you seen her?"

"Seen who, sister?"

"Fourth council sister, she's escaped. I've searched every inch of this ship. She's not here, which means she's there."

"What, how? No, I haven't seen her. I've been asleep all night."

"She had help. Help to get out of the Brig and to the surface. - There will be no mercy."

"I will look around, of course, but I will need help."

"I will be there presently."

"I will wait for you, sister." She closed the call, imagining the blast.

On the ship, it was chaos, with frightened crew, workers, and warriors continuing the search.

"Come with me to the surface. You know your way around the facility better than I do. Have a squad of warriors meet us in the hangar in five minutes," she said, calling third sister.

"Yes, sister."

As she marched to the hangar, she called the training officer on the surface to have him select some warriors to help her with the search. She got to the hangar at the same time as third sister and the squad.

"Let's go," she said.

Out of the corner of her eye, she saw the first officer run in. "First council sister, one moment I must speak with you, now," he said, out of breath.

His insistence surprised her. "What is it, first officer?"

"I need to show you something."

"It can wait, first officer."

"No, first council sister, it can't."

Third sister took a sharp breath. His lack of respect would cause a vicious outburst.

Her movement was a blur, and she was on him. "What did you just say?"

He could feel her hot breath on his face. Somehow, he kept his nerve. "I know who helped her, first council sister," he said. She released him and backed away.

She stared hard. "Really?" she said.

"Yes, first council sister, and I apologize for my lack of manners, but I thought you would want to see this first. In case it gets, err, mislaid before you get back."

"Right," she said. "Sister, take the warriors and begin the search. Send the shuttle back for me."

"Yes, sister."

"Well, first officer, lead the way."

Third sister ordered the warriors onto the shuttle, she followed them, and the first officer led first sister to the hangar's observation room. She watched the shuttle leave.

"Here, first council sister." He pressed play on the hangar's surveillance recordings.

"I see nothing," she said.

"One moment, first council sister, please watch."

Two figures, one struggling to walk, appeared. They were trying to avoid the cameras.

"Had I not changed the angle of this camera when I had it cleaned, they would have got away unseen."

"Who? Who is it?"

She squinted, trying to focus on the faces of the two figures in the shadows. As they got closer to the camera, she saw them. - Fourth council sister, and the commander.

"Where is he?" she said.

"In his quarters, first council sister."

"Take six warriors and bring him to me. I want to..."

A deafening explosion rocked the ship. On the ground, second sister smiled as the shuttle disintegrated. In the observation room, she and the first officer grabbed the table to steady themselves, and on the monitor, a fireball that had once been a shuttle burned itself out.

"Get him, first officer, and take him to the council chambers."

"Yes, first council sister."

She got a string of calls, one after the other, from her sisters onboard, asking what had happened. She told them to meet her in the council chambers immediately. The realization that if she had been on that shuttle, she'd be dead hit her. He'd tried to assassinate her, and she was sure it was fourth sister's idea. She was alone, and for the first time, felt vulnerable. The feeling made her angry, and she called for a warrior escort.

The first officer had saved her life, but there was still the loss of life. Not third sisters, but the life from the egg she wanted to harvest, which upset her more.

If the commander could attempt to kill me, who else might try? She wondered. She'd felt untouchable. That feeling had gone, replaced with something that would make her more dangerous paranoia. The two warriors arrived. "Do not leave my side," she said, and they escorted her to the council chambers.

On the surface, second sister sauntered over to the warehouse. She felt free for the first time since they'd arrived. She would make this their new home, help the humans evolve, teach them, and instead of forcing them, ask them for help to save the Szateth. Here they could live together in peace.

She looked over at the compound. All the warriors and workers, crowded together, were looking up, wondering who was on that shuttle. The training officer came running up.

"Excuse me, second council sister. Do you know who was on that shuttle?"

"No, I was about to call the ship for information and ask if they needed our help."

"We think it was the first council sister, along with some of my warriors."

"Why do you think that, training officer?"

"First sister called me to assemble a team of warriors to help her conduct a thorough search for fourth council sister. She called me a few minutes before the shuttle explosion."

"Let's not jump to any conclusions. We don't know for sure."

"We are ready to help with the search, second council... or should I say, first council sister."

"Let's hold off on that, training officer. Stand your warriors down."

"As you wish, first council sister," he said. He bowed and marched back to the compound.

It was the first time she'd been called first council sister. She liked it.

Her communicator buzzed. *Ah, the news of her death.* With a deep breath, she prepared herself to act shocked.

The caller ID on her communicator read - FIRST SISTER. *What? No - Can't be.* The shock became real. Her mind fought to understand as her communicator buzzed again, demanding attention.

"Sister, thank goodness, you are alive. We feared the worst," she said, answering the call.

"No, thanks to the commander."

Her sudden demotion was crushing, and everything instantly went back to how it was. "You're safe? Who was on board the shuttle?"

"Third sister and some warriors. - I have the commander. I'd invite you up to witness his execution, but I want you, the training officer, and his warriors to search for fourth sister. She's there somewhere. She tried to have me killed, and you have to find her for me."

"Has the commander said anything?" she said, trying to compose herself.

"Not yet. I'll let you know. Start the search and report back when you find her. She's there somewhere."

"Yes, sister. I'm pleased you're..."

The call went dead, as did her hopes for the humans and the Szateth.

Now, instead of celebrating with fourth sister, she had to get her away. There wasn't much time. She had dismissed the training officer, but first sister would have called him by now to start the search.

Sauntering turned into sprinting. No one could see her with fourth sister. There was no one in the warehouse, and she slid the racking to the side to get to the door of the hidden room. She was still asleep.

"Sister," she said, shaking her. "Sister, wake up. You need to move."

"What, what is it?"

"She's not dead. The commander failed, and they're looking for you. Come on. You need to get to the colony." She pulled to help her get up.

She groaned, holding her ribs, and bent forward to escape the pain.

"You have to move, sister. Here, take some more of these." She gave her more painkillers and a glass of water. "Come on, sister."

She needed the hidden room, so she closed the door and slid the racking back, while fourth sister leaned against some sheeting.

"You're going to have to get there yourself."

"You're not coming with me?"

"No, I'm supposed to be searching for you, remember? If I'm with them, I can stall and give you time to get away," she said. She heard voices. It was the training officer with his warriors. They were close. "Now, go sister, and stay at the colony until I come for you."

Fourth sister limped, and holding her ribs, disappeared into the long grass, as the warriors came around to the front of the warehouse. Second sister stood in their path, blocking the view of the direction she'd gone in.

"She isn't in the warehouse."

"Are you sure, second council sister?" the training officer said.

"Quiet sure. Have you checked the facility fully?"

"I believe so, second council sister."

"All the shelters in the compound, my shuttle, the tunnel, and the cavern?"

She could see him thinking. "Well, have you?"

"No, second council sister."

"Quickly then, she's getting away, and you must apprehend her. I will search my shuttle."

He bowed. "Let's go," he said, turning back to the facility.

She looked back to where she last saw her sister. *I bought you a couple more hours.*

Her thought focussed on self-preservation. She needed to know if the commander had told first sister anything. She called her.

"We are still looking, sister. Has the commander given you any information that might help us with the search?"

"Not yet. He's with us now. I'll let you know if he tells me anything."

"Thank you, sister. We'll carry on."

"Good," first sister said, cutting off the call. "Now, commander, tell me who helped you. I know you wouldn't have sabotaged the shuttle without someone forcing you to. Who was it?"

He stood in the corner of the council chamber, naked and shackled. "No one. No one helped me."

The other sisters watched in silence as she probed him for information. With the same calming tone she used just before ripping the throat out of a meal, she lied to him. It was chilling.

"Sure they did. Who was it, commander? Tell me, and I'll let you go."

"No one," he said, looking at his shackled wrists and the stump where his finger used to be.

"Oh, come now, commander, someone must have. I can understand why you'd agree to it. My treatment of you has been excessive. I apologize for that, and in compensation, I'd like to give you what you love - a female, or maybe two, to use as you like."

He looked at her.

"Tell me who forced you to do this, and all this will be over. You want that, don't you, commander?"

"Yes, first council sister," he said and looked down again.

"Well then, tell me, who was it? Was it fourth council sister? I know the two of you were close. Or someone else? Tell me, commander, who made you do it," she heard a fearful murmur from the sister behind her.

He paused, staring at the stump, and remembered the pain. "No one," he said.

"I'm trying to help you here, commander. You could help me root out a traitor. The reward for the one who helps me do that would be substantial."

He looked straight at her, hardening his eyes. "No one. I did it myself."

"Pity," she said, stepping closer to stroke his body. "Are you sure?" He didn't see her draw her knife, and he said nothing else.

She held his stare, then rammed the dagger up, stabbing under his chin, through his mouth, and into his brain. She held him up as he squealed and jerked. Blood poured down her hand, pooling on the floor, and she watched as life left his eyes. He went limp, a dead weight. She pulled the knife out, and his body collapsed to the floor.

The sisters fidgeted as she closed her eyes, savoring the taste of his blood on the blade before casually re-sheathing it. "Someone else is behind this. I will find out who. There will be no mercy," she said with the same calm, chilling voice. She looked at the body, then at the sisters. She'd made her point.

"Have this body cleaned away, sisters," she said, leaving the chamber with her bodyguards.

With the guards stationed outside her private chambers, she sat on her lounger, wondering who or how many of her crew and sisters wanted her dead. *How dare they challenge me? I am the first council sister. Still, you're all going to be harvested soon,* she thought, gripping the edge of the cushions until her knuckles went white. *I will find you.*

She called second sister. "Have you found her?"

"No, sister, not yet. We carried out a thorough search of the compound, the facility, the warehouse, and my shuttle. She's not there."

"She's there somewhere. Find her."

"We will, sister. The training officer sent his warriors to search the tunnel and the cavern. Did the commander give you anything for us to work with?" She squeezed her eyes.

"No, and we won't get anything out of him now. I'm coming down. Maybe I can find ways to motivate them."

"Yes, sister, good idea. Your help would be invaluable. I'll watch for your shuttle."

"I will use the Meta-gate from now on. I will be there shortly." She ended the call.

"Second council sister, are you there?" the training officer said, calling to her from the bottom of the shuttle's ramp.

She appeared at the top, looking down at him.

"She is nowhere, second council sister. We can't find her,".

"Perhaps you can tell first council sister that when she gets here. I'm sure she'll forgive you for your failure."

"She's coming down?"

She took a deep breath, smelling his fear. "Yes, training officer, and I suspect she's in no mood to accept that you've let her get away."

"We'll look everywhere again."

"That would be a good idea. I'll talk to her about how well you've performed so far, and that fourth council sister must have had help to escape your exceptional tracking skills."

"Thank you, second council sister."

"Carry on, training officer."

He bowed and ran back towards the compound to begin again, getting back as first sister came through the Meta-gate with her bodyguards. She didn't see him, but could hear him barking orders to the warriors and workers as she walked up to the shuttle.

Second sister saw her coming and was leaning over the survey map the late third sister had prepared, pretending to be looking for places fourth sister may have gone when she walked in.

"Anything?"

She looked up and saw the warriors standing on either side of her. "No, sister. She may have fled to the mountain, and possibly further beyond after this long a time."

"I doubt it. She's suffering an injury she got in the Brig that would limit her movement."

"Injured, how?"

"A mishap, I was told."

"A mishap? I see."

"It's irrelevant. I want her back in the Brig by nightfall. Am I clear?"

"Yes, sister. The training officer has been very efficient so far. I'm surprised, based on what you've told me, that he hasn't found her. If she couldn't get far, it must be a serious injury?"

"Hmmm, I see what you're saying. It's bad enough to slow her down, for sure. He's an exceptional warrior, so he should be able to find her?"

"Yes, sister. He is."

"And he's found no sign of her?"

"Not any he's mentioned to me, no."

"Hmmm. You know she's had help?"

"I didn't, no. Other than the commander? Who else?"

First sister stared at her, waiting for her to catch up with what she suspected.

"Surely you don't suspect a sister?"

"I don't know. I'm not ruling it out. There's something rotten in the council. But they'll be gone soon enough. Maybe there are others, and you were closest to her."

She could feel her paranoia rising. "Surely, you don't suspect me, sister. Do you?"

She didn't answer.

"I'll speak to the training officer now. Call him here, for me."

There was an awkward silence between them while they waited.

"Report, training officer," first sister said the moment he walked in.

"We haven't been able to find her, first council sister."

"Maybe you don't want to find her?"

"We have searched everywhere, first council sister, more than once. She is not in this facility."

She and her bodyguards closed in on him. "You know how I love to be entertained before a meal, training officer. Can you dance?"

He knew what she meant. "But first council sister, I've always done everything you've asked me to do."

"Except this, the most important task I've set you."

He said nothing.

"You have until dawn, training officer, or I'll have you brought to the ship to explain why you've failed me, and to dance."

He knew if he said anything, the excuse would enrage her more.

"I'll leave you both now, and expect to hear that you have her soon."

Without another word, she and her bodyguards left the shuttle and marched back to the Meta-gate.

The training officer looked at second sister. The expression on their faces questioned their futures.

"I have searched everywhere, second council sister."

"I believe you."

"Why would she turn on me like that? I've done everything she wanted me to do."

"Like spy on fourth council sister and me, you mean?"

"Yes, second council sister. I did that for her. She doesn't trust you. She insisted I do it, or lose my rank."

"She doesn't trust you either, it would seem, judging by her threat."

"You don't think she means it, do you, second council sister?"

"In my experience, training officer, she means every word. I've never known first council sister to make idle threats. Add to that the recent attempt on her life, and right now she believes everyone is against her. Yes, she means it. Are you sure you've looked everywhere?"

"Yes, second council sister. I don't know where she could be."

"I'm sorry for you then."

"Oh no, I don't want to die. - I'll run, find a place to hide, like fourth council sister." He frantically scanned the survey map.

"What are you looking for?"

"A place to hide. What do you think? She will not take me without a fight." He knew his life was on the line, and the expected respect required when speaking to a council sister was gone. Like her, he was thinking about self-preservation. "Where?" he said out loud. "Every good place is too far away to get there before dawn"

She could hear the mounting anxiety. "What if there was somewhere? Somewhere she couldn't find you?" She was taking a risk, but she needed an ally, and he wanted a way to stay alive.

"What do you mean? Do you know of a place?"

"Maybe I overheard fourth sister talking to the commander about somewhere."

"Where? Where is it?"

"I don't know, maybe I miss understood, when I heard her mention a place she'd built, close by, for some males she'd helped to escape."

"Tell me. Show me where it is on the map."

"This is my life I'm putting on the line for you, training officer. Give me a reason to. You've already stood against me, so it better be good."

"I'll do anything, second council sister. I give you my word, and I'll be in your debt - you know a warrior always does what he says he's going to do."

"That is true, training officer."

"Please, second council sister, help me survive."

"You'll do anything I ask of you?"

"You have my word."

"Very well, and I'm going to keep you to your word."

She told him about the colony and pointed to its location on the map.

"It's on the other side of the mountain. I'll never get there in time."

"You will," she said.

Well, I've committed myself now. Might as well tell him the rest. She told him about the entrance to the escape tunnel in the cavern, the cave network it led to, which took him under the mountain, out the other side, and to the colony.

His eyes lit up as she told him. "That's incredible, second council sister."

"One more thing. I hope that's where you'll find fourth council sister. She is on foot and is probably just getting there now. If she sees you, she and the males may attack, thinking you've found them. She's been training them to defend themselves against your warriors and another gathering. But first council sister has injured her badly. I'll give you some medication to take for her. Tell her I gave it to you. It should stop her and the males from attacking. Tell her what's happened."

"I will, second council sister. I owe you my life."

"Yes, you do, and I will keep you to your word, training officer."

"You have it. It will be my honor to keep it."

"Let's get you that medication. Come with me."

She gave him all the painkillers she had left. "Before you go, take this." She handed him a communicator. "Call me when you get there and have seen fourth council sister. Now, go."

"Thank you, second council sister. I will do whatever you ask of me," he said.

She watched him walk back to the compound and into the serum room. From there, he could go back down the tunnel from the secure area to the cavern and use the escape tunnel. *That's the easiest escape ever,* she thought. There was nothing more she could do. Now she had to wait.

Two hours ticked by and she hadn't heard from him. She was trying to convince herself she'd made the right decision to bring him in, but doubts were creeping in. *Why is it taking him so long?* She had to take her mind off it.

It was dark outside now. The lights in the facility and the compound lit them like daylight as the warriors and workers continued the search. She went down to call it off for the night.

"Are you sure, second council sister?" the head construction worker said. "First council sister was very clear we should not stop until we find her."

"And have you?"

"No, second council sister."

"Have you looked everywhere for her?"

"Yes, second council sister, multiple times."

"Then she's not here, is she? Look, we are all tired. Best we get some rest and begin again at first light. I will clear it with first council sister. I commend you for your diligence again, head construction worker, and I will relay it to first council sister."

"Thank you. Goodnight, second council sister."

Her communicator buzzed. "Goodnight," she said. "I must take this call."

The caller ID was the training officer. She walked away, making sure she was far enough, so the worker didn't hear. "At last. I was getting worried."

"I apologize, second council sister, but I have been attending to fourth council sister. I am sorry to report she has passed away from her injuries."

"What, she's dead?"

"Yes, second council sister. I'm sorry. Her injuries were too extensive. I was too late to stop the internal bleeding. She must have been in excruciating pain. On foot, I'm amazed she made it this far. She was one tough council sister to survive a beating like that."

"First council sister did this."

"Yes, second council sister. I believe so."

"She will pay for that," she said, then paused.

"Are you still there, second council sister?"

"Yes, training officer. This is what I want you to do. My sister can still play a role, one that will ensure your safety. I want you and some males to carry her to a place not too far from the warehouse. Lay her in a place where your warriors will find her body. Make sure you cover your tracks. It must look like she was the only one there. In the morning, I'll widen their search, so they find her. First council sister will not bother searching for you once she has her. Can you do that?"

"Yes, of course, second council sister. It will make her death honorable and give it meaning. I will do it."

"Thank you, training officer. I will be in touch in a few days. Please continue their training. I want an army, a human army, trained by the best. An army capable of resisting your warriors, an army of rebels. Ready for when I need them. Will you do that too?"

"It will be my pleasure, second council sister."

"Just call me sister - and you will be my General."

"Thank you, seco... sister. I look forward to our next conversation."

"I look forward to meeting my rebel army. Goodnight, General."

Neural Blockchain Journal Entry #932

I want all the males. I can't believe how incompetent my engineers are. My satellite is useless, and now I have no way of contacting the fleet. I will take what I want and leave this planet decimated.

There is a plot to have me assassinated. I don't know how many assassins there are, but they will not kill me. I've already got rid of the commander. It's a pity about fourth sister's egg, another one lost after third sister's death. With the 6 females and the five remaining eggs to be harvested, there will still be enough for me to have all the new sisters in my charge.

Second sister is managing the building of my other Meta-gates and holding facilities. She will do what I want her to do, although she has taken the death of fourth sister badly.

As long as I get my new warriors and my new sisters, everything will work out fine once we're away from here.

There is an experiment I want to run on the females before we leave. It should be fun.

First Council Sister - Szateth leader
Advanced planetary research fleet.

Neural Blockchain Journal Entry #108

———————————————————————

She killed my sister.

All my sisters are against her now. That sham of a confidence vote was just her way of harvesting fourth sister. Between the General and me, her death will have a purpose. First sister lost another egg, after third sister's death, and she'll stop looking for her training officer.

My rebel army will grow, trained by the best. I think there could be a future for my General and me.

I'm sure once the females have given birth, she'll want to harvest my other sisters. I don't think I can stop that.

The females are doing well after their blood transfusions and should give birth to healthy, happy Szatethess.

I still don't know what she has planned for them after they deliver our new sisters, and it scares me.

If I can, I will rescue and move some females to the colony too.

Her paranoia is growing. She sees enemies all around her, and she's right, they are all her own making. It didn't need to be this way, but her hunger for power and dominance had consumed her. She would sacrifice the Szateth to get what she wants.

The General is well and truly on my side. He's training the males in the colony, and soon I'll be able to build a bigger one with a Meta-gate and facilities of its own and move them all there.

My army needs to be strong.

There's a rebellion coming.

Second Council Sister

Advanced planetary research fleet.

Part Three

Rebellion

Fourteen

The Harvest

Their screams brought first sister running, and second sister pushing the shuttle's engines to their limit. They were the screams of labor pains. The six females were giving birth.

It was the day first sister had been waiting for, and second sister had been looking forward to and dreading at the same time. She would welcome new sisters but would have to watch as they suffered a worse pain: having the babies they'd carried and loved taken from them, and a new, as yet unseen, future.

The shuttle docked, and she hit the button to lower the ramp, jumping off before it finished.

"Welcome aboard, second council sis..." the first officer said.

She waved, sprinting past him and crashing through the hangar door into the corridor, determined to get to the females before first sister had the time to subject them to her third-rate medical skills. She got to her lab just in time.

"Ah, sister, I was just about to start."

"To start what, sister?" she said, trying to catch her breath.

"To give them pain relief and prepare them for cesarian sections."

"Surely it's better for them to give birth naturally, sister?"

"Why? I want my new sisters to be born quickly and safely. I'll cut them out."

"Naturally is the safest way, sister. Unnecessary medical intervention and the risk of complications associated with it should be a last resort."

"It's the way it's always been done. I see no reason to change it now."

"They will recover more quickly if they give birth naturally," she said. Wanting to spare them from her butchery. "Especially as you have further plans for them." A devious grin came over first sister's face, and she instantly regretted saying it.

The other sisters arrived, clucking around the mothers of the next generation of Szatethess. Their happy chattering broke the growing tension.

The grin on first sister's face disturbed her, but right now, she had to make sure the females gave birth on their own terms. "It's so good to see you, sisters. There isn't much you can do, other than to support them with ice chips and water if they ask for them," she said.

"It's lovely to see you too," fifth sister said.

"Especially on an exciting day like this," eighth sister said.

The others nodded, eager to be useful.

"Yes, yes, enough with the pleasantries," first sister said, her voice drowning the others. "How do we speed this along?"

The lab fell silent. Her impatience killed the joy of the moment.

"We don't," second sister said. "We wait, and let their human nature take its course."

"Right, well, how long then?"

"It could be hours, sister. But it is better this way."

"Ridiculous, I've got better things to do than to wait for them to push the babies out. I'll get some workers to prepare their chambers. Call me when my new sisters are here."

Once she and her bodyguards had gone, the excited chattering and cooing started again.

Second sister took notes and started her stopwatch every time they groaned. Over the next few hours, the time between their pains shortened. She noted their pains were in sync. *It's as if the babies know they need to be born together today,* she thought. The females moved about the lab to find a place and body position to prepare for the final contractions. The sisters followed as they looked for somewhere safe to give birth, then helped them get comfortable. There was a combination of sitting, squatting, on all fours, and lying. She wrote in her notes: Their natural instincts have taken over. They are nesting and looking for a safe place away from predators. This is what they must do when they give birth on the surface.

"It shouldn't be long now," second sister said.

The sisters smiled and clapped as the females scowled and groaned when another contraction started. They provided help, water, or anything else the females asked for while they waited for the babies to arrive. In the small hours of the morning, they gave birth to six healthy screaming Szatethess human hybrids.

Second sister weighed and examined each of them, noting their light olive skin, the soft scales on their faces, and the newly forming sharp needle-like teeth folded back against the roof of their mouths. Otherwise, they had ten fingers and toes and looked like perfect little human females.

Fifth sister called second sister to one side. "We should inform first sister our new sisters are here."

"We should, yes, but let's wait awhile," she said, "and give them some time with their babies before she comes and ruins their lives."

"Is that wise, sister? Isn't it better to separate the mother from the Szatethess baby sooner rather than later? It's the way it's always been done."

"Yes, but I wonder if we should change that. As a species, we are at the point of extinction because of the way things have always been done. We have to do something different if we are to avoid getting into this situation again in the future. Sister, I believe the human species is the key to our survival, but their nature is to nurture and guide their young, keeping them close until they can look after themselves, and not have others bring up their babies away from them."

"Well, that may be so, but first sister won't like that. With our new sisters here, she's got everything she wants, including a plentiful supply of human males for warrior conversion. It makes me nervous wondering what she's going to want next."

"Hmm, I know what you mean. She's got something planned for these females, but she won't tell me what. But just look at them, sister, see how happy they and the babies are?"

"Yes, you're right. Perhaps a few minutes before we—"

"Aha, they are here, my new sisters," first sister said, marching into the lab with her bodyguards, and a troop of warriors. "Look at them, my future council sisters."

Her sudden appearance stunned everyone into silence, and the babies started crying. She took one out of the arms of her mother. "Welcome sister. You and your sisters are going to help me build a Szateth empire that will rule for millennia," she said in a baby-like tone no one had heard before.

"Do they have any defects I should know about?" she asked.

"No, sister. They are perfectly healthy," second sister said.

"Good." She looked and smiled at each of them before handing the baby to a warrior.

"Give me back my baby," the female said.

"Your baby?" first sister said.

"Give her to me. Now," she said. Her eyes were wild.

The other sisters stood back. They knew what was about to happen.

"Take the babies to their chamber," first sister said to the warriors.

Too tired and weak from giving birth, they couldn't resist as the powerful warriors pulled the screaming babies from their arms. They looked in horror at the sisters for help, but they could do nothing.

"Lock these females in that cell," first sister said.

"Surely they should go to their room to recover in comfort, sister?" second sister said, stepping between the warrior and the female nearest her.

"What? - they've served their purpose for the moment, so no, I want them secured until I'm ready for them again."

"Again, you want them again? For what?"

"Watch your tone and remember your place, - unless you think you can challenge me too?"

Her bodyguards stepped closer. The menace in their eyes made her bow her head.

"That's what I thought," she said. "Take them to the cell."

The remaining warriors dragged the sobbing females to the cell and locked them in.

"Well, if that's all?" she said as if nothing had happened. "You'd better get back to the surface. I think you've still got one or two holding facilities and Meta-gates to build for me?" She waved her away. "The rest of you follow me to the chambers. We need to get my new sisters settled." She and her bodyguards marched out, followed by the silent sisters.

Alone, second sister couldn't hold her emotions in anymore. Tears of frustration, anger, and fear poured out. With her head in her hands, she sobbed. Overwhelmed by the pain of failing them for a second time, she vowed it would be the last.

No one could see her like this, and she struggled to pull herself together. The water she splashed on her face was cold, making her shiver as it washed away her tears. With a deep breath, she composed herself before walking with the air and grace of a council sister back to the hangar.

She nodded as she walked past the first officer who had just come back on shift. He wished her a safe flight as she boarded the shuttle. Dawn was breaking as she left. It was the start of a new day and a new determination to make Project Residentz her priority.

∞

First sister had instructed workers to convert the late third sister's private chamber into a nursery, and the sisters could hear the babies crying as they got closer.

Over the screaming, first sister said, "once these new sisters take their place on the council, they will be the ones to ensure our continued domination of the universe."

"That is a few years away, sister. They'll need the intense education we had before taking our seats," fifth sister said.

"You are correct. I will supervise their education myself. What I need you sisters to do," - she looked at each of them - "is to take care of their daily needs, food, entertainment, and all the other things Szatethess infants need."

"On top of our duties for the running of the ship?" seventh sister asked. "That is a lot, sister."

"Why? Is it too much for you, then?" She took a step toward her.

"No, sister." She looked at the floor.

"Good." She looked at the others. "I promise you won't have to do it for long."

They knew from her tone not to rile her more and accept their added responsibilities.

"Alright then. I want you to take an infant each, and care for her as if she came from your own egg. Fifth sister, as you are the youngest of the sisters, you will take two."

In the chamber, the warriors standing next to the cribs snapped to attention when the sisters entered. "You can leave now," first sister said.

They bowed, relieved to be going, and marched out.

"Choose the one you want."

The infants seemed to recognize the sisters as they stood over the cribs and stopped crying.

"I suggest you keep them together in here, so they develop that sisterly bond we all enjoy," first sister said with a sarcastic chuckle.

None of them said anything.

"Fifth sister, you are in charge of their welfare. Get whatever you need to ensure they are happy and healthy."

"Yes, sister."

"Good. Their education will begin in a few weeks."

∞

In the conference room of her shuttle, second sister didn't waste any time. She spread the map showing the location of the holding facilities and Meta-gate on the conference table. She tapped the map at the locations she'd chosen for her new colony. Remote, cold, and desolate.

It was going to be a challenge, and it would take some time and construction materials to build it, but it was the perfect place.

First sister had her new sisters, and no doubt was getting her claws into them already. Whatever she had planned for the females would happen soon; whatever it was, it wouldn't be good. Then there's the harvesting, and she'll increase the frequency of the gatherings once the last two facilities and Meta-gates are complete. She sighed. *There's not much time.* She called her new general.

"Can we meet in the warehouse late today?"

"Of course, sister. It will be early evening by the time I've hiked in. Is everything okay?"

"Yes, General, I have some plans I want to go over with you."

"Right, I'll leave now. Shall we say we meet at eighteen hundred hours?"

"Good. Can you bring a couple of your most trusted soldiers?"

"Yes, sister."

The wind and rain battered the shuttle, and looking over to the warehouse, the weather was as bad as she'd seen it since she first landed. *It's going to be horrible, but it will give you cover when you get to the warehouse.*

There was time to check the warehouse for what they'd need to build the meta-gate at the colony before they got there. She put on her heavy robe, but it didn't stop the icy wind from cutting through as she walked over. Some parts for her Meta-gate were already in the hidden room. She'd put them there when fourth sister was alive, and as the head construction worker had done an inventory since and noticed nothing missing, she knew she could take more.

She collected the other part, slid aside the racking covering the hidden room's door, and put them in with the others, ready for the

General. She checked the time. It would be some time before they would get there, and it was too cold to stand around waiting.

She called the first officer. "I need a shuttle first thing in the morning to take the workers and warriors to the next locations for first council sisters new facilities."

"Of course, second council sister."

"I'll need it for two days. Make sure it's fully fueled."

"I'll see to it myself, second council sister. I didn't know you could pilot a shuttle."

"There's a lot you don't know about me, first officer."

"I didn't mean to imply that you couldn't, second council sister. I apologize."

"No need first officer, just have the shuttle brought down first thing in the morning. I'll fly the pilot back after I've dropped the workers and warriors off."

"Yes, second council sister."

She secured the room, tightened her robe, and bracing herself ready for the wind, walked out toward the living compound. The first officer was right; she didn't know how to fly a shuttle. But with more facilities to build, it was the perfect opportunity to use it to transport the General and his soldiers to the new colony in the mountains. *Nothing a trip to the metaverse can't sort out*, she thought.

The howl of the wind made it hard to hear if anyone was moving about, and squinting she couldn't see any warriors or workers in there. The training officer had told her most of the warriors were out on a gathering training exercise, and the workers were busy doing maintenance and cleaning inside the facility.

No one saw her as she entered the Meta-gate room. She smiled. *Well, the timing couldn't be better*, she said to herself, opening the gold pin box that was in her pocket. She pricked her finger and squeezed a drop of blood to the surface, smearing it onto the infinity symbol on the frame above the entrance. The blood disappeared into the symbol and lit up. Moments later, the solid rock-colored surface inside the frame vibrated, accompanied by a sound, like sand being shaken in a can, changing the solid surface into something that looked like a mirror. The sound stopped, and in silence, the open gate shimmered. It was beautiful. She stepped into the metaverse. Inside, she had access to infinite knowledge. With a thought, a block linked to her neural blockchain, and she knew how to fly.

It had been a long time since she was last in there and she had forgotten how the transition from the physical to the digital world and back again made her body tingle. She gave herself a moment to enjoy the feeling before touching the infinity symbol again. The shimmering stopped, making the surface look like blue ice. The symbol dimmed, and the gate closed.

She shivered in the cold and left the gate room. The compound was still deserted, and she walked back to her shuttle unseen. She was just warming up when the General called. They were in the warehouse.

When she got there, he introduced her to three of his finest soldiers. They were still primitive humans, but understood his orders and her authority.

"Tomorrow General, I want you to build two Meta-gates, one at our new colony, the other where you and your soldiers are now. The new colony will be for us and humans, not our rebel army. I'll take you there by shuttle. Once it's built, call me and I'll come to get you and take you back to build the other in the forest colony. I'll network them and teach you how to use it."

"Sister, I don't know how to build a Meta-gate."

"I know," she said. "I'll teach you. Come closer and close your eyes."

She touched his forehead. He saw a brilliant light, felt the growth of new knowledge as his mind expanded, and he knew.

"I know how to build one, and a colony and, and something else." He touched his chest. "I feel different?"

"Yes, General. I have given you life. You and I are going to be working together for a very long time."

"I, I, don't know what to say. Thank you, sister. I will always do what I can for you."

"Yes, General I know. Now, everything you need for the Meta-gate is in here."

They followed her over to the empty racking. She slid it to the side and pushed on the panel behind it, opening a door.

"You and your men wait in here until I get you tomorrow morning?"

They followed her in.

"You'll be safe here, and here are all the parts you need to build the Meta-gate."

The general looked them over, knowing they were all there. "Yes, sister. We'll be fine."

"Thank you, General," she said, touching his arm. "I know I can rely on you. I'll leave you now and come for you around mid-morning."

The General and his men made themselves comfortable as she closed the door panel and slid the racking over. She looked back as she left the warehouse. No one would know they were there.

Back in the warm, she called the head construction worker. "Can you get a team of workers and a squad of warriors ready for tomorrow morning? We leave first thing for the next holding facility location."

"Yes, second council sister."

"Good, and order more construction materials from the ship. I've done an inventory of what we have and we don't have enough for two Meta-gates and facilities. They can bring it with them."

"Yes, second council sister."

"I have the shuttle for two days, so we can store what we don't need to construct the first facility in the warehouse before we leave and come back for it."

"Yes, second council sister."

There was nothing more she could do tonight. Tomorrow would be a milestone day. It would see the start of her new colony, and an end to first sister's plan to take every male on the planet. She took herself to bed, falling asleep the moment her head touched the pillow. She slept peacefully.

∞

It was just getting light when she woke. She felt a tingling lightness in her chest that had her dressed, and waiting for the shuttle, as the sun rose over the mountain. Workers and warriors marched from the compound as it landed. The warriors boarded, while the workers unloaded construction materials and loaded the tools they needed. They were securing the last as she walked over.

"I understand you are flying today, second council sister?"

"That is correct, pilot. I will take these workers and warriors to the new location, drop them there, then take you back to the ship."

"Very good, second council sister."

The warriors were checking their weapons when the workers boarded, taking their seats behind them. With everything secured, they were ready to go.

The head construction worker pressed the button to close the ramp, and she powered up the engines. As the shuttle rose, she felt her chest tighten as they flew over where the General had placed fourth sister's body.

Her death and the discovery of her body had first sister looking elsewhere for conspirators in her attempted assassination, giving her General the chance to train her rebel army and plan the new colony without interruption. She had everything she needed. Now it was time for action, to give fourth sister's death meaning.

She pushed the throttle levers forward, taking the shuttle to full speed over dense, lush forests, blue water, and ice sheets before arriving at the location. From the air, she could see the tribes of humans whose lives the Meta-gate and facility would destroy. *We'll save as many of you as we can*, she said to herself as the pilot marked their positions for future gatherings.

She hovered the shuttle over the landing zone, pressed the button to lower the landing gear, and descended. As soon as she landed, the workers sprung into action, unloading the hold while the warriors took positions guarding the area's perimeter. In seconds, the area was secure. *The General needs to train my rebels better than these,* she thought.

She called the head construction worker. "Are we clear to go?" she said, drumming her fingers next to the flight controls.

"Yes, second council sister, the hold is empty. You are clear to take off."

She opened the engine's thrusters, accelerating hard once clear of the trees. The shuttle shot across the sky.

On the horizon, she could see the ship. She had forgotten how big it was, and as they got closer, it blocked the sunlight, darkening the cockpit.

"An impressive sight, is it not, second council sister?"

"Indeed, it is, pilot. Be ready to disembark as soon as we dock."

She pulled the engine levers back, slowing the shuttle as they approached the hangar bay doors.

"First officer, this is the second council sister. Open the hangar bay doors," she said into the communicator on the instrument panel.

The enormous doors parted, and she flew toward the opening. As the shuttle docked, she could see first sister, her bodyguards, and the first officer waiting. She opened the ramp and walked off with the pilot.

"Good morning, second council sister, and welcome aboard," the first officer said, though his tone was anything but welcoming.

"I understand you've requested to fly the shuttle yourself. Why exactly?" first sister asked.

"I thought I'd visit each of the facilities and check on the warriors."

"Why? And why not use the Meta-gate in the compound? It's quicker and you won't use any fuel. Why would you want to fly?"

"Of course I could, sister, but sometimes, don't you think it's good to do things in a more, err, manual way? The flights over the landscapes can be breathtaking. This is a beautiful planet."

"I'm not interested if this planet is beautiful or not. What I want are the males, then to leave. I thought you knew that?"

"Yes, sister I do. However, the other advantage of flying is that I can map the tribes of humans from the air and direct your warriors. Unless your satellite is operational now?"

Her silence gave her the answer.

"Very well. You have the shuttle for one more day, and there's one more facility to build, correct?"

"Yes, that's correct, sister."

"One more day. Then I want my shuttle back here. Am I clear?"

"That's all I need."

"Well then, waste no more time here," first sister said, turning her back and marching away. Her bodyguard's eyes fixed on her for an extra second, as menacing as ever, before turning and following her out. The first officer smiled.

One day is all I need. She stared hard at the first officer, who instantly stopped smiling. She boarded and prepared to take off. *What a snake, running and telling tales.* She dismissed further thoughts of him as she flew out into the fresh air.

She called the General to be ready. As the shuttle touched down, she opened the ramp and ran into the warehouse. She slid the racking aside and opened the panel door.

"Let's go," she said.

They ran to the shuttle as she concealed the hidden room.

"You have what you need, General?" she asked, as the shuttle took off.

"Yes, sister. We are ready."

"I need you to build the Meta-gate as fast as you can, General. My flights, I'm sure, are being logged. I need to make it look like I'm doing what I said I'd be doing, so landings need to be fast."

"You get us there and we'll get it done, sister."

"I know, General."

Once again, she pushed the engines, accelerating towards the site of her new colony. The General and his soldiers began constructing parts of the Meta-gate in the shuttle's hold as they raced across the sky.

"We're getting close to the coordinates, General. Hold on to something as we land. Are you ready?"

He looked at the soldiers. "Yes, sister."

The landing was heavy, and the gear strained to cushion it. The General and the soldiers were on the ramp as it was lowering. In seconds, they and the gate's materials were on the ground.

"We're clear, sister," he said, into his communicator.

She powered up the engines and took off. "Call me once you're ready to be picked up, General."

"Yes, sister," he said, as the shuttle sped away.

She flew to two other facilities. At each one, a gathering was in progress and males were being pushed through the Meta-gates to be held in the cavern, ready for 'processing' as first sister liked to call it now. From the air, she could see how efficient the gatherings had been. First sister's goal of taking all the males would wipe out the local tribes.

Her communicator buzzed. It was the head construction worker. "We have completed the construction of facility eight, second council sister."

"Good work. I will be there to pick you up shortly."

Impressed and horrified at how quick they were, she set the coordinates and the shuttle turned toward them. There was only one facility left to build, and first sister would have a global network to plunder the planet as she saw fit. She and the General had to speed up if they were to save the Szateth and the humans. They had a day to finish their two gates.

Her mood darkened as she flew in. The building, the compound, the guard towers, and the Meta-gate were an ugly scab on the natural landscape around it.

The workers were waiting to load tools and machinery as she landed. They had everything in the hold in minutes. The head construction worker pressed the button to close the ramp. "We are ready to go, second council sister," he said.

Blue gravity waves pulsed from the engines, lifting the craft into the air. As it rose high above the tree line, she could see the tribes of unsuspecting humans happily going about their daily lives. Having seen what was happening at the other facilities, it was more important than ever to save as many of them as she could.

The glare from the mid-afternoon sun shone through the cockpit window, making her squint as she started the landing sequence back at the warehouse.

"Are we to load construction materials for location nine, second council sister?"

"I think we could wait until tomorrow. Time is getting on. It would be long into the night before you completed the construction if you started today. No, tomorrow will be fine."

"Very good, second council sister."

She pulled back on the thrusters and angled the engines to the floor. The gravity wave pulses slowed their descent.

"Be ready first thing in the morning. I'll fly you over early, so we can finish first council sister's holding facility and Meta-gates network."

The shuttle's suspension groaned, straining to absorb the hard landing.

"Yes, of course, second council sister," he said, reaching for the wall to steady himself.

"You and your workers should get some rest. Again, you have impressed me with your efficiency."

The hydraulic struts hissed as she pressed the button to open the ramp.

"Thank you, second council sister. I look forward to seeing you tomorrow."

He bowed and waved for the workers to follow. In a single file, they followed him off the shuttle.

The buzzing on her wrist made her jump. It was the General. She waited until the last worker stepped off the ramp before answering.

"Is it complete?"

"Yes, sister. We are ready for you."

"I'm on my way. Be ready General."

The ramp hissed again as it closed. The workers were a safe distance away, and pushing the thruster levers forward, the engines powered up, and she took off. *Just one more gate to build, General.* The hairs on her arms bristled. She pushed the engines to their maximum to get there.

The fierce mountain winds rocked the shuttle, and she fought to keep it steady. A pinpoint landing was impossible, and she came in hard. The soft ground under the landing gear absorbed some of the impact, but it was heavy.

The General and his soldiers ran on board. "It's good to see you, sister. The Meta-gate is complete and operational."

"Good work, General. Just one more to go. I'll land in the secure area. You'll need to take the tunnel to the cavern and from there to the colony. It'll be dark by the time we get there. The warriors are still out on exercise, and the workers should be in their huts, so there shouldn't be anyone around. You'll have some cover from the darkness."

"That's good, sister."

"Alright, let's get out of here."

The landing gear groaned in objection to the abuse she'd put it through as it rose into the belly of the shuttle. *Sorry shuttle*, she said, before pointing the nose toward the conversion facility and opening the thrusters.

Through the dark, the secure area's landing pad lights blinked their welcome. "Switch all the lights off back there, General. We need to go in dark."

She switched the shuttle's landing light off, hiding its approach.

"We're going to land."

As the shuttle touched down she said, "call me once the Meta-gate is operational, General."

"I will, sister."

The General and his soldiers started down the ramp as it lowered.

Their movements were as precise and efficient as the warriors at the holding facility. Her skin tingled as, in silence, they disappeared down the tunnel. *They are just as good, if not better.* She took off, maneuvering the shuttle low out of the secure area, over the compound, and landed by the warehouse.

∞

It had been a long day, and tying the belt of her sleeping robe, the inviting warmth of her bed chamber softened the tension she wasn't aware of until now. Her deep fur-lined lounger called to her, and with a drink, she sank into it, waiting for the call from the General. Her drink and the warm fur soothed away the strains of the day.

The beam of sunlight streaming through the window onto her face woke her. Still half asleep, she stood to escape it, yawned, and, stretching away the aches from being curled up all night, groaned as she pulled her body back into shape.

General, she thought, checking her communicator for a missed call. The screen on her wrist was blank. *Hmm, what's happened?* She looked out of the window to a clear blue sky. The workers and a squad of warriors caught her eye as they walked toward her shuttle from the compound.

She dressed, knowing they would wait without comment about her not being ready. She would leave them to wait a little longer.

She called the General. "Is the meta-gate online?"

"Yes, sister. We completed it moments ago. It's been a long night."

"I'm sure it has. Good work," she said, with a slow smile. "I will be on the shuttle and then on the ship for the rest of the day, so you and your soldiers should rest while you can. I'll link our Meta-gates when I return this evening."

"Yes, sister. They have earned it."

Her eyes sparkled. They were almost ready. "So have you, General. Later today, prepare what you need for the construction of the new colony, then we'll plan to get more humans to safety. I'll call you when I get back."

She ended the call, and pulling on her top robe, she walked to the ramp and pressed the button. The warriors snapped to attention as it lowered and the head construction worker moved to meet her as she walked down.

"Good morning, second council sister."

"As punctual as ever, I see," she said, her eyes still sparkling. "Shall we get to the last location, so I can report to first council sister that you've completed all nine of her holding facilities?"

"Yes, second council sister. It'll take us a few minutes to load what we need, then we'll be ready."

"Very well," she said, striding off toward the shuttle without waiting.

True to his word, they loaded everything and took their seats behind the warriors in minutes.

She typed the coordinates to the last location into the computer, pulled back on the engine's thrusters, and lifted off. There was no rush today, and as the landscape slid by beneath, she flicked on the autopilot and sat back in the pilot's chair, admiring the view.

Lost in thought over her plans for Project Residentz, the General, and her colonies, her lurching stomach told her the autopilot had begun the shuttle's descent. The unpleasant feeling brought her mind back to the job at hand, as she turned off the autopilot and took the controls to land.

"Use the Meta-gate once you've completed the construction to return to the compound. I need to return this shuttle to the ship," she said to the head construction worker as they touched down.

"Yes, second council sister."

She hit the button that lowered the ramp from the cockpit. The hydraulics hissed their anger at her treatment. She didn't care about any damage. The shuttle had served its purpose, and minutes later she was back in the air, heading for the ship.

As it came into view, her heart sank, the excitement and success of the last two days disappearing in an instant, as she wondered what horrors first sister had in mind for the females. Her sweaty palms brought the purpose of Project Residentz sharply into focus.

The first officer was there to greet her as she docked the shuttle. Her eyes narrowed seeing the sly grin he had on his face.

"Welcome on board, second council sister. It's good to see you again."

"Thank you first office," she said. "You look rather pleased with yourself?"

"First council sister has been very generous, second council sister, with her reward."

"Really? And what reward is that?"

"She's given me the pick of the females."

"What!" she said, her top lip curling, baring her teeth.

He stepped back, trembling. "She said, as I've been of great service to her, I could help her with her new experiment."

"Involving the new mothers?" she said, every muscle in her body tightened. "Have you taken her yet?"

"No, second council sister. I was going to choose one at the end of my shift."

"No - you're not!"

"But, first council sister promised me."

She struck forward, as fast as first sister had when she bit off the commander's finger. He stumbled back, falling, her needle-sharp teeth extending from the roof of her mouth.

"I won't. Please, second council sister, I won't."

The frenzied look in her yellow eyes had him cowering on the floor as a pool of urine darkened the front of his pants.

Her heart pounded as she fought the primal urge to kill. She held a deep breath and closed her eyes to calm down.

Wide-eyed, he stared as she opened her mouth, stretching the skin to retract her teeth and re-align her jaw. She exhaled, then opened her eyes, looking at him like he was prey.

"I give you my word, second council sister," he said and looked down.

He heard a guttural growl, the smack of her lips, then everything went black.

"Are you alright, first officer?" a small voice said.

His head shot up. It was one of his young hangar crew. He frowned, his eyes darting around the hangar. Second council sister was gone.

∞

With her reptilian senses in full hunt mode, she moved silently away from the pathetic sight of the first officer laying in his own waste, intending to confront first sister. She heard the marching slap of her sandals and the heavy thump of her bodyguard's boots before she saw her.

In a darkened corridor, she came up behind them. The bodyguards, sensing her presence, stopped, spun, and drew their weapons, shielding first sister. Their eyes and weapons tracked every movement she made.

"Stand down," first sister said.

They lowered their weapons but kept their menacing stare.

"I'm sure she doesn't mean any harm. Do you?"

"What have you done with my females?"

"You're females?"

The verbal attack had the bodyguards raise their weapons.

"You're giving them to the crew as rewards."

"Ah, you've spoken to the first officer? It was a bad idea, I grant you."

"So you're not giving them to the crew?"

"Certainly not."

"I thought, well... My apologies, sister. They're the mothers of our new sisters and deserve to be honored, not discarded like the leftovers of a meal." She unclenched her fists.

The bodyguards still had their weapons trained on her. "Forgive my warriors, sister. They are fanatically loyal, sometimes to a fault." She placed a hand on their arm. "And I don't want to lose you to a misunderstanding." She glanced at them, and they lowered their weapons. "Walk with me. I want to discuss," -she looked around- "well, maybe in the lower deck, seeing as we're heading that way?"

"Of course, sister."

The bodyguards stood aside, letting them pass, then followed close behind. At the end of the corridor, they stepped into an elevator.

The smell of damp vegetation and stagnant water got stronger as the elevator took them down to the lower deck. She knew first sister spent a lot of time down here.

Halfway along a brightly lit corridor, they stopped outside a set of double doors. First sister lovingly rested her hand on the handle. "This is my sanctuary. No one has been here except me. Here I can think and be who I truly am." She unlocked and swung them open.

Second sister stood frozen to the spot, open-mouthed.

"You two wait out here." Her bodyguards moved on either side of the doorway. "Coming?" she said, shivering at the welcoming warmth escaping into the corridor, and walked in.

Second sister couldn't resist following her through the doors. The humid air, damp ground, and dim red light had her senses tingling. The doors closed behind her, shutting out the sterile feel and mechanical sounds of the ship. It felt like she'd stepped into another world. It felt like home.

"I've had this entire deck converted, to look and feel like the swamps back home," first sister said, walking past her, and unbuttoning her robes. "Come and join me, and remember what it feels like to be totally free."

Instinct took over, and leaving her robes in a pile, she followed first sister into the trees. She caught up with her, sitting on a rock.

"Now you know why I come here."

"Oh my, yes, sister. I did not know it was like this."

"Here, I can think and hunt, as I used to."

"It's wonderful, sister." She stretched out, absorbing the heat of the rock.

First sister laid back next to her and for a few minutes, the two of them let the warmth, the moist air, and the smells remind them of days gone.

First sister broke the illusion. "Here is where I will hunt and harvest the others," she said, sitting up. "I need you, sister. We make a great team, don't you think? It's time for fresh blood on the council."

For a few blissful minutes, she had forgotten where she was, and who first sister was. She opened her eyes, and a chill ran down her spine.

"I'll bring them here, one at a time. If they're anything like you when they get here, they'll be easy kills."

"You're still going through with everything, then?"

Her voice went cold. "Do you doubt it?"

"No, sister I don't. And what about the females?"

"Don't spoil this for me," she said, narrowing her eyes as she looked down at her. "Very well. That's enough for today. Time to get back." She jumped off the rock, splashing into a shallow pool before disappearing into the trees.

"Wait for me, sister." She jumped over the pool and into the trees, but she'd gone.

"Where are you?" She stopped to listen. The silence felt heavy as she strained for any sign of her.

"This isn't funny," she said. The only sound came from the crunch of dead leaves as she stomped through the swamp toward the doors.

Her heightened sense told her she was being stalked. Without warning, a hand grabbed her wrist from behind and spun her around, taking her off balance. A forearm came across her throat, forcing her back, the air blasting from her lungs as she landed heavily with first sister standing over her.

"There, see, an easy kill."

"What did you do that for?" she said, struggling for breath.

"Practise." She reached out a hand to help her up.

"Well, I think you've mastered it." She grabbed it and pulled herself to her feet. "I need to get back. I've got work to do."

"Yes, there's a lot to arrange for the harvesting and the females. Let's get back."

She followed first sister out of the swamp.

"You still haven't told me what you intend to do with them."

"Who?"

"The females."

"Ah, yes. Come to my chambers later. I'll show you," she said with a devilish smile.

"I'd like to see the females whilst I'm here. Are they still in the cell?"

She could feel smooth metal more than dirt under her feet now as the swamp's vegetation thinned. Ahead were the doors and their robes.

"Yes, you'll find them in your lab," first sister said, dressing. "You won't recognize the babies. They've grown freakishly fast. They're walking and talking. Definitely not babies anymore. Their development has been unprecedented. I would say in the next week or two, they won't need the sisters to be their guardians." She reached for the door handles. "They will have outlived their usefulness. Which is why I bought you here today."

"I see." She looked back, staring into the swamp, as she slipped her feet into her sandals.

"Make sure the storage unit in your lab is operating correctly before you come and see me later. The eggs will need storing as soon as they're harvested."

"Yes, sister."

She opened the doors. The low hum of the ship's engines and the stark white light of the corridor invaded the tranquility of the swamp. Her bodyguards snapped to attention. "You understand why I have to do this?"

"I'm not sure that I do."

"I will have my army. I will have a council of sisters who understand what it takes to lead the universe, and I will bring the fleet back together, crushing any rebellion and growing my network of controlled planets. Then we'll think about preserving our species. That's what you want, right?"

"Yes, of course. But sister, humans are the best host species we've ever found in all the time we've been searching. They are not unlike us. I believe with time, genetic engineering, editing, and splicing, I can have human females giving birth to Szatethess naturally. There will be no more need to harvest eggs. The humans, sister, can save our species."

"Hmm, gene splicing, you're talking about creating hybrids. That's ambitious, even for you. You *will* need eggs for that. How fortunate that five are about to become available. I didn't realize you had such low regard for your sisters." She chuckled. "Make sure you come to my chambers just after dark, and we'll discuss it further."

"Their sacrifice will save us all, sister," she said with fake sincerity.

"Hmm." She pointed at the exit. "After you."

She locked the doors, and the bodyguards fell in behind as they walked back to the elevator.

Neither of them spoke as it rose, but she could feel the eyes of the bodyguards boring into her back. As the doors slid open, first sister stepped out and said, "I'll see you later, then?"

"Yes, I'll be there. I'm interested in finding out what you have in store for them."

First sister turned left towards her chambers. "Aha, yes. It's maybe an amusing shortcut that will save you some work. See you later," she said without looking back.

From the moment she boarded the ship, things had gone badly, and as she walked to the lab, she had the feeling things were going to get worse. The lights flickered when she flipped the switch, and a face she recognized appeared in the cell door window.

The mother stepped back as she unbolted and opened the door, her eyes fixed on her. The others looked up as she entered.

They were sitting separately from the other females and looked wretched. Filthy, naked, cut, and bruised. "What has happened?" No one answered.

"What has happened to you?" she said, kneeling next to the mother, who was holding her knees to her chest.

She shrank away.

"Please let me help you." She wrapped a blanket around her shoulders.

"What have they done to you?"

The mother, squeezing her knees tighter, didn't answer.

She stood. "Right, let's get you all cleaned up," she said.

She got a bowl of warm water, and with a cloth washed her.

"You abandoned us," one of them said, her voice cracking. "Left us here with that monster, and now she abuses us, every chance she gets. We thought you were our friend?"

"I'm so sorry." Tears filled her eyes.

"She's been taking one of us and one of the other females. It's going to be my turn soon, and when I get back, I'm going to have those same injuries."

"What does she do?"

"I don't know. They won't say anything. Whatever it is, it's bad."

"Will you help me clean them up?"

She took the bowl. "Will *you* help us?"

"I will find out what's been happening, and promise I will do what I can."

"Let's hope it's enough," the female said, kneeling, and unwrapping the blanket. The two mothers held each other's eyes as she washed away blood and dirt.

She stood and looked at each of them. Tears streamed down her cheeks as she witnessed the scene of misery and pain. "One of you is missing. Where is-"

"They came and took her, and one of the other females, a few hours ago. I don't know where."

The others began crying.

The color drained from her face. *Oh no, sister, tell me you're not doing what I think you're doing?* She felt a tremor of fear and fought to stop it. Then bitter anger took its place. "Clean up the others. I'll be back."

She wiped her face, and almost knocked the tray of food out of the head kitchen worker's hands as she shoved the lab doors open.

"Oh, careful," he said before he saw her. "Oh, excuse me, second council sister."

She stopped and seeing him tempered her rage. "No, no, my fault," she said. "I'm glad I almost bumped into you. Is this their last meal for the day?"

"No, second council sister. I will bring one more later this evening."

"I might ask you to do something for me then."

"Of course, second council sister. I'll be happy to do it for you."

"Let's dispense with the formality between us. You know how much I value your help. From now on, and when it's just you and I, call me sister."

"I am deeply honored," -a huge smile came over his face- "sister."

"Well, you are one of the very few on this ship who I know I can count on, and I thank you for that."

"What do you need me to do, sister?"

"I'll come and see you in the kitchen later before you bring them their meal."

"I'll wait for you, sister."

"Do you have a name I can call you by?"

"The others call me Aragam."

"Aragam, what does that mean?"

"A helpful, loyal being."

"Yes, exactly. The others are correct, Aragam."

"Do you have a name, sister?"

"No, just a ranking designation. But perhaps we should. A name that, like yours, reflects our character. Hmmm."

"That's a shame. We all have names in the kitchen."

"Well, at least I know to call you Aragam. It's a good name. I will see you later."

"I look forward to it, sister."

She held the lab door open for him. He bowed with a smile, almost tipping the food off the tray as he entered. His face reddened. She smiled and let the door swing back.

The sun was going down as she walked to first sister's chambers, and as the light faded, so did her willingness to bend to her any further.

Outside her chamber's door, the two bodyguards stood blocking the way in. They drew their weapons.

"Don't come any closer," they said, training their weapons in the center of her chest.

"She is expecting me."

"Is that second council sister?" came her voice from inside.

"Yes, first council sister. She says you are expecting her."

"Let her in."

They lowered their weapons, opened the door, and stepped aside, leaving just enough room for her to walk between them. First sister, sprawled on her lounger, wearing her light comfortable robes, had a plate of thinly sliced fresh meat on the floor, and a glass of her finest wine in hand.

"Come in, sister. Make yourself comfortable. Drink?"

The chamber was much warmer than the rest of the ship. She could feel its soothing, energizing effects straight away, and the dim red light relaxed her eyes. It was reminiscent of the swamp on the lower decks, and she struggled to keep her natural reptilian instincts in check.

"What do you have to show me, sister?"

"Relax first, sister. Sit down and have a drink. I want to hear more about your ideas for using human females for breeding. And I have some ideas of my own."

"Very well. I don't have long. I must get back to the facility."

"Ah, yes, talking of which, from tomorrow, there will be gatherings and new batches of males coming in from the holding facilities every day. I want it processing at full capacity."

She forced down a sick feeling. There was no more time.

"Tell me, how long will your suggestion of gene splicing and hybrid creation take?"

She took a deep breath, swallowing the wave of nausea. "Well, I'd need to sequence the human genome first, then identify where I can edit their DNA and add ours. It may be a matter of adding chromosomes. But I won't know without testing."

First sister fidgeted. "How long, roughly?"

"I'm not sure. Three to five years. Maybe less. I don't know until I get started," she said, trying to buy time.

"You realize that if it works, it would make us the last of the purebred Szatethess, don't you?"

"We've always needed a host species, sister. But as I would need to extract our DNA, destroying the last of our Szatethess eggs, we would no longer need a host. If that's what you're eluding to, then yes, you're right."

"So, you want to stay here for five years, maybe more, to run your experiments, do you?"

"It might not take that long. It depends on the result of tests, and the amount of work involved. But sister, I believe it's possible. There would be no need for a harvest ever again. We could gather a few willing females, the mothers could help me persuade them that what we're asking of them is a good thing. Sister, with the help of human females, our race need never be in this position again. They are the best opportunity we have."

She swallowed a large mouthful of her wine. "What if there's a quicker way?"

"I don't see how."

She put the glass on the floor next to her food. "Well, the new mothers have already been changed, and had some hereditary cognitive intelligence passed on to them from the eggs you implanted. You've altered their evolution, to make them capable of carrying a Szatethess. Am I wrong?"

"No, you are correct."

"Well, I've been studying how humans procreate. I find it fascinating, and they seem to enjoy it. We've got altered females and converted male humans, full of Szateth DNA."

"What are you suggesting, sister?"

"I'm suggesting they get together. You know, mate. Like they do in the wild. And rather than waiting for five years for the result of your experiments, which may or may not work, we'd know in nine months. If my warriors put babies in their bellies, they'd give us new sisters *this* year. Then other warriors could mate with them, freshening up the gene pool, and ensuring the continued survival of our race. "

"You're not serious?"

First sister stared at her and took another mouthful of her wine.

"My goodness, you're serious. But the mothers would never accept a warrior as a mate. Intellectually, they are far more advanced. There would be no attraction."

"I don't think you're getting my point. They don't need to be attracted to them, sister. They just have to mate."

"Well, I could ask them."

"I don't need their permission. They will do as commanded. I will not wait five years. I have what I need for this experiment, and I want to know now."

She clapped her hands, and workers wheeled two examination tables into the chamber. The lightly sedated females, squealing, fought against the straps holding them down.

"The warriors seem to like them to move a bit," she said with a smile.

She clapped again. The workers left, and two of the biggest warriors came in dressed in just their loin clothes.

A sudden heavy feeling in her stomach made her gasp when she recognized the mother, who was looking directly at her, her eyes pleading for her to help. She stood between the females and the warriors. “What is this, sister?”

“It’s a scientific experiment I’ve been running for a few days. Calm yourself, *second sister*, they are just humans.”

“No, this is wrong.” Her heart hammered in her chest. “There’s nothing scientific about this. It’s barbaric. You can’t treat them like this. Have you not heard a word I’ve said?”

She swung her legs off the lounger and stood. Her eyes, cold and emotionless, drilled into her. “No, it’s you who hasn’t been listening.”

“You cannot do this. They’ve been of great service to us. Providing new sisters for your council. You should reward them, not rape them. What are you thinking?” She moved closer to the mother, trying to shield her.

“They will be of service again. Now move.”

“Sister, they would be of service willingly, I’m sure of it. All I need is some of their DNA and the eggs, and I can edit their genes. Then, with some male sperm, I'll artificially inseminate them. If it works, we could have new Szateth and Szatethess repopulating our species, naturally and forevermore. You don’t need to do this.”

“All that sounds great, sister, and I commend you for the suggestion. This one,” -she pointed a finger at the mother- “has already had her DNA altered, if you remember. The chances of them getting pregnant through artificial insemination are low, and you know that. This way I get male sperm into them the way their nature intended. Besides, from what I’ve seen, they like it.”

“I’m sure they do, with males they chose for themselves. Please, sister, don’t force this on them.”

“It has to be done. Now, for the last time, move out of the way!”

“This is wrong, and it’s unnecessary.”

"Move!" she stepped towards her. "Guards, get in here." The door flew open, and drawing their weapons, they charged to her side.

"Second council sister is tired. Escort her to the hangar. She's leaving."

"This way, second council sister, if you would," one of them said, waving the barrel of his weapon in the door's direction.

"Think about what you're doing, sister. Everything we need is here. We can work *with* humans. Don't do this, I beg you."

"Get her out."

They moved to grab her. "Don't touch me. Alright, I'm going. I know the way." She glared at first sister, who met her gaze through narrowed eyes. She spun, barged past the bodyguards, and left without looking back.

Striding away, shaking, she knew what she had to do. "Aragam, I need to see you now," she said into her communicator.

"I am here, sister."

"Meet me in my lab as soon as you can."

"I'm on my way, sister."

They got to the lab at the same time. She pushed the door open for him, then scanned the corridors. No one had followed.

She went in. "No lights, Aragam." Stopping him as he reached for the switch.

"What's going on, sister?"

"Will you do two things for me, my friend?"

"If I can, sister, of course."

"When will you give the females their next meal?"

"In about an hour."

"Good. I want you to leave the door unlocked when you leave. Will you do that?"

"Yes, sister, but what for?"

"They can exercise on their own from now on. After the service they've provided for us, they deserve some freedom as a reward. Don't you think?"

"Well, yes. I suppose so, sister."

"So, you'll leave the door unlocked, then?"

"Is first council sister aware of this?"

"Of course. It was her idea."

"Ah, okay then. As you wish, sister."

"And talking of first council sister, can you give her something for me?"

Aragam nodded.

"Wait here, a moment." She went to the cabinet taking out the bottle of the modified paralytic. "First council sister has been under a lot of strain lately and her immune system is low. I want you to put this in her food next time you serve her."

"Oh, err, okay, yes. What is it?" he said, taking the bottle.

"It's just vitamins, Aragam. Nothing for you to worry about."

"Of course, sister."

"Don't mention it to her, though. She hates looking weak in front of us and the crew, so it's best if you add it to her food without mentioning it."

"I see."

She could tell he needed more convincing. "Can I tell you something in confidence, Aragam?"

"Of course, sister. You can trust me."

"I know." She looked around and lowered her voice. "What I'm about to tell you must not go beyond these walls."

Aragam leaned in.

"First council sister has been ill for some time. I have been treating her, but with me being on the surface so often and for so long, she hasn't been taking the medication I prescribed her. She hates taking it and hates showing weakness. She's such a proud leader."

"She is, sister. Yes."

"I'm leaving for the surface again shortly, and I don't know when I'll be back. Having come from her just now, and even though she won't admit it, I can see she's suffering. Those are slow-release vitamins and will give her what she needs to keep her healthy."

"I understand, sister. I'll pour them onto her next meal."

"And promise me you won't say anything to her?"

"I won't, sister. I'm honored to help you treat her."

"I knew I could confide in you, Aragam. I've needed to share this burden with someone I could trust for so long. Thank you."

"It is my honor, sister."

"And can you do one more thing for me?"

"Yes, sister. Of course."

"There will be a pilot transporting me to the surface. Could you give him a message saying I'll be a few minutes later than scheduled?"

"Of course, sister."

"You may need to wait for him, and it's cold tonight, so you should wait for him in the control room until he gets there."

"It will be my pleasure, sister."

"Thank you Aragam. Could you do that first, then get the food for the females? I need to get something from my old chambers."

With the bottle in his hand, he nodded and walked to the door.

"Aragam."

He turned

"Tell no one about first council sister."

He smiled and nodded, opened the door, and left.

Satisfied he'd do what she wanted him to do, she opened the cell door. "Sisters, in a few minutes, the head kitchen worker is going to bring you food. He will leave this door unlocked when he leaves. When he's gone, all of you make your way to the hangar. Make sure no one sees you. There is only a skeleton crew on at this time of night, so it should be easy enough if you're careful."

The mothers stood, wide-eyed.

"I will wait for you in the shuttle. If they see you, they will kill you. Do you understand?"

"What about our other sister?"

"Do you want to be free or not?"

They nodded.

"This is the only chance you're going to get. There isn't anything I can do about our other sister right now, and you have to be ready to move." She felt her stomach clench when she said it. "I'll try to free our other sister later. Move quickly and quietly as soon as he's gone. Do you understand?"

They nodded again.

"I can delay my departure for only an hour. After that, you'll be stuck here for first council sister to continue her 'experiment' on you. Don't be late."

She could see the fear on their faces. "Thank you, sister," one of them said.

"You will be safe with me on the surface, sisters. I will wait as long as I can."

They glanced at each other, and not wanting to endure the torture of the 'experiment' again, stood. "We will be there."

She smiled, in awe of their strength. "I'll see you soon, sisters." She locked the cell door and made her way to the hangar. The pilot was talking to Aragam in the control room. *Perfect.* She went back to the lab and listened for him to pass by before going back.

She knew the hangar had surveillance cameras recording everything and everyone in there. The mothers didn't. The cameras would pick them up the moment they walked through the door. She had to switch them off. The skeleton crew seemed thinner than usual, and looking through the door window, other than the pilot who had his feet up and eyes closed in the shuttle's cockpit, there was no one else in there.

She waited for the cameras to turn away from the door before rushing into the control room before they turned back. The cameras showed what they saw on a bank of monitors. She flicked the switch, turning them and the recorders off. Through the control window, she could see the pilot was still asleep. She strolled onto the shuttle and into the cockpit. *He's none the wiser*, waking him with her gentle chuckle.

∞

The warriors grunted, writhed, and drooled on top of the females. The mother had more fight than the other female and struggled hard. He pressed, squeezed, pinched, and dug his powerful hands into her soft flesh, forcing her down until her strength gave out. Motionless, with her eyes closed, she prayed he would finish quickly.

"Struggle for me," he said. "I like it when you fight."

She didn't respond. In the background, first council sister was laughing. She felt him finish. The sedation had dulled her, but she could feel the throbbing welts and bruises he'd inflicted. When he got off, she opened her eyes to be met by the face of another warrior.

"Struggle for me too," he said, as he licked her face.

She could feel and smell the foul stench of his breath.

"Struggle for me. Come on, move." His voice was deep and cruel.

Unable to fight anymore, tears of submission ran down the sides of her face. He tutted, unstrapped her, turned her over, and pressed a large hand between her shoulders. She heard more laughter before closing her eyes as it began again.

"I have more food for you, first council sister," Aragam said, entering her chambers.

"Ah, you must have read my mind. Put it here? And take this plate away."

He almost kicked her drink over, staring at the warrior grunting in rhythm as he pressed the female down.

"Like what you see?" first sister said.

His eyes blazed with excitement and he nodded, unable to take them off the act he was witnessing.

"I'm sure you'd like to take a turn," she said, taking a mouthful of the fresh meat he'd just bought for her. "Take this plate and get out."

"Yes, first council sister," he said, knowing better than to object.

The warrior's groans filled the room, and he heard the first council sister clapping and cheering them on. Unable to help himself, he slipped into the shadows to watch. The warrior backed away from the mother to catch his breath. He saw the mother face down, clinging to the sides of the table, and heard her sobbing. She didn't move.

"Well done," first sister said, as he tied his loin cloth. "You can come for another female tomorrow."

The other warrior groaned and got off the female, panting in satisfaction. He loosened the straps. Her eyes fixed in a faraway stare didn't move. He slapped her. There was no reaction.

"What is this?" first sister said, getting up from her lounger.

He moved further away. "I'm sorry, first council sister," he said, covering his genitals. "I don't know what happened."

"You held her down too hard, you idiot." She pressed her fingers to her neck. "And you've killed her." She sighed. "Well, that answers one question," she said, looking at the warrior. "Unaltered females aren't strong enough for my warriors."

They gave her an uneasy smile.

"Come back tomorrow, both of you, and you can go again with altered mothers," she said, looking at the lifeless body.

"As you killed her, you can take the body for cremation," she said to the warrior still covering his crotch. "And you take this female back to the cell."

"A cell in the Brig, first council sister?"

"No, in second council sister's lab."

"I'm not sure where that is. I'm sorry, first council sister."

She scowled, then spotted the head kitchen worker lurking. "Ah, well, you're in luck," she said. "You!" -she pointed straight at him- "Come here. You're the kitchen worker who takes the food to the females in the lab, aren't you?"

"Yes, first council sister,"

"Good. Show this warrior the way. As a reward, you can select the females for tomorrow, and stay to watch." She took a mouthful of the meat he brought her. Blood dripped onto her chin as she smiled.

"Yes, first council sister, thank you."

"Take this female and go with him," she said to the warrior who had abused her.

"Yes, first council sister," he said, fastening the last button on his tunic.

He leaned over the mother and prized her hands off the table. "Come on," he said. With a tight grip on her wrist, he pulled her along as he followed the kitchen worker to the lab. Aragam looked back and noticed her injuries. The corridor lights revealed the vicious cuts and growing bruises on her naked body. He smiled to himself, looking forward to tomorrow.

The ship felt deserted. They'd walked the entire length and hadn't seen a soul. Apart from the low humming from the air ducts, it was quiet. He checked the time. *Ah, that's why,* he said to himself. The night shift had just taken over. The only crew working were those monitoring essential systems.

The lab was dark and as quiet as the rest of the ship. They found the cell door open, and the mothers were gone. Aragam thought little of it. He'd left it unlocked as second council sister instructed.

"Get in there," the warrior said, pulling hard on the mother's wrist, catapulting her in through the door.

Aragam followed her in. "There is only one of you left who hasn't had the 'experiment' performed on her. It's her turn next."

The sedation had worn off and she could feel the pain from every injury. There was a bowl of water with a cloth on the floor, and she winced as she kneeled next to it. The cold water soothed the bruises but did nothing to soothe the contempt that filled her with hearing what he just said.

∞

"Here you are, ladies," Aragam said, setting the tray of food for the females on the floor, and the food for the mothers on the table.

The mother, with a blanket wrapped around her, gave a weak 'thank you,' while the others eyed him without a word. He had noticed over the last few days their usual enthusiasm to eat the moment he gave them food had gone. This evening was no different.

"Second council sister has told me you can exercise without a guard from now on, so I'll leave the door unlocked and you can take a stroll as and when you like. Just make sure those females don't follow. I'd hate for the warriors to hunt for them." There was no response.

"That was a joke, ladies." He raised his eyebrows. "Alright, well, there's your food," he said, waving a finger at it before walking out.

"We should eat quickly," the clothed mother said. She took a handful of meat and crammed it in her mouth before looking to see if the coast was clear. The others did the same and wrapped blankets to cover their naked bodies.

"It's clear." She looked back. The others were waiting for her word to go. "Come on."

The only sound was the gentle tap of bare feet against metal as they crept across the lab. The lead mother raised her hand for them to wait as she opened the lab door to check the corridor. It was quiet.

They followed her, hugging the wall as they tip-toed down the corridor. A little further, and the turn on the right would take them to the hangar. As they got closer, they could hear a male voice. They froze. It was Aragam. He would see them if they stayed there. They sprinted back up the corridor and through the lab door as he turned the corner. He would hear the swoosh if it closed. The last mother held it open just enough to prevent the noise that would give them away. She hoped he wouldn't see it, and they held their breath as he approached. They could hear him muttering something about *vitamins* as he walked past without looking.

She waited a few seconds, and opened the door a little more, to check the corridor. It was clear, and his voice was getting quieter. She nodded to the others, and they sprinted down the corridor to the turn. The lead mother peeked around the corner. It was clear. At the end was the hangar, and in seconds they were outside the door, looking in.

In the cockpit, second sister was talking to the pilot. The movement in the hangar door window caught her eye. She gasped and moved away from the window.

"Are you alright, second council sister?" he asked, following her.

"Oh, er, yes. I felt a blast of air hit my eyes," she said, rubbing them. "Could you check the air conditioner for me? Then we'd better go."

"Yes, second council sister. The unit is in the engine room. I'll be just a minute."

"Very good, pilot."

She waited for him to be out of sight before running down the ramp and waving the mothers in. They didn't hesitate. She directed them to the cargo hold and closed the door as the pilot returned.

"Everything okay, pilot?"

"Yes, second council sister. It's strange, the air conditioning system isn't in operation."

"Yes, that is strange. I hope you've checked thoroughly, especially after the explosion that killed third council sister. Are you sure it's safe to fly?"

"Yes, second council sister. I did the preflight checks myself. Everything looks fine."

"Ah, in that case, can we go now, please?"

"Yes, of course, second council sister." He powered up the engines, and the shuttle glided out of the hangar.

"Perhaps you could check the systems again after we land," she said, looking at the cargo hold door. "I don't think I could live with myself if something happened to you on the flight back. Would you check for my peace of mind, pilot?"

"Yes, second council sister. I appreciate your concern."

She pursed her lips, nodded, and took her seat. The landing was gentle, with none of the bumps or groans that happened when she'd flown it. "That was a lovely landing, pilot. Perhaps you could give me some pointers next time I need a shuttle?"

"It would be my pleasure, second council sister."

"Thank you. Now, would you check the systems again for me, just to satisfy my, what is I'm sure, irrational paranoia?"

"Of course, second council sister," he said, leaving the cockpit.

She opened the cargo hold door. "Quickly," she said, waving at them, and pressing the ramp button. "Wait in that building over there."

"Thank you, sister," one of them said, as they sprinted down the ramp and disappeared into the warehouse.

"Everything looks fine, second council sister."

"That's good," she said, exhaling in fake relief. "I'll sleep better knowing you got back to the ship safely."

As she stepped off, the hiss from the hydraulic struts raising the ramp startled her. She looked back and gave the pilot a wave as it sealed into the body of the shuttle. *The male species is so easily manipulated by flattery.* And with a painted smile, she watched the shuttle disappear into the night sky.

She called her General. "Are you there?"

"Yes, sister. It's good to hear from you. We were worried for a while."

"I'm fine, General. Can you get to the cavern? I'm sending the mothers of the new sisters to you. First sister has badly abused them, General. You must take care of them and keep them safe."

"Yes, sister. We'll be there to meet them."

"Have you got materials for the new colony?"

"There's some we'll take from here. We'll use what we have to start the construction."

"Perfect. Once first sister discovers the mothers are missing, I suspect time will get short."

"We'll have it done, sister."

"I know you will, General. The mothers will come down the tunnel to the cavern in the next few minutes."

"We'll leave now. Will I see you?"

"Not this time, General, but soon."

"We look forward to that day."

She closed the call and went into the warehouse. The mothers huddled together, shivering. "This is the last leg of your trip to safety, sisters. Can you make it?"

"We will do whatever we must, sister."

"Good. The workers should be asleep by now, and the warriors are out on a training exercise. No one should see us, but let's not take any chances. Follow me."

They wrapped the blankets tight and followed her outside. The white grass crunched under their bare feet as they ran to keep up with her.

"Wait here," she said, before opening the door to the facility. The darkness inside confirmed there was no one inside. "Come on." They slipped in behind her.

They made their way down the corridor into the serum room. "Wait by that door over there. I need to get something." They moved across the room, avoiding the examination tables that brought back the nightmare of first sister's abuse.

She took one of the vials of modified paralytic from the cabinet and sealed it in a cool bag. "Let's go," she said opening the door to the secure area. They ran across the sand and into the tunnel that led to their freedom.

"My General and a few of his soldiers, your males, will meet you at the other end and escort you to our colony. You'll be safe there."

"You're not coming with us?" the last mother said, holding back.

"Not this time."

"Thank you for saving us, sister."

"Give this to my General. Tell him to keep it safe for me." She handed her the cool bag.

The mother took it, then kissed her on the cheek.

"Yes, yes. Go now, go."

With a smile, she ran down the tunnel to catch up with the others.

And so the rebellion begins, she said to herself.

∞

The mother finished cleaning the cuts. The cold water, although soothing, brought bruises to the surface, swollen, purple, vicious bruises. She could feel Aragam leering at her naked body.

"If I had the chance to choose before, I would have chosen you." He licked his lips and continued to stare.

She took the blanket from the table and covered herself. Her movement jolted him from whatever fantasy was playing out in his mind, and looking away, checked the time. "Where are the others?" he asked.

She shrugged and turned her back on him.

"The other mothers aren't in here," he said, turning to the warrior sitting in the lab, with his feet on the bench. "Would you go look for them? They can't have gone far."

"Not my problem," he said, yawning.

Aragam tutted as he walked by. The corridor was silent. *Where could they be?* Second sister told him they knew their way around. *I'll just wait*, he said to himself. His communicator buzzed, and the name on the screen said, first council sister. He squirmed. It buzzed again. He had to answer.

"Yes, first council sister."

"Bring the females you've selected to my chambers now. The warrior you have with you will help if there's any trouble."

"Yes, first council sister." He felt his knees buckle, and he slumped against the wall. He looked up and down the corridor, hoping they would miraculously appear and save him.

The lab door swooshed as it opened. "What are you doing sitting there?" the warrior said.

"First council sister wants us to bring the next two females to her chambers, now," he said, struggling to get to his feet.

"Fine, where are they?"

"I don't know."

"Best you find them then."

"Best *we* find them. If we go back without them, no excuse will be good enough. She'll have us served on a plate - literally."

"Hmm, right, you go that way. I'll go this way. Be back here in ten minutes. They have to be around here somewhere."

They searched the corridors, opening every door they came across. Aragam searched the corridor on the right and into the hangar. He ran between the shuttles and checked in all the rooms. He came out of the control room just as a shuttle docked.

He could see the pilot frowning at him through the cockpit window.

"Who have you just transported, pilot?" he said, as he walked off the shuttle.

He pulled his shoulders back and stood over him. "Why were you in the control room? You're a kitchen worker and don't have the authority to be in there. Explain yourself."

"I am carrying out a search for first council sister. I have her authority to look everywhere."

"I see," he said, bowing to a higher authority. "In that case, I transported second council sister to the facility on the surface."

"Was there a group of females with her?"

"No, just her."

"Right, err, thank you," he said. *Where could they be?*

"Have a good evening," the pilot said, waving as he walked out.

Maybe the warrior has found them, he hoped as he went back to the lab. His heart sank when he returned alone.

He turned his wrist when his communicator buzzed. "It's her," he said. They looked at each other as it buzzed again. The color drained from their faces.

"Yes, first council -"

"Where are you? Why aren't you here yet?"

"The mothers aren't back from their exercise yet, first council sister."

"Well, call whoever is guarding them and get them to bring them back immediately. I want the females here now, kitchen worker."

He hesitated then said, "they are not being guarded first council sister. On your orders, I left the cell door unlocked for them to exercise unaccompanied."

"What! You did what?"

"Left the door unlocked as instructed, first council sister."

"I never gave that order."

"But second council sister said it was your idea."

"What!"

"Yes, first council sister, otherwise I would never have left the door unlocked. She said it was a reward for their service."

"You'd better find them, or the reward I give you will be the last thing you ever receive."

"Yes, first council sister."

The call went dead. They looked at each other again. "Maybe they've gone to the other private chambers to see the babies?"

"Oh, yes. Good idea. Let's go," the warriors said.

∞

What is second sister up to? She thought as she pulled on her top robe. "Come on, you two. Let's pay second council sister a surprise visit," she said to her bodyguards, who fell in behind.

They marched in perfect sync all the way to the hangar and into the room with the Meta-gate. She activated it and they stepped through, coming out into the gate room in the living compound on the surface. She loved the tingling going through the meta-gates gave her. Her bodyguards were not so keen, throwing up all over the gate room's floor.

She huffed. "You'll clean that up later," she said. "Let's see what second council sister has to say for herself." She stepped over the lumpy puddle. "Come on."

In the dark, she could see light coming from the serum room. *No one should be in there at this time of night.* She crashed through the door, closely followed by her bodyguards, who had their hands on their weapons. Second sister jumped and the smash of the glass flask echoed around the room.

"Oh, my goodness," she said, holding her hands to her chest.

"Clumsy," first sister said. "What are you doing?"

"Oh, err, I was just, err-"

"Spit it out. What are you doing in here?"

She took a breath to recover. "You scared me, sister. I was making sure everything was ready to process the males from tomorrow's gatherings."

"Right. Okay, yes, good." She raised her eyebrows.

She could see that first sister wasn't expecting such a reasonable answer, so pressed her advantage. "You startled me, sister. Did you need something? Can I get you a drink, to warm you?" she asked.

"You can tell me what you've done?"

"What I've done, sister? What do you mean?"

"Your attitude and compassion for the humans, especially the females, I find unbearable. You seem to have forgotten they are here to serve us, and after your display earlier this evening, I have concerns about our relationship. And now the rest of the mothers are missing."

"Missing, sister. How?"

"You ordered the kitchen worker to leave their cell door open. You told him it came from me. How dare you do that?" She took a step toward her. Her bodyguards drew their weapons. "And now no one knows where they are. Where are they, *sister*?"

She held her ground. "How would I know?"

"You were the last one to see them. Where are they?"

"Well, that's not right, is it? The head kitchen worker was the last to see them when he took them food. According to the mothers, he is very familiar with them. And yes, I asked him to leave the door unlocked so they could exercise alone. I think they deserved that. After that disgusting spectacle in your chambers, I came straight here to calm down and rationalize what you did. I suggest you question him, as he was the last to see them, not me."

"So you're denying any knowledge of their whereabouts?" first sister said, her eyes blazing.

She refused to look away. “Absolutely, totally. Why don’t you ask the shuttle pilot if I was alone? He’ll confirm I was. Or check the surveillance cameras in the hangar.”

“Watch your attitude.” She waved a hand and her bodyguards raised their weapons. “I’m wondering if fourth sister’s lack of respect has rubbed off on you?”

“Of course not, sister. I know *exactly* who you are.”

“As long as you do.” She waved her hand again, and they lowered their weapons. “So, they must be on the ship. Where might they go?”

“Have you looked in the sisters private chambers? If I was a mother, I’d want to see my children.”

“Hmm, that makes sense.” She turned to leave. “I’m returning to the ship. Carry on.” She left the door open, intentionally letting the icy night air in.

She breathed a sigh of relief, crossed the floor, and closed the door. She’d done some ‘self-preservation’ chemistry, but now had to work fast, packing more lab equipment, chemicals, and compounds into the boxes she'd hidden under the bench.

She called the General. “Do you have them?”

“Yes, sister. They are here and safe.”

“That’s good. Remember, they’ve suffered a serious assault and will need some time and care to recover from it. Please make allowances.”

“Of course, sister.”

“Can you send a couple of your soldiers back to the cavern and meet me at the end of the tunnel? I’ve some equipment I need them to take to the colony.”

“I’ll send them back now.”

“Thank you, General. And we need to get the building of the mountain colony underway. I suspect we’re going to need it sooner rather than later.”

"We'll make a start first thing in the morning, sister."

"Good. She's scaling up the gatherings from tomorrow, and we're going to need it."

"Yes, sister."

"Thank you, General. I have a feeling I'll be joining you all soon."

∞

The council chambers felt cold. She shivered as she sat alone, thinking about the betrayal before a simmering rage boiled over. "Guards." They ran through the door, hands on their weapons, scanning the room for a target. "We're going to the hangar."

"Yes, first council sister."

She knew cameras recorded every movement and went straight to the control room when they got there. Someone had switched them off. The recording had stopped just before second sister left on the shuttle.

She clenched her jaw. *I still think it's you, and if I find out it is, you'll join your sisters, you treacherous bitch.*

"Get the pilot of the shuttle that took second council sister down to the surface, and bring him to the council chambers. Don't ask. Tell him I want him now."

"Yes, first council sister." Her tone had the hairs on the back of their necks stand.

"Just one of you. You go," she said, pointing. "You stay with me."

They left the hangar immediately, going separate ways at the top of the corridor.

Back in the council chambers, she sat at the head of the table, drumming her fingers, waiting. The delay added to the ferocity of her rage. She could hear the pilot protesting as he and her bodyguard approached the council chamber. The bodyguard hustled him through the door.

"First council sister, I must object to -"

She drew her knife and stabbed it into the table. He fell silent. "Tell me, pilot, you took second council sister down to the surface earlier this evening, correct?" She squeezed the handle.

Her calm voice confused him. "Yes, first council sister, that is correct."

She stood, pulled the blade free, and walked around the table toward him. "And tell me, pilot, was there anyone with her?"

Paralyzed by the sight of the knife she was pointing at him, sweat poured from his forehead. He couldn't answer. She was in striking distance, and he closed his eyes.

"Pilot!"

His eyes flew open as she licked her lips. "Did you hear me? I asked you if she was alone."

"Oh, err, yes, first council sister, she was."

"Are you certain?"

"Yes, first council sister."

"Did you see anything strange in the hangar?"

"No, first council sister."

"You're sure?"

"Oh, well, I saw a kitchen worker coming out of the control room. He told me second council sister was going to be a few minutes later than she'd said. It gave me the time to do additional preflight checks," he said, not daring to tell her he took a nap. "Oh, yes, and then I saw him coming out of the control room again as I docked. He said he had your authority to be in there."

"Hmm. Anything else you want to tell me?"

"No, first council sister. The flight was fine. Second council sister was her usually polite self. It was a pleasure to take her."

"Yes, yes, thank you, pilot." She sheathed her knife. "You can go, now."

"Thank you, first council sister," he said, wiping the sweat on his sleeve. He almost knocked into the bodyguards in his hurry to leave. He heard them laughing as he scurried away.

She sat back in her seat. "Get me that kitchen worker. You stay with me this time, you go get him."

"Yes, first council sister."

He found him in the kitchen. "First council sister wants to see you."

He froze. "Me? Why?"

"Let's go." He grabbed his shoulder, spun him, and pushed him towards the door. "I warn you, she's not in the mood for waiting."

He shrank as he walked through the council chamber door.

"Do you know why you're here?" she said, glaring at him.

"No, first council sister," he said. His voice shaking.

"Because someone saw you in the hangar's control room."

"Yes, first council sister. I was looking for the females, as you instructed."

"No."

He hunched his shoulders, bowing his head.

"Earlier. The pilot saw you."

"It was cold. I was waiting for him. Sist- err, second council sister said I could."

"Was this before or after you left the door open for them to escape?"

"Before, no. After, no. Oh, I can't remember, first council sister."

"Did you see anything on the monitors in there?"

"Err, yes."

"Really, what?"

"Err, no. I don't know."

"You'd better know. Did you or didn't you?" The bodyguards pressed a hand on each of his shoulders, holding him still. He looked up. She drew her knife and grinned when he flinched. "What did you see?" She cleaned under a fingernail with the point. "It's okay, just tell me the truth."

"I don't know, first council sister," he said, looking up at the bodyguards, then at the knife.

"You don't know?" she said, turning the point towards him.

"I don't know, maybe. Or were they just blank? I don't know."

"So, they were blank? Were they blank, or did you see images on them?"

"I can't be sure, first council sister."

Her rage was clouding her judgment, and she couldn't tell if he was a genius traitor, or genuinely as stupid as he sounded. It didn't matter. Even alleged treachery meant he could serve another purpose.

"Take this traitor to the Brig. I'll question him again tomorrow."

"What have I done, first council sister? I was just following orders."

"It is easy to distance yourself from the consequences of acts of treachery by saying you were following someone else's orders," she said, knowing he had no answer. "Take him away," she said to her bodyguards. "Then go to the warrior chambers, rouse them all, and instruct them to search the ship."

She could hear Aragam pleading his innocence as her bodyguards dragged him away. She frowned and shook her head. *Second sister helped them escape.* She knew it, but she didn't know how, nor could she prove it. *With the processing facility, the holding facilities, and the Meta-gates, your constant questioning of my authority, and your pathetic love for the humans, your usefulness had ended. You, second sister, will share the same fate as the others.*

∞

"Why are we different from you?" the child said to fifth sister.

"You are no different. You are Szatethess. Soon you and your sisters will have a seat on our ruling council with the rest of us, and have a big ship like this one of your own to command."

"Is that what we're called, Szatethess?"

"Yes, child. You are a female of our species. Szatethess like you and me are born and we rule. We convert our males from other sentient species into warriors and workers. They are Szateth and serve us."

"I'm hungry."

"You're always hungry," she said, laughing. "Here, speak into this and order what food you want." She raised her communicator. "Press this button, then speak."

"I want meat."

"Yes, fifth council sister, I'll bring it immediately."

"He thought I was you," she said, her eyes sparkling.

"Well, you used my communicator, and it shows up as me on his."

"Can I get one?"

"First sister will give you one of your own when you join the council."

"She's really mean."

"Sometimes it might sound like she's being mean, I'm sure, but she's not. She's teaching you to be good Szatethess, to be powerful."

"Like you?"

She chuckled. "Yes, child, just like me."

"She says we're here to make more warriors. Then we're going to go to other places to get more. She said we can watch her convert one of these humans into a warrior, then we could have him. It sounds like fun."

"I'm sure it will be."

"She said, second sister, loves the humans more than us and lives on the surface with them. Why doesn't she love us?"

"Of course she does, silly. Second sister is a scientist. She's experimenting with the humans to have the human females give birth to Szatethess without having to use our eggs. We only have one. That's why there aren't very many of us. She's trying to make sure we survive. That's the main reason we're here."

"Did I come from your egg?"

"No, child, we only release our egg when we die, and because we can live for a long time, there aren't new sisters very often. So you, my child, are special." She could hear the chatter of the other children before they came in. Fifth sister told them she'd used a communicator to order food.

"Can we have a go, sister?"

"Maybe later, children."

"Oh, please. She's had a go."

"Later. Now it's playtime. Off you go."

"Oooh?" The toys saw their disappointment disappear.

The other sisters walked in and huddled around her. "Have you heard, sister?" seventh sister asked.

"Heard what?"

Eighth sister looked around to make sure the children couldn't hear. "The human mothers of these children are missing."

"What do you mean, missing? We're on a ship thousands of feet above the surface. How can they go missing?"

"Keep your voice down, sister. First sister has got the warriors out looking for them."

"And she's got the traitor who helped them escape in the Brig," sixth sister said.

"When did all this happen?"

"Yesterday, where have you been, under a rock?" ninth sister said.

"Ah, there you all are. Good." first sister said marching in. Her bodyguards blocked the doorway. "And where are my young sisters?" She scanned the room.

"There you are."

They stopped playing, and hearing her voice hurried into a straight line facing her.

"Look how big you're getting. Are you ready for tomorrow's lesson, young sisters?"

"Yes, first sister," they said together.

The other sisters broke from their huddle around fifth sister. "I hear you have found a traitor, sister. Congratulations," fifth sister said.

"Carry on, young sisters."

She turned to address them. "Yes, and that's why I've sought you out. I think we should have some entertainment and a celebration to mark the end."

"The end, sister. Of what?" ninth sister asked.

"The end of all treachery on board this ship," she said, narrowing her eyes and fixing them on her.

"Well, in that case. I think it's a great idea," sixth sister said.

Distracted by her enthusiasm, she blinked, relaxed her eyes, and shifted her gaze to see them all. "Good, Tonight then. Just after dark, in my chambers. This celebration is going to taste so sweet."

Their mouths watered, and for a moment, their reptilian instincts took over and they shivered in unison.

"Oh, and sisters, I have a special reward for you, for your most excellent guardianship of our young sisters. Look at them. They are wonderful." Her voice purred. She'd set things up for the next stage of her plan. She bowed to hide the malicious pleasure that was written all over her face, turned on her heels, and marched out.

"It's going to be a good night tonight," sixth sister said, rubbing her hands.

"I'm sure the meal is going to be excellent. I don't know so much about the reward. There's always a price for her generosity," fifth sister said.

"You're right, sister. Well, whatever it is, we're going to find out soon enough," ninth sister said, staring at the door.

∞

Followed by her bodyguards, first sister marched to the lower deck, barely able to contain her excitement. They took position outside the double doors after she'd gone in. She stripped off her clothes and ran through the swamp, feeling the exhilaration and careless freedom her private homage to home gave her.

She stopped at the flat rock where she and second sister had laid, absorbing the beauty of the atmosphere. It felt smooth as she ran her fingers over the surface, feeling its warmth. *I'll bring them here.* She grinned. *They will love it, and won't suspect a thing as I slit their throats and watch them bleed out.* She imagined the feel of their warm blood coating her hands.

Every fiber of her body was looking forward to the kills, and as she walked back to the doors, she made a mental list of the things she needed to bring and hide: her favorite blade to do the killing, the surgical tools to remove the eggs, a small cool box to store and keep them safe until she had all five. Then she would call second sister back to the ship and take hers. Her mouth watered. *Calm, calm,* the voice in her head said. *Soon.*

As she dressed, she glimpsed the time. It was getting late, and she still needed to prepare the kitchen worker for the evening meal. "You wait here, and you come with me. There are some things I need from the lab." The bodyguard waiting drew his weapon and stood in the middle of the doors. No one was getting in.

She marched at double time, and he struggled to keep pace. He was pleased to see the elevator. She continued at the same pace when they got out and marched to the lab. "Wait here," she said to him. He guarded the door, thankful for the break. In a bag, she put scalpels, scissors, clamps, spreaders, forceps, and a pair of bone shears, along with a cool box and some ice bricks. In her pocket, she put a vial of sedation fluid.

The lab door flew open. "Let's get back," she said. "There's more I need to do."

The frantic pace didn't let up. She ordered him to guard the doors with her other bodyguard as she went in. She hid the bag in a bush next to the shallow pool, then secured her knife under a lip on the edge of the rock. With a last look around, her whole body tingled. *One last thing to do, and everything will be ready.*

She jogged back to the doors, where her faithful bodyguards were waiting. They marched to the kitchen. "Which one of you is taking the food to the traitor in the Brig?"

"It is me, first council sister," said the youngest of the kitchen workers.

"And where is his food?"

"Here, first council sister." He picked up the plate of leftovers.

"I'll take it to him."

"Thank you, first council sister," he said, handing it to her.

"You look young for this job."

"Yes, first council sister, but I'm strong and can do it."

"Yes, you are," she said, feeling the muscles in his shoulder. "I'll keep my eyes on you. Can you dance?"

"A little, first council sister."

The kitchen fell silent.

"Good," she said, licking her lips. "Can you learn some more?"

"As you wish, first council sister."

"Good. I'll take this now. Maybe we'll see each other again soon."

Red-faced, he bowed as she left. With the plate in one hand, she broke the top off the vial of sedation fluid with the other and poured it over the food.

As soon as Aragam saw her entering the Brig, he protested his innocence again. "I only did what you council sisters told me to do. I touched nothing, I did nothing wrong. What have I done, first council sister? If I've offended you, please tell me how to make it right. I will do anything you ask of me."

"Calm yourself," she said. "I know it wasn't you. I apologize for the misunderstanding. You won't have eaten. I've bought food for you. It's not much. I can't be seen doing favors for prisoners. It's only leftovers, I'm afraid. Here." She passed the plate through the hatch.

"Thank you, first council sister. It's good of you." He took the plate, scooping handfuls of food into his mouth.

She shuddered, watching him. "There is one more service you'll do for me."

"Anything, first council sister," he said, spitting food from his mouth as he spoke.

"You've already done it." She threw her head back and laughed.

His eyes glazed over, he dropped the plate and slurred, "what's happening?"

"I want you to get him cleaned up, and when I call you, walk him to my chambers. He won't give you any trouble," she said to her bodyguards.

"Yes, first council sister."

"You come with me. I want you to announce the council sisters as they arrive."

The sun had just gone down, and she'd pushed the last of the loungers into a circle when her bodyguard announced fifth and ninth sister. "Come in, you're right on time." She clapped her hands and workers appeared with glasses and jugs of the best wine.

"The others are right behind us, sister," fifth sister said.

"Perfect. Once you've got a drink, please take a lounger and make yourselves comfortable."

The bodyguard appeared and announced the other three.

"Drinks for everyone," she said to the workers, who handed out glasses and poured wine.

"Please, everyone, take a lounger. Before tonight's entertainment begins, I'd like to raise my glass to you, my sisters, for all your support and hard work, especially with our young sisters. I'm sure you'll agree they'll strengthen and enhance our reputation across the universe. I am gratified to have such wonderful sisters by my side. So, to you." She raised her glass.

"To us," sixth sister said.

The others murmured something similar, raising their glasses in polite acceptance.

"As you know -" first sister said.

"Where is second sister? Shouldn't she be here too?" ninth sister said.

First sister's face dropped. The silence before she spoke was long enough for the atmosphere to become very dark. "Second council sister is otherwise engaged this evening. This celebration, ninth sister, is in honor of those here."

"But it was her who made this celebration possible, sister."

"On my orders, ninth sister, or have you forgotten?"

"No -"

"Very well then, can we enjoy our evening? I want to give you all something special. Let's not have the evening marred by someone who hasn't done what you've done, and who isn't here."

Her stare and unnatural silence were enough to stop ninth sister from pressing her further.

"As you know, over the last few months there has been an attempt on my life, which cost a loyal sister hers, a challenge to my leadership, and now, helped by a traitor, the escape of our young sisters mothers."

The uncomfortable shifting didn't go unnoticed. She saw the nervous smiles, the swallowing, and the hunching of shoulders.

She lifted her chin and, baring her teeth, said, "who, until now, had remained hidden?"

She lifted her wrist. "Bring him to us," she said into her communicator.

The workers refilled everyone's glasses. All eyes were on the door.

The bodyguard shoved the unsteady Aragam through the door, accompanied by disbelieving gasps, as he staggered to the center of the room. He stood swaying in front of first sister's lounger. He gave her a weak, drug-induced smile, unaware of what was happening.

"This? This is the traitor?" fifth sister asked.

"We spotted him twice in an area that is strictly off-limits to a kitchen worker. He insists he was just following orders, an order from me, and an order given to him by second sister. I gave no such order, neither did second sister."

She gestured for him to spin so they could inspect him.

"He had, on both occasions, been in the control room in the hangar. Sisters, the surveillance cameras were off. He switched them off to prevent us from seeing where the mothers went from the hangar. As you know, from there, they can access the rest of the ship, and we have yet to find them."

"Why would he do that?"

"The mothers told second sister he'd become overfamiliar with them, touching and suggesting things over the weeks he brought them food. I have witnessed his perverted voyeurism myself during one of my experiments with the females and the mothers. I can testify to his unnatural fantasies."

"So, you're saying he helped them escape so he could enact his fantasies?" ninth sister said.

"Exactly. He knows what he did, and his capture brings an end to all treason and a return to trust on this ship. There is only one sentence for a creature as low as this. Don't you agree, sisters?"

They slid forward to the edge of their loungers, their skin prickling, and excited eyes inspected their prize. It was the answer she wanted. With the effect of the drugs wearing off, confusion and paralyzing fear replaced compliance. They could smell it, and their mouths watered as his eyes drifted from one sister to another.

First sister stood. He could feel the warmth of her body close behind him. She wrapped an arm around his stomach, pulling him closer. The fingers of her other hand lightly combed through his hair, coaxing his head over and exposing his neck. "Thank you for your service," she said. Her hypnotic voice, so soft and relaxing, made him close his eyes. She looked at her sisters and smiled. Their drooling mouths opened as she sank needle-sharp teeth deep into his neck, ripping out his life.

As always, she fed first, taking the best meat. "His fear has made him sweet, sisters," she said, lifting her head out of his body's cavity, warm blood spilling from the sides of her mouth. "Take what you want."

The sounds of their feeding frenzy filled the chamber. In minutes, all that remained of Aragam were a few splintered bones. Full and contented, they returned to their loungers.

"Sisters, before we rest, I would like to invite you to the lower deck to feel and remember home. There you can be yourself, without the expectations, or the restrictions we have on us as council sisters. For a short while, you can let your natural instincts free. I would like to invite you individually for an hour each, tomorrow afternoon. Once there, I promise you the strains of the ship will become a distant memory."

"And we don't have to do anything for it?" ninth sister asked.

"You are such a cynic. No, of course not. As I have said, this celebration and reward will bring an end to treachery on board this ship."

"Forgive me, sister. It will be my pleasure to join you."

"I can assure you, sister, the pleasure is mine. As the wisest and oldest of us, would you like to come first, at midday?"

"Thank you, sister."

"I will send one of my bodyguards to escort you. Then an hour later would you like to come fifth sister, followed by you, my sisters, in rank order?"

With wide satisfied grins, they agreed.

"Rest now, sisters. Tomorrow is going to be a monumental day."

Their heavy eyes closed, savoring and digesting the sweetness of the meat that filled their distended bellies.

The chattering of cleaner workers roused the sisters when they opened the blinds. Their waking groans surprised them. They expected the room to be empty, but five pairs of squinting eyes adjusting to the assault of the sunlight confirmed it wasn't.

"Forgive us, council sisters. We didn't think anyone would still be here," the head cleaner worker said. "We'll come back later." She waved at the others to leave.

Fifth sister, more awake than the others, said, "no, no. It is we who should be leaving. You carry on."

The others yawned, extending their needle-like retractable teeth as they realigned their jaws. They eyed the cleaner workers, who fidgeted uncomfortably.

"Come on, sisters," she said, interrupting their fun. "First sister has already gone."

The workers bowed low as they left.

"She let us sleep in," sixth sister said, as they walked through the corridor to their chambers. "There's only a couple more hours before you get to spend some time on the lower deck, sister. You must be so excited?"

"I admit, I am," ninth sister said. "I'm not sure what to expect, but I imagine first sister will have created something as close to the real thing as possible. Yes, I'm looking forward to going down."

"You'll have just enough time to get cleaned up," sixth sister said, nodding toward her clothes.

She looked down at her blood-stained robes. "My goodness, he was a juicy one. Looks like I'm wearing more of him than I ate."

The others did the same, breaking into childish laughter.

She was fastening her freshly laundered robe when the bodyguard appeared.

"First council sister is ready for you now, ninth council sister, if you'd like to follow me."

"Lead the way." With fingers laced across her stomach, she walked tall, as befitting the oldest council sister, a couple of paces behind him. As they exited the elevator, the other bodyguard came to attention in front of a set of large double doors.

"First council sister is waiting for you inside." He opened the doors.

The warmth, smell, and moisture transported her mind back home the instant she walked in.

"Welcome, sister," first sister said, standing naked.

The bodyguard closed the doors, shutting out the sterile atmosphere of the ship.

"This is my sanctuary, sister. I come here to think and decide. Here we can be free. Remove your robes, sister. Leave them here and let us roam as nature intended."

Hypnotized by the beauty and surfacing memories of home, she undressed. Warmth and moisture bathed her body as she stood there, staring into the swamp.

"Come, sister, let me show you to the resting place. It's a flat rock where we can bask and soak up this wonderful atmosphere."

"I never knew all his was here, sister. It is truly wonderful."

"I knew you, of all the sisters, would appreciate it the most."

They walked through the swamp, coming out through the bushes into a clearing. In front of them a shallow pool mirrored their reflections, and In the middle was the flat rock.

"Let's rest and bask for a while," first sister said, leaping over the pool and crossing to the rock.

"I can't imagine a better way to spend an hour," she said, following.

"Sit there, sister," she said, positioning the unsuspecting sister for the kill. "Now, close your eyes and feel the heat as it rises through your body."

She sat next to her, close to the edge, feeling for the lip and her knife.

"Ah yes, sister, this is wonderful." She closed her eyes, leaned back on her hands, and took a deep breath, remembering the wonderful scents of home. "You have everything you want now. An endless supply of males for your warrior conversion facility, new young sisters to mold how you want, and you caught the traitor who tried to kill you." She smacked her lips. "You were right. He was so sweet."

"Yes, he was." she pulled the knife free, gripping the handle tight.

"What more could you want, I wonder?"

"There is one more thing."

She opened her eyes and scowled. "What more is there?"

In a swift, precise movement, she plunged the knife into the front of her throat. Only the bones in her neck stopped it from penetrating right through. There was no time to defend herself. Air and blood bubbled over the blade. Her eyes flew open. First sister leaned close. "Your egg," she said, twisting the blade and staring deep into her eyes as their light faded. "Thank you for your service."

Her last breath gurgled as it escaped the gaping wound. Her lifeless corpse fell back, slipping off of the knife. The back of her head hit the rock hard, cracking open. A pool of fresh blood oozed from the wound, as lines of warm blood from the hole in her throat ran down, joining it.

For a moment, she stared, mesmerized, as the pool got bigger. "Perfect, sister." It was a moment to savor. She closed her eyes to relive the moment the life left her body. "Yes, perfect." Drunk on the feeling killing gave her, she wiped the knife's blade on her dead sister's skin, then secured it back under the lip.

The blood from the wounds lapped over her fingers. The warm sensation made her shiver. She slid off the rock and stood at the side of the body. "Alright then, back to work. Careful now, sister, we don't want to do anything that will damage that precious egg, do we?"

She couldn't resist leaning over and pressing her palms into the warm red liquid. The metallic smell drifted into her nose, and the urge to taste it, to suck it off her fingers, was almost too much to bear. *No, no, no, there's work to do* but promised herself a taste before she finished with them all.

She walked around to the top of the rock, pulling the body further up, laying it out flat.

"I'll be back in a moment. You won't miss me, will you?"

She giggled to herself as she retrieved her bag from the bush.

"Only straight cuts and clean incisions, I promise," she said, putting the bag next to the body and arranging the tools in order of their use.

"Now, let's get started. Ready? Oh silly me, my hands are slippery. That won't do at all." She went and rinsed her hands clean in the shallow pool.

"That's better. Here we go then. Let's find that egg, shall we?" With the scalpel, she sliced open her abdomen, reached in, and pulled out most of the organs, placing them next to her head over her right shoulder.

The body jerked and shook as she cut and gouged to remove more flesh. "Are you not comfortable, sister? Hmm, perhaps a cushion." She cut out her liver and kidneys, and cut off a breast, placing them under her head.

"There. We don't want you moving now. We're at the most important part. I just need to find your uterus and cut it out with your fallopian tubes, take your egg, and we'll be done. Not long now, sister."

With her scissors and scalpel, she carefully snipped and cut through the remaining viscera in her pelvic area, exposing the Uterus.

"There it is. Well, done sister." She lifted it free with the tubes attached and felt for her prize. "It feels perfect, sister."

She cut the tube, freeing the egg, reverently placing it in the cool box, and covering it with ice.

"Look at you, sister, displaying yourself like that. If only everyone could love you as I do like this." She took a mental picture to savor the sight again when the work was over. "Well, there's more to be done, and your sisters will join you shortly."

The body had to be moved before the next sister arrived. They knew she was a stickler for time. According to her communicator, she had fifteen minutes.

"Time enough." She leaned over the body, rolled it towards her, stepped back, and let it drop onto the grass. She looked around. *Where shall I put this?* The bushes on the other side of the clearing were thick enough to hide the body. *Ah yes, in there.*

"You're much lighter, sister. Have you lost weight?" Her cackle echoed as she dragged the body away. She put her tools in the bag and hid them back in the bush. The entrails were slippery, but she scooped them up and then let them slide through her fingers over the body. Only drying blood remained on the rock.

Fifth sister appeared through the door, just as she threw ninth sister's robes into the bushes. "Ah, fifth sister, welcome."

"Well, I don't know what to say. I have no words," she said, her wide eyes trying to take everything in at once.

"I know what you mean, sister. I feel the same every time I come here. Would you like to see more?"

"Show me everything, sister."

"I'll take you to the very end. Now, remove those robes, be free, and let me show you my most favorite place, my resting rock."

Without a word fifth sister stripped off, leaving her robes in a heap by the doors. As they walked through the swamp, fifth sister asked how she had brought a taste of home on board the ship.

She wrapped an arm around her waist. "Well, it wasn't easy, I can tell you. I've had to tend to it, care for it, all these years to make sure it stayed alive. I planted it when this ship was under construction."

"It's ancient?"

"Well, yes. I suppose it is." They stepped out into the clearing. "This is it, my resting rock."

"What happens here?" she said, stepping over the shallow pool and looking at the rock's blood-stained surface.

"Sometimes I hunt here, sister. Like we did back home." She moved to the side of the rock and reached for her knife, holding it behind her back.

Fifth sister ran her fingers over the stains, breaking the scabbed surface where it hadn't dried. She looked at the wet blood on the tips. "You hunted here with ninth sister?"

She moved in behind her. "Something like that."

She spun, her reptilian instinct sensing the danger. The blade was already on its way to her throat when she saw it glint. She caught first sister's wrists, just as the point pierced her windpipe, stopping it. She squealed, resisting hard. But being the expert killer, first sister slammed her other hand onto the back of fifth sister's head, pulling it onto the knife, and like ninth sister, she gurgled her last breath and slumped to the floor.

"Thank you for your service," she said, pulling the knife free.

She stood over the crumpled body, gritting her teeth. Drips of blood from the knife splattered the body.

"This won't do," she said, stabbing the knife into the ground. "Damn it, sister, now I've got to lift you onto the rock, Damn it! The least you could have done was to sit first, like your other sister." She took a deep breath, hooked her arms under the shoulders, and heaved the body onto the rock, letting it flop back.

"Damn it, Damn it, Damn it!" She walked back to the pool and scrubbed her hands, turning the water a deeper red, grabbed her bag, and stomped back to the body.

Still shaking, she spat at the face of her lifeless sister, ripped the knife from the ground, and screaming, gashed her face in every direction, mutilating her beyond recognition. She ripped open her abdomen in a deep, jagged cut. Intestines spilled through the gash. The sticky, slimy sound as they bubbled up made her stop. *What have I done to you?*

She took a deep breath. "We could have really ruined things, sister," she said, waving the tip of the knife at her before putting it back under the lip. After another deep cleansing, breath, "Let's start over, shall we?" She got her bag and laid out the tools as before. With small snips and precise cuts, she preceded with the evisceration.

"I have it, sister. Thank you," she said, looking at the displayed body and taking another mental picture. There was more time for the cleanup, but shaking her head and closing her eyes, she knew how close she'd come to ruining things.

The killing of the other three sisters was uneventful, even boring, she thought. Her work done, she hummed and smiled to herself as she washed her hands in the blood-saturated pool, leaving eighth sister's corpse displayed on the rock. With her prized eggs carefully packed in the cool box, she made her way to the doors.

She dressed, and while caressing the cool box, she marched back to the lab with her bodyguards. The cell door was still open when she went in. Her nostrils flared, and gritting her teeth, she reminded herself who the real traitor was. It was the only egg that remained. *I'm going to take yours too, sister.*

Neural Blockchain Journal Entry #933

All opposition and threats to my authority on board are gone.

I have new sisters now who will help me get what I want, what we the Szatethess deserve.

I will take all the males, leave this planet, find my fleet, conquer new ones, and suppress rebellion on any of the others.

There's one more thing I have to do before we go, deal with second sister. I trusted her and she played me. The other sisters were too stupid for it to be one of them. It had to be her. Only a council sister could have set up the commander, scared the first officer, and used a crew member like that. I know she freed the mothers and got them to the surface.

Now, it's her turn to join the harvest.

First Council Sister - Szateth leader
Advanced planetary research fleet.

Neural Blockchain Journal Entry #117

This will be my last recorded journal entry for the ship's logs.

She knows it was me. There's no use denying it anymore. She refused to see how important humans are to our survival. What I did, I did to save our race from extinction. I have no regrets.

I am going to stay here. With the help of humans, I will alter their evolution and save our species.

Second Council Sister
Advanced planetary research fleet.

Fifteen

Control, capture, and awkward conversations.

The communicator on her wrist buzzed. The caller ID read 'First Sister.' She pressed her lips and frowned. *What can she want?* She ground her teeth as it buzzed again.

"Yes, sister."

"Ah, you're there. Good. I can see the facility is in full swing from the numbers I'm getting."

"I have nothing to do with it. The workers run it for me."

"They are efficient. The worker serum works very well. I'm coming to see you."

"Why?"

"We need to clear the air."

"I will not change my mind about the humans."

"I'm aware."

"What is there to talk about, then? I'll stay here and you can stay up there. We don't need to see each other."

"That doesn't work for me. I need to do things face-to-face. I'll be with you in an hour. Be ready." She ended the call.

She knows. I'll be ready alright. There was little time, and she was fastening her outer robe as she ran down the ramp and across the wet ground to the serum room. Inside, it was full of warriors, workers, and males strapped to tables. Every room, every table, and every syringe were full. She grimaced, trying to block out the groans of pain. The workers avoided making eye contact. No one challenged her as she took the vial of modified paralytic from the cabinet.

It was clear from the lack of respect usually afforded a council sister when she entered a room that first sister had instructed them not to acknowledge her. More proof that she knew. It was something she wasn't used to, and it made her feel uncomfortable, invisible, like she was a ghost. A quick, disgusted snort took away any feelings of guilt.

With the vial in her pocket, she returned to her shuttle, hoping she'd never have to go there again. From the cockpit, she waited for first sister to appear, and predictably, as the minute clicked over, completing the hour, she came marching out of the compound, with her bodyguards and a half dozen warriors. She would want to talk and arrest her in the most formal room on the shuttle, the conference chamber, keeping up the pretense of authority to her warriors.

She sneered, watching her march in front like a great General. *You can play your game, sister, but I have one of my own.* She moved out of the cockpit and went over to the drinks cabinet in the conference chamber, took two glasses and a bottle of their best wine, putting them on the table.

"You have this coming, sister," she said, wanting to hear her own voice say it, as she cracked the top off the vial and poured half its contents into one glass. She could hear footsteps on the ramp and poured the wine into the glasses.

"There you are, sister," first sister said, marching into the chamber with her bodyguards close behind her.

"I am prepared for you, sister."

"I have harvested the others. I have their eggs safely in storage and you're going to implant them."

"I see. Did you make them suffer?"

"Of course not. I'm not an animal." She grinned.

"If that's what you think," she said, looking away and reaching for the glasses.

"What did you say?"

"I said, would you care for a drink?"

"Hmm. Well, I suppose one won't hurt before we go."

She handed her a glass, and together, they emptied them in one go.

"I know it was you."

"You know it was me, what?"

"Who got the mothers off the ship?"

"Really?"

"Yes, really. The first officer told me what you said to him. You set up the kitchen worker to take the fall for you, didn't you... I thought I was a master of manipulation, but you... If I didn't need you for the implantations, you would be kill... err... ki..." The sharp barking cough made her squeeze her eyes shut.

She leaned in close. "Tell your bodyguards to wait outside... Do it now."

She opened her eyes, frowned, and coughed again, this time fighting to draw breath.

"Tell them, sister."

Her eyes bulged. "You two." She coughed, leaning on the table. "Wait outside."

They looked concerned, but left without question.

"What is this? What have you done?" She gripped her throat.

"Just a little insurance, sister. What you're experiencing now will wear off in a few hours. I promise. Do I have your full attention?"

She stared, sipping in the air in short gasping breaths, unable to speak.

"Good. let me tell you what's happened and what's going to happen. Before you enjoyed Aragam, the head kitchen worker, I had him slip you a little something in one of your meals. It was a paralyzing agent which I'd altered with a biological inhibitor, just for you. It is harmless until a second component, a depolarizing agent, meets and activates it. You've just had a tiny dose and you're feeling the effects of it right now. Just in case you thought I was bluffing."

She waved the vial in front of her face.

"At which point, and if you were to have a full dose, as it does in human males, the paralyzing agent will slow and eventually stop *all* your muscles and organs from functioning. It would be a slow, painful death, sister."

First sister forced herself to stand straight, staring with a hard, intense gaze, as her breathing became a little easier.

"There, as you can see, I keep my promises, sister. It'll be a few hours before it has completely worn off. For now, though, I suggest you don't speak." She patted her shoulder, then moved the glasses before sitting on the table, facing her. She touched her forehead.

First sister saw a blinding flash in her mind. Its intensity made her gasp and close her eyes.

"Open your eyes, sister. I've given you a gift, - of sorts."

She opened them, trying to focus and ignore the pain caused by the light.

"I have added life blocks to your neural blockchain. That means you will live for a very long time, sister. *I want you to suffer, sister*, and watch as I help the humans evolve. I want you to remember what you did to our sisters, and live with the fact that I could take your life anytime I want. You will never know who's going to administer the other half of the agent, nor when you have taken it. For now, you are safe. However, if I am arrested, imprisoned, killed, have an unfortunate accident, or just inexplicably disappear, I have given instructions for the full dose to be given to you. Do you understand?"

She nodded, holding the stare.

"Good. From now on, sister, I hold your life in my hands. Now, this is what's going to happen next. I will come with you to the ship to collect the eggs. Once I have them, I will leave. No one will get in my way, or try to stop me, sister. Am I clear so far?"

She nodded sharply.

"Once I leave the ship, you will not follow me. Do you understand?"

The tension in her body told her she did.

"Good... Hear me now, sister," she said, curling her lips. "For murdering my sisters, for betraying our primary mission, for trying to decimate this planet, for putting our entire species at risk for your own ends, you will never leave this planet. That ship will be your home and your tomb when you die."

She coughed in pain and tried to speak, but when she couldn't, spat at her.

"Charming, sister... I told you not to speak." She wiped her face. "Let me be clear. If I see you again, or the ship tries to leave, you will die."

Her stare grew colder as she clenched her fists.

"Oh, I know you want to kill me, sister. I'm certain every thought in that twisted, sick mind of yours is listing ways you would do it. But you can't, and I want you to feel that torment and frustration for the rest of your long life... Now, shall we go?"

The intense stare gave way as her eyebrows pulled together, the crease between them deep and clear. The color draining from her face left her looking haunted.

"Guards, can you come in, please?"

The door opened instantly.

"First council sister is unwell. Can you help me get her back to the ship?"

"Yes, second council sister. Should we get her to medical?"

"No, that's unnecessary. It's just something she's eaten or drunk. It will pass. Take her to her chambers the moment we get back and let her rest. Do not disturb her and do not let anyone else disturb her, either."

"Very well, second council sister."

She led the way. They took an arm each and followed. The squad of warriors fell in behind, and they marched back to the gate room.

The bodyguards didn't throw up this time as they stepped through the gate. The warriors were not so lucky.

"Clean this mess up," she said

The warriors jumped to attention.

"And once you're done, go back to your bunks."

"Yes, second council sister," they said.

"You two, bring first sister, and follow me."

The warriors were busy on their hands and knees, mopping up vomit as they left the room and went into the hangar. She saw the first officer in the control room, and, catching his eye, scowled, then bared her teeth. He looked down and carried on with what he was doing, visibly shaking. They walked past the control room window and the memory of making him beg, soil himself and pass out made her smile as they left the hangar.

"Come with me to the lab first. I'll give her something to help her rest, then take her to her chambers."

First sister looked at her warriors trying to shake her head.

"Don't worry, first council sister, we'll get you to your chambers soon," one of them said.

Too weak and out of breath, her head slumped forward.

In the lab, she filled a syringe. "Hold her up." They lifted her and she slid the needle into her arm.

"What is that you've given her, second council sister?"

"It's just a sedative. It will make her sleep, then wake as if nothing had happened. She might have a headache, so give her these if she does." She handed over two painkillers.

"Thank you, second council sister."

"Of course. Now, take her, please." A relaxed smile crossed her face as they left with her.

Once they'd gone, she put gloves on and lifted the lid of the storage unit. The burst of cold air stung her face as she held her breath and reached in, taking the harvested eggs, all the P9R, and packing them into a large cool box before closing it. The warm air soothed her skin, and she breathed again. *There's plenty of time. What else do I need?* She collected instruments, scanners, computer pads, drugs, compounds, and chemicals — everything she needed for a fully functioning lab at her mountain colony — and loaded them onto a cart. *That should do it.*

With a last look around, she was about to switch the lights off when she heard crying from the cell. *Can't be, can it?* She unlocked the door. *My goodness, it is.*

The mother was sitting in the corner, on the floor, wrapped in a blanket. She raised her head when the door opened, beamed, and sobbed when she saw who it was.

"Come with me, sister. It's time to get off this ship," she said, stretching out a hand.

They embraced, the mother unable to speak through her tears. "There, now. You're safe, and we're going to join the others. Are you ready?"

The smile in her eyes told her she was.

"Come on, then." They left the cell. "You can't go wearing that. Wait here a moment." She took coveralls and boots from the closet and handed them to her. "Put these on and push the cart. If anyone stops us, you're my assistant for the day. We're going to the hangar."

The first officer was still in the control room when they got there. He looked across when the cart bumped through the door. She glared at him, and he looked away again, not daring to challenge her. The room with the Meta-gate was now spotlessly clean. She activated it, and they pushed the cart through without looking back. The Meta-gate room on the other side was empty, and taking advantage of the privacy, called her General.

"Yes, sister. Good to hear from you," he said.

"I need you, General. We have to move everything to the mountain colony. There is a window for a few hours and a lot of equipment. Can you and a few soldiers meet me, where you left fourth sister's body?"

"Yes, sister. We'll leave now."

"You'll have to come around the mountain on foot. The facility is about to get the latest batch of gathered males, and there will be warriors in the cavern."

"It'll take us a couple of hours to get there if we double-time it. But we'll be there, sister."

"I have a few things to get from the shuttle. We'll meet you there."

"We?" he asked.

"I have a surprise for the mothers."

"They could do with something good to happen."

"Say nothing to them. Let it be a surprise. We'll meet you soon."

"So, it's starting then?"

"Well, I've started something, and she's going to want blood. We better be ready. She's going to come for us soon enough."

She heard him snort. "Well, she is in for a hell of a surprise when she does," he said.

∞

It was dark when she opened her eyes. The effects of the paralyzing agent and sedative made her sleep heavily.

"Guards, get in here," she said, croaking through the pain in her throat.

In seconds, they were by her side. "Thank goodness you're awake, first council sister."

"How long have I been asleep?"

"A whole day, first council sister."

"A whole day. Why didn't you wake me?"

"Second council sister told us you were not to be disturbed."

"That treacherous bitch." She sat up and threw the blankets off. Her legs buckled as she tried to stand.

Her bodyguards reached to help her. "Don't touch me." They snatched their hands away. She sat scowling, waiting for the dizziness to stop before finally getting to her feet.

"You," she said, looking at one of them. "Get the medic and bring him here. And you get me some water and fetch me my robe."

"Yes, first council sister," they said and set to their tasks.

Still feeling light-headed, she staggered to her lounger, lay, and closed her eyes. *I'm going to find you, torture you, and rip your egg out while you're still alive.* She drifted off again.

In her sleep, she could hear a distant voice. "How long has she been like this?"

"More than a day."

"First council sister, can you hear me?"

"Let me sleep..."

"Come now, you've slept long enough."

She felt a sharp stab in her arm. "Aargh, what are you doing? I'll kill you for this," she said, slurring.

"Well, perhaps when you're more able... You two help me get her up. We need to get her walking, so the effects of the drugs wear off more quickly."

They lifted her, and she hung her head, complaining she wanted to sleep, as they dragged her around her chamber.

"Keep her moving," the medic said.

They did as instructed, encouraging her to walk, until eventually, her legs moved, and she could bear her own weight. She lifted her head. "You can let me go now."

Still a little unsteady, she leaned on the back of the lounger.

"How are you feeling now, first council sister? The injection I gave you will flush your body of toxins."

"I think it's more complicated than that. I need you to run a full screening of my blood."

"What am I looking for, first council sister?"

"Anything out of the ordinary. I believe there is a dormant paralytic agent in my blood."

"I see. Let me take some and run some tests."

"How long before you know?"

"For a full screening, two days."

Her head cocked to one side. "You have twelve hours."

"I don't think you understand, first council sister. Some tests take twenty-four hours to yield a result. I can't make it happen any faster."

Her reply was instant. "No, it's you who doesn't understand, medic. I will give you your twenty-four hours. If you can't give me a definitive answer by then, I will personally throw you out of the airlock and watch you fall. Am I clear?"

"Yes, first council sister. Can I get some help?"

"Use whomever you want. Time is ticking, medic."

The medic's hands shook as he approached the vein with the needle. She gripped his wrist, steadying the shake. "Calm yourself, and do it right." She guided the needle into her arm, and he took what he needed.

"Thank you, first council sister," he said, putting the vials in his medkit.

"Go, now."

He bowed and left without another word.

"I need you two to fetch the first officer, the chief engineer, and the new commander of the warriors and bring them to the council chambers," she said to her bodyguards.

"Yes, first council sister."

Alone in her chambers, she felt frustrated and vulnerable, and for the first time, she wasn't the one in control. It was exactly what second sister said she would feel. She lifted a glass of water to her lips, then stopped, fearing what might be in it. With her heart pounding, she smashed it against the wall. Second sister had threatened her life, and like a cornered animal, she knew of only one way out - attack.

Anger and thoughts of murderous revenge held her tall as she marched to the council chambers, - she knew killing and liked it. The others hadn't arrived when she got there, and her thoughts darkened as she paced, waiting.

"Sit," she said, stabbing a finger at the chairs the moment they walked through the door.

They took their seats, and her bodyguards joined her at the head of the table. None of them said anything. This was not a social gathering.

"What is the status of the shuttles?" she said to the first officer.

He tried to match her sense of urgency with his answer. "Other than some minor maintenance, and the one on the surface, the other eight will be ready to fly in a matter of hours, first council sister," he said.

"Make sure it gets done."

"Yes, first council sister."

"How many more warriors can we accommodate, commander?"

"Space is getting tight, but maybe another couple of hundred."

"And if you had an empty deck?"

"Three, maybe four battalions, four thousand more warriors, first council sister."

"You'll have it."

He smiled, leaned forward, and met her eyes. She answered his smile with a sharp nod.

"I want more holding facilities and Meta-gates built. At least four times the number there are now," she said to the chief engineer.

He squirmed uncomfortably.

"Is there a problem?"

"Materials and energy to power them, first council sister."

"Take it then."

"The ship generates just enough to power those online now, first council sister. If we add more Meta-gates, there won't be enough, and the entire network will fail."

"So, you need more power. Can you build generators on the surface for the Meta-gates?"

"Well, yes, I suppose we could..."

"It's a closed question, chief engineer. Yes, or no?"

"If we have the right materials, then yes, first council sister."

"Good, what do you need.?"

"I could build large power generators with resonance chambers using the planet's natural frequencies to generate the energy. I could have them built using natural stone. We'd need to quarry that. So I'd need workers... And Gold, lots of it for the capstones to transmit the energy to the Meta-gates. That would need to be found and mined."

"So, you need workers, right?"

"Yes, first council sister, and materials."

"Re-task the satellite to find what you need, and have the facility workers use the worker serum. Convert as many males as you need. Tell the facility manager I've given instructions for him to use worker serum on the next batches of gathered males until you have what you need. Tell him if there's an issue with that to speak to me. The materials you can get from the planet?"

"Yes, first council sister."

"Good. Take what you need, chief engineer, and make it happen."

"There will be a side effect to all the energy production and transmission, first council sister. Global warming."

"I don't care about that, chief engineer. For us, that's a good thing. Just get it done." She coughed and leaned on the table, staring at the commander. "You two, you know what you need to do. Get on with it. Commander, you stay here."

She waited until the engineer and the first officer left. "Commander, I want you to send two of your best warriors to watch second council sister on the surface. I want them to report what she does. Who she speaks to, when, and what she says. I don't want her to leave their sight. I want to know everything."

"Yes, first council sister."

"I will have the lower deck made ready for more warriors, commander, and once the Meta-gates get built, you will have your battalions and we will leave this planet, find the fleet, and put them to good use."

"Thank you, first council sister. I'll assign my best warriors and send them under the cover of darkness tonight."

She nodded. "Leave me now, commander."

He bowed and left.

"Come on, you two," she said to her bodyguards. There was nothing more she could do until she got the results of the blood tests, and she tried to relax the tension in her jaw as they marched back to her chambers.

"Wake me, mid-morning. No one except for the medic is to disturb me," she said, struggling to keep her eyes open. Adrenaline and her plans for vengeance had gotten her through the meeting. Now, alone in her chambers, her body crashing from the high of the Adrenaline dump, she slumped on her bed and slept like the dead.

As always, they carried out their orders to the letter. When she woke and called them in, they informed her that the commander was waiting outside to see her.

"Send him in."

"Good morning, first council sister," he said, standing to attention.

"Report, commander."

He stood at ease. "I sent my warriors as requested, but when they got there, second sister was nowhere to be seen. They questioned the workers and the warriors at the facility, but none of them had seen her."

"Damn it!"

"What would you like me to do, first council sister?"

"Organize a search, commander, a small party, do it quietly, use your best trackers. Tell them they are not to engage when they find her, but to report to you immediately."

"Yes, first council sister."

"Start with her shuttle, commander, then have it flown back. I want to deprive her of her shelter."

He nodded and marched out.

Her stomach growled, letting her know she was hungry, and she pressed her hands on it when it growled again. Would second sister have spiked her food with the depolarizing agent purely out of spite? She didn't think so, but she didn't think she'd betray her either. If it had been her, she would have. She daren't take the chance. Hunger and thirst she could deal with. The need to kill second sister and the ache for the need for patience were what she struggled with the most.

She needed a distraction. "To the hangar," she said, marching past her bodyguards. "Let's check on the shuttles first. Then onto engineering, and medical."

The first officer met her in the hangar bay, and together they inspected each of the shuttles. "As you can see, first council sister. There isn't much to do, short of maintenance checks and refueling."

"Perfect, first officer. Have the pilots on standby, and make sure they are ready to go at a moment's notice," she said, walking down the ramp of the last shuttle.

"Yes, first council sister."

"Right, let's get to engineering," she said to her bodyguards, leaving the first officer at the bottom.

On the way, she noticed some garbage and flickering lights out in the corridors. These were things the sisters had managed. "Make a note... Find out who's in charge of the cleaning and maintenance, and tell them to sort these things out."

"Yes, first council sister," they said, producing notebooks.

"Have you tasked the satellite chief engineer?" she said, her voice booming as she walked through the door.

"We've just stabilized the uplink, first council sister. We're sending it new instructions now."

"Good, show me."

"We're hoping the explosion didn't damage the shielding too much. We're detecting an increase in solar radiation and meteor activity. Here, first council sister, you can see the code we're sending on this screen."

"You've repaired the ship's sensors as well? What about the long-range communications array?"

"There are still a few bugs in the sensor systems, but they are operational over a short range. As for the communications array, I'm afraid not. The damage is significant and we don't have the materials to repair it fully."

"Right, well carry on, I want it fixed. This is the code? Ah, yes, it's just a few lines. Is that all it needs?"

"Yes, as you can see, it's fairly simple. I've sent additional instructions for the satellite to notify us when it detects the Gold. Then I'll send the workers to mine it."

"Have you instructed the facility manager on the surface?"

"Yes, first council sister. I understand they began converting workers last night. The first should be ready for mining and construction engineering education in the Meta-verse in a day or two."

"Wonderful. Ensure your workers are capable, but don't deploy them or start construction until I tell you."

"Of course, first council sister."

Through the porthole, the light was fading. "Good work, chief engineer. I commend you."

He bowed as she left.

She called medical on her communicator. "I hope you have some results for me, medic. I'm on my way."

"Yes, first council sister," a shaky voice replied.

She was on a mission, and her pace to get things done was frenetic. He heard the slap of her sandals in the corridor and opened the door, bowing as they entered.

"Please come to my office, first council sister," he said.

Her nostrils flared as the distinctive smell of death and disease mixed with the sterile sting of antiseptic assaulted her nose. For a moment, it took her breath away.

"This way, first council sister."

She followed, taking shallow breaths, hoping to escape it.

"Tell me," she said.

"You are correct, first council sister. There is a dormant paralytic agent in your bloodstream. It has been very invasive."

"How do we get it out?"

"A blood transfusion is the only way. Do you have any left from when the other council sisters donated for the mothers? I can synthesize more if there is not enough."

"No."

"I am sorry, first council sister. There is nothing I can do. It will remain dormant until it meets with a depolarizing agent. I assume you know what will happen if it does?"

"Yes, medic. I've experienced a small taste. How would it get in?"

"In food, drink, injection, and if whoever made this is clever enough, it could even be an airborne agent," he said.

She frowned and forced a knowing laugh.

"I see," he said. "Might I suggest a food taster, and you filter all your air?"

"What good is doing all that if he doesn't have the paralyzing agent in him, too?"

"I can create something similar and give it to him."

"Hmm. Do it."

She looked at her bodyguards.

"You are the only ones I trust. Which of you will volunteer for this?"

They looked at each other, then stepped forward.

"I will create enough for two doses. Give me a few minutes," the medic said.

"I commend you both. When this is all over, I will reward your loyalty."

They rolled up their sleeves when the medic appeared with the injections and didn't flinch as the paralyzing agent invaded their bloodstream.

"Is there anything else I need to be aware of, medic?"

"I will try to devise an antidote, first council sister, but I have to warn you I'm not sure it's possible, and there's not much I can do about the air. Other than that, you are perfectly healthy."

"Very well." She stood to leave, knowing second sister had the better of her. She also knew sometimes you had to let your enemy think they'd won before getting the chance to crush them. The thought warmed her.

She looked back at her loyal bodyguards as she marched to her chambers. Loyalty was the one virtue she valued above all else, and theirs had never wavered. They had taken the worry over contaminated food and drink off her, and short of wearing a helmet that filters air all day, every day, which she would not do, there was no point in worrying about it.

Her mind drifted back to her teacher when she was young. 'Worry is a waste of energy, child. If you have a problem that you can solve, why worry about it? Do what you need to do to solve it. Equally, if there is a problem, and there is nothing you can do about it, worrying about it won't solve it, and you must let it go. Either way, never worry, it is the leech of sanity.' She smiled at the memory of her teacher's wise words.

Her bodyguards positioned themselves outside her chamber's doors, as always, as she went in. She sat on the edge of her bed, her mind screaming with rage and thoughts of revenge. Second sister's threat was real. She knew that for sure. *There has to be a way out of this.* Her mind gripped with the need to kill her, prevented any solution from showing itself. She closed her eyes, laid back, and slept, hoping her subconscious would find it.

When she woke, sleep had done its job, she had a solution. She knew she couldn't leave. Part of her 'punishment' was to have to stay. Her subconscious had wrestled with this knowledge as she slept, playing back all the conversations she'd had with second sister before a solution presented itself. Second sister knew she hadn't called the fleet, but she didn't know about the text message she transmitted before the explosion, giving their position and telling them to come. It wasn't the most satisfying solution, and she wouldn't get to kill her, at least not for a very long time, but it was a solution.

She sat up. The denial of instant revenge knotted her stomach, and she fidgeted to shake it off. With a deep breath, she focussed her thoughts. First, she would start a global warming program. The chief engineer told her a side effect of the power generators around the planet would be to warm it. She would build more to speed this process up, blanketing the entire planet in a warming, climate-changing net. Second, if second sister's predictions about the future growth of the human population were right, she would take advantage of her love for these creatures, converting and educating them in the ways of the Szateth. Third, when the fleet arrived, this planet would become part of the Szateth empire, its inhabitants subjugated and used.

She gritted her teeth and accepted she could still have everything she wanted if she reined in her need to kill her now. Second sister, without knowing it, had given her the way she would have everything she wanted - a long life. All she needed to do was to switch her strategy to play the long game. *A change of tactics, sister, one that you won't see until it's too late, then you are mine.*

She called her chief engineer. "Meet me in the council chambers."

"Yes, first council sister."

She placed a breakfast order with the kitchen for it to be delivered to the council chambers and marched out with renewed purpose. The food arrived as she did.

"I'll have it here," she said, to the worker pointing. The meat swimming in warm blood sloshed in the bowl as he placed it in front of her.

"Try it," she said to her bodyguards, who took some slices and ate without hesitation. She waited for any reaction. When none came, she wolfed the rest.

"Good morning, first council sister," the chief engineer said as he walked in. The bodyguards stared, chewing, as blood dripped from their mouths. He couldn't help the flinch as he wondered if he was there to 'entertain.'

She closed her eyes and swallowed her mouthful, relishing the feeling of the blood-soaked meat as it slid down her throat. With a smile, she opened her eyes and between picking meat from her teeth and sucking her fingers, thanked him for coming, and gestured he should take a seat.

"I have a question, chief engineer," she said.

"The satellite is already scanning first council sister, and I have my best teams on the ship's communications array and sensors," he said, choking his words out.

She didn't reply. It amused her to watch him squirm as he bit his bottom lip. She held up a hand. "I'm sure you have. That's not why you're here. My question is what you would need to construct more Meta-gates and power generators, many more, all over this planet?"

His shoulders dropped. "Oh, I see," he said, taking a huge breath. "Well, the process is simple enough, first council sister. All I would need are the materials, workers, and time."

"Will this planet yield the materials you need?"

"I believe so. Our preliminary scans show there are likely some large deposits of Gold around the planet. I will know for sure in a few weeks, once the satellite has completed its passes over the land masses. As for the construction stone, there is an abundance of limestone, granite, and Basalt, easily quarried."

"How much time do you need to build them and get them online?"

"The climate in the northern and southern regions of this planet would make the building more difficult, and we'd have to transport a lot of materials, and -"

"If you stick to the tropics, it's warmer there, right? You could build faster, then we could spread north and south from there."

"Yes, of course, first council sister. That makes perfect sense. May I ask what we will use all this energy for?"

"The Meta-gates, of course, so I can feed males directly into the cavern, and I'm very interested in the secondary effect you mentioned, the climate change and global warming."

"With that much power dispersing into the atmosphere, it will certainly do that, and travel around the planet will be easy too."

"Good. How long?"

"If I was to estimate, and it is just a guess, first council sister. I would need thousands of men, millions of tons of materials found, quarried, and mined, then there's the construction. Hmm, I'd guess a few months, maybe a year."

"You will have what you need, chief engineer. Make a start. Send all the shuttles out to scout for construction sites. Tell the facility manager to only convert workers from now on. Start today. That will be all."

She took a handful of meat and fixed him with a stare as she pushed it into her mouth. He stood, almost knocking the chair over, apologized and bowed, turned on his heels, and left. She chuckled.

∞

The General was getting the latest escapees settled when second sister stepped through the Meta-gate. The liberation of males from the cavern had gone unnoticed, so much so that both colonies were growing successfully.

"How are the mothers, sister?"

"I don't think I've ever seen sisters so happy to see each other, General. They are helping each other heal, and have been such a help to the humans in the colony. I don't think we'd have been as successful so quickly without them."

"Well, that's good," he said with a smile.

"You should see the effect P9R has had. It's given humans an evolutionary leap that's surprised me, to be honest. They learn so quickly."

The shadow of a shuttle washed over them. As they looked through the canopy, the shadows of seven more followed before turning and flying off in different directions. She frowned. *Where are they going? What are you up to, sister?*

"That's the first movement I've seen in a long while," he said, scanning the skies.

"Hmm, either they are looking for me or she's scouting for new holding facility sites."

"General!" A soldier ran into the clearing. "Five warriors, lightly armed, headed this way." He leaned on his knees, panting.

"Both it would seem," she said.

"Prepare the ambush we've trained for," he said to the warrior. "Use one of your squad as bait. Let them see him and make sure they follow him to the kill zone. I want their weapons."

"Yes, General." He ran back into the trees.

"It's about to get bloody, sister. Better you conceal yourself in case things go sideways."

"Very well. We need information, General. Keep one alive, and bring him to me."

"As you wish, sister." He darted into the trees, following his soldier.

She hid with a view into the clearing. It must have been two hours, and he still hadn't returned. She was worried. Other than her General, her soldiers had rudimentary weapons. Even lightly armed, the warriors would carry plasma pistols, wear body armor, and be among the best warriors. They would not survive in a standup fight. She thought about leaving through the Meta-gate when the General and four of her soldiers, holding plasma pistols, pushed a prisoner through the trees.

"On your knees," the General said, pointing his and the warrior's own plasma pistol at his head. He dropped. "Cross your left leg over your right, lace your fingers behind your head."

His cold eyes studied the general as he complied.

"Are you here, sister?"

"Yes, General," she said, leaving her hiding place.

The warrior turned toward her, and his mouth fell open.

"I know you," she said. "You were one of the first nine warriors converted in my lab. First council sister killed one of your comrades in cold blood before you for no reason."

He looked pained as the memory of first council sister gutting his comrade replayed in his mind.

"You remember him, don't you, General? You were his training officer."

"My goodness, sister. You're right." He lowered the weapons. The warrior looked at the General, then back at second sister.

"Why are you here, warrior? Tell me."

He said nothing, but she could see he was struggling with the conflict of what he felt over his murdered comrade and his warrior training.

"Come now. This doesn't have to end badly. It's a simple question. You have nothing to fear."

He shook his head. The General raised the butt of his pistol. She stepped in, raising her hand.

"Look at me," she said. "I know you're loyal. It's the one thing I admire most. But let me ask you, does she show you the same?"

He glanced down.

"I thought not. Look, do you even know why you will fight, and yes, die for her?"

He met her eyes, and she softened.

"She wants to ship you off to war on some faraway planet, where you'll fight and die, just another inconsequential number, used and forgotten. But it doesn't have to be that way."

He was visibly shaking.

"Stand," she said. The General stepped forward, raising his pistol. "It's fine, General." He lowered it, keeping a firm eye on the prisoner.

"Stand up."

He stood and closed his eyes.

"Are you out here looking for me?"

"We were.".

"Did you report you'd seen someone?"

"No, there was no time before your soldiers attacked." His eyes flashed open. Out of nowhere, he had a blade in his hand and he lunged.

The smell of burning, cauterized flesh filled the air. He was dead before he hit the ground.

"Thank you, General," she said, as he shot the corpse again. "Pity, at least we know. Has there been sightings of any other warriors?"

"No, sister. This is the first contact." He leaned over the body. "And with this level of equipment, she sent them to observe, nothing more. Other than this weapon, this communicator, and these rations. He had nothing else on him. They were to find you, track your movements, and report."

"Let me have the communicator." He handed it to her. "How long will it be before they realize they are missing?"

"That's a three-day ration pack." He kneeled and opened it. "With a day of it eaten. They'll allow for a couple of days over, so I'd say four more days."

"Will they have called in their current position?"

"No, they train trackers to keep silent until there is something to report. Then they dig in and wait for reinforcements."

She studied the communicator. "Can they trace its location?"

"No, sister, not this model. They're too old."

"So, they won't know where or when they went missing. Hmm. Take this body with the others into the forest. Let the Dire Wolves eat well tonight."

"Yes, sister."

"Good work, General. I'll be back at the mountain colony if you need me." She activated the Meta-gate.

"I need you to set up more observation posts outside," she said to the guard when she stepped through. "There's been warrior and shuttle activity around the forest colony, and I want to know if anyone or anything is sniffing around here."

"Yes, sister," the guard said, coming to attention. "I'll inform my superiors at once." He smiled at the mother who he was talking to and double-timed away.

"I guess I should wait awhile before going back to the forest colony, then. Are we likely to have visitors here, sister?" she asked.

"No, I doubt it, and I don't think her warriors would find our colony here, even if they were looking for it. But it pays to be cautious. You like him?"

"Yes, sister, he's a pleasurable distraction." She looked away coyly. "Although this is much more than a colony. Look what you've built," she said, looking back over the growing expanse of buildings. "It's an underground city. - You've done so much for us."

"Well, it'll all get undone if she finds us. And you're right to wait before going to the forest colony. The General will tell us when it's safe."

They walked back together, parting ways when she got to her home. She poured a warming drink and sipped it, studying the communicator. The day's events were troubling. First sister was planning something. The warrior confirmed she was looking for her, which the General and her soldiers could handle, but what were the shuttles doing? She took the communicator out of her pocket, touched the power button, and it came to life. She swigged the rest of her drink and made a call.

∞

In the council chambers, first sister was teaching a lesson. "Can any of you young sisters tell me what is most important in the life of a Szatethess?"

Six little hands shot into the air.

"Yes, you." She pointed.

"To expand our empire by whatever means necessary."

"Yes, very good. And what do we do about insubordination, or, even worse, rebellion in our empire?"

The eager little hands went up again.

"Someone else this time, err, you young sister."

"Crush it, first sister. Kill whoever dares show a lack of respect, and in a rebellion, kill the ringleaders and their families, and enslave their followers."

"Yes, well done." She clapped, and they giggled.

There was a knock on the door. The bodyguards drew their weapons and the little sisters fell silent. "Who is it?" first sister said.

"Forgive the interruption. It's the chief engineer, first council sister. I have some satellite survey and location results I'd like to share with you."

"Come," she said, rolling her eyes at the young sisters. They giggled again.

He opened the door to the sound of their childish voices and stares as he walked in.

He rinsed his hands and looked down. "Forgive me, first council sister."

"Quiet," she said, and the chatter stopped. "It's alright chief engineer, give me your report."

He slid the rolled-up map from under his arm and spread it on the table. "I've marked all the suitable locations for the power generators, first council sister."

"So, I see. And the network will cover how much of this planet when they're online?"

"Approx seventy percent, first council sister. To complete the coverage, we'd need to build either side of the tropics into the polar regions."

"Excellent, chief engineer. Is that enough to begin global warming?"

"Oh, yes, first council sister, more than enough."

"And where do we stand with materials and workers?"

"The number of workers I need to begin construction is well underway. Over the last few days, I have had ninety percent converted. They are in the Metaverse today learning the skills they need. I'll have enough to break ground at the first few locations in a day or two. The other good news is that I can locally source the material for the constructions."

"Well, that is good news. Look, young sisters, see how well the chief engineer has done with the task I set him." They leaned in and looked at the dots on the map.

"There is an issue I would welcome your advice on, first council sister."

"See how he shows the proper respect, young sisters?"

They giggled again.

"Ahem." The giggling stopped. "What is the issue, chief engineer?" she asked.

"The satellite has detected the largest deposits of Gold in three of the four corners of this planet. Here, bottom right on this continent, top right on this vast continent, and here, top left of these two continents," he said, tapping the map.

"So, what's the problem?"

"They are also the coldest regions on the planet."

"I see. Hmm, yes, that is a problem," she said, looking at her class. "What would you do, young sisters? How would help the chief engineer get the Gold he needs from these cold continents?"

"Gather any humans in these cold areas. They'll be used to it. Convert them and send them back to get the gold."

"Aha, there did you hear that, chief engineer? How amazing a child's mind is! With little responsibility comes clarity of thought."

He nodded and bowed at the young sister, who beamed at the respect he gave her.

"Very well done. You have seen a solution to a problem that will further our goals."

The chief engineer rolled up the map. "With your permission, first council sister, and yours, young council sister. I will send shuttles for the gathering."

"Carry on, chief engineer. Inform me once the constructions have begun." He bowed and left.

"That will be all for today, young sisters. Go to the dojo and carry on with your combat training."

They stood and bowed. "Yes, first sister," they said and filed out.

She slumped back in her chair, closed her eyes, and smiled at the ceiling. *Things are going well.* The buzzing of her communicator interrupted her self congratulations. It was the commander of her warriors.

She sat up. "What is it, commander?"

"The team of trackers is missing first council sister."

"What do you mean, missing?"

"They've been gone for five days, first council sister. Their rations ran out two days ago and they haven't reported in."

"Maybe they just got lost, and will turn up, starving, thirsty, and embarrassed in a day or so."

"I don't think so, first council sister. These are elite warriors."

"You know what direction they went in, though?"

"Yes, at least the direction they started out in."

"Well then, send more trackers, find out what's happened. She's one council sister, out there alone, commander."

"What should we do if we find her, bring her in?"

"No, commander. Under no circumstances is she to be challenged. I just need to know where she is - for now."

"And if she attacks?"

"Didn't you hear me, commander? Make sure your trackers see her first. She must not know I know where she is. They are to report, nothing more. Is that clear?"

"Yes, first council sister."

She ended the call. He couldn't help thinking he was sending another team to be slaughtered.

She stood. "Why can't everyone be like you two?" she said, looking at her bodyguards. "And just do what I tell them to do?" They followed her out of the chamber. They were just happy to be eating five-star food.

Halfway down the corridor, her communicator buzzed again. She stopped. It was the commander. Her finger stabbed the answer button. "What is it now, commander?" she said through her teeth, forcing restraint.

"You had better come to my office, first council sister. I've had a call from one of the missing tracker's communicators."

"So, so what? That's good. They've found her then."

"No, not exactly first council sister. The call was *from* second council sister. She wants to speak to you."

Her eyes darted to her bodyguards. "I'll be right down." She swallowed and ended the call. The march to the commander's office was frantic. They were jogging to keep up with her by the time they got there.

"What did she call you on?" she asked, crashing through the door.

"On this communicator, first council sister. We use it to receive calls from teams in the field."

The blank screen of the communicator staring at her from the desk meant she had to wait. She stared at it. "Do you know where she called from, commander?"

"No, first council sister. There are no tracers in those communicators."

"Did she say when she'd call back?"

"No, first council sister. But I sensed some urgency in her voice."

"Right."

It buzzed, the metal desk amplifying the sound, as the screen lit with an incoming call. She pressed the answer button.

"Are you there?"

The sound of second sister's voice grated on her. "Yes, I'm here," she sneered.

"Why are you looking for me? I thought we agreed not to contact each other again."

"Can't I want to know where you are, sister?"

"There is no need for that. It is enough that I know where you are. Besides, I have my science to save our species, and you have considerations for your continued survival to keep us both busy. Neither of us needs to be part of the other's lives."

"Pity it has to be this way, sister." She snarled.

"It's the only way. Your lust for complete control will extinguish our race if I permit you to carry on. You've lost your way. We tried to reason with you, tell you, and warn you, but rather than listen, you got rid of your opposition. I took steps, just like you would have done, to make sure you couldn't get rid of me, too. Now I'm the only one left and you know my threat to your life is real if you step out of line. - And now you know what will happen to your warriors if you send them to look for me."

"There is no need for this animosity between us. You have made your point."

"You are right, there is no need for a conflict between us - as long as you keep your end of the bargain."

"Bargain? A bargain suggests a deal agreed upon through negotiation, where I give you something in return for something you give me. We have no bargain, sister. You've dictated terms with a consequence attached if I disagree. That is not a bargain. That's oppression."

"Now you know what it feels like. Look, let's not waste each other's time. You know we will never agree."

"Why call then?"

"To let you know I can."

"Well, good for you."

"And I have a question. - What are you using the shuttles for?"

"Ah, you saw them, did you? Well, as I may not leave, I need more power, and this planet emits a frequency we can use to generate it."

"To keep the Meta-gates working?"

"If you like, yes."

"I will allow it, - for now. Though I suggest you send no more warriors to search for me."

"Thank you, sister. I will take that under advisement."

"I think we can agree on one thing, however. There is no council of sisters anymore, is there? You saw to that. Therefore, I am not your sister, and will not be on a council you manipulate for your own ends. Your callous stupidity would be the end for us all. I won't allow it."

"There's no need to get nasty. So if you're not my sister, what do you want me to call you?"

"I'm sure by now I am more than *irritating* you. However, my friends see me as giving them a chance for new beginnings. You remember the head kitchen worker you had 'entertain' you?"

"Oh, yes, I can still taste him." She smacked her lips so she could hear.

"There, that's exactly what I'm talking about, callous. His friends called him Aragam. It meant helpful, loyal being."

"Well, he was *helpful*, right to the end. You have friends?" Her laugh rumbled the speaker.

"Enough! The lack of value you place in the lives of others is unbearable. Never call me sister again. From now on, you will call me Margaret. It is the name of a precious jewel that started life as an irritant for its host, as I have for you. I think it's fitting." She laughed back. "You will address me with that name every time we speak, now and in the future. You can add it to the list of things that irritate you about me... unless you wish to feel the consequence of disobeying."

Her silence was enough of a reply.

"I thought not."

"Do you have a name in mind for me, - Margaret?" The sound of her saying it made her cringe.

"You see yourself as a pure being. A pure Szatethess. I admit it is something I admired about you. But it has twisted and corrupted you. So I will call you - Karen."

"Karen, hmm."

"It means the pure one."

"A back-handed compliment, Margaret? Forgive me if I don't seem appreciative."

"Your appreciation isn't required, Karen. Just your compliance."

"Anything else, Margaret?"

"No. I will call when I want something from you, - Karen." She ended the call.

She sat motionless for a few seconds, then squinted at the commander. "Which direction did the shuttles fly in before they dispersed?"

"I don't know, Karen," the commander said.

The shrilling scream froze him. A hand clamped around his throat and he was flying backward. The back of his head slammed into the wall. The hand tightened, closing his windpipe, and the hiss he heard made him open his eyes. Her needle-sharp teeth were all he saw, and he surrendered to his death. It didn't come.

She released him, and he slumped to the floor, gasping for air. When he looked up, he saw her mouth open, the skin of her cheeks stretching more than was natural. Her teeth retracted back into her mouth as she re-aligned her jaw. "Of course you don't," she said, smacking her lips. "Send the trackers, commander. If they don't come back, keep sending them until you find her. And commander, if you value your life, never call me by that name again. Are we clear?" she said, her eyes burning.

"Of course, first council sister. My sincerest apologies." He coughed, rubbing his throat.

"Come on, you two, to the hangar," she said, smoothing her robes.

She left the commander clutching his neck. *I have the food and drink situation covered, and there's nothing I can do about the depolarizing agent if it's airborne. Is that even possible? If it's not, her consequences have no meat. Unlike her, and I'm going to strip it from your bones, Margaret.* The thought of killing her put a determination in her step as she entered the hangar.

"Which direction did the shuttles fly off in when they left, first officer?"

"To the east side of the mountain, first council sister. Then they dispersed."

How careless sister, now I know where you are. She called the commander. "I have a direction for you to send the trackers, commander. She's somewhere between the facility and the east side of the mountain. Start there and keep going until you find her."

"Yes, first council sister. They leave within the hour," he said, his voice rasping.

She called the chief engineer. "Are your workers ready?"

"Yes, first council sister. They begin construction today."

"Have a squad of warriors accompany them and all the construction gangs."

"Are they to expect trouble from the local tribes?"

"Unlikely, but it pays to be cautious."

"Very well, first council sister. I will inform you when they break ground."

"Good. I instructed your predecessor to prepare cryo-stasis chambers. Did he do it?"

"Oh, err, yes, first council sister, nine of them. Are you planning on entering cryo-sleep?"

"Hmm, well, at least he did something right." She ended the call.

Neural Blockchain Journal Entry #934

Just a few more things to do until sleep to wait until the fleet gets here.

- Get the generators online and warm the planet. It'll be habitable by the time they arrive.

- Teach and prepare my young sisters for the fleet's arrival.

- Find second sister, or Margaret, as she now wants to be called.

Hopefully, the medic will find an antidote beforehand. I can't have the threat of death constantly hanging over my head. But I will not worry about it, there's nothing I can do. Then it'll be time to sleep. At least sleep will suspend this consuming need to kill Margaret. The crew can fend for themselves. They probably won't survive long after the cryo chambers lock the ship down, but that's of no concern.

Your death is coming, Margaret.

First Council Sister - Szateth leader
Advanced planetary research fleet.

Sixteen

Discovery, denial, death and memories

The General and his squad stepped through the Meta-gate at the mountain colony. Still wearing his combats and body armor, his olive skin glistened with sweat from the last skirmish with first sister's warriors.

"Take these weapons to the armory," he said to his lieutenant, handing him the blood-stained bag of plasma weapons they'd captured. "The rest of you get cleaned up and get some rest."

"Yes General," they said and marched towards the barracks.

He unbuckled his heavy body armor, letting it fall to the floor, before wiping the sweat out of his eyes. *That was a close one,* he said to himself, doing up the clip securing his plasma pistol in its holster. He rested his armor against the side of the Meta-gate and went to find Margaret in her lab.

“I don’t think she’s ever going to stop sending trackers to find you, sister,” he said, slumping in the chair next to her. “We’ve had to deal with five teams in as many weeks.”

“I know General. She doesn’t care about their lives. How are your soldiers? Any losses?” she asked.

“No, thank goodness. Humans are the bravest creatures I’ve ever fought with. And we’ve added more weapons to the cache.”

“They are an amazing species. What about you?”

“I’m fine. We’ll be ready to go again after some food and rest.”

“You look tired." She gave him a sympathetic smile. "At least we’re growing our arsenal.”

“It’s just small arms, sister. We’d have much bigger problems if they came at us with anything with real firepower,” he said with a faint sigh.

“I wonder why she hasn’t? Her attempts to find me feel half-hearted, like they’re more of a distraction. If she was serious, wouldn’t she send a whole battalion of heavily armed warriors?”

“I would, sister. I’m glad she hasn’t. Perhaps we’re missing something.”

“Hmm, maybe. - Have the shuttles continued to fly over?”

“Yes, with more frequency. Do you think there’s more behind the building of all these power generators?”

“More than likely,” she said. “Have you or your men seen or heard anything from the warriors?”

“No, not really, although thinking about it, it feels like there’s been a change in the atmosphere. It feels different, warmer and dryer. Have you felt it, sister?”

“No, not here. Hmm, interesting. The generation of large amounts of power can do that, and building them seems to be more of a priority than finding me. Tell me how it feels.”

"Sometimes it feels like my hair is standing up, and I'm getting a few static shocks off metal surfaces."

"Interesting. I'll take some measurements. I'll keep you informed."

"Thank you, sister."

"I've been thinking that we should adopt proper names for each other. Names that have meaning. I have chosen the name Margaret, and for you, General, I want to call you Thaider."

"Thaider?"

"Yes, it means honorable, decisive, and ingenious. All the things that you are as a General to my army, Thaider. It is my honor to have you by my side."

"I would be nowhere else, - Margaret."

"We would not be here without you. - I will find out what Karen, that's the name I've given first sister, is doing. Where is the nearest power generator to you, Thaider?"

"At the conversion facility."

"Alright, I'll get some measurements from there and find out what she's doing."

"It's too risky for you, Margaret. I'll get them if you bring the instruments here."

"I can't ask you to do something I'm not prepared to do myself, Thaider. We'll go together."

With not much to do, the wait for the time to enter cryo-sleep was drawing on her patience, and her march to engineering had more urgency.

"Where are we with the construction of the power generators, chief engineer?"

"Four more are coming online today, first council sister."

"Good, how many more until we reach the coverage we need to influence the warming of the planet?"

"Minuscule atmospheric changes will already happen with those online now, but another twenty or thirty, first council sister, then we should begin construction in the polar regions. They'll complete the network and we will have complete coverage when they come online, speeding up the rate of change."

"So, how long?"

"For complete coverage, I'd say three months."

"You have one?"

"First council sister, I'll need many more workers and much more material to build with."

"Take what you need. Impress upon your workers the need to work faster chief engineer. A month chief engineer is all the time you have, literally, if you fail me."

"It will be done, first council sister."

"I hope so, chief engineer. Although my mouth is watering at the prospect of either outcome." She watched his face pale. He bowed low as she left with her bodyguards sniggering.

"Get those four new power generators online. And please, for your sake, as well as mine, do it now," he said to an engineer, unable to control the tremor in his voice.

He knew he'd over-promised, even as he was agreeing to it, the voice in his head was telling him to stop, then that same voice, knowing she would have him 'entertain' her that night if he did, told him to keep talking. *Maybe I can do it?* His inner voice said, trying to comfort him. Every engineer was looking at him. They'd heard his fear. As he looked at them, his logical mind told him the truth. *You idiot, she's going to feast on you*. His every instinct told him to run.

"They are coming online now, chief," his engineer said.

Escape was all he could think about. He needed to get off the ship. His mind searching for an opportunity was racing with questions if he did. *Maybe I could hide in the forest and live off the land until the ship left.*

"Chief, did you hear?"

"Oh, err, Yes. Good. - Thank you. Erm, I'm going to the facility to take some readings and check the stability of the network." An opportunity had presented itself.

He almost bumped into first council sister as he rushed through the doors. He stopped dead, and looked at the floor, unable to look her in the face. "Forgive me, first council sister."

"I hope the reason you nearly knocked me off my feet is to give me good news, chief engineer?"

Her bodyguards chuckled again.

"Yes, first council sister. The new generators have just come online. I'm going to the surface to measure its output. I think you'll be satisfied."

"Oh, I know I'll be satisfied," she said, grinning. "Tell the first officer to send you down in a shuttle."

He bowed, then walked around her as fast as he could. Their laughter made him more determined to get away.

"Let's see how the medic is getting on with an antidote, shall we?" She didn't wait for an answer.

Her nose wrinkled as the hideous smell of the medical department assaulted her again. "Medic, have you got an antidote yet?"

"No, first council sister, the agent is in every cell in your body. It's wonderful in its simplicity, and resistant to anything I've used to kill it. I'm afraid a blood transfusion won't free you of it."

"I see, so you're saying I'm stuck with it."

"It looks that way, first council sister, although I will keep working on it to see if there is another solution."

"Good. What about the depolarizing agent? Could it be in the air?"

"It would take some advanced chemistry and a specialized delivery system. It is unlikely, but yes, it's possible."

"Hmm. Thank you, medic," she said. "Looks like you two are going to have to stay with me for the rest of your lives," she said to her bodyguards.

They smiled.

∞

Margaret stepped through the Meta-gate in the forest colony, clutching her power output scanner. Thaider and a squad of soldiers were going over their attack plan as the gate closed behind her. They came to attention, and Thaider walked over.

"I wish you'd stay and let me go instead, Margaret. There will be warriors guarding the generator, and you should not put yourself at risk."

"No, Thaider. Besides, if I take the measurements, it'll get done much more quickly. Give me a weapon. I can take care of myself."

He knew she wouldn't change her mind. "Very well. It'll take a couple of hours if we double-time it. We are ready to go when you are." He handed her a plasma pistol.

She tucked it into her robe. "After you," she said.

Thaider took point, disappearing into the trees, followed by Margaret and the squad. His pace was relentless. As an ex-council sister, it was her duty to stay fit, but he was on another level. They reached the place where they'd left fourth sister's body well within two hours. His hand signaled for them to come close and crouch. The squad, like Thaider, was unaffected by the speed march, but she was pleased to get the rest.

"The generator is just over this rise. We go carefully and silently from here. Our biggest advantage is surprise. Margaret, you stay in cover. Once the generator is secure, I'll signal you in." She nodded and they moved out.

The slower pace gave her time to fully recover, and she held back from the attack squad as they advanced on the generator. Near the top of the rise, he halted the advance and crawled to the top. As expected, four warriors guarded the generator. They'd stacked their plasma rifles next to the fire they'd lit, were laughing, and playing some game that had their full attention. He snorted. *That would never happen on my watch*, he thought. *This is going to be easy, and I want those rifles.*

He crawled back and split the squad into two teams, telling Margaret to wait at the top of the rise until he signaled her down. They moved out as Margaret crawled to where Thaider had been to watch the attack. They closed in on two sides. The guards had no clue they were about to die.

They were about to launch the attack when a shuttle appeared through the clouds. Thaider clenched his fist, holding it at eye level, - they froze. The landing shuttle distracted the guards, and he signaled the teams to regroup over the rise. Margaret stayed in position to see who came out of the shuttle. It was someone in a white coat, and when no one else came out, she joined the squad.

"It's an engineer," she said. "Probably here to take the same measurements I am."

"If we attack and they board that shuttle, we're screwed," Thaider said. "We should wait till it leaves."

"Or, we take it," she said.

Thaider looked at her, narrowing his eyes. "Why would we do that?"

"There's a lot of useful tech, weapons, and supplies on that shuttle. I'll fly it and hide it in the mountain colony."

"Won't Karen come looking with her army to find it? We couldn't withstand a full frontal assault."

"Dead warriors are going to spark a response, Thaider, just as much as a missing shuttle. She isn't aware of you, the colonies, or our army. She only knows about me. We could hide it."

"I'm not sure we're ready for a war, Margaret."

"No one ever is, my friend, but unless we retreat from our mission today, war is coming. Actually, no, not a war, a rebellion. She'll see it as open resistance to her authority by me. We'll still have the element of surprise."

"That shuttle and those other weapons, we sure could use them," he said, biting his lip.

"Let's take them then?"

"Alright, let's split up again and move into position."

"Or. - Or I could walk in," she said, raising her eyebrows. "The warriors will see my council sister's robes, distracting them long enough for you to launch your attack."

"Use you as bait? No, I don't like that, one bit!"

"The unexpected appearance of a council sister will send them into a panic. Then you attack This way there's a lot less chance of us getting hurt and more chance of getting what we need."

He shrugged. "I want those weapons, and if there's more on the shuttle... it's still not worth the risk of you getting hurt, or worse."

"Of course it is. Look, it's just sitting there, General, waiting for us to take it." She glanced over. "I'll wait for you to get into position, then walk in. Once the guards and I are talking, you attack. Don't forget the pilot in the shuttle."

He licked his lips. "Alright, you win. Are we ready for this?" he looked at his soldiers, they were smiling. "Let's go."

She moved back to the top of the rise, waiting for the teams to move into position. Thaider looked back at her and nodded. She broke cover and walked with the poise of a council sister across the open ground.

"You there - guards."

The authority of a council sister's voice had them jump to attention. Her appearance had the desired effect. The engineer was not so easily rattled.

He recognized her as she got closer. "You're second council sister," he said, pointing at her. "What are you doing here?"

The informality in his tone jolted the warriors out of their total obedience. "Stand still," one of them said. He reached for his pistol as the others went for their stacked rifles.

Bursts of white light and the smell of burned flesh followed. The only one left standing was the engineer, as her soldiers moved in.

"The pilot, Thaider..."

He ran up the ramp and a bright white light lit the cockpit. Moments later, he reappeared and nodded.

"Second council sister, I can't believe it's you. I'm so pleased it is."

She drew her pistol and pointed it at his head. "And why is that engineer?"

"I'm trying to get away from first council sister. I was to be her next *entertainment*."

"Really?" she said, pressing the muzzle of the pistol against his temple. "Why would that be, I wonder?"

"I'm afraid I exaggerated my ability to complete the work in the time she wants it done."

"And what work is that?"

"I am her Chief Engineer. She instructed me to build the rest of the power generators and Meta-gates in a month."

"I see. So, she's speeding up the gatherings."

"Partly yes, second council sister."

"Partly? What do you mean?"

"She's more interested in the secondary effect of producing so much energy."

"And what's that?"

"Warming the planet."

She took a step back and dropped the pistol by her side. "Did she say that? That she wants to warm the planet?"

"Yes, second council sister."

Her eyes glazed and stared. "Terraforming. Of course." She raised the weapon. "Has she ever talked about the fleet?"

"The planetary research fleet?"

"Yes."

"Not to me -"

"Why terraform then," Margret said, frowning at the floor.

"There was a text message sent by the satellite before the communications array went offline."

"What text message? What did it say?"

"It was our coordinates in this galaxy and an instruction for them to come here."

She lowered the weapon.

"Is everything okay, Margaret?" Thaider asked, running over.

"They're coming," she said.

"Who's coming?"

"The Szatethess fleet, Thaider, and if they take this planet, which they will, she'll gather all the human males, convert them, and enslave or kill the females. It would be the end of humankind and the end of our species."

"The fleet is unlikely to receive the message for many years," the chief engineer said, hearing her distress. "They are light years away, second council sister; when they do, it'll be thousands of years before they get here. So I think..."

"Let's take the measurements and get out of here, Thaider," Margaret said, switching on her scanner and pressing it against the sloping wall of the power generator. "This can't be right." She tapped the scanner, not believing the reading was correct, before pressing it against the wall again.

"Look at these readings," she said, showing them to the chief engineer.

"The new generators that have come online have amplified its output. I designed the network to do that."

"Are you crazy? Why would you do that?"

"The generation of all the energy and the release of the waste from that energy production into the atmosphere would initialize global warming."

"Are you sure that's all it does?" she said, taking another measurement.

"Margaret, there's movement coming from the facility," Thaider said. "We need to leave, now." He pointed to the soldier closest to the bodies of the warriors. "Grab their plasma rifles and side arms, and let's get out of here."

"Take me w-with you, - p-please?" The chief engineer said, unable to control the tremor in his voice.

"Why?" Margaret said, already walking away.

"Please, I have nowhere else to go, and I could be useful to you."

Margaret looked at Thaider, who just rolled his eyes. "Alright, come on."

He ran up the ramp behind them. She powered up the engines and lifted off. From the cockpit, she could see the squad of warriors checking the bodies of their comrades. They looked at the rising shuttle, their faces twisted in anger and confusion. She closed her eyes, offered a silent prayer for the dead, then ripped the cables off the shuttle's transponder so the ship couldn't track it, pushed the levers forward, and sped toward the mountain.

"She'll know I've gone, and she'll think I killed her warriors and stole the shuttle," the chief engineer said to Margaret.

"Well, you're in it with us now, engineer. Welcome to the rebellion." She put the coordinates into the autopilot, letting it take over. "How many more power generators are being built?"

"Thirty," he said.

"We'll need to take energy output measurements at other generators to monitor what's happening."

A ball of light, with its tail of fire, roared across the sky. They watched as it disappeared over the horizon.

"I believe you're right," he said, as another roared and burned out in the atmosphere. He scanned the horizon. "This planet is entering the meteor swarm, the ship's sensors detected."

"A swarm? How big?"

"The sensors were still malfunctioning, so we don't know."

"It's big enough if the sensors detected it. That's all we need." She switched off the autopilot, banked hard right, accelerating towards the mountain colony. In her mind, she was fearing the worst. As she approached the colony, neither the wind nor her piloting skills had improved as she fought to land. *Thank goodness for suspension*, she thought as she landed with a thud.

"You know where the other generators are, right?"

"Yes, second council sister," he said.

"Stay here," she said to him. "Thaider, rearm the squad. We're going to another generator site. I need a few more instruments. I'll be back in a few minutes." And she ran down the ramp.

"What's going on? What was that in the sky?" Thaider asked, entering the cockpit.

"Oh, err, just a couple of meteors," the engineer said, checking the sky.

"Are they dangerous?"

"Tiny meteors hit planets and moons all the time. Usually, they go unnoticed. But those were bigger than usual, I'd say."

"Will there be more?"

"I hope not, but if this planet gets close to, or goes through, the middle of the meteor swarm, there could well be."

They both looked. "Well, it's clear now," Thaider said. "Show me the area and terrain around where we're going next?"

"Yes, of course." He brought it up on the navigation monitor.

"It looks similar to the terrain around the conversion facility. Pretty flat and this ridge running around the top will give us plenty of cover on the approach," Thaider said.

"I found fairly uniform locations, so it would be easy to build on."

"We'll land the shuttle here and walk in," Thaider said, touching the screen.

"You two look like you have a plan," Margaret said, putting the case of instruments on the table.

"It's the same plan as the one we just carried out. The engineer has designed construction sites that will make attacking easy enough."

"I don't think they were ever expecting to be attacked, Thaider. However, I'm sure they'll know what happened at the conversion facility. They might be more on their guard this time," she said.

"Hmm. could be. As I was saying, if we land here and walk in, it'll be dark by the time we get into position, giving us more cover. And we're better armed now."

She set the coordinates into the autopilot. "Let's hope you're right. Let's go."

They flew from daylight into darkness, and as they closed in on the coordinates, they didn't have to search for the generator. It was lit up like a beacon. They could clearly see the gold cap on top of the generator with its blue halo flashing, sparking, and shimmering. As they flew closer, they could feel a change in the temperature and hear a faint buzzing making their hairs stand on end.

She put the shuttle in stealth mode and descended to the landing zone. As soon as it touched down and the ramp opened, fully armed and ready for a fight, they double-timed to the ridge. Thaider crawled to the top, and looking over, didn't see any guards. In fact, there was no one there at all.

He crawled back. "Looks like they've abandoned the site. Just turned the thing on and left it."

"You're sure?" Margaret asked.

"Positive."

"Is that likely?" she said to the engineer.

"I suppose. There only needs to be workers and warriors here while it's being constructed. Once it's activated, which we do from the ship, there's no need for anyone to be here. It's self-sustaining."

"Right then. Let's get these readings and get back," she said.

"Wait, Margaret, let me and the teams get into position. Just because we can't see them doesn't mean they're not there."

"Very well, Thaider. Ever the General. Thank you."

"You know what to do," he said to the two teams. They nodded and moved out.

Margaret and the engineer waited for his signal at the top of the ridge. A few minutes later, he waved them down. They ran to the generator across the open ground, surrounded by Thaider and her soldiers. He gave the signal for them to cover the area. They formed a circle, and facing into the darkness, swept their rifles through an arc of fire, keeping her protected. She couldn't help feeling impressed by their skill while she and the engineer took the measurements. She measured the generator's energy and waste output, while the engineer took atmospheric and seismic measurements. He looked at her and nodded. He'd got what she needed.

"We're done here Thaider. Time to go," she said, putting the instruments away.

They fast marched back to the shuttle in silence. Not that they had warriors to worry about, but Margaret's mood and the engineer's discovery created a tense atmosphere. They didn't speak on the flight back to the colony, either.

"Thaider, take the weapons and the soldiers back to the forest colony. Make sure we arm every soldier with everything we've got." She didn't look at him as she spoke.

Her mind was somewhere else, and wherever it was, it was dark and dangerous; he thought. "Yes, Margaret," he said, then told the soldiers to take everything from the shuttle.

"We may have to go back," she said.

"We'll be ready."

"Engineer, come with me," she said, looking at the ramp. "We need to make sense of these readings. I pray I'm wrong."

The polite assured Margaret was not standing in front of them anymore. Her eyes were hard and focused. Whatever had unnerved her made everyone concerned. They followed her off the shuttle, not knowing what to say. Thaider activated the Meta-gate and as the soldiers stepped through, he looked back at Margaret with a feeling that things were about to change.

In her lab, she downloaded the measurements into the computer and twitched nervously as they waited for the results.

"I presume you had me check for the movement of the planet's crust?"

"Yes. Energy generation on that scale does more than produce it and release waste. It's likely to agitate a planet's mantle, causing movement of its tectonic plates."

"Causing quakes and volcanic eruptions?" the chief engineer said.

"Exactly. And worse, if it continues, it will completely destabilize this planet, killing everything and everyone on it. This planet would become uninhabitable."

"Surely first council sister knows that?"

"Possibly, although she was never much of a scientist, so she may not, and I doubt your engineers considered it."

"No, we're all too afraid of her and tell her what she wants to hear. That's how I've ended up here. If she knows, then she'll know it'll take thousands of years before that happens."

"Time enough for the fleet to arrive. Take all the humans and leave with everything she wants." Then it hit her. "She hadn't changed her mind, she'd changed the time frame."

"But why not take all the humans now and just leave?"

"Because she can't. I saw to that," she said.

"You're keeping her here against her will?"

"Yes. She can't leave." She looked up from the computer monitor, staring off into space, then shook her head. "Very clever, Karen," she said under her breath.

"Karen, is that the name you've given her?"

"What? Oh, err, yes. There is a limit to how long I can control her, though. - The lifespan of the crew."

"What do you mean?"

"Has she had the cryo-stasis chambers activated?"

"Yes, nine of them, but one of them is malfunctioning."

"Damn. I see what she's doing."

The computer beeped, and they both stared at the numbers on the monitor. "The energy production and its waste have started global warming, but you knew that already, didn't you?" She glared at the engineer. "We have a baseline number from the seismometer. How long until the next generator comes online?"

"There are teams of workers building now. At least one more will join the network today, and every day after."

"We need to go back and take the same measurements again."

She called Thaider. "Meet me at the shuttle. We need more measurements. We're going back."

"Yes, Margaret, we'll be there in a few minutes."

"Come on, engineer, I want you to see the results of your work firsthand. Bring the instruments."

Thaider and the squad of soldiers were waiting at the shuttle when they got there, armed to the teeth.

"We're going back to the same generator, Thaider. We know there's no one there, so you won't need your weapons."

"Well, it'll be good training then, to see how we perform fully armed."

She leaned forward and said softly, "let's get on with it then."

The soldiers took their seats while Thaider and the engineer joined her in the cockpit. The somber mood kept conversation to a minimum during the flight.

Once they'd landed, Thaider and the soldiers led the way. He insisted they followed the same route and expected resistance, and a firefight once they got to the generator.

"We will not get caught with our pants down," he said.

She knew he was right. Fortunately, no one was there, and no one else had to die. Despite them being warriors of the Szateth, they were once human, and she felt every one of their deaths.

"Take the seismic reading, engineer," she said as she took the others.

As soon as he placed it on the ground, the needle on the instrument's screen whip-sawed wildly. He looked at her, his expression told her it wasn't good news.

She looked at the meter on hers. "There is another marked increase in output, and the look on your face tells me seismic activity is increasing too."

"Yes, second council sister, I'm afraid it's confirmed."

"Alright then, we have no choice. We have to stop this. Thaider, are you carrying explosives?"

"Yes, Margaret."

"Enough to destroy this generator?"

"Enough to level it."

"Good. Set it and let's go."

"You and the others should head back to the shuttle. I'll catch up, and we'll blow it remotely," he said.

"Very well. I have a call to make before we destroy it."

She and the others jogged back to the shuttle and waited for him. "Give me the detonator, Thaider," she said as he entered the cockpit.

He handed it over. "It'll destroy the generator, the meta-gate, and leave an enormous crater in their place. We should be a long way away before you press that button."

"Thank you, Thaider. I'll need you to bring all the soldiers, the females, and children to the mountain colony." She raised the ramp, powered up the engines, and took off.

"We have one more cavern escape mission planned and ready to go. I'll liberate as many males as I can and bring them, too."

"Good." She pushed the control levers forward, and the shuttle sped up. "How many soldiers can this shuttle carry?"

"Fully armed, thirty, I'd say."

"Enough to win in a battle against a defended construction site?"

"With speed, aggression, and surprise, - yes. After the first, though, and without the element of surprise, we'll face more heavily armed warriors. Plus, they'll be able to send reinforcements through the Meta-gate. It could get bloody."

"How many warriors will be at the sites, engineer?" she asked.

"A squad of twenty, maybe," he said.

"So when we attack, we need to destroy the Meta-gate, subdue the guards, round up the workers, then blow everything up, losing none of our soldiers. Does that about cover it?"

Thaider caught her sarcasm. "Yes, just about."

"Impossible," the engineer said.

"And yet it has to be done," she said.

"We know what we signed up for, Margaret."

"I know that Thaider. Let's just hope it doesn't come to that. I have got a call to make. In the meantime, make a battle plan and prepare the soldiers."

They were coming up on the landing pad, and she pulled the throttle levers back, slowing their approach. The wind had dropped, making the shuttle easier to control, and the landing softer.

"Get everyone and bring them here, Thaider."

"Of course, Margaret."

"Engineer, consider yourself conscripted into the army." She saw him fidget. "Give him a rifle and teach him how to shoot, General."

She felt the weight of what she had started. With a deep breath, she pulled herself tall and walked off with the defiant steps of a rebel leader.

The innocuous-looking communicator on her table was about to be the instrument of rebellion. She hesitated before picking it up, knowing the call she was going to make would spark a deadly response. She also knew she had no choice. Her finger squeezed the power button, and the screen came to life.

She pressed the call button. "Get me Karen." her heart raced as adrenaline surged through her.

For what felt like a long time, there was no response.

Then a voice barked. "Who is this?"

"Get me Karen. Tell her it's Margaret, and she needs to speak to me now."

"I don't know anyone going by the name of Karen."

"Do not mess me about commander, you know perfectly well who I'm referring to. Call her to your office, now."

"The first council sister is busy today, second council sister."

"When she finds out what's about to happen if I don't get to speak to her was because *you* stopped me, what do you think she's going to do, commander?"

"I'll call her."

"That would be wise."

The line fell silent, but she knew he was calling her.

Her legs were restless, waiting for a reply. "Please wait, second council sister. She is on her way."

She took a deep breath to calm herself, but in the long silence, self-doubt crept in. *Maybe they weren't ready for a rebellion. Maybe she should just let Karen have what she wants. She didn't know about Thaider, the liberation of males from the cavern, the soldiers, or the colonies. If she handed herself in, at least they'd survive.* She took another breath as a familiar voice broke in.

"I'm here Margaret, what do you want?"

"I know what you're doing, Karen."

"Really? And what is that?"

"Terraforming."

"Don't be ridiculous."

"Don't you lie to me, Karen! I have your engineer. He's told me everything."

"That sniveling worthless creature will say anything to keep breathing."

"Except that it's not a lie. I have measurements that confirm it."

"It was you who killed my warriors and took my shuttle! How did you-"

"I am sorry for that. Do you know what you've set in motion?"

"I don't answer to you, Margaret, but you will to me when I see you again."

"There is no time for idle threats, Karen. Humor me, prove you're not the third-rate scientist I believe you to be."

"So you know about the global warming effect of the power generators? It's of little consequence."

"Yes, Karen, but what else? What else will your science experiment do to this planet, and sooner than you hope? Come on, Karen, prove me wrong."

"I'm going to peel the skin off your body, slowly remove your bowels, and make you watch while I roast them in front of you before letting you die."

"Yes, yes, and I'll do the same to you, blah, blah, blah. You don't know, do you?"

"I'm going to rip the heart from your pathetic little body -"

"You really are a third-rate scientist, Karen. So let me tell you, let me educate you on the extent of your stupidity. - Your energy generation, and the waste it produces, are not only raising the planet's temperature, it's also agitating the mantle below the crust. All these generators are going to cause quakes and volcanic eruptions, on the land and in the seas. The more generators you build, the more quakes and eruptions will happen. You will kill everything, and it will be uninhabitable well before the fleet arrives."

"What are you talking about? My engineers would have -"

"Your engineers tell you what you want to hear because of what you are, Karen. A sick, deranged Szatethess who believes in her own omnipotence. Unless you stop now, stop your construction, and deactivate the generators. You will kill us all."

"Haha, just like fourth sister, how ridiculous you are."

"Have you listened to a word I've said?"

"You are ridiculous and I'm going to find you."

"Then you leave me no choice." She took the detonator out of her pocket.

"What can you do? I have dealt with your threat to my life, and soon you will be mine."

"Really? You've dealt with it, have you?" She laughed. "I'm sure you have food tasters, but there's more than one way to get the agent into you. I will be here when you wish to speak to me." She pressed the button to end the call.

She stared at the detonator with her thumb over the button, fighting the temptation to press it. If she pressed the button now, it would be satisfying, but Karen would know she could destroy the generators, and it would have less of an impact than if they attacked a construction site and they destroyed that too. It would be safer for him and even more satisfying knowing it would send her into fits of rage and frustration. She put it back in her pocket and called Thaider. "Are your soldiers ready?"

"Yes, we're about to come through the Meta-gate now."

"That's good. I will meet you all there."

She called on the mothers next door to her lab, and together they walked up to the meta-gate to welcome the refugees. As they came through the gate, the mothers took the humans into the city to begin their education, while Margaret and the soldiers boarded the shuttle.

The engineer was about to take his seat with his squad. "Show me where the nearest generator construction site is, engineer," Margaret said.

He slung his rifle and joined her and Thaider in the cockpit. He pointed to the location on the navigation monitor. "It is there, second council sister. It'll join the network today."

"Call me Margaret. You have earned it." She powered up the engines, and the shuttle slowly rose.

"Land us here," Thaider said, pointing to a clearing on the monitor.

She typed the coordinates into the navigation computer and engaged the autopilot.

"Take me through the attack plan, Thaider," she said.

"I assume I can't persuade you to stay in the shuttle when we attack?"

"Your presumption is correct."

"Hmm. Very well. The construction site is a good hour's march from the landing zone. We'll attack under the cover of darkness, during the changing of the guard at two am."

He tapped the monitor, zooming in on the construction site.

"We'll launch a three-squad, three-pronged attack. As they've laid the construction site out in a rectangle, squads one and two will attack the left and right front corners of the site. Squad one will attack first. Once the warrior's attention focuses on squad one, squad two will attack their flank. The surprise will disorientate and confuse them, forcing them to retreat behind the generator, where squad three will be waiting."

"Sounds simple enough," Margaret said.

"They will not be expecting us, and a three-pronged attack will minimize casualties. You, Margaret, will be in squad three, waiting to take prisoners. Our squads have their orders, and we are ready. Questions?"

Neither of them spoke. The autopilot beeped. They were coming up on the landing zone.

"Thirty seconds," he said. "Time check. Zero One fifteen hours..." He looked to make sure the soldiers were checking theirs. "-set."

With time in synch and a last check of their weapons, the squads stood ready to deploy as Margaret guided the shuttle into land. As soon as the ramp lowered, the squads were down and into the trees.

In the distance, they could see the lights of the construction site. Thaider signaled the squad to split and move to attack positions. There were still twenty minutes before the two am attack time. In position and waiting, Thaider could see the massive smooth sloping side walls of the generator and unarmed warriors talking, eating, and laughing. While gangs of Workers were busy moving enormous stone blocks. He saw the glint of gold as other workers covered the pyramid-shaped capstones. They were totally oblivious to what was about to happen.

Dead on two am, squad one charged in, firing over the bewildered warriors and workers heads. Some reached for their weapons and began firing back. Then, squad two attacked, overwhelming any resistance, forcing them behind the unfinished generator and straight into the arms of squad three. It was over in minutes, and no one died.

Margaret watched as squads two and three collected weapons, and held the warriors and workers under guard, while Thaider and squad one set the charges to destroy the meta-gate and generator. He walked over and handed her the detonator, then pointed his weapon at the prisoners.

She held the detonator above her head. "First council sister is using you. She doesn't care if you live or die. If you continue to build these Meta-gate and power generators, you are sentencing yourselves and this planet to death."

The kneeling workers murmured, and the warriors spat on the ground.

"I give you a choice," she said. "You can stay here and face first sister's anger when I destroy this place, or you can join me in our rebellion to save this planet."

The silence was painful. Not one of them moved or looked at her to accept her offer. She looked and nodded at Thaider.

"On your feet," he said, prodding the nearest warrior with his rifle. He slowly stood, followed by the others. "Move." He pushed the warrior toward the trees. The rest of the prisoners followed, surrounded by the soldiers.

"What do you want to do with them, Margaret?" he asked.

"Escort them to the shuttle, then we'll leave them. I'll detonate the explosives you laid here and at the other generator once we're in the air.

They'll have to fend for themselves and deal with Karen's rage, and I wouldn't want to be on the receiving end of that when she gets here."

"No, me either," he laughed.

The march back through the forest guarding prisoners was slow going, but as they entered the clearing, they were all accounted for.

"On your knees," Thaider said, his voice booming in the night air. The workers obeyed immediately, but the warriors refused. "Cross your left foot over your right, and lace your fingers behind your head." He slammed the butt of his rifle into the back of the nearest warrior's knee. He groaned and collapsed. There was no more resistance after that.

"I'll give you one more chance to join us," Margaret said, looking at each of them. No one moved. "As you wish."

"Let's go," Thaider said.

Margaret boarded first, then one by one, the soldiers peeled away, running up the shuttle's ramp. Thaider, the last to board, walked backward pointing his weapon. He joined her in the cockpit as they lifted off, watching the workers and warriors get to their feet and run into the trees.

"I think we have enough altitude," Margaret said. "There's the construction site." The shuttle hovered as she pointed at it in the distance. She took the detonators out of her pocket and gave one to Thaider. "You've earned this, my friend."

He took it. "On three?"

"To the rebellion," she said with a smile.

He counted "One, two, three." They pressed the red buttons together.

The intense flash from the detonation stabbed their eyes, making them turn away. Then pitch darkness. Moments later, the shuttle rocked from the power of the blast.

"Wow," she said. "Did you use as much explosive at the other site?"

"Yes. I wanted to make sure."

"Well, that will get her attention." She turned the shuttle and headed back to the colony. More lights streaked across the sky as they flew into the mountains.

"More meteors. Is everyone here from the forest colony?" she asked Thaider as the shuttle touched down.

"Yes. We're all here."

"Are you sure? We can't leave anyone behind," she said, looking up as another shower of lights lit up the dark sky.

"Yes. If Karen finds it, it's empty."

"Billet the soldiers until we can build a permanent base camp, then send the engineer to my lab at lunchtime tomorrow. I need some sleep."

"Yes, Margaret."

She walked down to the city, tired and dirty from the night's action, looking forward to a hot shower. The water was hot and soothing, and clean night robes made her feel civilized again. Her warm, soft bed lulled her off to sleep as soon as she got in.

∞

The last few days had taken their toll. She'd felt the roller coaster of a soldier's emotions, the adrenaline rush of battle, and the exhaustion from the comedown. Here in the mountain colony, they were safe and her body knew it, giving her the much-needed sleep to recover. It was mid-morning when she woke. She was relaxed and comfortable and didn't want to get up, but there were things to do. She stretched and sat up. Freshly laundered robes waited for her in the closet, giving her the incentive to start the day.

Rest had cleared her mind, she felt it on the walk to her lab. A sharp clarity that the stresses of the last few days had clouded. Focussed and refreshed, she smiled seeing the mothers and nine other females waiting for her.

"And who do we have here?" she asked.

"Volunteers Margaret. They want to give you some of their DNA to help with your experiments," a mother said.

"That's very good of you," she said. "If you'd like to come this way." She opened the lab door, walked in, and switched the lights on. "Please take a seat over there and roll up your sleeves."

"Thank you for doing this," she said, taking a vial of blood from each of them. The communicator in her pocket buzzed and vibrated frantically in her pocket.

"Thank you, ladies." She took the insistent communicator out of her pocket and frowned. "Would you mind telling the mothers outside where you're staying in the city, in case I need you again?"

"Yes, Margaret," one of them said. They stood, rolling their sleeves down, as the small black device buzzed again.

She pressed 'answer,' as the ladies filed out. "Karen, - I have been expecting your call."

"Do you think destroying two generators will stop me?"

"No, of course not, but I bet they made one heck of a bang. I needed to get your attention. Karen, please, one last time, you must stop. Have your engineers take seismic readings. You'll see the effect for yourself."

"You are pathetic, Margaret. Nothing you say is going to stop me. I'll replace anything you destroy. I'm just getting started."

"Are you really that stupid? Let me use small words so you'll understand. If you build more generators, in a few years, the seismic activity will overwhelm this planet, killing everyone and everything on it. By the time the fleet gets here, it will be a useless, lifeless rock. You must stop, now."

"You should know I have my best trackers on the ground, Margaret. Look, there is no need for us to be enemies. Make yourself known to them. Come back to the ship and let's talk. We can sort this out. When I see you, I'll make things right. What do you say?"

"You must think I'm as stupid as you are, Karen. I know exactly how you would make things right. My work is underway. I have the eggs, and with the help of the humans, I will alter their physiology, their DNA, and their evolution and make them capable of giving birth to Szateth and Szatethess hybrids naturally. Fourth sister was right. We should have removed you when we had the chance. But here's the good news, Karen. You are bringing your reign, your life, and the lives of your warriors, workers, and crew to an end all by yourself, and I will get to watch your failure."

"Your pitiful threats are pointless. I will replace any warriors or workers you kill. Your insignificant rebellion is nothing. I am going to find you, torture you. The last thing you'll see as you die is my smiling face."

"Well, good luck with that. It seems we both have work to do. Best we get started." She ended the call and put the communicator in the desk drawer. She sighed, clenching her fists. The vials of fresh blood on the desk caught her attention. The precision of DNA extraction would calm her.

The vials made a satisfying whirring as they span in the centrifuge, and she watched as the red blood cells separated from the white. She poured the red cells away. Locked in the white cells, the fragile DNA wouldn't reveal itself. It needed to be coaxed out with some chemicals, a bit of vibration, and a final round in the centrifuge. Before an agonizing wait, to see if it had worked.

There you are, she said to herself as white fluffy DNA formed in the tubes. She leaned back in her chair. What she held in her hands, in these tiny tubes, was the future of her species.

She had viable human DNA to work with. Next, she would extract DNA from a Szatethess egg and begin the engineering to develop a hybrid. With all the care they deserved, she placed the tubes in the storage unit next to the eggs. She visualized injecting the new DNA and altering the female, so she produced hybrid eggs and gave birth to human Szateth and Szatethess hybrids. It was possible. In her mind, she saw it, and she saw something else.

She looked at the time and smiled. The extraction had taken a couple of hours. The focus calmed her. In that focus, her mind told her what she must do. It showed her how to deal a devastating blow to Karen's global warming plans and save this planet. This mission was as dangerous as it was crucial. *We're going to destroy all her power generators and Meta-gates in one go.*

She called Thaider. "Do you have a command post set up yet?"

"Yes, Margaret, of sorts. It's more of a tent and a table, really."

"Can I meet you there? I know what we need to do next."

"I'm here now. Am I going to like it?"

"Probably not. But Karen won't either, and we could end her plans in one go."

"I see. I'll see you shortly, then."

She ended the call, and opening the lab door, saw the mothers and the nine females talking. "I'm glad you're still here, ladies. I'd like to thank you for the best DNA samples I've had. Would you be willing to donate more blood in a few days?"

"Yes, Margaret, just let us know when," one of them said.

"Perfect." She waved as she walked away and said, "I'll send for you." As she walked to Thaider's tent, she came up with a basic plan for the raid.

"I have a plan," she said, as she flicked open the tent flaps and marched in.

He turned and smiled. "Tell me."

"We're going to destroy the conversion facility, all the power generators, and Meta-gates, all at once."

"Right, well, that sounds good. How?"

"Have you got plans for the conversion facility?"

"I do." He took them off the shelf, unrolled them, and spread them out. "With the help of the engineer, we've added the power station, see?" He stood aside so she could join him.

"Ah, yes, perfect."

"So, how are we going to destroy all of them at the same time?"

"Well, we fly in using the shuttle and take them by surprise. They'll think it's Karen making an inspection. Especially if we go in, in broad daylight."

"That's bold. Okay, what about the guards at the generator?"

"There won't be many during the day, and the warehouse will give us cover from the compound. If we can take them quickly and quietly, there won't be much resistance. Then plant explosives before anyone knows we're there."

"So far, so good. What about the meta-gate? It's here in the compound." He pointed. "We shouldn't have any problems dealing with workers, but we've got to get across this open ground," -he slid his finger from the warehouse to the fencing- "unseen, otherwise we're sitting ducks, for the warriors in the guard towers."

"There'll be quite a few warriors out looking for me, so there shouldn't be as many to worry about."

"Okay." He rubbed his chin, staring at the layout. "A better idea would be to land late in the afternoon just before sunset. It'll still be light enough for the guards at the generator to be unconcerned with a shuttle landing, and if we fly in with the sun behind us, it'll blind them to any signs on the shuttle that it's not Karen. Then we take the guards at the generator and wait till dusk. In two teams, we go *around* the open ground instead of across where there is more cover."

"Yes, yes, much safer," she said.

"Assuming we reach the compound without a firefight, that is." With his finger, he guided Margaret through the rest of his plan. "A small team will head inside first to the Meta-gate room and plant explosives, then -"

"Not quite," she said. "Before that, I need to activate the Meta-gate, go into the metaverse, and add some code so I can remotely open all the gates at the same time."

"That means holding the Meta-gate room and risking you. No, there must be another way?"

"I said you wouldn't like it. - And someone needs to stay behind to send the explosives through once I open them."

"No! We cannot risk you, Margaret. Without you, we're all dead. What about the engineer? Can't he do it and stay to send the explosives through?" He said. His eyes holding hers, desperately hoping he could.

"He can stay and send them the explosives, but he won't know how to write the code. I'm the only one who can do that. And I'll want him to volunteer, Thaider. I won't order someone to stay behind."

His eyes hardened. "I'm sure he will."

"If we pull this off, think about the lives we'll save."

"Damn it, I hate it, Margaret." They stared at each other. The moment of silence felt like a lifetime.

He took a deep breath and forced himself to look away. "If that's the only way I'm going in with you."

"I wouldn't want anyone else," she said, touching his arm.

"If we're going to do this, then once we're inside, the rest of the team will have to secure the towers, go hut to hut, disarming and corralling the warriors into the conversion room. They'll have some heavier weapons we can take, too. Once we're done, we'll join the squad in the conversion room, then lock all the warriors and workers in the secure area. While we place enough explosives to demolish the buildings and everything in them, you open the Meta-gates and get back to the shuttle, and we wait for the engineer. Then we'll blow the place and everything else like before, from a long way away."

"Do you think we can do it with no one getting hurt?"

"Damn, Margaret," he said. He paused and leaned on the plans. "If we time it right and avoid a firefight with the guards at the generator and in the towers, we stand a good chance of getting everyone back."

"Oh, I hope so Thaider. If we're successful, it will put an end to her plans."

"Good, and she'll lose a lot of trained warriors and workers she won't be able to replace in the blast."

"Maybe I should give them the same offer as the others?"

"You could, but I doubt they'll accept."

"I'll send them down the tunnel to the cavern. I hate the idea of killing for killing's sake."

"Deaths are unavoidable, Margaret. You'll have to accept that, especially as we face a force of well-armed and well-trained warriors."

"I know, and I'll feel each one more deeply because of it."

"This is the only way?"

She stood tall. "Time is running out for the planet. I believe so, yes."

"Alright then. I'll brief the squad and get everyone geared up. We'll leave in an hour."

"I'll get what I need and meet you at the shuttle."

The squad was boarding and taking their seats when she got there.

"You're sure about this, then?" Thaider said, meeting her at the bottom of the ramp.

"No, but it must be done." She walked past him.

"The sun will just be going down as we get there," he said, following her into the cockpit, where a fully armed engineer met them.

"You know what to do?" she asked him.

"Yes, Margaret, the General has given me my instructions."

"I'm glad you're with us," she said, pressing the buttons to close the ramp and start the engines. "Here we go then." She pulled the thruster levers back, and the shuttle rose.

The three of them squinted as she turned into the sun. She dimmed the windows, flying full throttle straight at it. Their flight path took them parallel past the facility before turning one hundred and eighty degrees to head back to the facility with the sun behind them. She slowed and descended, imitating the approach of a shuttle from the ship.

"Thirty seconds. Standby," Thaider said. The soldiers cocked their weapons and took attack positions at the top of the ramp.

As the shuttle got close, the four guards at the generator looked up, shielding their eyes. The sun blinded them. They knew of first council sister's fearsome reputation, and taking no chances, stood to attention as the shuttle touched down. The soldiers charged down the ramp, opening fire. They were dead before they realized what was happening.

The soldiers in two squads waited for dusk. As the sun set, Thaider gave the order. On either side of the open ground, taking advantage of the sparse cover the long grass gave, they approached the compound.

At the fence line, the soldiers aimed their weapons at the guards in the towers while Thaider cut the links, making an opening. He froze, waiting to see if the tower guards had seen them. They hadn't.

The first squad went through. The others waited, covering their entry, while they took positions at the bottom of the towers. Then followed them in. A pair of soldiers prepared to storm each hut. Margaret, Thaider, the engineer, and a soldier approached the Meta-gate room. As they reached it, the door opened.

"What the..."

Thaider grabbed him from behind, covered his mouth, pulled his head back, and slit his throat before he could say anything else. He held the unsuspecting worker's dead body up while the soldier entered the gate room. A shout from inside broke the stillness, followed by two flashes of white light, then silence.

The guard in the nearest tower looked over. "Who's there?" he said, his voice cutting through the quiet.

"Keep the noise down," a voice from a hut said.

There was a rumble of boots, then a groan. The tower team silenced him.

Thaider dragged the body of the worker quietly into the gate room. Margaret followed, and the engineer closed the door.

"Let's hope that's the last of them," Thaider said, standing over the body. We'll guard this entrance. "You and Margaret do your thing," he said to the engineer.

From outside, he could hear the shouts of his soldiers as they pulled and shoved the warriors from the towers and their huts. Most of the warriors from the huts were naked and more concerned with covering themselves than fighting back.

The rustling sound of the Meta-gate opening captured Thaider's attention. As he looked, the solid rock in the center of the gate frame changed into a blue ice color. The shimmering hypnotic beauty of it held his gaze. He heard a voice in the back of his mind, a warm, calm voice he knew he could trust.

"Thaider."

"W what?" he said, blinking and forcing himself to turn toward the voice.

"Did you hear me? I said we're going in now. We may be a little while."

"Oh, err, yes Margaret, we've got you."

She and the engineer stepped through and disappeared into the metaverse.

"Check what's happening outside. I'll stay and guard the gate," Thaider said. The soldier nodded, opened the door, and left. He gripped his weapon and looked around. For the first time, he felt the cold of being alone. The weight of the silence dulled the beauty of the open gate as he breathed heavily to regain control.

He heard a creak from behind and whipped around, ready to fire. He let out a breath. It was his soldier coming back in.

"Report," he said, his heart hammering in his chest.

"We have corralled the warriors, General. No injuries."

"Good work. Have them moved to the secure area. Round up all the workers and keep them all together. Place all the explosives. Guard them well, and wait for further orders."

"Yes, General." He saluted and left.

He could hear the shouting as his soldiers moved the prisoners through the serum room and outside. As the noise died down, Margaret and the engineer stepped back through the gate.

"We're all set," Margaret said, holding up two black boxes with red buttons. "This one opens the gates and sends the explosives through.

This one detonates them. Where are we Thaider?" The rumble of the Meta-gate closing filled the room.

"The warriors and workers are being guarded in the secure area. If you still want to give them your offer, best we do that now."

The engineer opened the door. A flash of white light hit his shoulder, sending him sprawling into Margaret. His scream and the smell of burned flesh filled the room. The plasma shot had cauterized most of the wound, but it was severe. She could see his collarbone and blood poured from beneath it. He collapsed.

Another shot blasted through the door, catching Margaret's sleeve, slamming her arm against the wall. The remotes flew from her hand.

"Shit!" She reached for them. Another blast cracked into the floor, destroying the gate's remote. They were sitting ducks.

"Engineer, are you alright?" she said. Another blast shot through the door, just missing him.

Thaider returned fire through the hole, covering Margaret as she grabbed the engineer by his collar, pulling him out of the line of fire.

"We cleared the compound. Who are they?" Thaider asked, firing again.

"They must be a team of trackers returning. Karen told me she'd sent some." She ripped off a piece of her robe and pressed it hard on his wound.

He groaned and opened his eyes. "Well, this isn't how I thought today would end," he said, grimacing.

"Quiet now. We'll get you out of here soon," she said. "Hold this cloth here." She put his hand in place of hers.

Another shot exploded through the door, showering them in splintered wood, making the hole bigger.

"Will there be more?" Thaider asked.

"Maybe," she said, drawing her pistol.

"We have to get out of here. Margaret, I'll cover you while you make a run for the conversion room door."

"I'm not leaving him."

"Leave me, Margaret," the engineer said.

"No!" she fired through the door.

"We must." Thaider grabbed her arm.

"Leave me. I'm dead anyway. You'll need someone to open the gates manually. Leave me here, I'll do it."

"You must go, now!" Thaider said.

She leaned down and whispered. "Just press the infinity symbol, and the code will do the rest. You are a hero, chief engineer. I will never forget you."

She met his eyes again. He smiled and nodded.

Thaider switched his rifle to automatic fire, sending rapid bursts of white-hot plasma through the hole. "Margaret, now, - get to the door."

She grabbed the explosives detonator and moved to the side of the door.

"I'll fire three bursts, then you go, and don't look back."

She put the detonator in her pocket.

"Ready?" he said.

"Ready."

He fired, pinning the enemy down. She threw open the door, firing as she dashed through. He fired again, kicked the door closed, and fired again.

Shots flew at her from a new angle as more warriors arrived, forcing her to take cover before reaching the door. Thaider fired again. To her left, the facility door opened. Margaret and Thaider opened fire to keep their heads down as her soldiers ran out, firing volleys of automatic fire into the enemy's positions.

"Thaider, - come on," her voice barely audible over the weapons fire.

"Wait till we're clear, then open the Meta-gate," he said to the engineer.

"Yes, now go."

"Covering fire!" All hell let loose as plasma bursts flashed and exploded into the warriors. He ripped the door off its hinges, screaming and firing as he ran to Margaret.

"Let's get out of here before more of these bastards arrive." He held a hand out to her.

With plasma bursting all around, he looked magnificent. She grabbed it. A true leader she would have followed anywhere. They broke cover.

The entire squad was now with them, led by Thaider. They cut a path through the warriors, killing all that stood in their way. Once through the fence, Margaret looked back and saw the gate open as a warrior entered and fired. She stood looking at all the death and gore that lie around her.

"Grieve later, Margaret. We're not done yet. Come on," Thaider said, pulling her out of her heartbreak.

They reached the shuttle and were under fire again. Warriors and trackers appeared, opening fire from all directions. She hit the button, closing the ramp. Plasma shots cracked into the hull.

From the cockpit, she saw warriors running forward. Thaider squeezed her arm.

"Blow it now," he said, looking deep into her eyes.

Her eyes filled as she took the detonator out of her pocket. "For the engineer," she said, looking at Thaider. He smiled and nodded.

She closed her eyes and pressed the button.

Nothing happened.

∞

An alarm sounded, and blips flashed on the sensor's screen.

"What now?" she opened her eyes. Shuttles from the ship hovered above, pinning them to the ground.

"Did it work?" Thaider asked.

"There should have been a very large flash. I don't know?" She pressed the button again, then again. Still, nothing happened.

Bolts of white-hot plasma splattered against the cockpit window as the approaching warriors concentrated their fire on her.

"The explosives haven't detonated?" Thaider asked.

"Doesn't look like it," she said. "We need to get down there."

"Are you crazy!" He pointed at the warriors running toward them.

"We have to get off this shuttle, Thaider. We're going to have to fight our way out of this. Look." She pointed to the sensor monitor.

"Where did they come from?" he said, gripping his rifle.

"We're sitting ducks in here, Thaider," she said. "If we get to the serum room, we can escape through the tunnels back to the forest colony. Come on, before they surround us."

"Alright." He gave his orders. "Two squads. Squad one, as soon as the ramp opens, I want suppressing fire to the front. Get their heads down, give them everything you've got. Squad two, as soon as one opens fire, move to the right, around the warehouse, flank, and engage as soon as you're in position. One advance as soon as two engages. We'll come together, form a wedge, and we don't stop until we reach the serum room. They won't be expecting an attack. Maximum rate of fire, maximum aggression. Margaret, you're in squad two."

They prepared themselves, plasma rifles ready as she held her finger over the ramp's button. "Ready?"

A defiant chorus of *ready* rang out. She hit the button.

Squad one rushed forward. As the ground appeared, they opened fire before the ramp touched down. The stunned warriors paused, creating a window squad two took advantage of, jumping off to the right, sprinting to the warehouse, and making their way around.

It wasn't long before the firing started again. Desperate to join the fight, she and the others ran the length of the warehouse. The warriors were advancing just around the corner. They crawled around each other into firing positions and ripped into the warriors with automatic fire.

They had turned the tide, forcing the warriors to retreat. Squad one, led by Thaider, moved off the ramp, firing from the hip, and pressed forward. Squad two blasted them with covering fire. As they pushed the warriors back, she saw shuttles landing.

They left the cover of the warehouse and joined squad one. "Thaider, the shuttles," she said.

A bolt of plasma hit him. "Aargh." He dropped his rifle and fell.

"Thaider!" She reached for him.

A soldier grabbed her arm. "Leave him, he's gone. We've got to get to the facility," he said, pulling her away. He pulled her down the hill toward the facility door. She couldn't see him anymore. Without warning, warriors poured through like ants, opening fire as they spilled out.

"Take cover..." he said, pushing her away. A plasma bolt burned a hole through his chest, silencing him forever.

She screamed her rage and sprayed the door with deadly fire. The bodies mounted, but there were too many of them.

Weapon's fire was coming from the front, the facility, and from behind as the warriors from the shuttles closed in. She could hear the groans of the dying all around. Warriors surrounded her. She stopped firing.

"Hold your fire," a horribly familiar voice said.

She turned, confirming her worst nightmare. The hot muzzles of two plasma rifles pressed against her chest. "Drop your weapon," a warrior said.

"Ah, Margaret. How nice to see you," Karen said with a huge smile as she and her bodyguards marched toward her. "Have your soldiers drop theirs too."

"Drop your weapons," she said, her ears still ringing with the sounds of battle. Her remaining soldiers stood and did as ordered.

"Good. Collect their weapons and have them lined up over there," Karen said to one of her warriors.

He raised his rifle. "Move," he said, waving it to where she wanted them. With their hands raised, they complied.

"Now what?" Margaret said, spitting blood from her mouth.

Karen took her warrior's rifle. "This." She opened fire, killing the soldiers in cold blood.

She closed her eyes and turned away.

"Put her in shackles and take her to my shuttle," Karen said to her bodyguards.

She felt their cold steel lock around her wrists and ankles. "Let's go," the bodyguard said, pushing her. Her steps shortened by the chains made her stumble. "Move," he said, wrenching the chain between her wrists. She winced as they dug into her flesh.

"Oh, and thank you for returning my shuttle," Karen said, laughing.

It was over.

Slumped in her seat on Karen's shuttle, she felt the loss of Thaider, her soldiers, and the weight of the chains.

"Cheer up, Margaret, you and I are going to spend many hours together," Karen said, sitting next to her as the shuttle took off.

She didn't reply.

"I, for one, am looking forward to our time together." She patted her knee. "I've got plans for you. It's going to be fun."

Tears filled her eyes. Not for herself, but for what Karen would do to the humans and the Szateth. She felt the shuttle come to a stop as it docked.

"Take her to the council chambers," Karen said to two warriors behind her. They stood to attention and saluted.

"Get up," one of them said.

She lifted her arms and wiped the tears on her sleeve. The cold chain brushed her cheek, and she flinched.

"Come on, get up," the other warrior said, grabbing the chain and pulling it like a leash.

The pain was too sharp to resist, and she followed in the direction he dictated. They rubbed and tore at her skin, cutting deeper with every step, leaving footprints of blood as she shuffled to keep up.

"Welcome aboard, second council sister," the first officer said, smirking at the bottom of the ramp. "I wish I could be there to watch."

She looked straight ahead. The warrior pulled her along the corridors until she stood behind the seat that was once hers in the council chambers. She stood with defiance and the elegance of a council sister.

Karen and her bodyguards were whispering and glancing sideways at her when the young sisters marched in. "Ah, there you are," Karen said as they sat around the table. "I'm going to teach you a most important lesson today."

They stared at Margaret's dirty, torn robes and the shackles. "Is that second sister?" one of them asked.

"It was," Karen said, circling her prey. "Now, she's the ringleader of a rebellion. And what do we do with those?" she asked, taking her seat at the head of the table.

Their little hands shot up.

"What should we do with her?"

"Kill her." They sang.

"Yes. You're right. We should kill her." She stood, drawing her knife. "But she has done something far worse. She has conspired against me and killed a council sister. It is the worst crime a Szatethess can commit. I should make her suffer first. Don't you think?"

They sat wide-eyed, not sure how to answer.

She waved the point of her knife at her. "Warrior, remove her robe."

He stood behind her, reached around, grabbed the collar, and ripped it open, exposing her upper body.

She stabbed the tip of her knife into the front of her shoulder, above her breast, breaking the skin. A trickle of blood ran from the wound as she twisted it deeper.

The young sisters gasped.

"Do you think she should have a quick death, young sisters?" She looked at each of them. None of them answered.

"No, she must suffer first, as a warning to others." She drew the blade down, cutting deeper into her breast, and looked for the pain in her eyes.

It was searing, and she cried out.

Karen smiled, her mouth watering at the thought of what was to come. "There will be no mercy for traitors," she said, before looking at the young sisters. They looked away.

She cleaned her knife on Margaret's robe and put it away. "I will continue this in the brig," she said to the warriors. "Prepare her for me like you did fourth council sister. I will be along later."

"Yes, first council sister. It will be our pleasure," one of them said. He pulled her chain, forcing her to turn. He smiled and licked his lips, seeing the blood and her breasts.

"There will be plenty of time for that," she said. "Just soften her up, nothing more. Am I clear?"

"Yes, first council sister," they said, and pulling her along, marched out.

"You must not concern yourself with her, young sisters. She is a traitor and you must never have sympathy. You must be hard and send a message. Everyone must know what will happen if they stand against you. You will understand when you're older. - Now, shall we have some food?" They clapped and squealed. Her bodyguards grinned.

∞

"Get in there, traitor," the warrior behind her said, pushing her into the cell. The shackles on her ankles cut deeper as she stumbled, trying to stay on her feet.

They forced her to sit in the chair in the center of the cell. She looked around. There was no other furniture. This wasn't a cell to hold a prisoner. "You don't have to do this," she said.

A fist slammed into her jaw, knocking her to the floor. "We know," one of them said, lifting her back onto the chair.

"But we want to," the other said. He pushed his fingers into the cut on her breast. "I can feel bone."

She screamed.

"Silence," the other one said, slapping the other side of her face.

She whimpered as he pulled his blood-covered fingers out of the wound and wiped them on her face. He punched her again.

She could feel the side of her face swelling, and her eye closing. "Alright, please, no more."

"That's what I like to hear," he laughed, punching her again.

She could hear a voice in the back of her head, "second council sister, sister wake up." And felt little slaps on her face as she regained consciousness. She was on the chair.

"Ah, welcome back," one warrior said. He poured a cup of water, while the other dipped a cloth in a bucket and wrung it out.

He dabbed it on her face. She winced. "Yes, I'm sorry, second council sister, it's got salt in it. Don't want you to get an infection now. It might kill you." The echo of their laughter hurt her ears.

"You must be thirsty, second council sister. Here, drink this." She turned away. "Drink. It's not poisoned, if that's what you think." He took a mouthful.

"I'm going to take a piss," the other warrior said, leaving the cell.

"Alone at last, second council sister," he said. He caressed her breast. "Hmm, nice. I always wondered what a council sister would feel like." He squeezed hard.

Tears ran down her face as he continued his assault on the rest of her body.

They both heard the thud. "We'll continue with this later," he said. "What's going on out there? Stop messing about. First council sister will be here soon."

When he got no reply, he went to see what caused the noise.

She looked up as his body hit the floor. She could see a figure standing in the doorway, but her eyes refused to focus.

"Come on, sister, let's get you out of here," the figure said.

She knew that voice. "Thaider. How?"

"Can you walk?" he asked, covering her with her torn robe.

"I'll damn well walk out of here."

"That's the spirit," he said. "There's a skeleton crew, so if we're lucky, we'll make it to the hangar without having to deal with another of these." He spat on the dead warrior.

"Thaider, how are you here?"

"Later. Let's get these off you first." He took the keys off the dead warrior and unlocked the shackles. "Now, shall we get off this ship?"

She reached for his help to get up and gripped his shoulder. She felt the wetness of blood. "Thaider?"

"It's fine. Come on, follow me before we get seen."

He paused by the door, listening. The only sound was the low hum of the air vents. "It's clear," he said. They hugged the walls and ran when they could, reaching the hangar door unseen. He peeked through the window.

"The first officer's back. I don't see anyone else."

"He's mine," she said. "Then we'll take Karen's shuttle."

They waited until he went into the control room and then opened the door enough to slip through. "Your injuries, sister. Are you sure you can take him?" Thaider asked.

"Watch if you doubt it."

Her movements were smooth, powerful, and silent. Her reptilian nature was in full ambush mode as she closed in on him. She was behind him before Thaider knew it. He deserved what was coming, and she wanted him to see her, to know it was her before she tore him to pieces. She blew on the back of his neck.

His hand reached around to feel what was there, then he turned. His eyes flew open. "What, how..."

She struck forward, her needle-sharp teeth sinking into the top of his shoulder, ripping out the muscle as she squeezed his throat. Blood spurted from the bite, spraying the window. There was no sound as her teeth replaced her hand, tearing out his throat. His warm flesh and silky metallic-tasting blood triggered a feeding frenzy, and she gorged on his dead body.

"Sister, we need to go," Thaider said.

She spun, her eyes staring, full of the desire to feed. Blood dripped from her mouth as she chewed.

"Margaret, we must go."

She blinked and swallowed. "Yes. Thaider, I hear you." She wiped her mouth and smiled at the frozen look of terror on his dead face.

"Which one is her shuttle?" he asked.

"This one." She pointed at the grandest of them all, and they got on board.

You're not getting this one back, she said to herself, as she powered up the engines and ripped the wires off the transponder. "At least we have a shuttle again," she said. When he didn't answer, she looked over. He was unconscious. As soon as they left the hangar, she set the autopilot for the mountain colony. The wound on his shoulder was bleeding more than before.

"Thaider." She shook him and he groaned. She found the med kit under the instrument panel, squirted cleaning fluid onto a gauze, patted the wound clean, and covered it with a fresh bandage. "Hold on, my friend. We'll soon be home."

∞

Thaider opened his eyes, like every trained soldier he knew not to move until he'd assessed his body for injuries. He felt the pain and the smell of burned flesh from a wound on the back of his shoulder. Everything else seemed okay.

There were weapons firing some distance away, and he tried to sit up. Pain shot through his body, but he had to see. He reached over and grabbed his rifle, wedged the butt into the ground, and pulled himself up. The firing had stopped by the time he could see. Bodies of dead warriors were everywhere. He saw Karen point a rifle down the hill at his soldiers, and he gasped when she pulled the trigger. His heart was pounding in his ears as his soldiers fell, and her bodyguards led Margaret away in shackles, with Karen laughing. He had to rescue her.

Everyone thought he was dead, and that gave him an advantage. They would take her to the ship, where Karen would enjoy torturing her. He had to get up there. Adrenalin surged through him, dulling the pain as he crawled on his belly back to the shuttle. The wet ground made it harder to grip, but he got there. Once inside, he grabbed the med kit from the cockpit and hid in the engine room.

He grimaced, pressing a dressing onto the wound under his jacket to hold it in place. If he was to function, he needed to control the pain. The med kit was well stocked, and he filled a syringe with a cocktail of painkillers and antibiotics, stabbing it into his thigh. He grimaced again, feeling the chemicals burn as he squeezed them into his leg.

He was pain free by the time he heard the muffled voices of warriors coming up the ramp. There was no reason for anyone to come into the engine room, but he pointed his rifle at the door, anyway. The engines rumbled louder as they powered up, and the shuttle lifted off.

There wouldn't be much time to free her, and he knew he had to time it right. He looked at the screen on his communicator for the time. It was late, the skeleton night shift crew would have taken over by now. He felt the shuttle come to a stop and heard the ramp open. The warriors got off, and he heard voices.

"Last to get in again," someone said. He thought it was the first officer.

"Hmm, like always," a warrior said.

"One day you'll surprise me."

"I doubt it," he said with a sigh. "Come on, you lot, let's go get a drink."

He heard boots marching away.

Patience, he said to himself. If first council sister ran true to form, she would humiliate her first before having warriors beat her half to death in the brig. He prayed she'd survive the beating and checked the time again. *One hour.*

It was the longest hour he'd ever experienced. With his ear to the door, he listened for movement. Satisfied it was safe, he crept into the cockpit. Through the window, the first officer appeared out of the control room. He ducked and watched him walk out of the hangar. He scanned around again. It was clear.

He knew the ship's sensors would detect weapons fire, so he propped his rifle against the instrument panel and drew his knife. Staying low, he took a last look out the window. It was clear. He ran to the hangar door, checked the corridor, through the window, and slipped out.

"Aargh." He caught his shoulder as he went through, dislodging the dressing. He froze, listening. No one had heard him. He reached over and slid his fingers under his jacket, feeling the wound. They came out covered in blood. "Damn."

The painkillers were still working, and he ran through the corridors to the brig. As he got to the entrance, he heard a voice.

"I'm going to take a piss."

He tightened his grip on his knife, stopped, and waited. The door to the bathroom was just inside, and he heard it open. He followed the unsuspecting warrior in.

From behind, he reached around his head, pulled it back, and tried to stamp on the back of his knee, but he was heavy, and his injured shoulder restricted his movement. The warrior stepped back, thudding him against the door.

The warrior broke free and turned, reaching for his dagger, but not fast enough. He rammed his knife through the front of the warrior's throat. He gurgled, trying to scream a warning, but it was too late. His body flopped to the floor with a thud.

The pool of blood made it easy to pull the body away from the door. He heard another voice.

"What's going on out there? Stop messing about. First council sister will be here soon."

He opened the door and hid in the shadows, waiting for the warrior that spoke. The moment he was close enough, he stabbed his knife, one, two, three, four, five times in his belly, once to his heart, and a deep slash across his throat. He never stood a chance.

He stood in the doorway. He could see her in the chair, beaten and half-naked. "Come on, sister, let's get you out of here."

∞

A shower of meteors roared across the night sky. The flashes of light lighting up the shuttle's cockpit brought Thaider around.

"How long have I been out?"

"A couple of hours," Margaret said. "We'll be back at the colony in a few minutes. Then we'll get you patched up."

Another flash lit up the cockpit. "What's going on?" he asked. He got out of the chair and joined her, looking out of the window.

"A meteor shower, a big one. It's been going on for a while."

"Is this Karen's doing?"

"No, and I was afraid of this. I think the planet is moving through a meteor swarm."

The blast from a meteor entering the atmosphere washed over the shuttle, shaking it like a maraca. They gripped the side of the instrument panel to stay on their feet.

"That was close, and they're getting bigger."

"Will any of them hit? They must have felt that on the ship," Thaider said, picking computer tablets and paper off the floor.

"I'm sure they did," she said, looking at the instrument panel for damage warning lights. "We seem to be in one piece. Let's get back and get you treated, and I'm sure Karen is going to be mad. You've spoiled her fun."

"I hope so. After watching her kill our soldiers like that. If I ever get my hands on her, I'll cut her throat and smile as she bleeds out... And we should lay a memorial tablet for the engineer in the next few days. Perhaps you could say something at the service."

"It will be an honor, Thaider." As the shuttle turned for the mountains, she couldn't help but notice what looked like three new stars in the sky. *Oh, no!* "We have to get back. They are going to hit," she said, pointing at them and opening the thrusters to the maximum.

"Oh, shit. Are we going to die?"

"No, we'll be safe below ground. But when we get back, make sure everyone stays inside. I'll be in my lab. I've got a call to make."

∞

She was just dropping off to sleep when she heard the glass on her nightstand shaking. Then her communicator buzzed. She sat up and put her feet on the floor and felt the vibration. It buzzed again.

"What's going on?" she said, answering the call from her new chief engineer.

"It's a meteor shower, first council sister, and some of them are big."

"Is the ship in danger?"

"It might be, first council sister."

"My generators, are they still online?"

"Yes, first council sister."

"What did you disturb me for then?"

"I'd like to request we move the ship to a safe location."

"Why?"

"The meteor shower might get worse. If we get hit, it might damage the ship, first council sister."

"Is that likely?"

"It might be possible, yes, first council sister."

"I don't work with might's and if's, Chief engineer. Call me when there's something to talk about." She hit the end call button.

She laid back down, closing her eyes, thinking about how much she was going to hurt Margaret before she let her die. Her communicator buzzed.

“This better be good, or it’ll be the last call you ever make,” she said to the commander of her warriors.

“I’m sorry to report that second council sister has escaped the brig, first council sister.”

“What!” She jumped out of bed. “Lock down the ship immediately.”

“I’m afraid it’s too late, first council sister, your shuttle is missing. We think she’s on the surface. Two warriors are dead, killed by someone who is skilled with a blade. She had help.”

He heard crashing and smashing and screams of rage. Then the voices of her bodyguards, followed by silence.

“Who, commander?” she said in a voice so calm it made him shiver. “Who helped her?”

“I don’t know yet, first council sister. I was about to go to the control room in the hangar to view the recordings.”

“Do that, then meet me in your office. I want to make a call from your communicator.”

“Yes, first council sister.”

She ended the call. “Wait outside until I get dressed properly,” she said to her bodyguards.

Through the window, she noticed the light from what looked like three big stars. She had to squint. They were so bright.

“We need to go to the commander’s office,” she said as she opened the door. They followed as she marched past. By the time she got there, she was shaking with rage.

“Well, commander?”

"You should see this, first council sister." He tapped the play button on his monitor.

"It's the old training officer," she said, pointing. "How did he get on the ship?"

"He must have got on a shuttle," he said.

The communicator on her wrist buzzed. "Not now, chief engineer."

"But, first council sister, it's..." She cut him off.

She snatched the communicator off the desk and squeezed the call button. "Are you there Margaret?—Answer me."

After a moment of silence. "Well, well, I was about to call you. Hello Karen, is everything alri..."

The communicator crackled with static interference.

Her wrist buzzed again.

"Margaret," she said, holding it close to her mouth. "Margaret."

The sound returned. "Yes, Karen. What do you want?"

"You escaped this time."

"I did. It was easy. You need better warriors."

"You had help from the old training officer, I see. You're too weak to have gotten away by yourself."

"It pays to have friends. Maybe it's something you should think about."

"You won't be so lucky next time." Her wrist buzzed again. She tutted.

"Am I keeping you, Margaret?"

Static cut out the sound again. "What's going on?" she said to the commander. Her wrist buzzed again.

The communicator crackled back to life. Margaret was laughing. "Seems to me I don't need to stop you. Looks like the universe is going to do it for me. Your global warming project is about to take on a whole new meaning, Karen. You've seen the meteors, right?"

Her wrist buzzed again. "What, chief engineer?"

The alarm from the ship's sensors screamed in the background.

"What is that?"

"We have three large objects approaching the planet, first council sister. The ship's sensors have just picked them up."

"Only just picked them up? I saw them out my window. They're meteors, like before?"

"No. Bigger, first council sister, much bigger. They are chunks of an asteroid, miles wide. If they hit, they will cause an extinction-level event on this planet."

"Sounds like you've got your hands full up there, Karen. The universe is going to do my job for me. Just know that I will save our species with the humans and without you. Enjoy your failure in the short time you have left. Goodbye, Karen." She laughed and ended the call.

Bitch, we'll I'm not done yet. "Are they going to hit, Chief engineer? Tell me now."

"We suspect they might, first council sister, they are growing large in the sky."

"How long?"

"A few hours, first council sister."

"We need to leave the planet for orbit, then."

"It's too late, first council sister. They are too big and too close. We didn't detect them in time. And hundreds, if not thousands, of meteors are showering the planet. We won't avoid all of them. At the speed they're traveling, even with the shields, they'll damage the ship. We need to hide."

"The ship will protect us. We will be safe," she said, pacing, trying to convince herself. "Can we land?"

"When they hit, first council sister, *everything* on the surface of this planet will burn. I would not recommend it."

"Prepare the cryo-stasis chambers."

"Yes, first council sister."

She ended the call. *If we can't land on the surface... What about under it? Yes, underwater, in the deep ocean.* She called the bridge.

"Pilot, I need you to bring the propulsion engines online, raise the shields, and look for a location to submerge the ship."

"Already on it. I have the perfect place, first council sister. An underwater mountain ridge between two of the biggest continents. The volcanic activity along the ridge is spreading the ocean floor. Hydrothermal vents, along with the new Magna, will warm the surrounding water, giving us the protection we need. We can take shelter there. Might I suggest twenty-five degrees North, seventy-one West?"

"I commend you, pilot. Prepare the ship. Take us there, now."

"Yes, first council sister."

∞

Protected from the impact of the asteroid fragments, they could feel the rise in temperature. Margaret leaned on Thaider as they walked through the city. Her swollen face throbbed with every step.

"I wouldn't want to be up there, right now," Thaider said.

"Mmm," Margaret said, staring at the ground as they walked. She knew if she felt the heat this far down, everything on the surface would be gone. "All her generators, facilities, and Meta-gates. There'll be no trace of them."

"Should we take precautions?" Thaider asked.

She touched his arm. "No, my friend, we're quite safe."

"How long will we have to stay here?"

"A long time, Thaider. We're going to have to wait until the surface heals. Hopefully, I'll be healed by then, too." She touched her battered face and tried to laugh. They stopped and watched the humans going about their business around them. "Generations of these people will be born, live, and die before we can emerge," she said.

"What about Karen and the ship?"

"I think we can assume her sense of self-preservation will mean she'll do anything to save herself."

"Really?"

"Oh yes. It's the one thing she's good at." She carried on walking, and they reached the edge of the city.

"So, what do we do now?"

She stopped and looked at him. "We live, Thaider. You and I are going to be the guardians of theirs and our future." She looked across the city. "It's going to take a long time for me to create a human Szateth hybrid. It's a new science, I don't understand, yet. And over the time we're here, we'll teach them how to become a civilized society. Then once on the surface, we'll teach them how to use this planet's resources so they become independent of us, and the hybrids can evolve naturally."

"Then what?"

"We'll still be here when the fleet arrives, and we're going to have to help them all over again when it does. I know what I need to do. We'll have help next time."

"How can I help? I don't know enough."

"You know how to build a Meta-gate."

"Yes."

"Then, for now, you know enough. I will make sure that by the time they get here, the humans have enough knowledge to understand our technology, so they won't be at as much of a disadvantage. We'll guide them in the meantime."

"You mean we'll be like parents? You will be their mother. Their Terra Mater, their Earth Mother."

"Earth Mother, hmm. Yes, okay. But Thaider, we must resign ourselves to the pages of legend and history. This planet is theirs, and once I've finished my work, we'll need to stay in the shadows until they need us again."

"I will teach some of them the skills to make them strong, disciplined soldiers capable of defending themselves."

"The one good thing to come out of this is that I'll have time to do what I and my other council sisters set out to do. Karen never understood how important the Human species are to us. Now, there's no rush. We have what we need and enough volunteers for me to complete my work. Come on Thaider, we've got a lot to do."

They walked back into the city.

"Together we'll watch, wait, and teach for the time when a few of them must face my sisters again. They must be ready, or everything we do from now on will be useless."

"We have time, Margaret,"

She squeezed his arm and looked at him. "I just hope it's enough. We need to secure their future, Thaider. Build a Meta-gate in my lab. Only you and I will know how to use it and tell no one what it is. That'll be a good start."

"I'll come in the morning." They stopped outside her house. "What about the crew and the warriors on the ground? She wouldn't leave them to die, would she?"

"Of course she will," she said, her voice devoid of emotion. "She cares for no one but herself."

"Yes." He looked away.

"She'll promise a few something to get them to help her, then once she and the young sisters are safe, she'll betray them. It's her nature."

"Is she really that sadistic?"

"I'm afraid so." They stopped outside her house. "I'll see you then. Get a good night's sleep. Our work begins tomorrow."

Her cuts and bruises made sleep uncomfortable. She could have created a neural block and healed herself, but wore them as badges of honor to remind herself why the work she was going to do was so important.

The pinging of her alarm woke her. She sat up, and for a moment, had forgotten about them before they reminded her. They throbbed and the dressing on her chest needed changing. She got up and looked in the mirror above her sink. The purple and blue clashed with her olive skin. *Well, that's attractive*. She filled the sink with cold water and soaked a cloth. She groaned as she held it against her cheek.

The cold numbed her face, but the dressing, stuck to the wound, was anything but painless as she peeled it off. *Ahh, damn it. - Good, none of the stitches pulled out.* The soreness eased as she dabbed the wound with the cold cloth. With a new dressing, she felt better, and she put on fresh robes.

She called on the mothers on the way to her lab.

"Morning ladies. Would you bring those females to my lab, please? I have another request to make."

"Yes, sister," the first mother said. "I know they'll want to help. We'll be along shortly."

"Thank you, ladies. I'll see you soon."

She flicked the lab's lights on, switched on her computer, and, humming, opened a new spreadsheet to record the results of her experiments.

Thaider and a few soldiers came in carrying materials, tools, and equipment to build the Meta-Gate.

"Good morning, General Thaider," she said.

"Good morning, Margaret." He put his tools on the table next to her. "What was that you were humming?"

"Oh, nothing. I'm just feeling that today we're going to make some actual progress."

"Sounds good. Where would you like me to build it?"

"Behind the screens over there. It'll be out of sight if anyone looks in."

"You men put all the equipment and materials over there. Then you can resume your normal duties."

"Yes, General," one of them said.

Through the noise of equipment and materials being stacked, he heard giggling behind him. When he turned, he saw nine females watching his muscular soldiers, laughing and covering their mouths as they whispered to each other.

"It's human nature, it seems," Margaret said to him, with a curt smile. "That'll do ladies. Take a seat if you please."

"Hurry you men, duty calls." They marched past him and out of the lab, stared at by an appreciative giggling audience.

"I'll make a start on the build," Thaider said, squinting his eyes at the females. They looked away.

"Yes, thank you, General. Now ladies, thank you for coming in again. The blood you gave me has progressed my work more than you can imagine. Now I have a further request to make."

"Whatever we can do, Margaret," the one who had taken charge of the group said. The others nodded.

"Before you agree, you should know what I'm asking of you." She looked at each female. "I want to give each of you a memory, a genetic memory, one you will pass down through your genes to your children, who will pass it on to theirs and on through time."

"What sort of memory?"

She's a natural leader. "A memory of what's happened here, a memory of our arrival, our treatment of your species, and what is coming in a future time. Each of you will get a memory that emphasizes a particular event."

"Is it going to be painful?"

"Not for you, but for the future generation who will need it. They will suffer in childhood until they meet each other."

The nine shuffled in their seats.

"If you agree to this, your descendants will be the leaders of the second rebellion. They will be the heroes and saviors of mankind, but they will need to know what's coming to prepare their army."

"Why us?"

"Because you ladies volunteered to help. That loyalty to me and your species makes you the best among you, and because of that, I believe you are genetically strong enough to pass the memory intact through time."

They looked at each other, and then at their leader. "We agree."

She breathed a sigh. "Thank you, ladies. May I start with you?" she said to the leader, dragging an empty chair in front of her. "Please sit here."

She sat, and Margaret touched her forehead. She saw a brilliant light, and the memory of *all* that had happened, and what was to come, burst into her mind. When it was over, tears streamed down her face.

"Now you know," Margaret said. "And you know what must be done."

"Yes." She got up and offered the chair to the next female.

One by one, they sat in front of her, receiving their memory and weeping once they knew.

"You are special, ladies. Your bloodline is the most precious of all. You now carry the burden of future knowledge. General Thaider and I will be here to help you cope with the weight of it if you need us."

The nine wiped their tears, then Margaret added. "Tell no one what you know or what's happened here today. Your reward is knowing that your descendants will be the saviors of humankind."

In their minds, they could still hear the faint echo of Margaret's warm voice. *Remember the Rebellion.* They sat in silence, trying to come to terms with what they knew. What they knew for sure was that whatever happens in the future, Margaret and Thaider were going to be there.

∞

"Your time will come, Margaret," Karen said, muttering to herself as she marched to engineering.

She called the pilot. "Are we at the coordinates?"

"We're arriving now, first council sister."

The continuous roar of meteors crashing and exploding rocked the ship.

"Good. Submerge as soon as we're in position. There's no time to waste."

"Yes, first council sister."

"Bring the young sisters to engineering," she said to her bodyguards.

"Yes, sister." They reached out for a wall, feeling the ship descending.

"Quickly now. I don't want to be kept waiting. I'll meet you outside engineering."

"Yes, sister." They carried on down the corridor to their chambers when she turned off.

She didn't have to wait long. "Ah, there you are, good. Now, wait for me in there." The young sisters filed through the door.

"I would like to give you a part of your reward now," she said to her bodyguards.

Their eyes lit up.

"In second council sister's lab, you will find some females. Take them to my chamber. I will order food and drink for you. Use them. You know what they're for."

"Oh, thank you, thank you first council sister," they said.

"There is something more for you to look forward to in the future. Go now."

They bowed low and marched away. One of her eyebrows pulled upwards, and turning her back on them, she snorted and walked into engineering.

"We're all about to sleep for a while, young sisters," she said to them as they gathered around her.

"But we slept already, first sister," one of them said.

"This is a very special sleep. It protects, heals, teaches you, and helps you grow. When you wake up, you'll be older, cleverer, and bigger."

"Like you, first sister?"

"Well, not as old." She laughed. "And maybe not as clever, but certainly as big as me."

"Ooh, that sounds like fun."

"It is. The chief engineer here is going to show you where we're going to sleep."

"You're going to sleep too, first sister?"

"Yes, that's right."

"This way, young council sisters, if you'd follow me." He walked past the flashing lights and wall of monitors.

They looked at first sister for her permission. "Yes, yes, off you go. I'll be with you soon." She shooed them away, and their little legs scampered to catch up with him.

"There is one for each of you," he said, pointing to the row of cylindrical glass tubes. "You can choose whichever you like."

Their excited squeals made him smile as they climbed in. He pushed the button to activate the chambers. The lids came over and sealed. In moments, the young sisters were in cryo-sleep. He checked the readings on each of the chamber's monitors, then slid and locked them into their housings behind the wall. Three chambers remained.

The ship came to rest on the ocean floor. The hull groaned as the shields adapted to the immense pressure of the water surrounding it.

She called the pilot. "Good work, pilot, I commend you. Secure the ship, then come to engineering. There is a spare stasis chamber."

"Thank you, first council sister," he said.

The chief engineer returned. "The young sisters are in cryo-stasis, first council sister," he said, looking at the red warning lights flashing on the screens. "Are we safe under all this pressure, first council sister?"

She made a few adjustments to the control settings, and one by one, the lights went out. "Yes, here the ship can withstand more than this planet can throw at it. Show me the stasis chambers."

"This way, first council sister." He led her past the monitors, to the secluded cryo-stasis area, usually off-limits to the crew.

She saw the sealed doors to the tubes that housed the sleeping sisters, and the three open chambers. "This one is mine?"

"Yes, first council sister," he said, pointing at the panel in the chamber. "Here you control the ship's systems and the parameters for the sleep cycle and waking program."

"Very well, chief engineer, you have done well, I commend you. As you can see, even though the stasis chamber on the end is offline, there is one spare."

"Yes, first council sister, thank you."

she climbed into her chamber and began programming the ship's system to power down and sleep.

"You have been valuable to me, chief engineer, and I think you could be so again in the future. Take this." She handed him her dagger.

"Thank you, first council sister. It has been a privilege to serve you. When will we wake?"

She typed commands into the computer as she spoke. "Once the ship sensors detect a stable climate warm enough for us to live. When there is a resumption of life for food and a life form suitable for conversion."

"Why do I need your dagger, first council sister?"

"The ship is secure, first council sister," the pilot said, running in. He saw her in her chamber and looked at the chief engineer and the spare chamber. "I thought this was for me?"

She grinned. "I hope you win," she said to the chief engineer, then activated her chamber. As she started recording her last neural-blockchain journal entry, and the chamber slid into its resting place, she saw the pilot lunge at the chief. She and the young sisters were safe. She didn't care about anyone else, although she looked forward to seeing who won.

Neural Blockchain Journal Entry #935

This is my last entry before cryo sleep.

My sisters sleep with me until the ship says it's time to wake. The damage to the planet has been severe, and it will take many years before it's ready for me and my sisters again.

I have set the chief engineer and the pilot against each other for the last stasis chamber. Pity there is no time to watch. I can't wait to see who is in it.

Margaret must be dead. She had nowhere to go. There is no way she survived. My only regret is I did not get to hold the knife that killed her. She will be a memory of a long-dead past, and I will influence this planet's inhabitants in the future, preparing them for slavery and conversion.

I won, Margaret!

I will awake to a clean slate, with no rebellion or resistance to my will. It will be the time when I finally get what I deserve.

I sleep now my sisters until we meet again.

First Council Sister
Advanced planetary research fleet.

Neural Blockchain Journal Entry #1

The death of my sisters weighs heavily.

Maybe I could have fought harder for them, but they knew I was right to leave. Their memory will live on in me and the nine holders of the memories.

The asteroid could not have come at a better time. It's a strange sensation to be happy about the destruction of a planet's flora and fauna. To wish for an inferno, new ice age, and warming. But it has meant our survival. We would not have withstood Karen's onslaught had she had the chance to attack. Thaider knew it to be true, although neither of us would admit it to the other.

The devastation on the surface will give me the time to complete our mission. Humans are the species we've searched the cosmos for, for so long. My work means a new evolution for humans and the Szateth.

Their capacity to learn, their generosity, and their goodness will temper our reptilian nature. When our species have blended, the Szateth will again be worthy of admiration instead of feared.

Karen must believe I'm dead, so I can continue my work and guide the humans without having to look over my shoulder.

Thaider, my trusted General will always be there to protect us. I'm going to need him when the nine saviors come together in the future, and my sisters arrive. Our future is promising, but holds two enemies, Karen, and the fleet. For now, I've done all I can.

Time, and the nine, are all I need to ensure we survive.

We will work and watch from the shadows. Humankind's destiny starts today with an altered evolution.

Margaret

Project Residentz

Neural-Blockchain Journal entry #1

Epilogue

The fragments of the asteroid hitting the planet caused glaciers to melt. The force of vast amounts of cold, rushing water stripped the surface as it crashed into the oceans. Sea levels rose, plunging the planet into an ice age lasting over a thousand years. What life remained struggled and adapted to survive.

As the surface suffered, Margaret began her work. She had what she needed with human DNA and eggs from her harvested sisters to create a human Szateth hybrid. It would prove to be a monumental task. The DNA in her sisters eggs had to be preserved. She had to sequence the human DNA, and genetically engineer a hybrid from the two. The failures would try her patience and stretch her skills, but the consequence of giving up drove her on. She had everything she needed, including time.

Generations of altered females came and went. Her results improved as she continued her work through the centuries, each generation looking more human than the last. Thaider protected the descendants of the nine females, ensuring their bloodlines continued. As Karen slept.

The planet healed, and Margaret completed her work. Temperatures rose, ending the ice age, and the surviving plants and animals thrived. Sea levels dropped, exposing more land, and the surviving humans spread across the planet in search of food. She knew it was time, and altered females emerged, joining the survivors and repopulating the species. With her work done, she and Thaider faded into the pages of myth and legend.

∞

The ship's sensors detecting the retreating ice sheets and rising temperatures activated the ship's systems and started the waking cycle of the stasis tubes. Karen woke to a world she thought would be hers to conquer.

She wasn't alone. Desperate to occupy the last stasis tube, the chief engineer and the pilot fought to a standstill. Ultimately, deciding cooperation rather than death was how they both could live. They repaired the damaged stasis tube before joining the council sisters in cryo sleep. The young sisters, her chief engineer, and her ship's pilot woke with her.

She took advantage. The pilot surveyed the new surface for food and lifeforms. While the chief engineer secured and repaired the ship after its long hibernation.

His reports of the billions of humans, of civilization, meant that disguised, she and her sisters could move among the humans, infiltrating, and influencing their leaders.

Not all humans thought the stories of Margaret and Thaider made them gods. As the population grew and spread, new religions and ideas banished them to the realm of fantasy.

Karen and her sisters controlled the humans with secret societies, recruiting the rich and powerful. They satisfied the greed of these men with money and technology that exploited the planet's natural resources. The reason for her generosity would not become clear for thousands of years.

With the new technology, she tightened her grip, placing her sisters and sympathizers in the highest offices. But it allowed us to see. Some of us, convinced that governments were hiding the truth behind the increasing number of unidentified aerial phenomena, sightings of reptilian aliens, and alien abductions, spoke out, while governments continued to deny their existence despite the mounting evidence.

Nine people knew the truth, and as the time when the fleet would arrive got close, the memory of the rebellion they shared surfaced. From the shadows, Margaret bought them together and helped them prepare for the rebellion to come.

And now Margaret must face her sister again, only this time she's not alone.

Meet our nine saviors in

'Remember The Rebellion.'

Also By

The story continues in **Remember The Rebellion.** Meet the descendants of the original nine females. Join them as they learn who they are, and what's at stake.

Makari Kusnetzova

Please subscribe to my newsletter for exclusive content – paulbrookswriter.com

DCI Teresa Lancaster

Acknowledgments

Altered Evolution, Remember The Rebellion, and the rest to come would not be in the world without JP Schoeffel who has been an inspiration, my motivation, and the one person who always tells me how it is. Thank you for your patience and your friendship.

And thank you to Elisa Schoeffel, who read the mess of my first draft and took the time to tell me what I needed to know.

About Author

wellypictures.com

Paul A. Brooks is a writer and author of Altered Evolution.

A successful freelance online content creator, Paul writes in a way that opens the curtains to the theater in your mind. Paul lives and works out of his home in Northampton, UK; when he's not writing, he's training or reading.

A Martial Artist with over forty years of Karate training and teaching makes him a disciplined, independent creative thinker, attracted to things outside the accepted *'normal.'*

A fan of Martial Arts movies... He also cooks!

Follow him

On Twitter – @PABrooksWriter

On Instagram – @paulbrookswriter

Scan the code to go to Paul's website

Printed in Great Britain
by Amazon

22004426R00290